MORE PRAISE FOR *WELCOME TO NIGHT VALE: A NOVEL*

"This is a splendid, weird, moving novel. . . . It manages beautifully that trick of embracing the surreal in order to underscore and emphasize the real—not as allegory, but as affirmation of emotional truths that don't conform to the neat and tidy boxes in which we're encouraged to house them."
—NPR

"Longtime listeners and newcomers alike are likely to appreciate the ways in which *Night Vale*, as Fink puts it, 'treats the absurd as normal and treats the normal as absurd.' What they might not foresee is the emotional wallop the novel delivers in its climactic chapters."
—Austin Chronicle

"*Welcome to Night Vale: A Novel* masterfully brings the darkly hilarious, touching, and creepy world of the podcast into the realm of ink and paper."
—Asbury Park Press

"A marvelous book. It's a book that manages to have a real plot—about children and their relationship to their parents, and about parents and their relationship to the world their children are growing up in. Like the podcast, the novel is full of people we love and root for, full of frightening things, and full of dramatic tension that pays off beautifully with resolutions worthy of any great tale of traditional conflict."   **—Boing Boing**

"A wonderfully creepy tale filled with revelations about the nature of the town and its residents."
—AV Club

"This is the kind of book that'll make you say ALL HAIL THE GLOW CLOUD. Whether you're a fan of the strange and upsetting *Welcome to Night Vale* podcast or you're new to Night Vale and its quaint desert conspiracies, it's never a bad time to visit Night Vale."   **—Bustle**

"Fans will find it refreshing to see Night Vale from different perspectives . . . but knowledge of the podcast isn't required to follow the story. This unusual experiment in format-shifting works surprisingly well."
—Publishers Weekly

"Take Conan's Hyboria, teleport it to the American Southwest, dress all the warriors in business casual, and hide their swords under the floorboards—that's Night Vale: absurd, magical, wholly engrossing, and always harboring some hidden menace."

—John Darnielle, author of *Wolf in White Van*

"They've done the unthinkable: merged the high weirdness and intense drama of Night Vale to the pages of a novel that is even weirder, even more intense than the podcast."

—Cory Doctorow, author of *Little Brother*
and coeditor of *Boing Boing*

"This is the novel of your dreams, a hypnotic travelogue that shimmers and changes as you read. A friendly (but terrifying) and comic (but dark) and glittering (but bleak) story of misfit family life that unfolds along the side streets, back alleys, and spring-loaded trapdoors of the small town home you'll realize you've always missed living in. When it says 'welcome,' it's mandatory. You belong here."

—Glen David Gold, author of *Carter Beats the Devil* and *Sunnyside*

"This small town full of hooded figures, glowing clouds, cryptically terrifying public policies, and flickering realities quickly feels more like home than home. You will want to live in Night Vale, even if that means you might be taken off in an unmarked helicopter or cross into a parallel universe by accident. There is nothing like Night Vale, in the best possible way."   —Maureen Johnson, author of *13 Little Blue Envelopes*
and *The Name of the Star*

"Brilliant, hilarious, and wondrously strange. I'm packing up and moving to Night Vale!"

—Ransom Riggs, author of the #1 *New York Times* bestselling
Miss Peregrine's Home for Peculiar Children

"I've been a fan of *Welcome to Night Vale* for years, and in that time writers Jeffrey Cranor and Joseph Fink have delighted me with stories that are clever, twisted, beautiful, strange, wonderful, and sweet. This book does all of that and so much more. It's even better than I'd hoped. I think this might be the best book I've read in years."

—Patrick Rothfuss, author of *The Name of the Wind*

ALSO BY JOSEPH FINK AND JEFFREY CRANOR

Mostly Void, Partially Stars:
Welcome to Night Vale Episodes, Volume 1

The Great Glowing Coils of the Universe:
Welcome to Night Vale Episodes, Volume 2

WELCOME TO NIGHT VALE

A NOVEL

JOSEPH FINK AND JEFFREY CRANOR

HARPER PERENNIAL

NEW YORK • LONDON • TORONTO • SYDNEY • NEW DELHI • AUCKLAND

HarperCollins
PUBLISHERS

A hardcover edition of this book was published in 2015 by Harper Perennial.

HarperCollins books may be purchased for educational, business, or sales promotional use. For information, please e-mail the Special Markets Department at SPsales@harpercollins.com.

FIRST HARPER PERENNIAL PAPERBACK PUBLISHED 2017.

Designed by Leah Carlson-Stanisic

Title page illustration by Rob Wilson

Library of Congress Cataloging-in-Publication Data has been applied for.

ISBN 978-0-06-235143-2 (pbk.)

24 25 26 27 28 LBC 13 12 11 10 9

To Meg Bashwiner
and to Jillian Sweeney.

The history of the town of Night Vale is long and complicated, reaching back thousands of years to the earliest indigenous people in the desert. We will cover none of it here.

Suffice it to say that it is a town like many towns, with a city hall, and a bowling alley (the Desert Flower Bowling Alley and Arcade Fun Complex), and a diner (the Moonlite All-Nite Diner), and a supermarket (Ralphs), and, of course, a community radio station reporting all the news that we are allowed to hear. On all sides it is surrounded by empty desert flatness. It is much like your town, perhaps. It might be more like your town than you'd like to admit.

It is a friendly desert community, where the sun is hot, the moon is beautiful, and mysterious lights pass overhead while we all pretend to sleep.

Welcome to Night Vale.

Pawnshops in Night Vale work like this.

First you need an item to pawn.

To get this, you need a lot of time behind you, years spent living and existing, until you've reached a point where you believe that you exist, and that a physical item exists, and that the concept of ownership exists, and that, improbable as all those are, these absurd beliefs line up in a way that results in you owning an item.

Good job. Nicely done.

Second, once you believe you own an item, you must reach a point where you need money more than you need the item. This is the easiest step. Just own an item and own a body with needs, and wait.

The only pawnshop in the town of Night Vale is run by the very young Jackie Fierro. It has no name, but if you need it, you will know where it is. This knowledge will come suddenly, often while you are in the shower. You will collapse, surrounded by a bright glowing blackness, and you will find yourself on your hands and knees, the warm water running over you, and you will know where the pawnshop is. You will smell must and soap, and feel a stab of panic about how alone you are. It will be like most showers you've taken.

Before you can offer Jackie your item, there will first be some hand washing, which is why there are bowls of purified water throughout the shop. You need to chant a little as you wash your hands. You, of course, should always chant when you wash your hands. It is only hygienic.

When you have been properly purified, you will lay the item on the counter, and Jackie will consider it.

Jackie will have her feet up on the counter. She will lean back.

"Eleven dollars," she will say. She will always say, "Eleven dollars." You will not respond. You are, ultimately, unnecessary to this process. You are, ultimately, unnecessary.

"No, no," she will say, waving her hand. And then she will name her actual price. Usually it is money. Sometimes it is other things. Sometimes it is dreams, experiences, visions.

Then you will die, but only for a little while.

The item will be given a price tag. Eleven dollars. Everything in the pawnshop is that price, no matter what she loaned you for it.

Once you are no longer dead, she will give you a ticket, which later you will be able to exchange for the item, or at any time you may look at the ticket and remember the item. Remembering the item is free.

You are leaving this story now. You were only an example, and it is probably safer for you not to be in this story anyway.

Jackie Fierro squinted out the window at the parking lot. There was no one coming. She was closing soon. Relatively speaking, she was always closing soon, and also always just opening.

Beyond the window was the parking lot and beyond that the desert, and beyond that the sky, mostly void, partially stars. Layered from her vantage, it was all distance, equally unreachable from her post at the counter.

She had recently turned nineteen. She had been recently nineteen for as long as she could remember. The pawnshop had been hers for a long time, centuries maybe. Clocks and calendars don't work in Night Vale. Time itself doesn't work.

For all her years as the newly nineteen owner of the pawnshop, she left the shop only when it was closed, and then only
to her apartment, where she sat with her feet up on the coffee
table, taking in the community radio and the local cable news.
Based on what the news told her, the outside world seemed
a dangerous place. There was always some world-ending cat-
aclysm threatening Night Vale. Feral dogs. A sentient glowing
cloud with the ability to control minds (although the Glow
Cloud had become less threatening since its election to the
local school board). Old oak doors that led to a strange desert otherworld where the current mayor had been trapped for
months. It seemed safer to not have friends or hobbies. To sit
at work, head down, doing her job, and then sit at home, glass
after glass of orange juice, radio on, safe from anything that
might disrupt her routine.

Her days were spent in silence, mostly void, partially thought.
Some days she would recatalog her inventory. Other days she
would clean the shelves. Every day she would sit and think. She
would try to think about the day she took over the store. There
must have been a day like that, but she could not think of the
specifics. She had been doing this for decades. She was very
young. Both of these were true at the same time.

She knew college was a thing nineteen-year-olds did. She
knew being unemployed in a difficult job market and living at
home was a thing other nineteen-year-olds did. She was con-
tent doing neither of those, so she continued on and on and on
at the pawnshop.

She understood the world and her place in it. She understood nothing. The world and her place in it were nothing and
she understood that.

Because of the lack of working time in Night Vale, she went
off her gut feeling about when the shop should close. When the

feeling came, it came, and the doors had to be locked, removed from their frames, and safely hidden.

The feeling came. She swung her feet off the counter. A decent day.

Old Woman Josie, who lived out by the car lot, had come in with a great number of cheap plastic flamingos. She had carried them in a large canvas sack and emptied them onto the counter like loose change.

"It is not for myself that I give up these little ones," said Old Woman Josie, addressing a bare wall several feet to the right of Jackie in a strong, formal voice, making the occasional sweeping gesture with her palm, "but for the future."

Josie stopped, her palm still out. Jackie decided the speech was over.

"All right, man, I'll give you eleven dollars," she said. Old Woman Josie tightened her eyes at the bare wall.

"Ah, okay"—Jackie softened, prodding at one of the flamingos and looking at its weak plastic belly—"tell you what, I'll give you a good night's sleep."

Old Woman Josie shrugged.

"I'll take it."

A good night's sleep was a wildly generous offer. The flamingos were worthless, but there were so many of them, and Jackie couldn't help herself. She never refused an item.

"Be careful not to touch those directly," Josie said, after she was finished being dead.

Using shop rags, Jackie laid the flamingos out side by side on a shelf, each one tagged with a single handwritten eleven-dollar price tag. Most things shouldn't be touched anyway, Jackie thought.

"Good-bye, dear," said Josie, taking the ticket that Jackie had filled out. "Come by sometime and talk to the angels. They've been asking about you."

The angels lived with Old Woman Josie, in her small tract ·home whose tract no longer stood, leaving it alone at the edge of town. The angels did chores for her, and Josie made a modest income selling items they had touched. No one understood why the angels lived with her. Very little was understood about the angels. Some things were.

Of course, angels do not exist. It is illegal to consider their existence, or even to give them a dollar when they forget bus money and start hovering around the Ralphs asking for change. The great hierarchy of angels is a foolish dream, and anyway is forbidden knowledge to Night Vale citizens. All of the angels in Night Vale live with Josie out by the car lot. There are no angels in Night Vale.

Around the middle of the day, Jackie had acquired a car. It was a Mercedes, only a few years old, and offered with urgency by a young man wearing a gray pin-striped business suit stained with dirt. It was impressive how he got the car onto the counter, but there is a way these things are done, and it had to go on the counter. He washed his hands and chanted. The water went brown and red.

She settled on an offer of five dollars, talking him down from eleven, and he laughed as he took the money and the ticket.

"It's not funny at all," he explained, laughing.

And finally a woman named Diane Crayton arrived late in the afternoon—almost closing time according to Jackie's gut.

"Can I help you?" Jackie asked. She was unsure why she asked this, as Jackie rarely greeted people who came in the store.

Jackie knew who Diane was. She organized PTA fund-raisers. Diane sometimes came by to distribute flyers that said things like "Night Vale High School PTA Fund Drive! Help give kids the municipally approved education they deserve. Your support is mandatory and appreciated!"

Diane, in Jackie's mind, looked just like a woman who would be an active PTA mom, with her kind face and comfortable clothing. She also thought Diane looked like a woman who would be a loan officer, with her conservative makeup choices and serious demeanor. She would look like a pharmacist if she ever were to wear the standard white coat, gas mask, and hip waders.

She looked like a lot of things to Jackie. Mostly she looked like a person lost in both a place and a moment.

Diane took a handkerchief from her purse. Without changing her upward, distant expression, she wept a single tear onto the cloth.

"I'd like to offer this," she said, finally looking at Jackie.

Jackie considered the handkerchief. The tear would dry soon.

"Eleven dollars. That's the deal," she said.

"I'll take it," Diane said. Her loose-hanging arms were now drawn up near her purse.

Jackie took the tear-dabbed handkerchief and gave Diane her ticket and the money.

After her brief death, Diane thanked her, and hurried out of the shop. Jackie tagged the tear with its eleven-dollar price tag and placed it on a shelf.

So a decent day. Jackie flipped the sign on the door to CLOSED, her hand touching the window, leaving its ghost upon the glass, a hand raised to say "Stop" or "Come here" or "Hello" or "Help" or maybe only "I am here. This hand, at least, is real."

She looked down to adjust the items on the counter, and when she looked up, the man was there.

He was wearing a tan jacket, and holding a deerskin suitcase. He had normal human features. He had arms and legs. He might have had hair, or maybe was wearing a hat. Everything was normal.

"Hello," he said. "My name is Everett."

Jackie screamed. The man was perfectly normal. She screamed.

"I'm sorry," he said. "Are you closed?"

"No, that's okay, no. Can I help you?"

"Yes, I hope so," he said. There was buzzing coming from somewhere. His mouth?

"I have an item I would very much like to pawn."

"I . . ." she said, and waved her hand to indicate everything she might have said next. He nodded at her hand.

"Thank you for your help. Have I introduced myself?"

"No."

"Ah, I apologize. My name is Emmett."

They shook hands. Her hand continued to shake after he let go.

"Yes, well," he said. "Here is the item."

He set a small slip of paper on the counter. On it, written in dull, smeared pencil, were the words "KING CITY." The hand-writing was shaky and the pencil had been pressed down hard. She couldn't stop staring at it, although she didn't know what about it was interesting.

"Interesting," she said.

"No, not very," said the man in the tan jacket.

The man washed his hands and quietly chanted, and Jackie forced herself to lean back and put her feet on the counter. There is a way these things are done. She looked a few times at the man's face, but she found she forgot it the moment she stopped looking.

"Eleven dollars," she said. The man hummed, and other small voices joined him, apparently from within the deerskin suitcase.

"Where did this come from?" she asked. "Why are you offering it to me? What would I do with it?"

Her voice was high and cracked. It did not sound like her at all.

The man was now harmonizing with the voices from his suitcase. He did not seem to register her questions.

"No, no, I'm sorry," she said, fully aware of, but unable to stop, her poor negotiating technique. "My mistake. Thirty dollars and an idea about time."

"Done," he said, smiling. Was that a smile?

She gave him the thirty dollars and told him her idea about time.

"That is very interesting," he said. "I've never thought of it that way. Generally, I don't think at all."

Then he died. She usually used this time to finish up the paperwork, get the ticket ready. She did nothing. She clutched the slip of paper in her hand. He wasn't dead anymore.

"I'm sorry. Your ticket."

"There's no need," he said, still possibly smiling. She couldn't get a good enough look at his face to tell.

"No, your ticket. There is a way these things are done." She scrawled out a ticket, with the information tickets always had. A random number (12,739), the quality of light at time of transaction ("fine"), the general feeling of the weather outside ("looming"), her current thoughts on the future ("looming, but fine"), and a quick sketch of what she thought hearts should look like, instead of the pulsing lumps of straw and clay that grow, cancer-like, into our chests when we turn nine years old.

He took the ticket as she thrust it at him, and then, thanking her, turned to leave.

"Good-bye," she said.

"KING CITY," said the paper.

"Good-bye," waved the man, saying nothing.

"Wait," she said, "you never told me your name."

"Oh, you're right," he said, hand on door. "My name is Elliott. A pleasure to make your acquaintance."

The door swung open and shut. Jackie held the slip of paper in her hand, unsure for the first time in however long her life had been what to do next. She felt that her routine, unbroken for decades, had been disrupted, that something had gone differently. But she also had no idea why she felt that. It was just a slip of paper, just clutched in her hand, just that.

She finished her paperwork; on the line that said "pawned by," she stopped. She could not remember his name. She couldn't even remember his face. She looked down at the piece of paper. "KING CITY." She looked up to get a glimpse of him out the window, just to jostle her stuck memory.

From the counter, she could see the man in the tan jacket outside. He was running out to the desert. She could just barely see him at at the edge of the parking lot's radius of light. His arms were swinging wildly, his suitcase swinging along. His legs were flailing, great puffs of sand kicked up behind him, his head thrown back, sweat visible running down his neck even from where she sat. The kind of run that was from something and not toward. Then he left the faint edge of the light and was gone.

There's this house. It's not unlike many other houses. Imagine what a house looks like.

It is also quite unlike many other houses. Imagine this house again.

Given that it is simultaneously not unlike and unlike other houses, it is exactly like all houses.

One way it is not unlike other houses is its shape. It has a house-like shape. That's definitely a house, people might say if shown a picture of it.

One way it is unlike other houses is also its shape. It has a subtly unnatural shape. That's definitely a house, but there's something else, something beautiful, inside that house, people might say if shown a picture of it. I don't know if *beautiful* is the right word. It's more like . . . like . . . It's actually upsetting me now. Please stop showing me that picture. Please, those same people might beg a few moments later. It is a terrible, terrible beauty that I do not understand. Please stop.

Okay, the person showing the people the picture might reply, because that person might be good and caring. It is hard to say who is good and caring when you know nothing about a person except that they show other people pictures of houses, but there's no sense in going through life presuming awful things about people you do not know.

It would be safe to assume that the house is an enclosed structure owned and built by people.

It would be weird to assume that the house has a personality, a soul. Why would anyone assume that? It is true. It does. But that was weird to assume that. Never assume that kind of thing.

Another way it is unlike other houses is its thoughts. Most houses do not think. This house has thoughts. Those thoughts are not visible in a picture. Nor in person. But they find their way into the world. Through dreams mostly. While a person sleeps, the house might suddenly have a thought: Taupe is not an emotional catalyst. It's practical and bland. No one cries at any shade of taupe. Or another thought like OMG time! What is time even? And the sleeping person might experience that thought too.

These thoughts may also be shared in the shower. Grumpy thoughts. Angry thoughts. Thoughts that should be unthought before interacting with the public. Thoughts like [low guttural growl] or [knuckles crack, fists clench, teeth tighten, eyes stop letting in any new information, and water runs down a rigid face].

The thoughts are everywhere. Sometimes they are quite literal and utilitarian. There's a rodent chewing on some drywall behind the headboard could be one such thought.

Another way it is not unlike other houses is that it houses people. It houses a woman, for instance.

Imagine a woman.

Good work.

It also houses a boy, not quite a man. He's fifteen. You know how it is.

Imagine a fifteen-year-old boy.

Nope. That was not right at all. Try again.

No.

No.

Okay, stop.

He is tall. He's skinny, with short hair and long teeth that he deliberately hides when he smiles. He smiles more than he thinks he does.

Imagine a fifteen-year-old boy.

No. Again.

No. Not close.

He has fingers that move like they have no bones. He has eyes that move like he has no patience. He has a tongue that changes shape every day. He has a face that changes shape every day. He has a skeletal structure and coloring and hair that change every day. He seems different than you remember. He is always unlike he was before.

Imagine.

Good. That's actually pretty good.

His name is Josh Crayton.

Her name is Diane Crayton. She is Josh's mother. She sees herself in Josh.

Josh looks like a lot of things. He changes his physical form constantly. In this way he is unlike most boys his age. He thinks he is several things at once, many of them contradictory. In this way he is like most boys his age.

Sometimes Josh takes the form of a curve-billed thrasher, or a kangaroo, or a Victorian-era wardrobe. Sometimes he amalgamates his looks: fish head with ivory tusks and monarch wings.

"You have changed so much since I last saw you," people often say to him. People say that to all teenagers, but they mean it more with Josh.

Josh doesn't remember how he looked the last time each person saw him. Like most teenagers, he always was what he happens to be in that moment, until he never was that.

There was a girl Josh liked who only liked Josh when he was

bipedal. Josh does not like always being bipedal and found this news disappointing. There was a boy Josh liked who liked Josh when he was a cute animal. Josh always likes being a cute animal, but Josh's subjective sense of the word *cute* was different than the boy's. This was another disappointment for Josh, and also for the boy, who did not find giant centipedes cute at all.

Diane loved Josh for all of the things he appeared to be. She herself did not change forms, only showing the gradual differences that come with gradual changes of age.

Josh sometimes tried to fool Diane by taking the form of an alligator, or a cloud of bats, or a house fire.

Diane knew to be on guard at first, just in case there really was a dangerous reptile, or swarm of rabid flying mammals, or a house on fire. But once she understood the situation, she was calm, and she loved him for who he was and how he looked. No matter what he looked like. She was, after all, the mother of a teenager.

"Please stop shrieking and swarming into the cupboards," she would say. It was important to set boundaries.

Josh sometimes appears human. When he does, he is often short, chubby-cheeked, pudgy, wearing glasses.

"Is that how you see yourself, Josh?" Diane once asked.

"Sometimes," Josh replied.

"Do you like the way you look?" Diane once followed up.

"Sometimes," Josh replied.

Diane did not press Josh further. She felt his terse answers were a sign he did not want to talk much.

Josh wished his mother talked to him more. His short answers were a sign he didn't know how to socialize well.

"What?" Josh asked on a Tuesday evening. He had smooth violet skin, a pointed chin, angular thin shoulders.

The television was not on. A textbook was open but not being read. A phone was lit up, a sharp thumb tapping across its keyboard.

"Come talk," Diane said from the cracked door. She did not want to open it all the way. It was not her room. She was trying very hard. She had sold a tear to Jackie that day. It had felt good to have someone explicitly value something that she did. Also, expenses had been higher than usual that month and she had needed the money. She was, after all, a single parent.

"About what?"

"Anything."

"I'm studying."

"Are you studying? I don't want to bother you if you are studying."

"Ping," the phone added.

"If you're studying, then I'll go," she said, pretending she did not hear the phone.

"What?" Josh asked on some other evening. It was a Tuesday, or it was not a Tuesday. His skin was a pale orange. Or it was deep navy. Or there were thick bristles that plumed from just below his eyes. Or his eyes were not visible at all because of the shade of his ram-like horns. This was most evenings. This was the incremental repetition of parenting.

The television was not on. A textbook was open but not being read. A phone was lit up.

"How are you doing?" Diane sometimes said.

Sometimes she said, "What's going on?"

Sometimes she said, "Just checking on you."

"Josh," Diane sometimes said, standing at his door, in the evening. Sometimes she knocked. "Josh," she sometimes repeated following a certain amount of silence. "Josh," she sometimes did not repeat following a second amount of silence.

"Dot dot dot," Josh sometimes replied. Not out loud, but like in a comic book speech-bubble. He pictured other things he could say, but did not know how.

For the most part, I do not like taffeta, the house thought, and Diane shared that thought.

"Josh," Diane said, sitting in the passenger seat of her burgundy Ford hatchback.

"What?" said the wolf spider in the driver's seat.

"If you're going to learn to drive, you're going to need to be able to reach the pedals."

The wolf spider elongated, and two of his middle legs extended to the floor of the vehicle, gently touching the pedals.

"And see the road too, Josh."

A human head with the face and hair of a fifteen-year-old boy emerged from the body of the spider, and the abdomen filled out into something of a primate-like torso. The legs remained spindly and long. He thought he looked cool driving a car as a wolf spider. He did look cool, although it was difficult to control the car. It was important to him that he look cool while driving, although he would not have been able to articulate why.

Diane stared him down. Josh took a fully human shape, save for a few feathers on his back and shoulders. Diane saw them poking out from underneath his shirtsleeves but decided that not all battles are worth fighting.

"Human form when driving the car."

Diane saw herself in Josh. She had been a teenager once. She understood emotions. She empathized. She didn't know with what, but she empathized.

Josh huffed, but Diane reminded him that if he wanted to drive her car, he would play by her rules, which involved not being a three-inch-long wolf spider. Diane reminded him of his bike and how that was a perfectly reasonable form of transportation.

Diane's task of teaching her son to drive took additional patience, not just because of Josh's insistence on constant reassessment of his physical identity but also because the car was a manual transmission.

Imagine teaching a fifteen-year-old how to drive a car with manual transmission. First, you have to press down the clutch. Then you have to whisper a secret into one of the cup holders. In Diane's case, this was easy, as she was not a very social or public person, and most any mundane thing in her life could be a secret. In Josh's case this was hard, because for teenagers most every mundane thing in their lives is a secret that they do not like sharing in front of their parents.

Then, after the clutch and the secret, the driver has to grab the stick shift, which is a splintered wood stake wedged into the dashboard, and shake it until something happens—anything really—and then simultaneously type a series of code numbers into a keyboard on the steering wheel. All this while sunglasses-wearing agents from a vague yet menacing government agency sit in a heavily tinted black sedan across the street taking pictures (and occasionally waving). This is a lot of pressure on a first-time driver.

Josh often got frustrated with his mother. This was because Diane was not the best teacher. This was also because Josh was not the best student. There were other reasons as well.

"Josh, you need to listen to me," Diane would say.

"I get it. I get it, okay," Josh would say, not getting it at all.

Diane enjoyed arguing with Josh about driving, because it was time spent talking, having a relationship. It was not easy, being a mother to a teenager. Josh enjoyed this time too, but not consciously. On the surface, he was miserable. He just wanted to drive a car, not do all of the things it takes to be able to drive a car, like having a car and learning to drive it.

And sometimes he would say, "Why can't my dad come teach me?" because he knew that question hurt her. Then he would feel bad about hurting her. Diane would feel bad too. They would sit in the car, feeling bad.

"You're doing a good job," Diane once said to Josh, in relation to nothing, only trying to fill a silence.

So every other time, I'm not doing a good job, Josh thought, because he didn't understand the context of her statement.

"Thanks," Josh said out loud, trying to fill the silence with graciousness.

"You still need to work on a lot of things," Diane did not say. "I'm sorry your father isn't here," she also did not say. "But I am trying so, so hard. I am, Josh. I am, I am, I am," she did not say. As far as things go, her self-control was pretty good.

I'm really good at driving, Josh often thought, even as he veered too close to highway barriers, rolled wheels up on curbs, and failed to yield to hooded figures, resulting in mandatory citywide ennui for hours. Night Vale's traffic laws are byzantine and kept on a need-to-know basis with civilian drivers.

Their driving lessons often ended in a "Good job" and a "Thanks" and a brief pause and a divergence into separate silent rooms. Later Diane would knock and say, "Josh," and Josh would or would not reply.

Diane hurt. She was not consciously aware that she hurt, but she hurt. "Josh," she said, so many times a day, for so many different reasons.

Josh loved his mother but he did not know why.

Diane loved her son and she did not care why.

Another way the house is unlike other houses is it has a faceless old woman secretly living in it, although that is not important to this story.

3

"KING CITY," said the paper.

Jackie had never felt fear in her entire life. She had felt caution, and unease, and sadness, and joy, which are all similar to fear. But she had never felt fear itself.

She did not feel it then.

She got to the work of closing: wiping down the bathroom sink, sweeping the floor, and adjusting the thick burlap covering up items that were forbidden or secret, like the time machine that Larry Leroy had stolen from the Museum of Forbidden Technologies, and the pens and pencils (writing utensils having long been outlawed in Night Vale for reasons of public well-being, although everyone still surreptitiously used them).

The paper was still in her hand. She hadn't realized it, had been going about everything without realizing, but there it was. Still there. Dull pencil. Smudged. Hurried handwriting. She put it down on the cracked glass of the countertop.

Now it was time to feed those items that were alive. Some of the items were alive. Some of them were dogs, and some weren't.

There were lights now, in the desert. Low bubbles of light coming and going. She had never seen them before. She ignored them, as she ignored all things that were not part of the small circle of her days.

There were always things she had never seen before in Night Vale. There was the man she passed in the desert using a pair of scissors on the top of a cactus, as if he were cutting its hair. There was the cactus that had a full head of hair. There was the day where the small crack that's always visible in the sky suddenly opened up, and several pterodactyls flew out. Later it was revealed they were just pteranodons, and all the panic was for nothing.

She finished her check of the inventory. The paper was in her hand.

"KING CITY," said the paper.

How did it get there?

"How did this get here?" she asked. The dogs did not respond, nor did anything less sentient.

She put the paper in a drawer in the back room, in the desk she did not use for the work she did not have.

There was nothing more to be done to close the shop. If she were honest, and she tried to be, she had been looking for excuses not to leave. If she were honest, and she tried to be, the floor had been clean enough to begin with. A glance out the window. The low bubbles of light in the desert were gone. Nothing there but a distant airplane crawling across the sky, red blinking lights, vulnerable in the vast empty, faint red beacons flashing the message HELLO. A SMALL ISLAND OF LIFE UP HERE, VERY CLOSE TO SPACE. PRAY FOR US. PRAY FOR US.

The paper was in her hand.

"KING CITY," the paper said.

Jackie felt fear for the first time, and she did not know what it was.

For the first time in a long time, she wished she had a friend to call. She had had friends in high school, she knew that, although the memory of high school was distant and vague. The rest of her friends hadn't stopped at nineteen. They had gotten older, living full lives. They had tried to stay in touch, but it was difficult as they moved on to adult careers and kids and retirement and Jackie just kept being nineteen years old.

"So, still nineteen?" Noelle Connolly had said, when they spoke on the phone for the final time. Her disapproval was clear in her voice. "Oh, Jackie, did you ever think of just turning twenty?"

They had been friends since sophomore Spanish class, but Noelle had been fifty-eight at the point she had finally asked Jackie that question, and spoke in tones that felt sickeningly parental to Jackie. Jackie had said so, and Noelle had become openly condescending, and they had both hung up, and she and Noelle had never spoken again. People who grow older think they are so wise, she thought. Like time means anything at all.

The radio came on by itself as she stood there, paper in hand. It always did at this time of night. Cecil Palmer, the host of Night Vale Community Radio, spoke to her. News, the community calendar, traffic.

She listened when she could to Cecil. Most of the town did. At home, Jackie had a small radio, only about two feet wide, a foot and a half tall. It was the lightweight portable edition ("under 14 lbs.!") with a mother-of-pearl handle and sharply angled, open-beaked eagles carved into the upper corners.

Her mother had gotten it for her whenever her sixteenth birthday was, however long ago that had been, and it was one of Jackie's favorite possessions, along with her record collection, which she never listened to because she didn't have a license to own a record player yet.

Cecil Palmer spoke of the horrors of everyday life. Nearly every broadcast told a story of impending doom or death, or worse: a long life lived in fruitless fear of doom or death. It wasn't that Jackie wanted to know all of the bad news of the world. It was that she loved sitting in the dark of her bedroom, swaddled in blankets and invisible radio waves.

Look, life is stressful. This is true everywhere. But life in Night Vale is more stressful. There are things lurking in the shadows. Not the projections of a worried mind, but literal Things, lurking, literally, in shadows. Conspiracies are hidden in every storefront, under every street, and floating in helicopters above. And with all that there is still the bland tragedy of life. Births, deaths, comings, goings, the gulf of subjectivity and bravado between us and everyone we care about. All is sorrow, as a man once said without really doing much about it.

But when Cecil talked it was possible to let some of that go. To let go of the worries. To let go of the questions. To let go of letting or going.

The slip of paper, however, Jackie could not let go of. She opened her hand, and watched it flutter to the floor. She stared at it. It was on the floor. "Dot dot dot," the blank back of the paper said, not literally, but like in a comic book speech-bubble. She stared and stared, and it sat and sat, and then she blinked her eyes and it was back in her hand.

"KING CITY," it said.

"This is getting me nowhere," she said, to no one, or to the dogs, or to the Thing that lurked in her corner.

She tried calling Cecil at the station, to see if he had heard anything about a man in a tan jacket, holding a deerskin suitcase. She couldn't remember Cecil ever mentioning a person by that description on his show, but it was worth a shot.

One of the station interns picked up, promising to take a message, but who knew if the poor kid would even survive long enough to deliver it?

"That's okay," Jackie said. "Hey, listen, I think the Arby's is hiring. Have you considered that? Their death rate is really low for the area."

But the kid was already hanging up. Oh well, not Jackie's job to worry about the life of someone foolhardy enough to be a community radio intern.

The shop was well and truly closed. At this point if she waited any longer she might as well lay out a sleeping bag and spend the night. Which, nope. So she stepped out into the parking lot, jumpy for sure.

There was a black sedan with tinted windows at the end of the lot—the windows cracked down enough for her to see two sunglassed agents of a vague yet menacing government agency watching her intently. One of them had a camera that kept going off, but the agent didn't seem to know how to deactivate the flash. The light against the tinted windows made the shots worthless, and the agent cursed and tried again and it flashed again. Jackie waved good night to them, as she always did.

Maybe she would take the Mercedes home. Drive with the roof down, see how fast she could make it go before the Sheriff's Secret Police stopped her. But she wouldn't, of course. She walked to her car, a blue Mazda coupe with double red stripes that had been washed, presumably, at some point before she owned it.

"King City," she said. The paper in her hand agreed.

It had been a mistake to accept what the man in the tan jacket had offered her. She didn't know what it was, or what it meant, or what information it was trying to convey and to whom. But she knew that it had changed something. The world was slipping into her life. And she had to push it out, starting with this slip of paper, and the man in the tan jacket.

She announced her intentions, as all Night Vale citizens must.

"I will find the man in the tan jacket, and I will make him take this piece of paper back," she announced. "If I could do that without having to learn anything about him or about what the paper means, that would be just ideal." The agents in the car, holding index fingers to earpieces, dutifully wrote this down.

Out in the desert, bubbles of light, low to the ground. The echo of a crowd arguing and then cheering. For a moment, a tall building, all glass and angles and business, where there had definitely been nothing but sand, and then it was gone, and there were more lights, shifting, warping the air around them. And the echo of crowds. And the lights.

She put the car in reverse, and pulled onto the highway, tossing the slip of paper out the window and watching with satisfaction as it fluttered into the night behind her, and then, snapping her fingers, caught the paper between them, where it was, where it had always been.

THE VOICE OF NIGHT VALE

CECIL: Hello, listeners, Cecil here, your voice from the darkness, the quiet whisperer in your empty night, speaking to you now from a booth at the Night Vale Community Radio station. Here to bring you all the news and community goings-on that you need to know, and hide from you all forbidden and dangerous knowledge.

Now, the news.

There are lights above our town, Night Vale. I am not talking here about the stars. No one knows what the stars are or what they intend, but they have remained in mostly the same order and have indicated no harm for as long as anyone around here can remember. Astronomers keep trying to explain that stars are distant suns in distant galaxies, but, of course, you have to take everything astronomers say with a grain of salt.

But these new lights are not stars. They are low bubbles of light coming and going overhead. They are not the same lights that sometimes hover hundreds of feet above the Arby's. Those lights are different. We understand those lights. The new lights, however, are concerning.

Witnesses reported the lights changed colors when commented on. Some people would say things like "Oh, look at those orange lights," and then point. And suddenly the lights would be yellow, and those people's friends would then respond, "No, that's definitely a yellow," but then they'd go back to being orange. And so on.

That was one such witness account, given by Chris Brady and Stuart Robinson of Old Town Night Vale. Chris added, "What do you think? They're orange, right?" The lights then turned yellow again, and Stuart concluded with "Why is it so important for you to always be right, Christopher?" before storming off, followed by a very apologetic Chris.

So far the lights seem harmless, unless you're directly under them, in which case, they're the opposite of harmless, whatever that means to you.

Last night, at a press conference, the City Council reminded everyone that the Dog Park is there for our community enjoyment and use, and so it is important that no one enter, look at, or think about the Dog Park. They are adding a new advanced camera system to keep an eye on the great black walls of the Dog Park at all times, and if anyone is caught trying to enter it, they will be forced to enter it, and will never be heard from again. If you see hooded figures in the Dog Park, no you didn't. The hooded figures are perfectly safe, and should not be approached at any costs. The City Council ended the conference by devouring a raw potato in quick, small bites of their sharp teeth and rough tongues. No follow-up questions were asked, although there were a few follow-up screams.

We have also received word via encrypted radio pulses about the opening of a new store: Lenny's Bargain House of Gardenwares and Machine Parts, which until recently was that abandoned warehouse the government was using for the highly classified and completely secret tests I was telling you about last week. Lenny's will serve as a helpful new source for all needs involving landscaping and lawn-decorating materials and also as a way for the government to unload all the machines and failed tests and dangerous substances that otherwise would be wasted on things like "safe disposal" or "burying in a concrete tomb until the sun goes out."

Get out to Lenny's for their big grand opening sale. Find eight government secrets and get a free kidnapping and personality reassignment so that you'll forget you found them!

And now, it's time for the Children's Fun Fact Science Corner.

Here is what we know about sentience. Sand is sentient. The desert is sentient. The sky is not sentient. Plants are intermittently sentient. Dogs are the most sentient. We are not sentient. The planet as a whole is sentient. The parts that make up that whole are not sentient. Holes are sentient. We are not sentient. Gift cards are sentient until they expire. States in which it is illegal for gift cards to expire have created immortal sentience. Money is not sentient. The concept of private property is sentient. Sand is sentient. The desert is sentient. We are not sentient.

This has been the Children's Fun Fact Science Corner.

Is your identity safe, listeners? With so much information being stored in databases these days, it's uncertain how we can feel secure that our identities are our own. There are scams galore to try to steal your credit card numbers, social security numbers, city citizen personal numbers, neighborhood resident tracking numbers, and so on.

Not a week goes by where we don't hear of some database being cracked open like a fresh egg on a granite countertop and personal information spilling everywhere, for identity thieves to just lap up like a dog who's allowed to be on a kitchen counter and who likes raw eggs.

Here are some tips for protecting your identity, Night Vale. Change your computer passwords often. Most of us are not legally allowed to use a computer, but change them anyway, just in case you suddenly are allowed to use one someday. Also, wear a mask when in public, and black out your house number with spray paint.

Finally, most identity thefts occur when databases are not securely managed. So, my advice? Don't ever end up in a database.

This has been Tech News.

Coming up after this break, some exclusive clips from my recent three-hour interview with myself, in which I interrogated myself on my motivations, where I am in life, why I'm not in a different place in life, whose fault that is, and why I said that one embarrassing thing once.

4

Diane had not seen Evan or Dawn at the office for a while. Days really.

Diane rarely talked to Evan. She sometimes talked to Dawn. They were not friends. They liked each other just fine. Dawn worked in marketing. Diane technically worked in marketing too, but she just ran a database.

The database was a list of names. It was also a list of personal details associated with names. It was also a series of personalized photos and histories connected to each name. It was fun to take each life and compact it to a single numerical ID and set of subtables. Because while hugely impersonal and reductive, when combined with tens of thousands of other numerical IDs and their hundreds of thousands of sets of subtables, a database could tell you a lot about how people behave.

Sometimes when she had a little extra time—she often had some extra time at work—Diane would look up information about people in her database. She would do research to find photos or stories or videos about them and index those data in their files. This wasn't necessarily helpful to anyone so much as it was a good way to get to know people. Between her work and raising Josh, she had limited time to make new friends or go on dates.

When the marketing department needed data from Diane's database, they could use extremely personal information in their mailings to not only customize a sales pitch to that person but also let them know "we care about you so much that we looked up everything we could find about you in real life." Customers were often so flattered by this gesture that they would send thank-you notes like "How did you find all this out?" or "Who are you people?" or "I have never told anyone this fact, so how did you know?"

Diane's boss, Catharine, read these letters and would sometimes let Diane know how happy everyone was to receive their marketing mailings and what a valuable asset Diane was to their company. Sometimes Diane wanted to ask Catharine what their company actually sold, but she knew it was not her place to ask a question like that.

Most people in Night Vale know there is information that is forbidden or unavailable, which is almost all information. Most people in Night Vale get by with a cobbled-together framework of lies and assumptions and conspiracy theories. Diane was like most people. Most people are.

Her desk was not in the same set of cubicles as the rest of the staff. Her desk was down the hall next to the server room. Her office outsourced their IT help, so it was just Diane alone near the constant hum of the servers.

This was nice because Diane could do personal work or make personal calls when she wanted. She rarely did this, but it is certainly nice to have the freedom to do what you want, when you want, especially if you are not the type to abuse this freedom.

Diane was not the type to abuse this freedom.

But because her desk was far away from everyone else, she often felt out of the loop. She certainly was invited to participate in regular office activities, like low-stakes betting pools on major sporting events (the Super Bowl, the Absurd Bowl, knifeball, poetry, et cetera), or birthday cake, or going-away parties where the exiting staffers would take swings at a piñata filled with bees.

But she was not part of the normal casual conversation of office life. She did not discuss the latest news topic each morning. Diane did not experience this camaraderie with her co-workers. She knew Martellus had a baby last year. She knew Tina liked to cross-stitch prayers written in long-forgotten languages. She knew Ricardo distrusted birds. But her interactions were limited by office geography.

She could have made an effort, over the years, to leave her desk and engage with her co-workers, but she had not done this. She was not shy, but maybe lazy socially. Not willing to seek out situations and connections that were not already part of her routine. Or maybe she was shy. How does a person discover whether they are shy if they never have the time to meet new people?

She worried often that, without another parent to provide a different example, Josh would learn only her shyness, and in fact he seemed to have trouble making and relating to friends. But better, she supposed, that he learn awkwardness from her than learn anything at all from his father.

Diane took the job six years ago because her job at the counter of Big Rico's Pizza was not making enough money to raise Josh on her own. The company took Diane because they needed someone who understood databases. Diane did not understand databases, but she figures things out quickly, so she lied to get the job.

The job market in Night Vale is difficult, what with mysterious hooded figures already doing many tasks (parking attendant, cartographer, dog watcher) that are more traditionally done in other towns by humans for pay. Like most citizens of

Night Vale, Diane found this situation frustrating, but was also gripped with an unspeakable, trembling terror that kept her from complaining about it.

Her first weeks on the job involved taking her work home and teaching herself database management. This was difficult because she did not yet have a license to turn on her computer at home, plus it took her attention away from Josh. Josh had tried to talk to her during those early days of her work, something about a concert he wanted to go to, and she had told him she was busy and to go away. She needed the job more than she needed Josh to like her.

Later she understood databases, having become the person she'd lied about being, and could get all of her work done during work hours.

When people asked what she did for a living, Diane would say, "I work in an office. What do you do?" And then she would guide interesting conversations about their lives, or she would talk about Josh. Raising Josh was what she did for a living, and the office work just allowed her to do that.

Diane never really spoke to Evan at work. She had seen him many times. They had shared comments at birthday and piñata parties like "Good cake, right?" or "Champagne at work! Great!" or "The sky seemed especially vast and unending this morning." The usual chitchat.

She didn't even notice right away that Evan was not at work. Same with Dawn. But as days passed, their absence overtook the mundane humdrum of office talk. Some thought Evan and Dawn had run off together. Diane was not comfortable enough with her co-workers to shame them for their gossiping.

Some speculated that Evan had left his family, that he had a secret life. Some thought he might just be going through personal issues. Some thought he had died and no one had caught the body yet.

Catharine, the division head, called a meeting to discuss the pair's absence. It was mostly practical, as they had work that needed to get done. Someone offered to drive over to their homes to check on them. Catharine said that would be fine.

Diane almost never thought of Evan. But she was thinking of Evan a lot one morning. Evan was thinking of her too.

Diane looked up that morning. Evan stood a few feet from the front of her desk. He was wearing a tan jacket. His belt was a darker brown than his shoes. His hair was recently cut. His face was clean and smooth. He was smiling, silent.

He was not smiling like one smiles at a co-worker or friend. He was smiling like one smiles for a photo in front of a touristy monument.

His teeth were white. Or, they were almost white. One, his left upper bicuspid, was a little farther forward than any other tooth. His teeth were not white, but they were close.

He was looking toward Diane. He was not looking at Diane, but in her vicinity. She could see his pupils. They were not dilated. They were dots. He was looking toward Diane, but his glance seemed to stop just short of where Diane was. He was smiling.

Diane said good morning to Evan. Evan turned his head slightly.

"It's good to be back," he said.

"Where is Dawn?" Diane asked, emphasizing the noun.

"Where is Dawn?" Evan asked, emphasizing the verb. His teeth were stained and crooked.

"Is everything okay, Evan?" Diane asked.

Evan stopped smiling and moved his left foot toward her without putting his weight on it.

Diane's phone rang.

Evan extended his left arm without bending his elbow. He kept his eyes on the point just in front of Diane.

Diane's phone rang.

Evan extended his fingers. He bent his right knee still without putting any weight on his left foot.

Diane's phone rang.

In his fingers was a slip of paper. A small bead of sweat formed along his upper lip. He was not looking at her.

Diane's phone rang.

Between rings, Diane could hear Evan's belabored breathing. His whole body was vibrating from the muscular strain. Evan set the small slip of paper on the desk. There was writing on it.

Diane's phone rang. She grabbed the receiver, interrupting its full ring.

"Diane Crayton," she shouted into the phone.

"Hi, Diane. It's me, Evan," said the tinny voice in her ear.

"Evan?"

Evan kept smiling, unspeaking. He released the paper.

"I can't make it into work today, Diane," Evan's voice on the phone said. "Can you tell Catharine that I can't make it into work today?"

"Evan," Diane repeated.

Evan stood up, breathed deeply in through his nose and deeply out through his mouth.

"I am not able to come to work today, Diane. Do you understand me?" said the voice on the phone.

"Yes. I think."

Evan smiled again. He looked at Diane. She saw the slip of paper on her desk. She could not read what it said.

"Am I being clear, Diane?"

"Evan, I don't know. Where are you? Where are you right now?"

"I can't make it in today."

Diane stared at the slip of paper on her desk. Evan looked toward Diane, smiling. Then he turned, no longer looking toward Diane, but likely still smiling. He walked quickly away from her desk, turning the corner and heading down the hall, out of sight.

"Evan. Hello?"

"Tell Catharine."

"Click," the phone said.

Diane hung up. She looked down at the slip of paper on her desk. It was not there.

She hurried to Catharine's office. On the way she saw Dawn.

"Hey, Dawn. Where have you been?"

"Hi, Diane. I was home sick for a couple of days. Feeling a lot better though."

"Good. We were missing you around here. Say, did you see Evan this morning?"

"Who?"

"Evan."

"Who is Evan?"

"Evan McIntyre. Works in sales. Sits in that cubicle right there."

Diane turned and pointed in the direction of Evan's cubicle. But instead of a cubicle, there was a fern and an empty chair beneath a framed photo of a cloud. She wasn't sure which cloud it was.

"I don't ever remember anyone named Evan ever working here," Dawn said.

Diane looked toward the cloud. Not at it, just short of it.

Dawn smiled. Her teeth were white. "You okay?"

The cloud did not say anything.

Jackie ordered coffee. Eventually coffee was given to her. These moments were related.

The Moonlite All-Nite was packed, as it always was in the morning. There were few places in town where one could quietly have breakfast in the company of so many other people also quietly having breakfast. There is nothing more lonely than an action taken quietly on your own, and nothing more comforting than doing that same quiet action in parallel with fellow humans doing the same action, everyone alone next to each other.

In her right hand was the coffee, served in a mug that said:

JONES BROTHERS WEED WATCHERS CO.
"WE WATCH YOUR WEEDS FOR SUSPICIOUS BEHAVIOR!"
24/7 AUDIO AND VIDEO MONITORING.

It was part of the Moonlite All-Nite's charm. They used mugs gathered from any number of sources. Sometimes those sources left strange stains or humming sounds on the mugs. This was also part of the charm.

Her left hand clutched the piece of paper, where it had been clutched since yesterday evening. Earlier, she'd tried burning the paper, but it came back from the ashes. She had placed the paper in a small lockbox, which she locked. It got out.

She tried showering the paper away. Taking a shower often solved problems for her. She would find herself with thoughts that seemed to come from outside of her, thoughts that would question decisions or offer suggestions or just consider life hazily in a way that made it seem like the thoughts could not possibly be her own.

When she'd held the paper directly under the stream of the shower, it had turned soggy and dissolved, falling into sludge that crumbled toward the drain. But then it was back in her hand. Over and over she destroyed it, and over and over it returned.

"Finally, a dependable companion," she said to the showerhead, and a thought popped into her head that was barely formed into words, more a general image of how often Jackie is surrounded by things she can depend on, and how little she thinks about them. She left the shower as most people leave showers, clean and a little lonely.

Sitting in the diner, out of hope for much else, she rolled the paper into a ball and shoved it into her oatmeal, along with the usual blueberries and salt cubes and cured salmon. She downed the entire bowl like she hadn't eaten in days, which might have also been the case. It was hard to tell, as she was hardly able to pay attention to much more than the paper. Her left hand twitched, and without looking down she knew.

"Dammit!" she said, stabbing the paper with her butter knife and then repeated "Dammit" a couple of more times in a hopeless decrescendo.

"KING CITY," said the paper.

"Yeah, yeah, so I've heard," she muttered. No one around her noticed. Teenagers shout things a lot while smashing knives near their hands, everyone knew.

The man on her left was poking the chipped countertop and whispering to it. His straw hat was set very far back on his head, so that his face seemed longer than it should be. On her right was a woman who had set her chair so it was facing the door to the diner and was making a checkmark on her clipboard every time someone walked in. All in all, no one cared about a young woman shouting and jabbing at her hand.

Coffee at the Moonlite in the morning was part of her usual routine. In about five minutes, she would put down whatever remained of the coffee, whisper into her water glass for the check, pull it out from under the tray of sugar packets, where it would suddenly be, then place it along with some cash back under the sugars, wait for the sound of swallowing to indicate the bill was paid, and then leave the restaurant. The typical diner rigmarole.

Then she would drive to the pawnshop, dig up the doors from where they were hidden, and replace them unlocked at the front just in time for opening time, which was the moment her gut told her the shop should be open. She would sit there all day, doing what she did and no more than what she did, and then she would stop doing that and go home. There wasn't much else to it, life. A person's life is only what they do.

But this morning she did not ask for the check. She did not pay it or leave. She stared at the paper in her hand and knew that she would not do any of the things she normally did this day. This knowledge came as a pain in her stomach and a fluttering on her neck. It was physical, this knowledge, as a strong knowing always is. It had more to do with an ache in her bones than a notion in her head.

The paper had disrupted her routine, and her routine was her life. Without it she was just a teenager who did not age and had no friends. She felt helpless before the paper's power, even as she did not understand what that power was.

"Fine!" she shouted at it.

"Okay!" shouted a man in a nearby booth at a stain on his tie.

In the kitchen, another man, in a floral apron and a hairnet, nodded at a tub of soaking dishes. "Yep," he said.

People often found themselves assenting to inanimate objects in the Moonlite All-Nite.

Jackie sat back on the cracked red stool that smelled of rubber and sawdust. She needed a plan. She turned to the man on her left.

"I need a plan," she said.

"What was that?" He looked up. His forehead was long and unwrinkled, and he appeared to be wearing a great deal of makeup.

"A plan, dude. I need my life back the way it was." She shook the paper in frantic demonstration.

"Ah. Okay, kid." He flicked his eyes back to the counter where he had been staring.

"I need the man in the tan jacket."

The man next to her narrowed his eyes. He presumably had two eyes.

"What was that you were just saying?" he said.

"I need to find someone else who saw him. There must be somebody in this town who talked to him and can tell me about him."

He stared at her with what was probably a normal amount of eyes.

"I'll need to start talking to people. All over town. Try to find anyone who knows him. Listen carefully to what they say and what they don't say."

"Did you just mention a man in a tan jacket?" he asked.

"Doesn't matter," she said, turning back to the front and re-establishing the wall between her and her fellow customers eating at a diner counter, or the "eighth wall" as it is known in the world of theater.

She decided to make a list of everyone who might know about this mysterious man. She pulled out the pen she used for writing tickets at the pawnshop. It was a promotional pen from a festival put on by the city a few years ago.

THE NIGHT VALE SHAKESPEARE IN A PIT FESTIVAL. FALL INTO THE BARD'S WORDS.

it said. The broken leg had been painful, but she did love the pen.

She searched her pockets for anything to write on and could find nothing. The blank tickets were kept at the pawnshop, and anyway they were only for writing claim tickets. There is a way things are done. Although that moment they were not being done. Her existence was premised on everything being the same, every day, and the paper was insistently different. It was impossible to sink into a blissful holding pattern with a mysterious paper in her hand.

There were no menus or place mats to write on, and then she looked down at her left hand and the paper. Of course. She put the paper on the counter, wrote "LIST" at the top of the blank side.

Or at least "LIST" was what she intended to write. Instead, she wrote "KING CITY."

"No," she said, to her own hand. She crossed out what she had written and wrote "LIST."

Except that it still looked a lot like "KING CITY."

"No," she said again. She would not accept it. Not this too.

Maybe it was the surface. She pushed the paper aside (where it immediately sprang back, the marks from the pen completely gone, into her left hand) and wrote directly on the counter.

"Hey," said Laura, the waitress, as she walked by. "I'll have to clean that later."

Laura had many branches growing from her body, laden with fruit.

"TEST," Jackie wrote on the counter. And again it came out as "KING CITY." She yelled in frustration. The man with the long forehead and the woman with the clipboard glared at her. Teenagers don't usually write things while yelling, they thought, worried.

"Shhh," said a voice from under the man's hat.

Even if she did go to the pawnshop, she wouldn't be able to write tickets for the customers, or price tags that said "$11." She felt utterly defeated, and this feeling made her angry and defiant. What had she done to deserve this? She punched the counter, and then held her aching fist.

Her phone rang. She pulled it out, and the woman next to her slipped in an earpiece so she could listen along.

"Hello, Mom?"

"Hello, dear!" Her mom didn't quite grasp that phones bridged the distance between people, so shouting was unnecessary.

"I'm sorry, Mom. I'm busy at work right now." The woman with the clipboard, one hand on the earpiece, raised an eyebrow at her, and Jackie waved it off. "Do you need something?"

"I can't just call my child? I have to need something?"

"Of course you can, Mom, that's not what I—"

"But now that you mention it . . ."

"See?" Jackie mouthed to the woman with the clipboard. The woman shrugged.

"What is it, Mom?"

"I need to talk to you."

"I'm glad we could talk then. Was there anything else?" Jackie wrote "KING CITY" on the counter again and cringed.

"No. I need to talk to you in person. It's important. I have something to tell you. It's about . . . Well, it's better if you just come and we can talk about it."

Jackie's eyes burned. She wasn't sure if it was an allergic reaction. She couldn't remember ever feeling this sensation. She touched the corner of her eye. It was wet. There was water coming from her eyes and trickling down her cheeks, and she knew she was crying but she wasn't sure if she had ever cried before. She let all the air that was in her out, without using her mouth to make that air communicate anything. This lack of communication communicated a great deal.

"Jackie, are you there?"

"Yes, I'm wherever I am. Here I am. Mom, have I ever . . . I mean, do you ever remember a time when I . . ."

She looked up and froze without actually stopping movement. The freezing happened inside.

One of the cooks was staring at her. He was tall and blond. His smile was wide and warm, and it unnerved her. He was flipping burgers (who was ordering burgers this early in the morning?), but he wasn't taking his eyes off of her, so the burgers were landing on the floor, in the sink, on the edge of the griddle, in a haphazard splash pattern starting from where his spatula tossed them. His smile was so wide and so warm. Jackie didn't feel safe.

"Jackie, come on over. I think this is a good time to tell you."

"Okay, Mom. Okay, I'll be there. I just have a few things I need to do first."

She shut off the phone and her mom was gone.

She would need to start somewhere. Old Woman Josie had mentioned that the angels wanted to see her, and even though no one could legally acknowledge their existence, they did tend to know what more legally existent creatures did not. It was, if nothing else, somewhere to start at. She got up to leave, glancing back to the kitchen.

The cook was still staring at her, a burger in midflip. Her quick glance did not take in its landing, and so, in her mind, it was always in the air, tumbling, never landing, never consumed, only spinning and falling, spinning and falling.

Catharine's office had two plants, three chairs, two desks, one hutch, six personal photos in standing frames, one of those clichéd motivational posters on the wall that had two crows tearing out the insides of a reasonably sized forest cat with the cheesy inspirational caption, "Unremittingly, you must stare into the sun," and a clay paperweight most likely made by Catharine's daughter (it was signed

by your seed

in adorable small-child handwriting).

Diane sat in one of the chairs that had no wheels. The other two chairs were empty. The computer was humming and glowing. Flashes of colorful dots disappeared and reappeared on the screen. A phone was ringing somewhere in the cubicle area. A phone was being answered in the cubicle area.

A tarantula inched between the keyboard and mouse, as if it were playing the game where it can only move one leg at a time, which is a popular game with tarantulas. Tarantulas are simple creatures, Diane's house thought, but no one was home to receive that thought. Josh was at school, not thinking about tarantulas. Diane was in the office, trying not to think about Josh.

The door opened and Catharine said, "Sorry about making you wait so long," but she said it in a way that a person says, "Sorry about the loss of your pet." Catharine was either expertly empathetic or completely disingenuous. It depended on what you needed a boss to be. In this way Catharine was a good boss.

Catharine sat down in the chair that had wheels and was between the two desks. She shoved papers and their paperweight out from the center of the desk, creating a small, clean triangle of oak desktop between her and Diane.

"How's Josh?" Catharine asked.

"Josh?" Diane was not expecting small talk. Nor did she expect Catharine to remember her son's name. She had always gotten along fine with her boss, but they had spoken only once or twice in her entire time with the company. Catharine had always seemed fair and kind, as things go, but also stressed and distracted.

"Josh, right? Your son? How is he? Still taking different physical forms all the time?"

"Oh, he's fine. Just fine."

"That's unspecific, but I will not press you for more if you do not wish to mix work and home lives," Catharine said, without moving her neck or eyes. "I legitimately am interested in Josh. I met him a couple of years ago, when we saw each other at the Ralphs. You were looking at different cereal packages, and Josh that day had—oh, I remember—such long fingers and ears, big dark eyes, and beautiful black wings. He was a handsome boy."

"Yes. He is a handsome boy."

"And I was buying metal cleaner and a thirty-two-pack of meat thermometers. I remember that day well." Catharine frowned, her eyes briefly sad before she was able to compose her face back to neutral. "How is he doing at school? He must be fifteen now. Is he dating yet?"

"I think maybe he has an interest."

"You don't have to answer that if you do not wish." Catharine raised one hand in the air, fingers together, palm facing Diane.

Diane looked at Catharine's forceful but caring gesture, and then up a bit along her arm. The tarantula, which had been near the computer earlier, was now on Catharine's shoulder. It had one leg in the air, pointing toward Diane. It was possible that the creature was still walking slowly, but Diane hoped it was instead mimicking its owner's arm gesture.

Imagining this, Diane smiled a small smile. Catharine smiled a small smile in unconscious response.

Catharine had no idea the tarantula was there. She was, in fact, terrified of spiders. She couldn't even look at a photo of one without panicking or possibly passing out. Diane misunderstood the situation.

Catharine thought she was connecting to an employee on an emotional level. Catharine also misunderstood the situation.

"Oh no, it's fine," Diane said. "He's fifteen. You know how it is. He doesn't talk too much about what kids he likes."

"That's probably for the best. It's tough to talk with parents about romance and sex and dating. I remember being that age. I remember being almost all of the ages I have been."

The tarantula had turned and was crawling down Catharine's upper arm. Diane thought it would be nice to have a pet at the office. Like goldfish. Could she take care of goldfish at her desk? They make a lot of noise, and you have to feed them mice every week, Diane thought. Maybe not.

"Tell me what I can help you with, Diane," Catharine said.

"I wanted to talk to you about Evan. About what happened last week with Evan and Dawn being absent."

"Right. Your insistence that someone named Evan worked here." Catharine tilted her head.

"Well, about the misunderstanding we had about Evan."

Catharine did nothing.

"It was a—" Diane weighed the difference between accepting

blame for an action and claiming that action. On the one hand, she could protect her job, her reputation. On the other hand, she could act based on what she understood to be a reality—that a man named Evan used to work in her office.

She had gotten in some arguments with her co-workers in both HR and finance over this issue. She wanted Catharine to help resolve it, but she also knew her insistence was beginning to reflect poorly on her.

Diane's head pulsed with what wasn't quite a headache. It sounded like her own voice was different, or like it belonged to someone else.

She also considered that in the place where she thought Evan's desk was, there was no desk at all. Maybe her co-workers were right. She began to sell herself on the idea that she must have lost her mind, or a part of her mind, for a moment. That perhaps she should see a doctor. Like most people in Night Vale, she wasn't sure what doctors did, exactly, but it was rumored that there were benefits to their secretive activities.

Diane had many thoughts in a breath-long conversational hesitation. The tarantula didn't even have time to take a step.

"—a mistake," Diane continued, the pause almost indistinguishable from a stutter. "I don't know how I thought that there was a man named, umm . . ."

And for a flicker she did not remember anything about the man, let alone his name.

"Evan," she recovered, "who worked here."

"I understand," said Catharine.

"But I'm curious. Was there ever an employee by that name, or a similar name? Was I close? Was I maybe conflating this person with someone else? I'm just trying to not, feel crazy, you know?"

Diane laughed. Catharine did not laugh.

"Not off the top of my head, no. I will look, and I will let you know. There used to be an Alan, I think, who was a sales associate."

"Oh, I remember Alan. No, not him."

"It will be difficult to help if you create a Culture of No, Diane."

They both laughed at this. It was an excellent dry joke, Catharine thought. I am connecting with people, Catharine thought. What in the hell? Diane thought.

"Seriously, I will look into it, Diane. I am glad Dawn is back and that we have our full staff together again."

"Yes, I was— Well, I don't know if you were, but it was stressing me out, not knowing."

"Not knowing?" The tarantula was stepping off the back of Catharine's elbow, trying to reach the armrest.

"You held a staff meeting where we discussed Dawn and Ev—— Dawn's absence. That she was missing for a few days and no one could get hold of her. We offered to drive to her house and—"

"When was this?" Catharine swiveled her chair around to her computer and jerked the mouse back and forth in three equal swipes. The colorful dots and darkness faded, and Catharine clicked on her calendar. The tarantula retracted its exploratory leg.

"Tuesday."

"Time?"

"Morning I think. I think it was a morning—"

"There's nothing on my calendar that morning. We had an operations meeting that afternoon, but you wouldn't have been at that. Nothing in the days around Tuesday. We had a staff meeting on Thursday, but Dawn was back that day. Dawn was only gone four days, and she had been calling in sick each day, Diane."

Catharine turned back from her computer. The tarantula, still on her arm, turned with her.

"Have you talked to Dawn?" she said.

"Yes. No. Not in detail."

"You should talk to Dawn."

"I will. I definitely will."

"Diane. You should also give yourself some time off. I want a healthy staff, a happy staff. I want you to take care of your migraines."

Diane had never had migraines and wasn't sure what Catharine was talking about. She thought that perhaps it was a different day than she thought it was, or that Catharine was not her boss but another person wearing a mask. Nothing seemed right.

"I will. I'll take care of . . . them. And I'll talk to Dawn."

"Wonderful." Catharine turned her chair back toward Diane again. "And, Diane."

Diane, standing to leave, paused.

"Thank you."

"No. Thank you, Catharine. Thanks for the . . . thanks for being patient. I was confused."

"You are welcome." Catharine's fingers were together again, fitting neatly into the cleared triangle of her desk.

The tarantula had reached the armrest and was just dragging its brown bulk onto the desk. It pulled itself next to a photo of a young Catharine and a younger boy.

"Catharine, can I ask an unrelated question?"

"Any time, Diane."

"What is her name?" Diane asked, pointing to the spider.

"Whose name?"

"Or his. I apologize. I shouldn't assume gender."

"Ah. Of course. This is a he," Catharine said with a rigid smile, reaching her hand out in the direction of the tarantula. The tarantula stopped. It seemed to stare at Catharine's hand. Or it could have just sensed motion above it and frozen.

Tarantulas are simple creatures, Diane thought, not knowing where the thought came from.

Catharine's hand wrapped around the side of the picture of her and the boy. The tarantula brushed one leg against Catharine's middle finger. She felt it but did not know what the feeling was and thus, like most things she does not understand, she ignored it.

"This is a photo of me with my son, Kim."

It took Diane a moment to connect her mental narrative with the visible reality. But when she processed that Catharine was talking about the photo of the boy and not the tarantula, she understood clearly.

"I understand clearly," Diane said.

"What a weird response."

"He's beautiful, I meant. I meant you are both beautiful in that photo."

"We were younger in that photo. There are other photos where we are older."

"Time." Diane guffawed.

Catharine reciprocated. "Right? What is time even?"

Catharine took her hand away from the photo frame. The tarantula set its foot back on the desk. Diane completed her movement to stand up.

"Go talk to Dawn."

"I will."

Catharine turned back to her computer knowing she had reports to write.

Diane left Catharine's office knowing she needed to talk to Dawn.

The tarantula stared at the ceiling not knowing at all what a ceiling is.

THE VOICE OF NIGHT VALE

CECIL: . . . which implied a lot while saying little. Indeed the same could be said for the rest of the planets in the solar system. None of them commented.

Our town is once again facing a serious tarantula problem. The Night Vale Unified School District indicated that fewer than one in five tarantulas graduate from high school. Indeed, most spiders never even enroll in public education, choosing to instead spin webs and eat smaller insects.

Tarantulas are simple creatures, thought PTA Treasurer Diane Crayton today, without ever voicing that sentence aloud to anyone, according to several reliable and invasive spy satellites that were scanning her brain at the time.

We reached out to the tarantula community for a response to Diane's privately held opinion, and were immediately crawled upon by several of them. I think they are gone, but I am feeling a vague tickling on my back that I am afraid to investigate.

Maybe I'm developing migraines. I should ask Carlos about that.

Listeners, the Sheriff's Secret Police are out in large numbers tonight in Night Vale. They are not looking for a killer or a missing person. There is no disaster or accident to handle. They are simply wandering around town in large numbers. Some of these police are working, sitting in patrol cars waiting for minor traffic infractions or calls to duty.

Some of these police are not working. They are out to dinner with their families, or watching a popular sporting event on a bar television with friends. Some are reading books or catching up on television shows. Some are working late in a secret precinct office probably hidden in that heavy-looking, unmoving cloud.

The secret police are out in large numbers tonight. Nearly every member of the secret police is somewhere in Night Vale. They all exist. We feel very safe.

More news next, but first a brief word from our sponsors.

Pepsi. A refreshing drink. A soft tone playing when you wake up, but then it is gone and you don't know if you dreamed it. A hallway glimpsed in the back of your refrigerator, but when you look again it is gone. The recurring feeling that your shower is losing faith in you. Desperation. Hunger. Starving, not literally, but still. That hallway again, lined with doors that you know you can open. Your fridge is empty. You haven't left your home in days, and yet you come and go. This isn't food. What are you eating?

Pepsi: Drink Coke.

The City Council held their third press conference in as many hours to reiterate the extreme dangers posed by angels.

"There is no such thing as an angel," said the council, in their unified manyvoice, "but if there were, what a dangerous and disgusting creature it would be. Think of its many legs and its ghastly voice. Think of an angel as a murderer hiding in your home. Think of an angel as the very concept of meaningless injury and death. You'll have to imagine all of this because angels do not exist."

"Stay away from them," they concluded.

We now return you to the sound of whatever is around you, which is probably a great deal more sound than you think, only some of which indicates future harm for you.

7

Old Woman Josie would come first. Jackie could visit her mother later.

Josie's house was near the edge of town, next to the used car lot. When a person was done with a car, and they didn't need to pawn it, they would park it in the used car lot, open the door, and run as fast they could for the fence, before the used car salesmen could catch them. No one ever came to buy one. The used car salesmen loped between the lines of cars, their hackles raised and their fur on end. They would stroke the hood of a Toyota Sienna, radiant with heat in the desert sun, or poke curiously at the bumper of a Volkswagen Golf, nearly dislodged by potholes and tied on with a few zip ties. The used car salesmen were fast and ravenous, and sometimes a person who meant only to leave their car would leave much more than that.

Jackie parked her car down the street to avoid any confusion with the salesmen. Her stomach hurt, not like she had eaten something bad but like she had done something bad. It was a stabbing pain on her right side. Maybe her appendix had burst. That's a thing, right?

Jackie was not at work. She had left her routines fully. In her hand was a paper. In her mind were vague memories of a man with a tan jacket, holding a deerskin suitcase.

She approached the house. It was a low bungalow, avocado green, with a neat lawn kept well watered in the dry climate at the expense of some other place far away and out of mind.

The lawn was surrounded by a border of pebbles, arranged into geometric patterns that were perhaps meant to ward away evil or might have just been the way earthquakes had left them. The fence between the house and the car lot was tall and chain link. A used car salesman howled, hopping from car roof to car roof with an animal joy. Jackie creaked open the metal gate into Josie's side yard, with an outdoor sitting area made of rusted metal rocking chairs with cushions whose fabric was faded nearly all the way to white by the sun.

"Can I help you?"

She turned. There was a being that was difficult to describe, although the best and most illegal description was "angel." Angels are tall, genderless beings who are all named Erika.

"I was just doing some trimming," the being said. They were holding hedge trimmers and standing by an empty patch of dirt. There were no plants of any kind anywhere near them.

"I'm looking for Old Woman Josie," Jackie said.

The being shifted. There was the crack of heavy wings flapping and a flash of a blinding, bright blackness, a darkness so radiant it seemed to Jackie her heart would break.

"Josie?" the being said. "Sure. She's around. Let me go get her." They didn't move.

"Ah, okay. Thanks, man," Jackie said. The being still did not move. "I'll just knock then?"

"No need," said Josie. "Erika got me." She was walking in from the backyard, hunched over a cane, her long hair in strings over her face. But there was something about her body that seemed powerful, like an Olympic athlete perched on an old woman's skeleton.

"Great," Jackie said. "Thanks, Erika." The being still did not move. A flock of birds took off from a tree on the street, bird after bird, more birds than could possibly fit in a tree. They seemed confused, cawing and flying into each other.

"What can I do for you today, young Jackie Fierro?" said Josie. "Finally taking a day off and enjoying yourself?"

"Nah, just wanted to ask you about some stuff." More pain. Maybe her appendix really had burst. Maybe she would die. "I have a . . . problem. Thought maybe someone else might be having it too."

"Almost always we are all experiencing the same problems as everyone else," said Josie, "and pretending we don't so that every one of us thinks we are alone. Come on inside."

She hobbled over to the front door. Under her arm was a cloth-wrapped bundle, with dirt clinging to it. As they entered the cool of the house, she set it on a kitchen counter and led Jackie into the living room.

"Take any seat you'd like in here," she said. "They're all the most plush thing your butt will ever experience."

Jackie chose an overstuffed easy chair with a paisley design.

"Wow," she said, settling back and back into fabric that continued to give. For a moment the pain vanished. Comfort was the answer to all life's problems. It didn't solve them, but it made them more distant for a bit as they quietly worsened.

"You wanted to ask me a question?" said Josie, who had put herself on the couch with a good view of the bundle on the kitchen counter. She seemed to be counting under her breath, keeping time with a tapping foot.

"Yes. What do you know about a man in a—"

"Ah, hold on, dear." A different being, just as difficult to describe as the one outside, was bringing in coffee and a plate of Oreos. "The only thing for company, of course. Coffee and Oreos. Would you like any?" Josie asked.

"No, thanks."

"No?" Josie frowned. The being may have frowned too. It was difficult to tell and, of course, impossible to describe.

"Well, sure then."

"Sure then?" Josie shook her head. "No, no. If you don't want the coffee or the Oreos then you don't take the coffee and the Oreos. Please take it away, Erika."

The being was gone. Presumably they walked away. Jackie must have just missed them walking away. Josie glared at the bundle on the counter.

"Don't you dare," she said.

"Don't I dare what?"

"I wasn't talking to you. Tell me your question."

"Josie, do you know anything about a man in a tan jacket, holding a deerskin suitcase?"

"The man in the tan jacket?" Josie's voice took on a new tone, one filled with interest and perhaps panic. Erika was back. Both of the Erikas. They sat on either side of Josie on the couch. Their faces were similar to the ones that a human uses to express fear. No, not fear. Concern. They looked concerned.

"Yes," Jackie said. "A man. In a tan jacket. Holding a deerskin suitcase."

The angels' eyes flared, which was an action as odd to witness as it is difficult to picture.

"Oh, my dear," said Josie. "I don't know if you should be asking about all that. Are you sure you wouldn't rather have some Oreos?"

"I wouldn't, no."

"Fair," Josie said. "Then we'll talk about a man in a tan jacket holding a deerskin suitcase." She clutched her left hand against her side like she had a pain there, but no pain registered in her face.

"We don't know anything about him," Josie continued. "Not Erika, nor Erika. Of course Erika never really knows anything about anything, but Erika's a sweet one, so."

"Do you know about him or not?"

"We know about him, we just don't know anything about him. We are aware that he exists, so there's that much, but his existence is the limit of it, the knowledge."

"Knowledge is made of limits," said Erika, the one who never really knows anything about anything.

"That's cool," said Jackie. She did not mean it, and she said it in a way that let them all know she did not mean it.

"Yes, it's pretty cool," said Erika, the sweet one, meaning it completely.

"Here is what it is," said Josie. "We have seen the man you are talking about many times. But we can never remember anything about him."

The Erikas nodded sadly.

"We were not even aware he was a man," said the Erika who was not sweet. "We cannot see gender."

This was not why they were sad. Their sadness was unrelated to the conversation. It was not unrelated to the dirt-covered bundle on the kitchen counter.

"Had the same problem," said Jackie. "Kept forgetting everything I knew about him moments after I had started knowing it. It, I dunno." She struggled to find a combination of words that would encompass how deeply the last twelve hours had unsettled her. She knew how she felt. She just needed to describe it in words. "It sucks," she said instead.

"Yes! Yes, it does suck," said Josie. Her face was limp and her mouth kept forming a smile only to lose it. This was related to the conversation.

She reached across and placed her hand on Jackie's.

"Erika? Erika? Can we have a moment alone?"

The two beings were no longer on the couch. Through the window Jackie could see one of them plucking absently at a tangle of blackberries, although their head was turned slightly back toward Jackie, presumably trying to hear.

"Jackie, there are things that I cannot tell you." Josie's hand was still upon Jackie's. Josie's other hand was clenched at her side. "I cannot tell you because they are secret, or because they are impossible to put into words, or because I do not know them. Mostly it is because I do not know them.

"Considering an entire universe of knowledge, worlds upon worlds of fact and history, I know almost none of it. And much of what I know is not the kind of thing that I'm aware I know, or think of as 'something I know.' What toast smells like, for instance. What sand feels like. Those are not the kinds of facts I would tell anyone, or even think to tell anyone."

Jackie didn't know what to say. She agreed with all of what Josie was saying but also didn't care about most of it.

"Okay" was all she ended up saying.

"All of this is to say that I am choosing to not tell you some of what I know. Or I am lying to you about it. And I want you to forgive me."

"We all want things," said Jackie.

Josie nodded sadly. She stood, which involved a complex re-arrangement of flesh and joints and muscles.

"Walk with me," she said. And Jackie did. They walked into the kitchen. Josie did not acknowledge the bundle on the table, and so neither did Jackie. If Josie wasn't going to express concern about something, then Jackie sure as hell wasn't going to either.

Josie produced a glass of water, through practiced manipulation of cupboards and valves and municipal plumbing. Neither she nor Jackie was impressed with the human miracle represented by how easily the glass of water was produced.

"Drink this," she said, extending it to Jackie. "It'll help with your migraines."

"I don't get migraines. I've got something much worse." She started to hold up her left hand.

"Drink."

Jackie did.

"I don't get migraines, though," she said after.

"Jackie, I'm sorry that this has happened to you when you are so young. For all those decades you have run the pawnshop, you have been so young and unaware of the cruelty of life outside of the equally but differently cruel bubble of youth."

"How many decades?" Jackie asked, mostly to herself.

"I know what you are looking for. I know what has happened. And it's going to be very dangerous. You may not live through it. And if you do, the you that lived through it will not be the same you that lived before it. In that sense, you will definitely not exist after, and I'm sorry."

The bundle started to float off the table. Josie rolled up a Cave and Cavern Decor and Accessories Catalog, the kind that clogged up so many Night Vale mailboxes, and slapped at the bundle. It plopped back on the table.

"Damn ungrateful," she said.

"What is?" said Jackie.

"Nothing. Nothing is. The man in the tan jacket is from a dangerous place. A place that no one can go to and return from. That's what we think."

Josie held out her left hand. In it was a slip of paper. It said the name of a place.

"You too?"

"There are many of us. We're not sure what's happening. We need to know more." Josie tossed the paper on the counter and sat down at a kitchen stool, the slip of paper already back in her hand.

"Where do we start?" said Jackie.

Josie told her. Jackie swore at her, and then apologized for swearing.

"The library, though." Jackie considered. "No. That's. That's." She indicated with her hands what it was.

"The search for truth takes us to dangerous places," said Old Woman Josie. "Often it takes us to that most dangerous place: the library. You know who said that? No? George Washington did. Minutes before librarians ate him."

Jackie opened the front door. The pain in her gut subsided for a moment, or perhaps only faded under the anxiety of thinking about the library.

The yard outside seemed so bright and so distant from the dim interior. The Erikas carried on with their yard work. There was a hole dug into the backyard that one of them was starting to fill. They stood motionless, muttering at the hole, and a bright black light enveloped the displaced dirt, nudging it back into its place.

There were hands wrapping around her. Josie was hugging her, but the angle was wrong, and there was a significant height difference. They both stood in the unnatural hug for a moment, neither wanting to acknowledge the misalignment of the physical affection.

When Jackie thought about where she had to go, she did not feel fear. But she felt an awareness of how tenuous it was, the collection of thoughts and habits that was Jackie Fierro. How easily those could all be taken away and rearranged into some other form of matter.

"Stay away from the man. Don't try to follow him to his city. It's a trap."

"Josie. I can't live with this," Jackie said, looking at the paper in her hand.

"It's going to be okay," said Old Woman Josie. "It will be."

She squeezed harder, and Jackie turned in to the hug, allowing herself to be comforted. Her stomach did not hurt anymore, or it hurt differently.

"That was a lie," said Josie. "That was one of those times I was lying."

"I know," said Jackie. "It's fine."

She was lying too.

8

Diane was filling her gas tank when she saw Troy. She didn't approach him, and he didn't notice her. She had not seen Troy in fifteen years, and had not wanted to see him ever again.

When she tried to put the nozzle back onto the pump, it kept falling off because her hands were shaking. She didn't feel anything at all, but she couldn't get her hands to stop shaking. By the time she looked up, Troy was already gone. He had gotten into his car (white sedan, broken taillight) and pulled away without looking at her once. She forced herself to stand very still and breathe slowly until her hands stopped shaking. Once they were steady, she put the nozzle back onto the pump, deliberately opened her car door, and drove away at a reasonable speed. The entire time she felt fine.

Weeks later, she stopped by her bank to get change for a PTA fund-raiser. Sitting behind one of the desks was Troy, wearing a dark suit and a plastic name badge. She tried to confirm the name on the tag without him noticing her staring but was unable to.

This time her hands did not shake at all. She actually felt fine, but she tasted blood. Without even noticing, she had been biting her lower lip so hard that the tooth had broken through. She wiped the blood away and walked past him with her withdrawal slip, not looking at him. Because she wasn't looking at him, she couldn't see if he was looking at her.

Just a few days after that, she and Josh went to the movies. This was a monthly tradition that went back to when he was seven. He had been acting glum, taking on oozing, gloppy forms that made a mess of the furniture and carpet, and asking her a lot of questions about his dad and where he had gone. She had been alternately terrified and exasperated by the moody creature that had appeared in place of her little boy, and she announced that, as a special treat, they would go to the movies.

That night at the movies was the first good night they had had in weeks. She hadn't been sure what to see and just asked at the ticket counter for whatever popular children's movie was playing. The joyful glow of being somewhere together and feeling like they were both on the same team had outshone the silly antics of the funny characters in the kids' movie (*No Country for Old Men*) up on the screen. They had left the theater, him walking upright, with non-oozing legs, and holding her hand with a human palm and fingers. He did not ask about his father again for months.

And so started their monthly attempt to recapture the lightness of that first night. Mostly it was good. Sometimes, especially lately, she had to remind him to keep his form short, and free of any broad wings or smoke emitters that might obstruct other moviegoers' views. He would always do what she said, but not without a lot of sighing and eye-rolling (he almost always took a form with eyes when going to the movies, although he had gone through a period where he preferred the experience of sightless listening).

This particular night, the theater was showing the sequel to that popular animated franchise about the trees that look like trees but have human organs and try to stop developers from razing their forest. The trees are unsuccessful at first, but in the end the construction crews learn their lesson after seeing the large quantities of blood, and hearing the mangled screams.

Later they are eviscerated themselves by vengeful arboreal spirits. Diane thought the movie wasn't as good as the original, but she adored the comical voice work of immortal cinema legend Lee Marvin. Josh said he thought it was boring, but he said that about most movies, and he seemed to laugh at most of the jokes and funny death scenes.

While sitting through the previews, Diane saw Troy enter. He was wearing a polo shirt and carrying a carpet sweeper. He crossed from one exit to the other. He seemed to be checking the floor lights along the aisle. One strip was unlit.

Diane tried not to look at Josh and immediately failed, turning to watch his silver, scaly skin, his flat nose and protruding eyes intent on the screen. Josh hadn't recognized Troy. Why would he? Josh hadn't seen Troy since he was a baby. She saw herself in Josh, and sometimes assumed he did the same.

Josh did not see himself in Diane. She knew this.

She put her arm around Josh, ostensibly out of affection, but subconsciously out of protection. He glanced at her hand hanging near his non-shoulder. He glanced back at Diane, confused but not upset.

Diane looked forward, toward the screen, thinking about how to not think about Josh's father. Her foot was tapping. She carefully stopped her foot from tapping.

Here is what it was about Troy.

Diane does not always have a husband. There was a time when she always had a husband, but now she never has one.

She always has an ex-husband. They were never married, but husband and ex-husband are the shortest-hand way to describe her relationship to Troy.

Diane is interested in the semantics of marriage and not marriage. This is why:

Diane always has two parents. Someday she will never have

two parents, but right now she always has them. They are mother and father to Diane, and grandmother and grandfather to Josh.

Her parents have never been married. They never want(ed) to be married. They want(ed) to be together and in love. They are almost always together and almost always in love. They never want(ed) to get a certificate or fill out paperwork or have their love and togetherness approved by a smiling god.

They, of course, value and respect others' love of a smiling god. (Is that a smile?)

They also fill out paperwork and get certificates when required to do so for, say, a job or a driver's license or Diane's birth or the times they're required to play the mandatory city-wide lottery whose winners are fed to the hungry wolves at the Night Vale Petting Zoo.

But they do not want to be married. Our life together is just that: our life together, they might say if you asked them to succinctly grandstand about their choice. They might, but they probably wouldn't. They aren't sanctimonious or vociferous. They simply love each other, and that is enough for them to believe in.

Diane too wanted to be with someone and be in love with someone. She wanted to do these things without being married. She still does. She saw herself in her parents. She saw how she could be, how life could be, how love could be.

There is a correlation between seeing what could be and experiencing what is. But, as the well-spoken scientist who is often interviewed on the news says: "Correlation is not causation" and "Past performance is not a predictor of future results."

Diane's parents are also two different races. It matters which races, but it matters only to Diane and her parents and their family and friends, not to those who do not know them. Not everyone gets to know everything about everybody.

Growing up in the Southwest, Diane saw a few mixed-race parents, mixed-race children, but she did not always have the opportunity or inclination to befriend these families. When she was a kid, friends were still determined by City Council decree, based on the numerology of each child's name, which had been considered the most solid foundation for a lasting friendship.

Sometimes she was teased, called terrible names by other children. Sometimes, those children were not the same race as one of her parents. Conversely, those same children were often the same race as her other parent.

As Diane became a teenager, she continued to hear not only about her race but also about her body.

She was a girl, not yet a woman. She was fifteen years old.

Imagine a fifteen-year-old girl of mixed-race parents.

That's pretty good. That's very close, she might say to anyone who described what she looked like. Diane didn't know what she looked like. She never cared to know. Many people would tell her anyway.

When her body won the race to womanhood against her person, Diane began to hear that she was tall, short, fat, skinny, ugly, sexy, smiled too much, smiled too little, had bad hair, had beautiful hair, had something in her teeth, dressed nice, dressed cheap, had duck feet, had elegant feet. She was too dark. She was too pale.

She heard a lot of different descriptions of her, and she took them all as truth.

You must never need to get any sun, Diane, a person might say as they playfully (and jealously) batted their sleeved arm at her. You don't look like who you are, Diane, a different person might say as they playfully (and scoldingly) batted their unsleeved arm at her.

Teasing about race came less and less. Or rather, it disguised itself as simple assessment. You sound like a regular person on the phone, someone might say to her on the phone.

She also heard about the non-marriage of her parents. You're technically a bastard, right? people sometimes asked when they heard her parents were unmarried.

Were you an accident? other people (sometimes the same people) might ask. Do they not love each other? other people might inquire, earnestly. Well, they've got an easy escape if things ever go wrong, still others might joke, unearnestly. Are they swingers? some might joke and others might ask sincerely.

But most common was the assumption that she would never fall in love. You'll probably never meet someone, some assumed, because your parents didn't teach you the importance of marriage.

She did find true love. His name was Troy. He was seventeen. She was an older seventeen.

Imagine a teenager named Troy.

That's not bad. He's a bit less athletic, but it doesn't matter. Troy looked like what he thought he looked like. Troy always looked exactly how he thought he looked. He never loved Diane until they met. Then he always loved her. Until later, when he never loved her.

"I will always love you," he sometimes said.

Later he didn't say this at all. He wasn't even there to say it.

They were always together and always in love for the eight months they first knew each other, working summer jobs at the White Sands Ice Cream Shoppe. Then Josh, not yet named Josh, began to form. He began first as scattered cells. Those cells joined and began to multiply into billions and billions of cells until they were shaped like a single, giant cell.

Those cells added more cells from Diane's cells, and those cells began to make eyes and feet and kidneys and tongues and wings and gills, growing and expanding into a Josh-like shape. People pointed out to Diane how different she looked on the outside. She did not feel she looked any different.

Then one day Josh came out of Diane.

She was a girl, finally a woman. She was eighteen years old.

Imagine an eighteen-year-old mother.

Imagine a seventeen-year-old father.

Troy couldn't. Troy couldn't see himself anymore. He looked at Josh, whom he named after his uncle, a retired Army Ranger he vaguely thought of as "cool," and Troy saw a mirror out of sync. A face stared back, making different gestures, different motions than Troy made. It was his face, but it did not look like him, act like him.

Troy had never experienced discord. Or he had never known he had experienced discord until that moment.

Troy moved out of Night Vale when Josh was one year old.

A month later, Troy sent Diane a letter. It said something about a military family. It said something about being children. It said something about mistakes. It said something about remembering each other. It said something about never forgetting her face.

She doesn't remember if he said he would never forget her face or if she should never forget her own face. Either way, neither happened.

Some people told her they knew she would never keep a man. Some told her that good parents would have insisted Troy marry her. Some told her she dressed inappropriately. Some told her she was too tall. Most told her she would never get married now.

This was fine with Diane. This is still fine with Diane.

We meant to say you'll never meet anyone now, let alone get married, most would clarify.

Josh was always curious about who his father was. He understood, based on what his friends had told him, that many children had two parents, and there were periods where it was clear he felt one short. Often he would ask questions. Sometimes those questions were out loud.

Diane sometimes hears that Troy is an actuary. Sometimes she hears Troy is a florist. Sometimes she hears Troy is a cop. A toll collector. A professor. A musician. A stand-up comedian. Once she heard a terrible rumor he became a librarian, but she could not imagine Troy becoming the darkest of evil beasts, no matter what he had done to her. Is it even possible for a human to become a librarian? Diane wondered.

And now she and Josh in the movie theater, and Troy, unnoticed by Josh.

The dark strip of floor lighting turned back on. Troy, still not looking her way, gave a big thumbs-up to somebody out of sight, just around a dark corner. Troy's teeth shone in shadow. He did not look at Diane. Troy exited the theater slowly, still grinning, thumb still extended.

She looked back at Josh, her arm reflexively tightening around him. He squirmed and glanced at her.

"I'm sorry," she said, and removed her arm.

"No, it's fine," he said, looking down at his half-eaten Twizzler.

"Really?" She put her arm back around him.

They waited quietly for the movie to start.

Later, Diane would return to the theater on her own.

9

Jackie started her car in the direction of the library, but soon it strayed. Or she strayed it. Whatever the verb is to cause to stray. Corrupted. She corrupted her car toward her mother's house.

Her mother had called, and being a good daughter was as convenient an excuse as any. Anything to avoid the library.

She turned onto Desert Elm Drive, a name which was evocative of nothing real. She drove past the Antiques Mall. The antiques in the window were especially cute, wrestling with each other and playfully snapping at each other's tails. But she could never seem to justify the money for an antique, and besides she was rarely home, so how would she care for one?

Her mother lived in the neighborhood of Sand Pit, which was between the developments of Palm Frond Majesty and the Weeping Miner. It was a neighborhood of single-family homes, with small front yards, mostly kept gravel by water-conscious residents, and backyards that rose steeply into hills unsuitable for planting without extensive and time-consuming terracing.

Her mother's house was like any house that was pink with green highlights, or any house with a manually opening wooden garage door fallen half away to splinters, and any house with a rosemary bush slowly encroaching its way into every other plant in the yard, and a front gate that sagged into rusted hinges, and a thick green lawn that frustrated her water-conscious neighbors. Her house could easily be mistaken for any other house that happened to be identical to it.

Jackie felt unease she could not express with any sort of co-herent gesture or incoherent word when she eyed the house. Something about the house was unfamiliar to her. Her heart was beating in her chest, which is where it usually beat. She got out of the car and thought about all else that she could be doing now. Like driving through the desert in that Mercedes that was in her pawnshop, destination unknown (or no, glanc-ing down at her hand, she knew exactly the destination, didn't she?), with the top down, searing air and dust running through her hair, pretending that the discomfort of driving with the top down was enjoyable because it, as an action, signified enjoy-ment. Or finally treating herself to a nice prix fixe dinner (with wine pairings and complimentary antivenoms) at Night Vale's hottest foodie spot, Tourniquet. Or standing very still out in the dunes at night until the lights came down around her and she felt herself lifted by cold alien hands, taken away somewhere secret and far away for research, never to return. All the fun she could be having, except she had never done any of those things, and if she were honest, and she sometimes was, she had never wanted to. What she liked was routine. Her routine was her life.

If she thought about it, her life hadn't added up to much at all, but she never thought about it. Except now, every time she saw that paper in her hand, she thought about it. It was ghastly, all this thinking.

Her mother was waiting at the open door.

"Oh, Jackie, I'm glad you came."

Jackie followed her inside. The house was immaculate, as though no one lived there. Some people prefer to make their homes so neat that there is no evidence of life anywhere at all.

"You had something to say, I think," Jackie said. "I came by to hear it."

"You were always quick to the point. Even as a child."

Her mother led Jackie into the kitchen, which was as pristine as the living room. The colors were teal and raspberry, the same as every other room in the house, with accents of mint. It resembled a model home, and Jackie wondered if the perfect oranges perfectly arranged in the glass bowl on the counter were just wax.

Jackie looked again at the oranges, the kitchen, the clean walls and furniture. She was not sure she had ever been inside this house. Of course, she must have grown up here. Unless her mother moved after she had grown old enough to move away, but she would have heard about it, probably been involved in the moving process, possibly even the process of picking a new place. Also, at nineteen, she couldn't have moved away from home very long ago. But nothing about the house was familiar to her. She looked around the kitchen trying to guess which drawer held the silverware, the surest sign of kitchen familiarity, and she hadn't a clue.

"Do you remember years ago, when we had your best friends Anna and Gracia over for a birthday party and you were annoyed because your birthday wasn't until the next day?" asked her mother.

"Ah," Jackie said. "Mmm," she said. She slipped open a drawer, trying to appear like a person who casually knows where the silverware is. The drawer was full of dish towels.

"I tried to explain that the next day was a school day, and the elementary administration sends armed posses of schoolchildren after truants, but you just wouldn't listen. Always stubborn, you." Her mother's eyes were wide and her lower lip was folded under her teeth. Her fingers were pressed pale into the Formica counter.

Jackie tried another drawer. It was full of an opaque, fatty liquid, simmering from some invisible heat source.

"No," Jackie told herself. She hadn't been looking for the hot milk drawer. The silverware drawer. If she knew where that was, then she knew the house. If she didn't, then.

"I've never been inside this house," she said. Her mother didn't look surprised.

"When you were ten you hit your head on this counter here. I thought you'd be hurt but instead you were laughing. You said it reminded you of a character in a movie doing a funny fall, and that picturing it that way, from a distance, made it hurt less. You couldn't stop laughing."

"How did I even know how to come here?" Now Jackie was afraid again, and it made her angry. In her anger she slammed open another drawer, but again not silverware. "This is where silverware should go, if you think about the kitchen in terms of workflow. And who even has *two* hot milk drawers?"

"You had a knack for hurting yourself but a natural tendency to not really feel it," said her mother. "I remember when you got stung when your birthday piñata was filled with bees. That taught you a valuable lesson about birthdays in general. Remember that?"

"I remember the pawnshop. I remember days at the pawnshop. Going back and back. What I don't remember is where your silverware drawer is. Where is it? Where is the drawer?"

There had never been information more important to her. She crumpled the slip of paper in her left hand, and then fanned herself with it, not a single crease in it.

"I don't have one, dear. You know that. We're both getting worked up. You'd better sit down. We'll figure this and everything else out if we just have more water. It's important. It will help with your migraines."

"I don't get migraines!"

Her mother glanced out the window, and Jackie followed the glance, physically, to the window. Her anger was a creature now, and it walked behind her, pushing her along.

There was her mother's yard, neat grass bordered by gravel. The grass kept alive with an artificial life-support system of pumps and machines stretching hundreds of miles to the nearest reservoir, its roots barely clinging to the sandy topsoil, mixed heavily with chemical fertilizer. Beyond the lawn, terraced on the steep hill, were plants more suited to the climate. Cacti, and sagebrush, and metallic trees that changed size each day.

"I'm not sure I've ever been out there," she said as she sat down at the kitchen table with her mother.

"Of course you've been out there," her mother said. "Let's talk together about memories you have of being out there."

Her mother rolled an avocado back and forth on the spotless tabletop. The floor and the tabletop and the walls were all the same clean color, and everything was equally clean and unused. The avocado was, of course, fake, as all avocados are.

Then her mother looked up with pleading eyes. She gestured with the avocado, as if that were what she was trying to say, or at least an approximation of that.

"When you were five years old, we held a birthday party for you in Mission Grove Park, in the birthday party area. The one that's fenced in and kept secure in case there's another one of those occasional birthday . . . accidents.

"It was a simpler time. Because I personally had less memories and so less to superimpose upon the world, and so it was much clearer, and also I was younger. Thus, the world was simpler. I'm getting lost.

"We had a birthday party for you. There were presents and guests and a banner that said: HAPPY BIRTHDAY.

"Your father picked you up and swung you around. Parents sometimes show love through velocity. I don't have that picture anymore, but at one point I did. Your father picked you up. It was your birthday. Do you understand?"

"I don't remember having a father."

"Well, dear. He left quite some time ago."

"I don't just not remember having a father. I don't remember you ever telling me I didn't have a father."

Her mother gripped the avocado and searched Jackie's face, presumably for some sense that communication had occurred.

"What ever happened to Anna and Gracia?" Jackie asked.

"Who?"

"The other girls from one of my birthday parties?"

"Oh, I don't know. We all lose touch with friends as we get older."

There was a sound of movement in the backyard. Her mother lowered her eyes as Jackie sprang up and went to look out again.

Still the backyard, and the lawn, and the plants, and the gravel. But now also a shape in the gravel, against the fence. At first, vaguely man-shaped. Then, specifically man-shaped. Her eyes filled in the details as they were discovered. Blond hair. A warm smile. Was that a smile? It was the man from the kitchen at the Moonlite All-Nite.

"Who the hell is this guy?" Jackie said, eyes and fists tightening.

The Sheriff's Secret Police were always easy to summon, as quick as shouting "Hey, police!" out your door or whispering it into your phone. The phone didn't even have to be on. But calling for help was not something Jackie Fierro was likely to do.

What she was likely to do, she thought as she did it, was charge out the back door directly at the man, shouting, "Coming for you, creep!"

There weren't even footprints in the gravel. That's how gone he was. She stumbled to a stop. No one. She jumped at a loud hiss behind her.

"I'm not afraid," she declared, and she wasn't. She was angry, which is the more productive cousin of fear.

The sprinkler popped up, and the water hit her full-on. And then the rest of the sprinklers, one by one, tossing their burden into the hot desert air to nourish the grass, or to float away and evaporate.

"I have definitely never been out here," she said, water streaming down her hair and face into her clothes and shoes. "How did I even know how to get to this house?"

Her mother, visible faintly through the kitchen window, took a deep, slow bite out of the wax avocado and, not looking back at her daughter, began with difficulty to chew.

10

"I'm going to the movies," Diane called at Josh's door, not stopping to wait for a response.

At first, when she started doing this, he would say, "Have
fun" or "I'm just going to stay home," because he could only
hang out with his mother every so often, not every other night.

"I'm going to the movies," Diane called out for the fifth or
sixth time in two weeks, and Josh began to resent her for going
out so much without him. This resentment was not conscious.
He just thought it was idiotic she was going to the movies so
often. Who does she think she is? Josh thought.

Who are any of us, really? the house thought.

Josh stopped answering, and Diane stopped expecting an
answer. She would simply go.

It was 8:00 P.M. The movie that evening was John Franken-
heimer's 1973 adaptation of *The Iceman Cometh* again. Diane,
like most people, had seen the film dozens of times in her life—
there were nightly screenings of it by Night Vale city ordinance.
She didn't love the movie as a movie, but she appreciated it as
a familiar comfort.

She would often cry, particularly when the character Larry
Slade said, "As the history of the world proves, the truth has no
bearing on anything." It is not a sad or emotional scene. In fact it
is quite a didactic one, but hers were tears of nostalgia. She would
mouth the line "It's irrelevant and immaterial" along with Larry.

Anyway, she wasn't there because of the movie.

Diane bought a ticket from the sentient patch of haze working in the box office. Her name was Stacy, and Diane had developed a sort of friendship with her, or at least the comfortable familiarity of recognizing each other without making a big deal of it.

Each time she went she would look for Troy while trying not to make it obvious that this was what she was doing. She sometimes was successful at keeping this even from herself, thinking as she looked around that she was just curious about new releases that had made it past the Night Vale Top Secret Censorship Board (which consisted only of a guy named Luis, who refused to watch any of the movies he judged on the risk he would see a forbidden idea or gesture) or the current price of a tub of popcorn (which Night Vale Cinemas kept strictly linked to the coal futures market for reasons no one in town understood). But really she was looking for Troy and she was not seeing him.

She waited for a night no one else was in line and no one else was in the box office with Stacy.

"Do you know a guy who works here named Troy?"

"Sure. He's not here tonight though."

"Oh, shoot. I'm an old friend of his. I was hoping to run into him here. Do you know when he usually works?"

There was a long pause. Stacy, a haze with no face or body to read, continued to drift around the box office booth. Diane did not know if she had made Stacy uncomfortable with the question.

"I'm sorry. You probably can't answer—"

"No no. I'm looking at the schedule right now."

Diane saw some papers rustling on a clipboard pinned to the wall.

"He's working tomorrow from eleven to four."

"Oh, great," Diane managed. She felt like she was choking, but she was able to breathe just fine. She nodded, as casually as she could. "Thanks, Stacy."

Diane's life at work was no easier. No one was talking about Evan. Nobody remembered Evan. She told everyone apologetically that she must have been confused.

"Because of your migraines?" asked Janice Rio, who was assistant director of sales and, more relevantly, whose desk was closest to her lonely outpost near the server room.

"No," said Diane. "I don't have . . . no."

"Hmm," hummed Janice. It was what she did when she didn't care what the other person had said but the rhythm of conversation demanded a response. She walked away before more responses might be needed.

Diane did not get much work done, which was not as responsible as she liked to think she was. Instead she spent a lot of time looking at a couple pages of notebook paper she had found on the floor of her car.

The top sheet had a phone number and an address in writing that looked like Josh's. The address was in Old Town Night Vale and had a unit number at the end. Josh had had a friend years ago who lived in that part of town, but Diane couldn't think of anyone he might know now who lived there.

On the second sheet of paper, a different handwriting, still by Josh. His handwriting regularly changed depending on the size and shape his writing appendage took. A tentacle and a wing and a human hand, even with the same mind behind them, will wield a pen differently through the sheer fact of mass and shape. Still, like with anything related to his transformations, Diane could always tell Josh's handwriting. There was always something at the core of it that pinged at the place inside her where she kept all the care she had for him.

The note said, "I want to meet this guy."

Below it, in handwriting that was not Josh's and written in a different color ink: "I'll get you his number, but don't call him yet."

Josh: "I won't. Duh. Does he have a picture? I want to know what he looks like."

[Who?]: "If he doesn't I can get one."

Josh: "What's his name?"

And then nothing more. Diane wondered who the boy was Josh was interested in. She didn't know if he had ever been on a date with anyone. He had never been willing to talk about dating with her.

Diane wondered how to bring this up to Josh, and then she wondered if this was even the kind of thing you bring up with a teenager.

"So you're interested in dating?" she could ask, but expecting what? A yes? Then what?

"What's his name?" she followed up in her daydreamed conversation.

"I don't know. Someone else knows," she projected him saying as he looked down his thin beak at his hands, which had twice as many fingers as her own.

"You wanted to ask what the boy's name was. Why didn't you pass the paper back to your friend?" she imagined herself asking.

"Why are you reading my notes?" she pictured him shouting. His eyes pink, his long teeth bared. He was crying, his wings flapping.

She imagined this conversation a few times at her desk, and it never ended any better.

She stuffed the note in her pocket and lied to Catharine that she was having a migraine (Catharine had said: "I can see that." Diane didn't understand how someone could even see a migraine.) and left work early—sometime between the hours of eleven and four.

She was anxious and driving fast, listening to the radio turned up to a loud but sensible volume. Cecil Palmer was talking to that scientist, who was explaining how clouds are made of moisture and aren't cover for alien crafts or appendages of a great sky being. It seemed ridiculous, like most things on the radio these days. He was bending facts to create an absurd argument just to get listeners stirred up.

She was disappointed, because Cecil and the scientist were dating, and interviewing your partner for a news program seemed to be a conflict of interest. And, more important, the scientist was talking nonsense.

" . . . tiny, tiny droplets that are invisible individually, but as a whole form a puffy white cloud," the scientist said.

That was when she heard sirens, which at first she thought were municipal censorship to spare regular citizens from having to hear this kind of talk on community airtime, but then she realized were actually on the road behind her.

She was doing almost fifty in a thirty zone. Okay, she thought, so this I deserve.

As she pulled her car over, she looked at the clock on her dashboard and realized there was no way she was going to get to the theater in time to see Troy. A feeling that had risen to the top of her chest slipped back down into her belly. She couldn't tell what that feeling was or if it was good or bad.

There are no regular police in Night Vale. There used to be, but it was decided that a regular police force wasn't secure enough. Everyone knew that the regular police existed; someone could use that information against Night Vale somehow. No one was sure how, but the threat was enough. There had been community meetings and then the police had vanished with no official explanation. A couple days later, the Sheriff's Secret Police force appeared around town, driving dark red sedans with gold racing stripes and black seven-pointed stars on the sides that say SECRET POLICE on them, staffed by the exact same people who had previously been regular police officers. Everyone felt much safer after that.

Which is why it was so odd that the car that had pulled her over was an old-fashioned police cruiser, light bar on top and Crown Victoria body. The officer getting out of the vehicle was wearing just a regular police uniform without the cape or blowgun belt.

She dug around in her glove compartment for her insurance card and registration, and then in her pocket for her license. She pulled out Josh's crumpled-up note.

She stared at the note. She must have stared at it for a while; she wasn't sure.

There was a loud tapping in her left ear.

She looked up, confused. There was a knuckle rapping on the window a few inches from her face.

She screamed, but she wasn't scared. Her body screamed before she could do anything about it. The knuckle stopped hitting the glass.

She held her hand to her chest. Her other hand pressed the window button.

"I'm sorry," she said, exhaling, long, slow breaths.

"License and registration, please."

The voice was vaguely familiar, but she was too in her own thoughts to care.

"Here you go."

Silence. Diane saw khaki pants, khaki shirt, a black leather belt, and elbows as he read her documentation, and elbows as he wrote out a ticket.

This took several minutes because, by law, police are required to describe the nature of the sunlight at the time of the infraction in verse, although meter and rhyme are optional.

"Searing, yellow, and there's a sort of purplish halo around it before it fades into the mundanity of sky. It is a reminder—this sun—of our near-infinite smallness in a near-infinite universe. But today, as I write this speeding ticket, I feel I could crush the sun like a grape underfoot, and that the universe is an umbrella that I may fold up and put away," the officer wrote on Diane's ticket.

Diane thanked the officer when he handed her the ticket, but her eyes were on Josh's note on the passenger seat.

"Just be careful, umm . . . Diane," he said, and her head cleared enough to recognize where she knew that voice from. She looked up.

He was blond and his teeth shone. They briefly made eye contact—or she assumed they made eye contact through his mirrored shades—and then he was gone, walking quickly back to his cruiser.

She tried to breathe in and missed.

It was Troy.

THE VOICE OF NIGHT VALE

CECIL: " . . . ALL HAIL, ALL PLANT YOUR FACE INTO THE FALLOW
EARTH AND WEEP IT INTO PROSPERITY," it concluded, before cutting
the ribbon to officially open the new downtown roller rink. A big thanks
to the Glow Cloud for its speech, and, of course, all hail the mighty
Glow Cloud.

A warning to our listeners: There have been reports of counterfeit
police officers on the roads, who, instead of looking after our interests,
work under arbitrary authority to unfairly target and extort those who
are least able, societally, to fight back. If you see one of these FalsePo-
lice, act right away by shrugging and thinking What am I gonna do? and
then seeing if anything funny is on Twitter.

And now some sobering news. Station intern Jodi was asked to al-
phabetize everything in the station as part of the Sheriff's Secret Police's daily census of every single item in Night Vale. Unfortunately,
Jodi was so assiduous in her work that she alphabetized herself as
well, and what was once a helpful and hardworking intern is now a pile
of limbs and organs, arranged part by gory part from A to Z.

To the family and friends of Intern Jodi: She will be missed. Especially since she alphabetized herself early in the process, and so most
of the station still needs doing. If you need college credit or a place to
hide from the dangerous world outside, come on down to the station
today, and start a long and healthy life in radio.

In other news, a woman wearing a bulky trench coat and aviator goggles, speaking on behalf of Lenny's Bargain House of Gardenwares and Machine Parts, announced that there may have been some slight problems with a few of the things they sold.

"Some of the garden fountains we sold are actually motion-activated turrets," she said. "Also it's possible that we put stickers on armed explosives that said SNAIL POISON. And while we stand by the fact that they will, in fact, kill snails, it should be noted that they will also kill any living organism within several hundred feet of the snails. We probably should have put that on the label. So sue us.

"On second thought," she said, "don't sue us. You don't even know what part of the government we work for. Who are you going to sue? And don't you think we've already paid off all the judges? You don't have a chance."

She cackled, waving an absurdly long cigarette holder terminating in an unlit cigarette. This went on for several uncomfortable moments. Her laughter subsided into a labored snorting and then a few long, intentional sighs.

"Oh man," she said. "I needed that. All right, I think that's everything. Oh yes, I forgot. Absolutely do not touch the flamingos."

She nodded to the few journalists in attendance and returned to her burrow near City Hall, where she was later driven out and ethically captured by the local Cage and Release Pest Control.

The Night Vale PTA released a statement today saying that if the School Board could not promise to prevent children from learning about dangerous activities like drug use and library science during recess periods, they would be blocking all school entrances with their bodies. They pulled hundreds of bodies out from trucks, saying, "We own all of these bodies and we will not hesitate to use them to create great flesh barricades if that is what it takes to prevent our children from learning."

The School Board responded by criticizing the use of PTA funds to purchase so many bodies, but PTA treasurer Diane Crayton said that sadness is eternal, that weakness is another word for humanity, and that all will pass, all will pass. She was holding a cup of coffee close to her chest and murmuring that to herself. I am not sure if she was referring to this current controversy, or if she was even aware of our presence. More on this story, somewhere in the world, always happening, whether we report it or not.

And a big thank-you to local scientist, certified genius, and, oh yeah, my boyfriend, Carlos, who came by earlier to explain clouds. Need something explained in language that for all you know could be scientific? Feel free to drop by Carlos's lab. Sometimes he'll be there. Sometimes it's date night, and he's with me. I am his boyfriend. I don't know if I mentioned that.

11

Jackie rolled open the car window (her car had manual everything except the transmission, which was some form one less than a manual, the works of which even her mechanic couldn't understand. "This isn't even a transmission. This is just a bag of rocks attached by string to your gear change. How does this car even drive?" he had said to her the last time she had gone in for an oil change. Her answer, as was her answer to everything that was outside the routine of her days, was to shrug and cease thinking about it the moment people around her stopped reminding her of it) and let the sun do its thing on her skin. The air as she drove felt good, sliding over her and feeling real in a way that nothing else that day had.

What she needed was someone who understood the world, who studied it in an objective way. She needed a scientist. Fortunately, Night Vale had, just a few years earlier, acquired a few of those.

They had come all at once, scientists being pack animals. Their leader was a nice man named Carlos, who had started dating Cecil, the presenter of the local radio station, after a near-death experience a few years before involving a brutal attack from a tiny civilization living under lane 5 of the Desert Flower Bowling Alley and Arcade Fun Complex. It was an ordinary enough way to begin a relationship, as these things go.

Jackie had always thought they made a sweet couple, even if Carlos was a bit too preoccupied with whatever "science" was, and Cecil was a bit too enthusiastic sometimes about, well, everything. The fact that Carlos was an outsider to Night Vale was unusual as well. Night Vale doesn't bring in a lot of new residents, and most people born there never leave. Everyone liked Carlos, as they liked most out-of-towners (or "interlopers," the affectionate nickname Night Valeans shout while pointing when they see someone unfamiliar in the street). He was likable enough, good looking enough, and smart enough to be reprehensible, but despite all of these things, no one feared or distrusted his clever science or perfect hair.

Because Cecil talked openly on his radio show about Carlos, their relationship was a point of near-constant discussion in Night Vale, all of their imperfections and faults, which made them individuals worth loving. They had built those faults into the usual messy, comfortable, patched-up, beautiful structure that any functioning long-term relationship ended up being.

This, the idea of relationships bit, was all conjecture on her part. She herself felt too young to try to figure out her own life, let alone someone else's life near hers, and so she had never even sought out companionship of that type. Jackie thought about dating from time to time in the distant way a person thinks about eventually becoming famous or owning a castle or growing ram's horns. They're all achievable, realistic goals, but by turning objectives into mere fantasies, she never had to go through the trouble of achieving or maintaining them.

She occasionally found herself thinking about love when staring at the many twinkling spy satellites in the night sky, or when the wind tasted like sour peaches for no understood reason, or when she said a word that seemed different than a word she would ever say. Then she would wonder what it might be like to join her life with someone, or even just a few minutes with someone, just a touch or a glance, just anything, just something.

I'd like to meet someone special someday, Jackie thought.

"KING CITY," the paper in her hand said.

Jackie crumpled the paper against the steering wheel. She hadn't been completely aware she was driving.

She pulled into a strip mall that only had two businesses: Carlos's lab and Big Rico's Pizza. Big Rico's had struggled ever since wheat and wheat by-products had been declared illegal. This was the result of a long and not terribly interesting story, but the gist is that wheat and wheat by-products transformed first into snakes and then into evil spirits resulting in a number of dead citizens.

Jackie parked the car on asphalt that had been lifted into sharp undulations by the roots of a nearby tree, which was transformed by the tires of her slowing car into a disquieting thumping that did nothing to improve her mood.

Carlos's lab was on the outskirts of the science district, which was a pretty run-down part of town. There were a few new laboratories being built, but the science community did not like gentrification, so they resisted new money, holding tight to their history and culture.

It was not uncommon for a single block to have not only marine biologists but also quantum physicists living next door to each other. In many other cities, this may seem like the makings of a civil disaster, but Night Vale's science district really made it work.

There were certainly some major disagreements and highly public conflicts between, say, the astronomers and the ornithologists, neither of which considers the other a real science. It's difficult sometimes for two scientific groups to get on well when the core tenet of one science is to disprove the existence of another science—such as it is with meteorologists and geologists.

Carlos's lab was helpfully labeled with a simple illuminated yellow and black LAB sign and a handwritten

WE ARE "OPEN"!

sign in the front window. The door was unlocked, and led first into a small waiting room, like a doctor's office but with fewer deadly traps. She passed through it into the lab itself.

Carlos and his team of five scientists were huddled around a table. There were rows of beakers around them, all bubbling, and a chalkboard covered in numbers and also the word *science!* in different fancy cursives. Some of the iterations had pink chalk hearts around them. It was much like any university-level science lab.

"Excuse me," Jackie said.

None of the scientists noticed her. They were all writing busily on clipboards and wearing lab coats. This is called "doing an experiment."

She walked up to see what they were experimenting on. Under some work lights was a pink plastic flamingo.

"Careful now," Carlos was saying. "We don't know what this or anything else does."

The scientists nodded in unison and scribbled on their clipboards.

"We understand very little."

More nodding, more scribbling.

"Excuse me, Carlos?" she said. He turned. There really was something blindingly handsome about him. His hair maybe.

Or his demeanor. People are beautiful when they do beautiful things. Perhaps he had spent most of his life doing beautiful things and it had really stuck. He smiled. He had teeth like a military cemetery.

"Jackie, hello. I'm sorry, I was doing science." He waved over at the flamingo. "This is all very sciency stuff. Just here is an equation," he said, indicating some numbers on the chalkboard. "It's important to have equations."

"I see that. How's Cecil?"

"Overenthusiastic, consumed with his work, has very little understanding of science. I love him a lot. The usual."

The scientists nodded and wrote on their clipboards. All information was important information, even if the reasons were not immediately apparent. The reason for anything was rarely immediately or even eventually apparent, but it existed somewhere, like a moon that had escaped orbit and was no longer a moon but just a piece of something that once was, spinning off into the nothing. The scientists were just then writing down that very metaphor. Metaphors are a big part of science.

"I need your help, Carlos."

"Jackie, there's little I love more than helping people. Science and Cecil are about it. But I'm in the middle of an important experiment, and I think if we just push through we might figure out why the experiment is important. Finding out why we are doing what we already were doing is an exciting moment, and I believe we may be almost there."

"All right, dude, but—"

"Besides, Josie asked us to look at this, and I owe her a few. More than a few. I owe her, I don't know, a high number. I would express it as an equation, but it's all figurative and figurative math is really tricky."

"Carlos, look."

She held up her left hand. The scientists all waited with pencils hovering, unsure of what observations they should be making at that moment. She did all her tricks with the slip of paper. She tossed it on the ground, tore it into pieces, flung it onto a Bunsen burner. Hell, she ate it. Why not?

Each trick ended the same way, with her holding the uncreased paper back in her left hand, where it had never really left.

Carlos dropped his clipboard.

"You too?" he said.

"Me too?"

"Let me see that."

He took the slip of paper and examined it closely. When he let go it was back in her hand. The scientists were staring, mouths open. Their clipboards were at their sides. One of them appeared to have overloaded and shut down completely.

Carlos rushed around the lab, turning on and off burners, and throwing switches frantically. The other scientists helped the one scientist reboot.

"We start immediately," Carlos shouted.

"Oh, good," she shouted back. "Why are we shouting?"

"Here is what we know so far. The composition of the graphite is what you would expect to find in graphite. The composition of the paper is exactly what you would expect in paper. All the parts are as we suspected, even as the whole astonishes.

"It does not appear to be physically dangerous. Mentally it exerts a hold stronger than even the fascination with its properties could explain. After all, and I speak as someone who came here for what was supposed to be only a short research fellowship with the local community college, this town is mostly made of the unexplained.

"Sorry, I'm getting distracted. Also, can you stop throwing the paper at me? I know it never actually reaches me, but it's still unnerving, and I'm helping you out here. Thank you. I'm sorry if I snapped. It's okay to say I did. No, it's okay.

"King City is a small town of a little over ten thousand people in Monterey County. You can see pictures of it online. Just search any phrase at all in image search and a picture of it will always be the first result. There doesn't appear to be anything unusual about it, any more than any other place where people live their unusual lives.

"You are not the first I've seen with these slips of paper. It's not important who else. It's important to them, but not to you. I haven't thought much about it, so I guess not important to me either. I just assumed it was another passing strangeness that would take care of itself before Cecil even finished the broadcast day of reporting on it. But it's been a few weeks now. And I didn't realize the paper did that. I wonder what else it does.

"You've reported feeling like your life is different since getting the paper. Like you are not yourself anymore, and the past is not your past, and the future you planned is now impossible. This is a common feeling, usually felt when we first wake up or when we receive thoughts that do not seem to be our own while showering. But with that feeling sustained as long as it has been, and the start of it aligning exactly with your receiving of the paper, it is safe to say that the two are connected.

"Here, look at this equation. I have no idea what it means. It's really long though. I'm going to add a couple more variables. Great, that looks really great. Nilanjana, please add that to the chalkboard.

"The next obvious step would be to go visit King City itself. See if all of this can be explained through simple physical proximity, or even if the slip of paper will react differently when it is proclaiming location rather than destination.

"Oh, and Nilanjana? Draw another 'Science' with a heart around it please. Put that next to the new equation. Thank you, Nils.

"But getting to King City is not as easy. Getting anywhere from Night Vale is a little tricky, as we have a vast desert around us and our reality does not seem to align exactly with the reality of the rest of the world, but King City is an especially difficult case.

"Look at this map. Stan, can you please put the map up on the projector? No, wrong slide. That's the picture of a bee with a label saying 'Blood Oath.' That goes with the apiology project. Yes, the next three slides as well. They're some free-writing I did about bees. That's why they're labeled 'Research Notes.'

"Okay, yes, good. There's the map. So this is a map of our region, with all roads and highways, and I want to show you all something. Let's start here with a laser pointer and try to make our way from Night Vale to King City. Head out on Route 800 and then turn here, and merge with this— But oops, we missed it. So we go back, maybe try cutting across on this little mountain road. You believe in mountains, right? Not everyone does. Either way, we end up miles away. You see? None of the roads connect. It is like they are two entirely different road systems that seem like they should connect but never do.

"Here, this next slide even brings us down to the level of horse and hiking trails, small ranch roads, stuff like that. I won't try to trace it all out right now, but believe me: there is no sequence of walking or driving or any other kind of transportation that would take us from here to King City. Even though, and this is very strange, we could easily follow any number of roads to get to, say, Soledad, just a few miles down the highway from our target. Okay, so easy enough, now that you got to Soledad, just head down the highway to King City. Well, if you're starting in Soledad you can do that. But if you start tracing the roads all the way back in Night Vale, then by the time you get to Soledad you can't find any way to get to King City.

"Scientifically speaking, wow. Big wow. This makes no sense, right? Do you think this makes no sense? Everyone nod if this makes no sense. Everyone's nodding. See, we are all in agreement that it makes no sense.

"But this is all laboratory work. And what does lab work tell you? Almost everything. Labs are very important.

"Something is wrong with King City. That's the most scientific answer I could give you. And I think that it would be dangerous to go. Which you couldn't do anyway. But even the attempt might do irrevocable harm to your person or to the consciousness within your person. Not recommended.

"You might try talking to our mayor. She's had some experience with other worlds. I can't think of anyone else who has. Besides, of course, me. I've had extensive experience. But I don't like talking about myself. It's personal and not scientific.

"Most people don't leave here. Most people only come and then stay and stay and stay. Honestly, I have no idea how long I've been here. Time doesn't work here and all that. But not long enough. I haven't stayed long enough.

"Oh, sorry, I have to go. Or you have to go. I'm going to stay here, this is my place of business. But it's just that Cecil's show is almost on and I never miss it.

"No, I think I haven't stayed long enough at all," Carlos said.

13

The Moonlite All-Nite Diner along Route 800 served okay coffee. Okay pies.

Some of the pies and coffee were invisible, and, for the people who like invisible pie or invisible coffee, this was a real plus. Here's what: If you like a thing, and only one place in town serves that thing, you're going to be pretty excited by that thing, regardless of quality.

So for people who like invisible pie, the invisible pie at the Moonlite All-Nite was perfect, despite being just okay.

Diane did not like invisible pie. Her friend on the PTA, Steve Carlsberg, was one of those people who championed the unpopular dessert. "It's an underappreciated pie, Diane," Steve would sometimes say between bites. "You develop a taste for it, like you do with scotch whiskey, or cilantro, or a salt lick."

Diane remained unconvinced. Her issue was not with flavor (the pie had none) but with texture (it had none).

But Diane was not at the Moonlite with Steve now. She was there to meet Dawn.

They rarely interacted at work and even less often outside of work. There were a lot of reasons for this, none of them interesting. Not everybody gets to be friends with everybody.

Diane was not friends with many people. She had drifted apart from her childhood and teenage friends, because of age and changing circumstance and the high rate of mysterious disappearance and death in Night Vale. In her mid-twenties, she found herself at the funeral of what was her last remaining childhood friend (Cynthia Yin, whom she had met in Music Censorship class in third grade and who had survived three UFO attacks, a year's incarceration by the City Council for voting incorrectly in a municipal election, and a direct encounter with a pack of street cleaners, only to die of a liver cancer which had gone undiagnosed for over a year), and she wondered whether it was worth it to have friends, to make any connections at all when the world so easily took them from her.

Since then, she had continued making friends, but they all, like Steve, were friends of circumstance. The people she worked with in the PTA. Regulars here at the Moonlite. Even the people and sentient patches of haze who often walked the same evening neighborhood route as she did, which was more of a distant nodding relationship than a friendship, but whose names she knew. (A few of them had even whispered some interesting secrets to her as they passed.)

Mostly she contented herself with Josh, who was not a friend, and was often not even friendly, but who filled her life until it couldn't fit much else. She looked with excitement and unease to the day when he would grow old enough that her heart could empty a bit of him and there would be a space left where someone else could fit, although she couldn't imagine who.

Anyway, Dawn was late. This was fine with Diane.

Laura, one of the regular waiters, was standing over a table, long leafy plants growing from her chest and arms and neck. The diners plucked the fruits from her branches, looking at each bright bulb for dents, smelling them for ripeness.

Diane had written down some things to talk to Dawn about. She wanted to know the obvious: how've you been, how's the family, do you have a family (written in parentheses, as Diane did not want to presume that everyone has a "family"), how are you feeling, name every person you've ever worked with, and so on.

But this was all leading to the real reason for their conversation. Evan. Was his name Evan? She looked at her notepad. "EVAN," it said in an unfamiliar hand.

"Evan," Diane said aloud.

"Hey, Diane," Laura shouted across the way, a family of five yanking blackberries and tomatoes from her sides. "Good to see you again. Somebody'll be with you in a minute, all right?"

Diane smiled and waved. Laura was bleeding along her wooden limbs. The diners stopped taking the food from her and stared in discomfort.

"Oops, sorry about that, let me get you another server. Be right back."

Laura bled her way toward the kitchen. A branch caught on a sink and snapped off. Laura begin to weep, still making her way toward the coffee machine, her face growing paler and paler as the stump of the branch spurted blood onto the coffee cups.

"Oh jeez," she said, tears falling from her face and landing like dew on her already blood-spotted leaves. "Clumsy me. Just a real Sally Knock-'em-down."

A blond man wearing a white apron, handsome in all of the expected ways (and in this way almost forgettable), followed behind her carrying a tray of used dishes. As he rounded the corner of the table, Diane saw it was Troy.

Diane got to her feet before she even knew that was what she was going to do. He did not look at her. He trotted with his dishes. She thought she was going to say something, but she didn't know what to say, so she just followed him. It was definitely Troy. Would she follow him into the kitchen? She wouldn't know until the moment came.

He was nearing the swinging silver door and they were well past the restroom arrow sign, well past the point where her presence could be excused, and still she hadn't said anything to him.

The man, and now she was starting to feel unsure that it was Troy, maybe just a man who looked similar, or even a man who didn't look that similar at all, turned around to face Diane. As he pressed his back against the door to open it, he looked at her.

"Excuse me," Diane said much louder than she had intended, "is this the restroom?"

He said nothing. The door swung shut, then open, in smaller and smaller increments. The man who looked like Troy was gone.

"What are you doing, Diane?" It was Laura. She was not smiling. Her branches were still bleeding a little onto the floor.

"Nothing. I just—"

"Restrooms are back that way."

Diane pointed at the door to the kitchen.

"Nope, back that way," Laura said, her face giving nothing away but bland service industry congeniality.

Diane walked toward the restroom, but she did not need to use it so she just slowed her way back into the restaurant and past the coffee counter, glancing into the kitchen area. She couldn't see anyone in it.

"They're right over there, Diane," Laura said from across the room. She pointed with a leafy arm, her face no longer congenial, her eyes unmoving, unmoved.

Diane turned and went into the restroom. She stood in front of the mirror for a minute, her hands gripping either end of the sink. It had been Troy, she knew it. Or, well, maybe it hadn't been. And anyway she was here to find out about . . . Ethan? Ellen? She couldn't remember the name. Nothing about herself seemed certain. She shouted into the sink. It did nothing in response. She shouted again, wondering if the people out in the dining room could hear her. No one came in, anyway. She wasn't sure she had even been shouting out loud, or if she had only thought about shouting. Her throat felt raw.

She ran the sink and then the hand dryer and then returned to her booth.

Dawn was there.

"The waiter told me you were in the restroom. She said to have a seat. Sorry I'm late."

"Hi, Dawn. It's good to see you."

Her throat was tight and sore as she spoke, and she tried to make her voice sound normal.

"What's this?" Dawn grabbed the notepad Diane had left sitting on the tabletop.

"No, you don't have to—" Diane started. "It's just some things—"

Dawn grinned as she read it.

"Well, first off, I am fine. How are you? Do you have a pen?"

Diane indicated the pen next to the salt, pepper, and sand shakers.

"Ah, great." Dawn took it and checked off the questions as she answered them. "The family's great. My sister is pregnant. My father retired and is making hammocks. As a hobby, you understand. He's made thousands, leaving them in a giant pile on his front lawn. The neighborhood association is upset because they think it's a political statement, some kind of conceptual art installation about the existence of mountains."

"Yikes. That's very controversial," said Diane, finding a gap in the conversation she could work her voice into. "I mean, I believe in mountains and all, but I understand it's a controversial viewpoint. I would never force that viewpoint on others."

"Right, well, that's not what he's trying to do at all. Don't get down on my dad. You don't know him. He just likes making hammocks and then putting them in a pile. That's something he's always loved."

"I'm sorry. That's not what I meant. I'm glad your father is happy."

"He says kids come by sometimes trying to steal hammocks from his pile to hang between two trees and lie on. He manages to chase most of those vandals away. He acts irritated when he talks about it, but, between you and me, I think he likes the challenge."

Dawn checked the next thing off the list and added, "Yes, I have a family. It might have made more sense to put that first."

Diane didn't think that anything about today was likely to make sense. She felt nauseous after that moment in the restroom and was extra glad she hadn't ordered any food, invisible or not.

"I'm feeling okay," Dawn said, pen over the next question. "I had a migraine recently, although of course I didn't know until someone told me."

"Of course," said Diane. Why of course?

"Also a bout of food poisoning. Had to miss a couple of days."

"You got a migraine from food poisoning?"

"What? No, how would that happen? It was just food poisoning. We have the salmon deliveryman come by every Tuesday, and leave fresh salmon on our porch. Lately the quality seems to be deteriorating. He used to put an entire live fish there and lumber away. We'd open the door to find a wet creature with panicked, unblinking eyes, flopping around outside our door. We'd kill it with strychnine and have delicious steaks and salads and pastas. But lately, he's just been leaving wet piles of torn, pinkish gray flesh that I hope is salmon. Honestly, I think he's just tossing it from the sidewalk, not even walking up to the porch anymore."

"I've never heard of any kind of meat causing food poisoning. Just wheat and its by-products."

"Well, me neither, of course, but after we ate this week's salmon delivery, and it was especially moist and spongy this week, Stuart and I both felt a bit sick. We couldn't get out of bed for days."

"Is Stuart your husband?" Diane asked.

"Who?"

"Stuart."

"Who is Stuart?"

"You just said his name is Stuart. The man you live with."

"I live alone, Diane. Single as single can be."

Diane suddenly felt like the words she was saying were twisting in her mouth and coming out as different words altogether. No part of the conversation was connecting with any other part. She might throw up after all, but she had just been in the restroom. It would look strange to run back to it so soon. The thought of that slight embarrassment kept her stomach in check.

"Who did you eat that salmon with the other night?"

"Nobody. Just me. Like I said, this is my first time out with someone else in over a month, I think. So glad you invited me."

"Right. I'm glad you agreed to meet me."

A gray-gloved hand rose over the edge of the table, holding two coffees. It quietly slid them in front of the two women. They pretended they did not see the hand, maintaining eye contact and waiting in polite silence as it pushed food they had never actually ordered onto the table: a Greek salad for Diane and a Denver omelet for Dawn. The hand made a subtle flourish of accomplishment and then disappeared back under the table.

"This is about"—Dawn looked back at Diane's list—"Evan?"

Diane moved the Greek salad away from her, one hand on her stomach.

"Yes. I remember working with Evan. I remember him going missing from our office the same time you were out sick. He called me the day you came back, and when I went to his cubicle, where I was certain he worked, there was no cubicle there. Just a plant and a photo and a chair."

"Mm." Dawn's mouth was full of omelet. She seemed very hungry. It must have been the recovery from the food poisoning.

"And neither you nor Catharine remember anyone named Evan working with us?"

"I'm sorry. I don't," Dawn said, having swallowed the mouthful of egg. Diane felt a surge in the back of her mouth and had to take a moment to keep herself together.

"It's just that," she said after that moment, "how can you sit so close to where someone worked and have no recollection of them?"

"Well, Diane, I—"

"You didn't call in. Catharine had some of us ready to go to your house to find you, Dawn. But then you get back to work and Catharine is like 'No, I was totally in the know,' and you were like 'Yeah, just food poisoning.' But I'm telling you the feeling around the office before you came back was that you and, and"—Diane glanced at her notepad—"Evan were both missing. We almost had to get the Sheriff's Secret Police involved."

Dawn set the pen down and slid the notepad back to Diane. Her lips were stern and thin and had a bit of egg on them.

"Diane, tell me what you remember about this Evan."

"I remember working with him. For years."

"Did he like sports?"

"I don't know."

"Movies? TV shows? Books? Certain types of dogs? What kind of clothes did he wear?"

"I remember a tan jacket."

"What else? What color shirts? How tall was he? Was he married? How old was he? What's a memorable thing he once said? Did he ever tell you a joke? Or maybe he had some insight during a meeting? What department did Evan work in, Diane?"

A long pause became a short pause became a quick beat became nothing.

"I don't want to make you seem crazy, Diane. I really don't. Listen, I'm just happy to have a friend to hang out with. I can't remember the last time I hung out with somebody. But I can tell you there was never an Evan at our office."

Dawn's face was flushed, and she was breathing hard. She seemed furious, but it might have just been the food poisoning.

Diane saw the familiar blond man ducking under the counter. She counted slowly to ten, but the man did not come back up. Maybe she hadn't seen anything. Maybe she had come into existence seconds ago and had made up every moment until this moment to explain how she came to be sitting in this booth in this diner.

Dawn took a sip of her coffee to cover the silence, which went longer than either of them had anticipated, so the sip ended up draining her mug. She set down the empty mug and wiped coffee and egg off her mouth.

"Sometimes the only things we can know for sure are the things we feel. I believe you, Diane. I disagree with you, but I believe you."

Diane felt a gentle hand touch her own, a sympathetic pat. Dawn had both hands on her coffee cup. Diane looked back down at her own hand, and saw the final quick motion of a gray-gloved hand disappearing under her table.

14

Jackie felt, as the door swung her back out onto the sun-cracked asphalt, that science had taught her little. Carlos had suggested seeing the mayor. It would mean going to City Hall, which would put her in dangerous proximity to the City Council, but the mayor herself was a comforting figure, and probably safe enough.

City Hall was certainly better than where Old Woman Josie wanted her to go. Anywhere was better than the library.

She sauntered to her car, not in any hurry to leave the mild warmth of the evening sunlight. The desert beyond the roads and buildings was going pink at the edges, orange farther in, and then a deep yellow glow where the setting sun met the horizon. It was all very pretty to look at, and so she did. As a result, she did not notice what was in her car until it grabbed her as she opened the door.

"Erika! You scared the shit out of me." Jackie had to intentionally restart her breathing.

The impossibly tall being, seemingly made of bright black beams of light, shrugged, and there was the flutter of hundreds of tiny wings all beating at once.

"Fear is a reasonable response to life."

Jackie didn't have time for general philosophizing from a being it was illegal to acknowledge existed. Or maybe she did have time. She wasn't about to pretend she understood anything at all about time.

"You're in my car, so explain why or get out."

Erika turned to look at her. Where eyes might be on a human being was a shadowy glow that Jackie could taste in the back of her mouth. It tasted like strawberry candy covered in mud.

"I come with a message on behalf of the angels. We are afraid. All of us. I am perhaps the most afraid."

Jackie forced herself to meet Erika's gaze directly, or as directly as she could given that she could not locate their eyes.

"Is that message supposed to be useful to me?"

"It is not supposed to be anything. It is just a message. Messages are for the sender, not the receiver."

"Then, dude, I hope it helped you out, telling me that. I really do hope that, but could you get out of my car? Or else you're going to end up at City Hall, because that's where I'm going."

The fluttering of wings again. A soft voice singing somewhere far above them.

Erika shrugged.

"Actually, I could use a ride. Do you mind?"

"Do you have gas money?" Jackie wadded up the piece of paper in her left hand and threw it into Erika's chest. It bounced to the window and then back down into Erika's lap.

"I am afraid of this piece of paper," said Erika.

"KING CITY," said the paper.

"Even angels are afraid," said Jackie. Erika stared blankly into a blank lap. Several listening antennas on nearby rooftops swung around to point at the car. A small blinking light on the dashboard repeated the warning

ANGEL ACKNOWLEDGED.

Jackie pushed the reset button to turn it off.

"Sorry, I meant even you are afraid," she articulated loudly for the listening devices. "Seriously, do you have gas money?"

"There was a time where I was extremely wealthy. One of the most wealthy people. But angels don't use money, as they keep telling me over and over." Erika folded their hands in their lap.

"Figures. All right, Erika, let's go."

She started the car, somehow, even though nothing about the engine should have started. "Rocks. This is just a bag of rocks," her mechanic had muttered during her last scheduled maintenance, tears running down his face.

As she pulled the car out, Erika pointed into the desert.

"Behold."

Out amidst the spectrum of sunset, the giant glass building had returned. There were others with it, a multitude of glass specters, and bubbles of light with a source that did not seem to be the rapidly departing sun. The voices of a crowd chanting something just on the edge of intelligible came with it.

"So?" said Jackie, continuing to navigate out of the parking lot. "Sometimes in my mirror I see brief flashes of a faceless old woman. These things happen."

"Not these things," said Erika. "This is all wrong. We are worried about Old Woman Josie. We are worried for her. I am terrified. I am terrified." A few of their long hands were rubbing together.

"I'm sure there's nothing to be terrified of about visions in the desert. It's just our eyes lying to us. Every part of our bodies lies to us constantly. Didn't you ever take a health class in elementary school?" Jackie said.

Erika turned in their seat to keep whatever they passed as

eyes on the spot in the desert where the lights had been until the desert was no longer visible. They turned back.

There was a comfortable quiet between Erika and Jackie, only breaths and breeze and faint traffic.

After a few moments of this, Jackie asked, "So, seriously, man, no gas money?"

"All right, I think I have maybe ten bucks," said the angel.

"What are you looking for?" Dawn asked to the back of Diane's head.

Diane stopped. She had felt fine a second ago, but now a sharpness of nerves hit her chest. She knew how this looked, crouched low, lifting up the trash can in the custodial closet near the office elevator.

"I lost something last week, a slip of paper."

"They'd have already taken last week's trash."

"I know. I just thought maybe it had fallen out. Loose paper. Never mind." Diane stood.

She was significantly taller than Dawn. At least five inches taller. Diane did not see herself as taller.

"What did you lose? Maybe I can help."

Diane hadn't exactly avoided Dawn since their conversation at the Moonlite All-Nite Diner, but she had allowed the natural processes of work to wear away any bridge that might have been formed between them. She was okay with distance. She was okay with being a stranger. And thinking about that day at the diner brought back the nausea; the egg on Dawn's lip, the two realities in Dawn's stories, and the blood dripping from Laura's branches. Dawn's face made her dizzy with memory.

"No, it's fine. It's fine. It was a small piece of paper."

"Like a receipt?"

"Yeah, but with handwriting, I think."

"So a note?"

"Yeah, a note."

"What did the note say?"

Diane was unintentionally not breathing. When she noticed, she started breathing again.

"It's fine. You don't have to tell me."

"KING CITY," Diane said without knowing how she knew to say it.

"King City."

"I think it said 'KING CITY,' in pencil, all caps."

"That's all it said?"

"Yes. It just said 'KING CITY.'"

Dawn stared at her, and Diane didn't know what else to say.

"I don't know how to help you, Diane," Dawn said, a perfect mix of confused and disappointed, and went back to her desk.

Diane stayed at work, not working on work, as everyone else left—Dawn, Catharine, the men (all named Shawn) who worked in sales, Piotr, Celia, Maya, Martellus, Ricardo, and Tina.

Once everyone was gone, she logged on to Tina's computer (as something of a party trick, she was excellent at guessing passwords based on a person's personality, and had long ago correctly guessed that Tina's password was "WhoAmIReally" followed by nineteen question marks), and looked up the office phone records.

She glanced up every few moments, to make sure no one was coming back for a forgotten jacket, or to use the Bloodstone Circle at the office so they didn't have to wait until home to use one. But the office was silent. She felt the silence more than heard it. In her tension it had become tactile.

There was no record of people who called in to the office, only outgoing calls, so that was no good. She then searched the payroll folders for all staff lists. Any sign of someone named . . .

Diane could not remember who she was looking for.

Evan. She was looking for Evan. Diane grabbed blank paper from Tina's printer and wrote "EVAN" in pencil, all caps, and slid it into a new manila folder.

A search of Tina's computer came back with no Evans. It found some usage of "griEVANces" in a folder titled "HR" and several usages of "relEVANt" in Tina's e-mail program. No "Evan."

Diane walked around the empty office again, to reassure herself that it was empty. She imagined being watched.

At Dawn's computer (password "A11isL0ss"), Diane opened the web browser and typed in the address of every phone provider she could think of. Two letters into her third guess, the browser autofilled the address of a log-in screen. When she hit enter, the browser had already filled in a user name and password.

Diane logged into Dawn's phone account as Dawn.

She looked up recent call history and found the four dates Dawn was gone but no record of her calling the office.

Of course, this did not mean Dawn did not have another phone at home. Diane tried looking up more phone and cable providers. There were no other autofills.

Outside Catharine's office, Diane gripped the doorknob, but it did not turn. She stared at the brushed-nickel knob.

She was not at all the type of person to break into her boss's office. Or rather, as it turned out, she was that type of person, but she had never considered herself that type of person. The type to do anything that anyone might consider wrong or that anyone might report to a local government agency or amateur surveillance club. She was responsible and quiet, she thought, as she quietly started on the responsibility of getting through the door.

She first imagined the old trick from television where a detective pops a lock with a credit card. Then she imagined having the power to walk through walls and, by extension, doors.

Then she imagined being a professional locksmith, with a small backpack full of short wires that she would shove carefully into a standard lock, grease smudges on her knuckles and face, a cold, concentrated look in her eye and a plastic-handled screwdriver hanging by its flat-headed tip from her teeth.

Then Diane imagined that a custodian probably keeps keys.

Inside the unlocked custodial closet, Diane found a metal cabinet. Inside the unlocked metal cabinet, Diane found a cluster of keys, a jangling rat-king on a yellow rubber coil.

Outside Catharine's office, Diane imagined that she would just know the right key, and it would be the first key.

Diane imagined the same thing with the second key, and the third through thirteenth keys. As she did, she imagined being watched. She looked up after every key, but there was no one. The Bloodstone Circle hummed a familiar melody in the corner.

On the thirteenth key, the knob turned. There was a moment, the door was open but unstepped-through, where Diane thought that she could still walk away and not become a person who had broken into anywhere in her life, but then she stepped forward and became that person forever. She shut the door, made sure the blinds were closed, and sat in the chair with wheels at Catharine's desk.

Catharine's computer didn't have a password. It just had the question "Are you Catharine?" with yes and no buttons. Diane clicked the yes button, and the desktop blinked up.

She ran a search for the name Evan. She got similar results to what she'd gotten on Tina's computer. She found no "Evan" as a name or former employee.

She searched for e-mails related to Dawn to see if there was any mention of Dawn's absence, any unusual notes.

Diane imagined she was a hacker, not an actual master of programming languages and network security, but a hacker from a movie, wildly typing, every finger expertly leaping from key to key as a long string of important secrets streamed down the screen in old-fashioned computerized font, her eyes flicking left and right, taking in every number and letter and significant bit of information.

She imagined finding more than nothing.

She felt a light itch on the hand holding the mouse. In the mild glow of the computer screen was the tarantula, one leg up on her little finger. The tarantula paused as if it was hesitant to move farther into Diane's physical space. She spasmed a bit out of shock, but then settled down when she was able to process it.

She would not have minded it, as Josh often appeared as any variety of arachnid, so she had no fear of spiders or most insects. She found it sweet that the animal appeared to be so shy or considerate.

In actuality, the tarantula saw large blocks of moving colors and shapes and sensed it had made contact with a creature much larger than itself. It felt great fear and was holding still out of the if-you-move-you-will-be-seen-and-if-you-are-seen-you-will-be-eaten instinct.

Diane continued looking up previous agendas and minutes from staff meetings. The tarantula took her movement as a threatening advance and scuttled away into the dark of the office.

Diane imagined finding great clues. She imagined film noir, dim but high-contrast light pressing through the blinds creating smoky, white slices across the pitch-black room. Diane imagined her face lit softly in blue by the computer monitor. She imagined not her own face but the face of a hardened detective wearing an archetypal hat.

She imagined being watched. She heard a soft thump from over her shoulder. She felt a warning zing up the back of her neck. She was being watched.

She did not turn her head. She did not move. She looked only with her eyes, pressed so far to the right it hurt her sinuses.

There was a shadow against the blinds. The blinds were closed. There was a person just on the other side.

The person was neither tall nor short. She did not know if the person could see her. They were not leaving.

If you are seen you will be eaten, the tarantula thought without human vocabulary.

Diane was unintentionally not breathing. When she noticed, she continued to hold her breath. Her hands stayed where they were.

There was a rapid clicking. The doorknob rattled back and forth. She couldn't remember if she had locked it. She was eventually going to have to breathe. The doorknob rattled.

She breathed. Her breath sounded so loud. Was it always this loud?

The computer flashed to a screen saver. She did not know if this change in light was visible through the blinds.

Again the doorknob rattled. Then a knock. Another. Three hard taps on the door.

There was nothing she could do. She stayed where she was. Did nothing. The shadow returned to the window and stayed for a long moment. She didn't know how long the moment was. It felt endless to her, motionless in the chair.

Then the shadow blurred as its source moved away from the window. Light began to come in around the blinds' edges.

She heard a muffled creaking, like wheels. Wheels on a cart. A custodial cart. The sound moved away down the hall.

Diane imagined that custodians worked long hours, and would not be out of the office for some time. Hours maybe. She turned off the computer monitor and waited in Catharine's office, quietly, alone, breathing.

THE VOICE OF NIGHT VALE

CECIL: . . . allergies to shellfish, dislike of shellfish, apathy to shellfish, philosophical disagreement with shellfish, or a general uncertainty about the whole concept of shellfish should let the event planners know when making their reservation.

And now a word from our sponsors:

We know that sometimes in life you find yourself with nothing to do but wait. Maybe you have hours to wait. Maybe you have hours to wait hiding in a darkened office until the custodian leaves so that you won't be caught snooping through confidential files at work. There's lots of reasons you could be waiting. It just happens to be that the reason you are waiting right now is that one. Yes, we know a lot about you.

Wouldn't this period of malfeasant waiting be better if you were able to use it, say, catching up on the latest episodes of your favorite TV shows? Think how less boring illegally breaking into your boss's office would be if you were watching TV right now, Diane.

We all thought better of you.

Hulu Plus: Good for criminals.

This has been a word from our sponsors.

And now a word about librarians. We are all, from our youngest years, warned that the most dangerous, untrustworthy creature is that which stalks our public libraries. We all remember as children having this told to us by frazzled men in rumpled suits clutching ancient tomes to their chests.

"Agggh!" they would say, pointing at a diagram that was just a square with the word LIBRARY written neatly in the middle of it.

"Ouuugh!" they would continue, pointing at the clearest photograph ever taken of a librarian, which is a blurry and badly burnt Polaroid.

"Oh! Oh! Oh!" they would conclude, pointing at the first diagram again. It was always a very short presentation.

Then the men would run from our classrooms, looking fearfully around and muttering, "There's no time, just no time," and never would be seen again.

These warnings, as playfully conveyed as they were, are serious matters that should be applied to your grown-up, serious life. Librarians are hideous creatures of unimaginable power. And even if you could imagine their power, it would be illegal. It is absolutely illegal to even try to picture what such a being would be like.

So just watch out for librarians, okay?

And now, let's have a look at traffic.

Here is a man with a new job. Here is a man. He has a new job. So new that he hasn't actually gone to it yet. He is now only in the process of going to it. It is his first day. Not as a human, but at this job. It is approximately his ten thousandth day as a human. And yet, for all his days, he is not yet very good at being a human. He still makes a lot of mistakes. All that time and he still is unsure of himself.

He drives to his job. His car is nice. Nicer than he can afford, but just as nice as he hopes he can soon afford. His car is aspirational. His gray pin-striped suit, his smile, his silver watch, the way he walks, these are all also aspirational. He doesn't think of himself as the him that exists in this moment but as the him that will exist soon. He is not far away from the him that he really is. He will be that version of himself very soon.

But then he sees something. It doesn't matter what. It's someone dying. It's sudden and not anyone's fault, but also could have been prevented. He is sitting in his nice car and he sees this death. And he does not go to his new job. He never does. In fact, since he never actually goes to it, it is not accurate to call it his new job. It is the job he never had. It is a future that, like most futures, never happened.

This has been traffic.

New statistics by the community activist group Citizens for a Transparent Government say that it is as difficult as it has ever been to get through City Hall alive and speak to Mayor Cardinal, that over half of citizens who have appeared before the City Council have been eaten by the council, and that the government is still not transparent.

"I can still totally see them," said Frankie Ramon, spokesperson for the group. "They're not even faint outlines in the air, they're still totally visible, totally opaque. It's like they're not even trying."

Next: a sudden loss of consciousness followed by a waking as a new person, living a new life, but with all the same old questions unanswered. Starting in one, two,

Jackie dropped off Erika across the street from City Hall. It wasn't safe for Erika to exist in such close proximity to the source of city law.

"Thanks," Erika said as they opened the car door.

"Hey," said Jackie. "Don't worry about it. Thanks for the cash."

"You're a good one, Jackie Fierro," they said. "And that makes the world a dangerous place for you."

There was that flutter of wings again, and a dark haze filled the air behind Erika. Once they had unfolded themselves from the car, they stood over seven feet tall, much more than could have fit in Jackie's compact.

"Be well," they said, as their feet and then the rest of their body melted down into the sidewalk. "Failing that, Jackie, simply be. Simply continue to be."

And they were gone into the earth.

"Why did you need a ride if you could do that?" Jackie sighed.

She pulled the car across the street and parked it in the small lot reserved for those visiting the mayor or looking to throw themselves on the terrible whims and absent mercy of the City Council.

City Hall was a majestic building when it was fully uncovered from the black velvet that shrouded it each night. When not covering the building, the velvet sat bunched up on the yellowing lawn. Jackie headed through the arched entrance, not bothering to check in with the guard by the door. The guard wore a mask that blocked all sound and sight, so that he would not see anything he was not supposed to see. Even if she had tried to check in, it would have just added minutes more of frustration to an already frustrating day.

The only way to the mayor's office was past the doorway to the City Council. She took that trip as quickly as her body could take it, scrunching the slip of paper in her hand. The doors were open, and she could see the misshapen forms and hear the predatory shrieking of the City Council at work. The hall smelled of chalk and burnt hair.

A new law had recently made a visit to the City Council the only possible way to petition a speeding ticket, and, as a result, citizens had taken to accepting speeding tickets given to them when they weren't even in a car, when they were sitting still on a bench, or sleeping in their own bed. Better to pay than to Pay was the general feeling.

She imagined running into the council chambers just then. Who can fathom the danger and pain of a visit to the City Council? Of course, who can fathom an inextricable paper that binds to one's hand and unhinges one's concentration and maybe one's life? Would the City Council solve the problem for her, one way or another? Would that be better, after all?

From somewhere on the meeting room table, amid the chaos of council members in mid-meeting, Jackie heard a soft whimper and a loud snap and decided to keep walking quickly.

The mayor's office was upstairs, in an area of the building that was decorated with a great deal of wood paneling and framed photos of lighthouses. The mayor's receptionist was an elderly man who nodded with a smile when she explained what she needed, and gestured at one of the plush club chairs lining the wall.

Perhaps at last she had come to the place that could help her. The elderly man behind the desk gestured toward the door, and then held up five fingers, and nodded again.

"No problem, I'll wait."

She picked up a magazine from the table in front of her. "Ten Ways to Redecorate Your Bloodstone Circle." "How to Lose Weight Without Losing Sight of Your Own Mortality." "A Cake Recipe That Only People Who Hate Our Government Will Want to Try So Mail Us Your Best Pictures of Making It and We Will Take You Away." Boring stuff like that, but diverting in the few minutes it took the mayor to be ready for her.

The elderly man rapped softly on his desk to get her attention and then gestured with an open palm toward the door.

"Thanks, man. You're my favorite person I've talked to all day."

He shrugged, turning back to the stairs and leaving her to the business of opening the door, which was tricky. It was one of those ones that required some mild bleeding.

"Ugh," she said as she entered the office. "There I am like an idiot thinking Push. No, pull. And I forgot entirely to just Bleed. There should be a sign or something."

The mayor, Dana Cardinal, was sitting in a portrait of official grandeur that had to be posed, her silhouette against the picture windows, and the light falling on the desk, and the papers spread out amid light and shadow. It was all perfectly staged to present her authority.

"I happen to agree, but try to get anything done in this building," said the mayor.

"Sure, yeah. Didn't mean you were doing anything wrong."

"Yes you did. It's perfectly fine. If we cannot be judged on our actions, then we cannot be judged. And let me tell you." The mayor turned to face her and leaned her elbows upon the desk.

"We can be judged. We definitely can. So, Jackie, you came to see me. Is something troubling you?"

Jackie sat down in the chair across the desk from the mayor and did the trick with the paper. On the floor. Back in her hand. Torn to pieces. Back in her hand. Mentally willed into flames. Back in her hand. The mayor nodded gravely, not appearing surprised.

"Yeah. So," Jackie said. "But that's just part of it. Here's something else: I'm not sure I've ever been to my mother's house. She asked me if I remember my childhood and I don't. I don't, Dana."

Jackie threw the paper in the hand-carved oak wastebasket next to the mayor's desk. The paper wad caught the rim and then rolled in. Jackie laid the paper in her hand down on the desk. "I can't write anything but 'KING CITY.' I can't think of anything else," she said. "Guess I gotta go there, but no one seems to think I should or even would be able to do that."

The mayor smiled a smile of comfort, not happiness. She looked out the window at the rapidly diminishing day.

"Jackie, those all are serious problems. I don't want to tell you those problems aren't serious. But I apologize if there's only so much I can do. It's a little bit hectic here, as you can see."

She waved her hand to indicate the absolute still of the office.

"My brother's sick. We're not sure what's wrong with him. I'd love to be home taking care of him, but I have to be at City Hall. We're not sure what happens if I don't go every day, but we think that whatever it is that protects us from the full wrath of the City Council involves the mayor being at City Hall every single day. So here I am. For my city. My brother has a fever and chills. He says he sees lights out in the desert. I told him we all see lights in the desert. He says, no, different lights. Not the same ones we usually see. Low bubbles of light coming and going. I don't know what to say to that."

"Low bubbles of light? Because I've—"

"He clutches this piece of paper to his chest. Won't show it to us. Says he doesn't want us to catch what he has. Always thinking of others even as he slips away. He's slipping away from us, Jackie. Also the big job fair is coming up. Tents to set up. All sorts of mysterious organizations that want the best booth placement so they can trick the young people of Night Vale into disappearing or incriminating themselves or at best becoming part of a mysterious organization."

"Your brother has a pap——"

"I'm sorry, Jackie. I didn't mean to complain." The mayor shook her head, and then nodded, and then shook her head again. "No, yes, I did mean to complain. I don't have anyone else to complain to. I'm young, Jackie. Did you know that about me?"

"Sure."

"I am. I'm young. And this job is hard. I don't know if I can help you because, and I'll be honest here, I'm struggling a bit to keep this all together. But it's my job too. I was chosen to be mayor. I was chosen and so I will serve my city the best way I can. And that means helping people like you when they come to me for help. I'm sorry, Jackie, I'm being a bad mayor."

"Oh, nah." Jackie paused slightly. "No, you're doing great." She leaned across the desk and held out a hand. The mayor did not take it. She continued to look out the window for a moment, her humanity and thoughtfulness tucked away inside a tight frown, an honest brushstroke in a boring painting. The mayor caught herself and set her face into something more official, less herself: a perfectly slight smile.

"Let's start again. Jackie, I will do my best to help you. I may not be able to help you. More often than not I can't. But I always try."

"That's great, dude, thanks."

The mayor rubbed her hands together.

"King City is becoming a problem for Night Vale. I know there are papers in hands and there is confusion and frustration and fear. No, not fear. Concern. There is concern."

"I'm not afraid and I'm not concerned. I'm ruined." Jackie tried the word on her tongue and found that it felt right, so she said it again. "I'm ruined."

"I don't know why King City has connected to Night Vale. Sometimes other places have a mysterious connection to our own. A little fishing town in Russia. Our unfriendly neighbor, Desert Bluffs. That desert otherworld which trapped me for months. We cannot always keep the outside world on the outside."

"So I should go to King City?"

"Sure."

"You think so?" Jackie was glad for an authority that would finally tell her what she should do.

"Probably not. I'm not even sure if it's a real place. It could just be an idea on paper."

"But I spoke with—"

"I don't know what a King City is," the mayor continued, yawning. "I don't know a lot of things. I do know there will always be problems for Night Vale. There are so many. Usually they pass. Often they kill many people, but what are people but deaths that haven't happened yet?"

"Births that already happened?" Jackie said without thinking.

The mayor laughed. She looked different when she laughed,

and then she stopped laughing and she did not look different anymore.

"Thank you, Jackie. I needed that. As for you. Well. I know you came here hoping that I would have an answer or a piece of advice that would fix things."

"So—"

The mayor stood, a wordless pre-good-bye. Jackie stood too, a wordless capitulation.

"You say your life is unraveling. Your life cannot unravel. Your life is your life. You haven't lost it. It's just different now."

"Do you feel the same thing about your brother? That his life cannot unravel? That it is just different now?"

Dana blinked. "Yes," she said. "I suppose I do."

"Fair enough, man, but I want my old life back, whatever my old life was."

Dana shook her head.

"You know, Jackie, before I was mayor, I was an intern at the community radio station. One of the only interns to survive that program. Being an intern at the radio station is dangerous and terrible work. But there are days, sitting in this office, with responsibility past my years, working in a system I barely understand, that I miss my time as an intern. At least I was allowed to be young. At least I was allowed to be Dana, not Mayor Cardinal."

"I hope your brother will be okay," Jackie said.

"He'll be what he'll be. And we'll all learn to be okay with whatever that is."

Jackie said good-bye with her eyes.

"Good-bye, Jackie," the mayor said with her mouth.

Jackie pulled on the door. It did not move. She pushed on the door. It did not move.

"Oh, right. Jesus. There really should be a sign," she said, bleeding.

Back out in the wood-paneled waiting room there was a blond man with a big smile sitting at the desk.

"Hey?" she said.

"Yes?" he said, his voice all customer-service politeness.

It was not the same man as when she arrived. She did not know where she had seen him before, but the sight of him made her uneasy.

"Wasn't there someone else here before? This old guy who didn't talk?"

"Oh, oh no," he said. His smile did not waver. "It's always just been me here. You have a good day, okay?"

"Sure. Okay," she said.

As she walked down the stairs, he pulled out some forms, picked up a pen, and silently smiled at the forms, writing nothing. Jackie did not even flinch passing the City Council doors this time. Nothing, not even the terrible council, was more frightening than the fact that no one seemed able to help her, least of all herself.

"You didn't come home last night."

Josh said this from the couch, book open across his legs. He had red claws and antennae. He was wearing baggy jeans and a Mountain Goats T-shirt, which Josh had once been kicked out of school for wearing, because of its strong political message siding with those who believe in mountains.

Diane stopped short of the kitchen. She hadn't expected Josh to be up already. She was running on three hours' sleep and had hoped to be up and out before him.

"I'm here now. I hate it when you wear that shirt."

"Mountains are real, Mom."

"I believe in mountains, Josh. It just reminds me of how I had to come pick you up from school and wait in the front office while the vice principal gave me a lecture about how inappropriate it is to raise a child to believe such nonsense. It was embarrassing."

"Well, I'm not embarrassed by my beliefs."

"I'm embarrassed to be told I'm a bad parent."

"You aren't home a lot these days." It was a swerve, not a response. He wasn't looking at her or his book. It was difficult to tell where he was looking because of the solid black eyes drooping from the ends of long, curved stalks atop his head.

Diane walked past him into the kitchen and started the process of making coffee. She always ground her own beans. She did not feel that her coffee tasted better because of this, she simply liked the process of grinding beans: the cool crumple of the bag from the freezer, the gentle rattle of beans across the countertop, the therapeutic release of pounding them into grounds with a hammer for several minutes.

As she removed her safety goggles and washed her hands, she called to the living room, "How's school?"

"You didn't come home last night."

She dried her hands. "I came home late last night."

"From what?"

"Work."

"You never work late."

"I did last night?"

She hated the question in her own voice but had never been good at lying.

"Doing what? What were you doing that you didn't get home until early morning and that you didn't answer my texts and that you didn't reply to my e-mails?"

"My phone was off."

"Okay. Why?"

She came back into the living room, and Josh stood to face her. He was tall, his jeans draping in baggy folds over his hooves.

Diane wished she knew what Josh looked like. She wished there was a single thing she could assume about her son. She wished Josh had a second parent to be ballast. Josh wished all of those things, too.

"I was on a date."

Josh didn't respond, so Diane nervously filled the pause.

"My phone died, and I was. Um."

"You just said you were at work."

Josh tried to fold his arms, but the claws snagged on each other, and so he awkwardly clasped them in front of him.

"Yes, I've been seeing someone. I know we don't talk about dating much. Mom and son, you know. It's . . . awkward. Right?"

"No, Mom, no. That's really cool. What's their name?"

A good lie requires two things: (1) assertiveness in delivery, and (2) narrative logic that cannot be unhinged by actual truth.

"Dawn," Diane said assertively, achieving one of those two things.

"Don?"

"Yes, Dawn."

Josh sat back down.

"How long have you been seeing Don?"

"A few weeks. Mostly seeing movies and having some dinner, getting to know each other."

Diane began to panic about Josh running into Dawn and trying to talk to her about their relationship. She mentally scheduled an ugly breakup with Dawn in the coming days. Or would that make Josh even more likely to talk to her? It would certainly remove Dawn from the list of possible future friends.

"And so you spent the night at Don's house last night?"

Right. She was still dating Dawn in the here and now, and had to focus.

"You're not allowed to ask me questions like that, Joshua."

"You're right. Gross."

She examined Josh's opaque, bobbing eyes, and his flagellum-lined mandibles. It was difficult to tell by his expression if he was being playful or aggressive, but she could hear a grin in his voice.

Her face relaxed.

"Yes, I've been dating a lot. I'm sorry, Josh. I sometimes don't tell you enough about what is going on with me. I get selfish."

"It's fine," he said, head tilting down, idly flipping his book open and closed.

He was embarrassed by how much he needed her. At his age, he felt he should be basically independent, but as she had spent less and less time at home in the previous weeks, he had become aware of how complete his assumption of her presence had been. It panicked him a little, and that panic had come out as a demand to know where she had been, and he hated himself for demanding to know but also couldn't stop himself from asking.

"Listen. This goes two ways, honey. It's just you and me and we have to trust each other. You're my baby—"

"Mom—"

"You're my baby. You're my pal. You're everything, okay? And that means when you close me out, I have nothing. I have a job and a house and some friends and a car and your grandparents. But also I have nothing."

Josh swung open his mandibles to speak.

"Hang on," she said. "I'm not saying you need to tell me everything. But, just: How is it going? How are you feeling? This can't be an easy time for you. Or maybe it is. I really don't know."

She sat across from him. There was a silence, and she let the silence happen.

"You could just ask," he mumbled.

"Josh, I ask all of the time. I asked just now. And I get one-word answers." She could hear her voice getting louder and tried to pull it back in. "Sorry. I just want us to talk about our lives. Not all the time. Sometimes. I promise not to get bored when you tell me about your"—she glanced down to his T-shirt—"Mountain Goats concerts, if you promise not to get bored when I tell you about the office copier breaking down halfway into my job."

"That sounds boring."

"It wasn't. It was R-rated for strong language and machine violence."

Josh didn't laugh, but he softened, which was all she needed a bad joke to do.

"So I'm dating Dawn," Diane said, thinking she was not at all the type of person to tell lies to her son but once again finding that she was a different person than she thought. "Mom going on dates. Gross, right?"

"It's not gross," Josh mumbled.

"We're seeing a lot of each other, but who knows how long it will last? Tell me about you."

"I don't know."

"You're not dating?"

"No." Josh forced a laugh.

"Interested in a boy?"

"No."

Diane didn't want to press Josh further, hoping he would enter the conversation on his own.

The silence thickened the air with the hums and thumps of bodies and appliances, the coffeepot, and a distant car honk, and a nearby bird exclaiming, and her blood moving in jerking, lurching steps under the skin of her neck, where she felt a slight tickle, and the faceless old woman that secretly lives in their home taking slow, careful steps on the second-floor hallway above them, and all the other sounds that silence is made of.

"Why do you think I'm interested in a boy?" Josh said.

"Well, you're fifteen. I assumed all teenagers do is think about other teenagers, don't they?"

"No, I am, I guess. I mean, not a boy. There was one but he was weird. I think I scared him."

Diane kept from saying anything, worried that it might stop this unexpected moment of communication. She let Josh tell his own story.

"There's a girl named Lisa who my friend Matt says likes me, but I think she's just really nice to everyone. I don't think being nice to someone means you like them, especially when you're nice to everybody. I mean Matt just only thinks about getting with girls and hooking his friends up with girls. All these girls are in love with Matt, and he sometimes sets them up on dates with his other friends, like he's a matchmaker. And they all go out with his friends, just so they can stay close to Matt, but they all eventually find their way back to him. I think that's his game, setting his friends up to stash future girlfriends. That's totally it. That's probably why he's trying to set me up with Lisa, because he's still dating Rosita, and if I can hang out with Lisa—"

"Josh."

"What?" He looked startled, like he thought he was alone.

"Do you like Lisa?"

"I guess. Yeah? I don't know her."

"Are you attracted to her at all?"

"I don't think so? A little bit? Not really?"

"Then don't feel pressure to go out with her. If you like her, then there's nothing wrong with it. But don't do it for Matt. That's his problem to work out. Not yours."

"Okay."

Silence again. Diane used the silence to scold herself for interrupting with didactic parenting. But also, wasn't it her job to interrupt Josh's life with parenting?

"I hate to ask you this," Diane hated to ask, "because I don't want it to seem like I was snooping."

Josh lifted his eyestalks until they were definitely, opaque blackness and all, looking directly into her eyes.

"I found a note in my car the other day."

Josh's shoulders tightened and his antennae pulled back.

"I think it fell out of your notebook. And it was short. Normally I wouldn't read something that looked this personal, but I saw it and took it all in before I could even tell what it was."

This lie also accomplished one of the two things that make a good lie.

"What note?"

Josh knew what note. He had been looking for that note. Dreading his mother would find that note. Hoping he would not have to talk about that note.

Diane would occasionally find notes he had written. This had happened before. Sometimes it was actually happenstance, and sometimes the faceless old woman who secretly lives in their home would move his notes to where Diane would see them because the faceless old woman was bored and found the troubles of others interesting. Always Diane said she believed in his privacy and always she meant it, but also it always happened that she had read the entire note before she realized what it was. This was not a pattern that she was aware of, but it was one that Josh was very familiar with.

"It was a note where you were asking your classmate about a boy. A boy you were interested in."

Josh started to sigh in relief and stopped himself just as the air was coming out, so that it came out sounding like an exasperated huff. The note was not about a boy, but a man. Here is what it was about the note.

When he was six, Josh had asked his mother who his father was. Diane told him he didn't have a father. Some kids have fathers and others do not. Josh was one of those other kids.

When he was ten, Josh had asked his mother where his father was, knowing at that age that it was improbable for babies to be born without a biological mother and biological father. Diane told him she didn't know.

When he was thirteen, Josh had asked his mother who his father was so he could track him down. Diane told him that would not happen. That he was not old enough to go looking for his father yet. When he turned eighteen and was living on his own, not under her roof, he was welcome to do whatever he wanted, but that he'd be much happier not trying to track down a man who didn't care enough to raise him in the first place.

Diane did not talk much to Josh for a couple weeks after that, except to ask him what time he was coming home and whether he had homework or choir practice or a Boy Scout function. (Josh was only a few tasks away from getting his Blood Pact Scout badge.)

Josh considered his mother to be a nice mother and person. She was kind and she smiled and she gave tender hugs and was concerned with his well-being. Josh also considered his mother to be a difficult mother and person. She was unforgiving and she demanded kindness back and she killed with silence and said sharp but subtle things that cut deeply.

"You still have a lot of *maturing* to do," Diane had said to the thirteen-year-old Josh, who was one of the last boys he knew to get through puberty. He had no defense because the only thing worse to a late bloomer than thinking about late blooming is talking about late blooming.

For her part, Diane did not have a good reason for why she wouldn't tell Josh anything about his father. She didn't have a good reason for most of what she did. Mostly, she went by what seemed right in the moment, and justified it to herself later, and in this way she was no different than anyone else she knew.

There were times—like that day in the movie theater or after her speeding ticket—when she had wanted to tell Josh about Troy, but the shape of his name felt wrong in her mouth, and the thought of talking about him made her feel dizzy, like she was waking up from a dream that had been almost exactly like her own life and was now trying to differentiate the two. She did not hate Troy. She did not hate anyone. But she just didn't want to talk about him, and so she didn't.

At age fifteen, Josh had not asked his mother who his father was. He did not want to upset her, partially for her sake and partially for his.

Instead, Josh wrote that note to a friend of his who knew some people who knew some of the hooded figures who knew an agent from a vague yet menacing government agency who had full access at City Hall. And that agent might be able to get some information on who Josh's father was.

Now his mother thought it was a note about a boy he liked. She seemed not upset at all, and he wasn't going to give her any reason to be upset.

"Oh! That note. I wrote that to my friend DeVon," Josh said, truthfully, before going on to fail at accomplishing either element of a good lie. "His cousin, um, Ty goes to the new charter school on . . . DuBois Road, near Route 800? And DeVon keeps telling me that Ty's single and really cute, and I said I wanted to meet him, and DeVon is like I'll see what I can do, and I'm like do you have a picture, and DeVon's like hold up, I'll get you one but just wait. Let me see if he's interested."

"Did you get a photo?" Diane said.

"Yeah."

"And?"

Josh was uncertain about the specifics of his imagined crush, and the lie faltered.

"Is he cute?" Diane did not blush about her boy getting old enough to date, although she would allow herself to blush later, when she was alone.

"Yeah," Josh said, before his mind had caught up. The last thing he wanted was for his mother to ask to meet this nonexistent Ty or, worse, for her to ask DeVon about his cute cousin.

"When do I get to meet him?"

"Mom!"

"Sorry. Sorry." And the conversation ended. They could both feel it, even though they continued to talk to each other. The connection, whatever had surfaced in the last few minutes, had sunk out of sight again.

"I'm not that interested anyway. DeVon's a good friend. It'd be weird to go with his cousin."

"Josh." She did not cry, although she would allow herself to cry later. "I'm so proud to have such a smart, considerate boy."

"Are you about to cry?"

"Nope." Diane stood up and walked toward the kitchen. She was already back to thinking about Evan, and where she could possibly look next for information on him. She was tired and suppressing a nascent panic. She needed time alone, time to think.

"I need coffee, and you need to get to school" was how she explained that out loud.

Diane drank her coffee from a chipped Night Vale Community Radio mug she had gotten a couple of years back during a fund drive. She didn't choose to donate to the station. But she had expressed her enjoyment of Cecil's show to a friend of hers. Her comments were picked up by one of the thousands of listening devices the station had hidden around town. Using a complex algorithm that measures age, net worth, and perceived enthusiasm for the station's programming, Station Management took a donation straight from Diane's bank account without her having to write a check or send off an envelope or even know the money was gone. It was a convenient approach to fund-raising for everyone involved. One day she received the mug and a shirt that had that famous Eleanor Roosevelt quote on it ("One day we will destroy the moon with indifference!"), and that's how she knew she was an NVCR supporter.

"Can I take the car today?" Josh asked, trying to cash in on the goodwill he'd built this morning.

"You cannot."

"Mom."

"I said no."

"You just said I'm smart and considerate."

"Right. I didn't say you're a good and responsible driver."

"But you want me to get better, right?"

"Is that what you do, Josh? I try to have conversations with you. I try to talk to you, and we have a morning of real progress. A real breakthrough where you're kind and articulate and charming, and what's the endgame? Just to borrow my car?"

Josh stood perfectly still. This was the moment he feared most. This was how conversations with his mother went. He just wanted it to be over and for himself to be out in the world, where he could keep looking for his father. He wanted to understand who he was in relation to the father that had abandoned him (had his father even abandoned him? He didn't know, and that was the point) as well as he understood who he was in relation to his mother, in all of its goods and bads. Then, seeing himself against and between these two people, he could start to figure out who he was beneath all of the forms he took every day, beneath whatever he looked like to the world in any given moment.

"I'm left to wonder if the only time you want to actually talk to me is when you want something from me. That's incredibly disingenuous."

"Mom. I—"

"Disingenuous means not genuine. Don't know if they've taught you that word in school."

"I'll catch the bus."

"Better hurry."

Josh threw his things in his bag and walked out the door.

Diane stared into her coffee, knowing she had ruined a lovely moment with her son, knowing he must loathe being around her when she was like this.

"I love you," she called, hoping it wasn't too late.

"I love you too," he said back, not loudly enough to be heard.

Now that science and civic leadership had failed to solve her problem, Jackie sat in her car in the City Hall parking lot, unsure of what to do. No one had fixed anything. No one had been able to help her.

She watched as workers rushed out of the doors to begin the long process of draping the black velvet over City Hall. It was nice to watch people struggle over a problem that did not involve or affect her at all. She didn't have to help or act or choose. Part of her wanted to just recline the seat as close to lying down as possible and sleep the night where she was. Stay in one spot and let the world go on with its strange and terrible business without her.

But before she had even finished having that thought, she was already turning on the ignition and reversing out of the parking lot. She wouldn't stop. She couldn't. There was something in her that made giving up feel as impossible as the most impossible of her problems.

Driving through Night Vale in the early evening was peaceful. There weren't many cars out on the roads, mostly just the agents from a vague yet menacing government agency starting their slow-cruising night patrol of the town. It wasn't late enough for the hooded figures to be prowling the sidewalks, looking for lone pedestrians to take and do whatever it was they did (almost no encounters were witnessed, and, if they were, the witness was wise to cover the witnessing part of their sensory systems until the whole thing, whatever it was, was over).

The lights were on in the various places of business along Route 800. The neon of the Moonlite All-Nite stood out as the day turned to night. A slab of mint light in the warm desert darkness, as the radio had once described it. She considered eating there, hunger being one problem that was simple enough to solve, but the thought of returning and seeing that man—the blond man in the kitchen—smiling at her made her nervous. Was he the same blond man she'd seen outside the mayor's office?

She shook her head, but the thought wouldn't leave.

The blond man, it said.

"KING CITY," the paper said.

A man in her mother's backyard. Blond hair. A smile. That was where she had known him from. Her heart was beating in her wrist, which was where it rarely beat.

Dots of light studded the hazy purple of the twilight horizon: red taillights, yellow porch lights, orange streetlights, the strange greenish white pulse of light hundreds of feet above the Arby's. In the distance a jagged line of soft blue light, like a crack in the sky. Above all of that was the clean, white brightness of the stars and the moon and the searchlights of surveillance helicopters.

Children in Night Vale grow up hearing the Dopplered whir of helicopters above, recording or monitoring or whatever it is that helicopters do. It's a comforting sound, knowing that you're well taken care of by unimpeachable judges of what is good and what is evil.

Jackie did not feel comforted, only inured. She was not thinking, only doing. Unaware of her car's speed, she turned off Route 800 onto an unnamed street that led, eventually, into the Sandwastes and the shantytown that was the barista district.

Before all that, though, the unnamed road went right by Jerry's Tacos.

The light of Jerry's Tacos was the most inviting thing she'd seen all day. It was a small stand, only recently reopened after an ugly incident a few years back involving a time traveler, but already word was around that the food was worth the years of waiting and silence that had preceded it.

She pulled into the lot, relieved to have so simple a task in front of her as ordering food and then consuming it. Reaching into her pocket, she added paper of a different sort and with a different kind of value than the paper already in her hand.

The only other car in the lot was a silver pickup. Full-size. Well worn. Tall. Long. The windows gray with dried dirt. She had seen it many times. It belonged to John Peters (you know, the farmer?).

He was at the window, already picking up an order of the house specialty, a mysteriously crunchy enchilada.

"Hey, John," she shouted as she walked up.

He turned, crunchy enchilada in hand.

"Howdy there, Jackie. How goes it with pawning?"

She posted an elbow up on the counter and waved away the shadow on the other side of the frosted glass that was waiting for her order.

"It goes. For sure it goes. I'm just, well, taking a break I guess. People take breaks. How goes it with, you know, farming?"

"Ah, it is what it is. It's farming, you know."

"Sure."

A big crunchy bite of enchilada.

"Man, that looks good." She turned to the shadowy figure behind the glass. "I'll take one of those and one Jerry's Special Taco. How much do I owe you?"

A receipt popped out from under the glass. She took a look at the price.

"Really? Jesus."

John Peters watched her force a tear out onto the receipt and push it back under the glass. The price paid, the food was delivered through a hatch moments later.

"Prices here have gone up a bit," said John.

"Tell me about it."

They both dug into their food. When nothing else works, eating sure does.

"What do you know about a man in a tan jacket, holding a deerskin suitcase?" Jackie asked, not wanting to break the easy quiet of eating, but also not wanting to hang on to the question.

John stopped chewing.

"Have you seen a man in a tan jacket, holding a deerskin suitcase?" he asked.

"Yeah. Except I don't remember much about him."

"No," said John. "Wouldn't suppose you would. He has that effect on people."

Jackie looked out from the pool of light they were standing in to the dark desert beyond. There was movement there. She swore that she could see the tan-jacketed man in question sprinting just at the edge of the light. More blur than person, but still with the desperate run that was away from something rather than toward.

"Is that—?" she asked what could only be herself, given that John wasn't looking.

She dropped her food on the counter and started away from the stand, but John stopped her with a hand on the shoulder.

"Don't bother. Wouldn't catch him, probably. And wouldn't remember if you did. He's dangerous."

"Dangerous?"

"If I were you I'd stay away from his town." He pointed at her hand. She held up the paper.

"King City?" Jackie asked.

"KING CITY," the paper confirmed.

"He's here because of Diane, I think," he said.

"Diane Crayton?"

"Don't know if he's helping or hunting her, but he certainly always seems to be lurking around wherever she is."

"Diane Crayton," Jackie repeated, in answer to her own question. She considered this information.

"Wouldn't go anywhere near that town of his if it were me," he said. "Who knows what you'd find, or what you'd find out and then wish you hadn't."

He picked up a Styrofoam cup full of horchata and took a long slurp from it, his eyes on where the man may or may not have been running.

"Mostly we don't get destroyed," John said. "Mostly we destroy ourselves."

Another car pulled into the lot. It was a well-preserved Chrysler from at least a couple if not a few decades past. Out of it came a woman about which much the same could be said.

"Mom?" Jackie said, as the woman entered Jerry's Tacos.

Jackie's mom smiled. She was wearing the exact same clothes as she had been that morning.

"Hello, John. How goes the farming?"

"Till we get some of that federal water here, mostly I grow imaginary corn. Grows just as well as anything else. Sells pretty well too. Plus doesn't take much work."

"I would not imagine it would, no."

Her mother said hello to the shadow (Jerry?) behind the

glass, glanced over the regular menu, and, not finding anything to her liking, said the code phrase to receive the secret menu.

"I am comfortable with secrets," she said, then did a quick scan of the proffered yellow page. "Well, I have to say, it all sounds so good. I'll take the number four, and I'll never tell a soul."

"Mom, did you always have that car?"

Her mother looked up from the menu.

"Yes, of course, dear. I've only ever had that car. Who ever would have more than one car in their life?"

"Right. Yeah, no. I know." But why did Jackie not remember it at all?

"Have to get back to farming I suppose," said John, standing in the open doorway.

"It's dark out," Jackie's mother said.

"Indeed it is," he said, shading his eyes and looking up at the night sky. "It's completely dark out. Well, better get back to it."

He winked, tossed the wrappers and cup into a trash can, and tossed himself back into his truck.

"Mom, you were saying earlier about me as a kid."

"Yes, dear, suppose I was." Her mother pulled some napkins from the dispenser and sat down. She didn't look at Jackie.

"What was that about?"

Her mother laughed. She kept laughing.

"Mom, what is going on? Why won't you tell me?"

Her mother didn't stop laughing. Also, she was crying. Jackie wasn't sure what to do. Her mother's food showed up and her mother was still laughing and also crying. Pausing several times along the way, Jackie moved toward where her mother was hunched at the counter, extending an arm and placing it across her mother's back. Jackie looked out the windows toward her own car. She wished she could laugh and weep, too. She felt as though everything had been taken away from her, even though only most things had.

Jackie stared past her car at the dust of John's departure swirling in the edge of light and darkness, where she could still see movement that looked like a running man.

"Diane Crayton," she said to herself. She couldn't hear her mother anymore.

19

Diane watches the local news quite a bit.

Even when the cable is out, she watches the local news. The local news has a strong broadcast frequency, so even if one did not have cable, one would still receive the local television newscast. Even if one had working cable, the local news broadcast would come in on all channels. Or even if one did not have an antenna. Even if one turned one's television off, sometimes the frequency is just so strong. So very, very strong. It is hard to turn off the news.

That's the local news station's slogan: "It's hard to turn off the news. Go ahead. Try. See?"

In any case, Diane watches local television news because it speaks to her. It literally speaks to her.

One of the morning news coanchors—who was wearing a necktie and a coat and who had hollow eyes and sharp teeth and who cannot see themself in still photographs—said, "Diane Crayton. Hello."

Diane said nothing at first, because she was eating cereal. It was the morning and she had just gotten out of the shower before work. In the shower, she had suddenly had a thought about all the space within the walls of a house and how much space that would add up to if it were all turned into one hollow cube. She had no idea where the thought had come from.

"Hello, Diane," said the coanchor's coanchor.

"Hi. Hello. Good morning," Diane replied, politely covering

her face and chewing the remainder of her mouthful of Flakey O's, cereal made by a local company known for its aggressive and controversial advertising.

"How is Josh?" said the second coanchor, who wore a brown suitcoat with ivory lapels, who wore their hair down, who had shiny maroon lips and nails and bright red eyes.

Josh had already caught the bus to school. The day after their talk was good. The day after that day was less good. The days after those days had returned to averted eyes and closed doors.

Diane had gotten some concerned calls from the school about Josh skipping classes and doing dangerous things like expressing public curiosity about the mysterious lights that pass over Night Vale at night, and trying to enter the City Council chambers without protective gear. He had also been coming home late each day.

She had tried to talk to him about Ty, but Josh looked annoyed when she brought it up. He would just roll his thin, yellow eyes, his long ears flat across the top of his skull, and say, "It's fine," or "Nothing new," or "I don't want to talk about it."

"Is Josh all right?" said the second news anchor.

"He's fine."

"How do you know?"

Diane did not answer.

"He's going through a lot, Diane," said the first coanchor, and the two coanchors shared a smile. (Was that a smile?)

"He had a crush on someone, I think, I guess, and it didn't work out," Diane said. She wasn't eating cereal anymore.

"Is that all that's bothering him? Just a failed crush?" the second coanchor pushed on, showing at least some background in journalism.

"I don't know. I wish I knew. I don't know. He seems different or like something has gotten off the rails inside him, and I don't know how to nudge him back. He's been texting in class. When he even shows up for class."

"Is he texting a particular person?"

"Not that I was told."

"Definitely check your phone records, Diane," the first anchor said, leaning farther over the desk than seemed possible.

"It's a little invasive."

"You're his mother. You are allowed to be invasive as long as he is living under your roof with you paying the bills," the second coanchor said.

"And it's not like you're averse to checking other people's phone records," the other added.

And here the two coanchors laughed tinnily, with trained rigor, and there was a low rumble felt by many people across Night Vale for the next few seconds.

"I don't think it's just about a crush," said one of the anchors.

"I agree with Tim," said the other.

"Thank you, Trinh."

"Last night, when I saw him," said Diane, "he was small, about the size of a basketball. And like a basketball, he was round. Unlike a basketball, he was smooth and dark and heavy. I don't know how to talk to him when he's like that."

"You do not know how many parents say that, Diane," Tim purred, smiling, eyebrow tilted. There was a rapid clicking sound from the back of Tim's throat, or "thorax" as news anchors call it.

"You must be there for him," Trinh said.

"But what does that mean? I stand outside his door. I knock. I say 'Josh.' I say it twice. I tell him there is dinner. I tell him there is television. He says 'cool.' That's all. Everything is 'cool.' And he stops going to class."

There was a high scream from somewhere in Diane's house,

and the sound of a mirror cracking. The refrigerator opened, and a carton of almond milk hit the floor as if it had been slapped off its shelf. (It had.) The faceless old woman who secretly lives in her home was on one of her rampages again.

"Dammit." Diane rolled her eyes and stood up.

"Relax, Diane. The milk is not a disaster. It does not need tending to right away."

"Yes, finish your story."

"Well, when he does come out of his room, he sits without speaking. His eyes retract. His hair grows long around his hands and feet, silky and straight and soft. His nostrils expand. What am I supposed to say to that? What is the right thing to do?"

She sighed, watching the almond milk spread across the floor.

"Honestly, there are times when I want to hit him," she said. She had not known she was going to say it.

The coanchors glanced at each other and shuffled blank papers on their fake desk. The almond milk pooled against the cabinets. She needed to get a paper towel to wipe it up but didn't feel like she could move.

"I mean I would never do that. I just think it. Does this make me a bad person?"

"You are only a bad person if you do bad things," said the second anchor.

"Thank you."

"That's not an acquittal, Diane. The counterpoint is that you are only a good person if you do good things."

"Turn off the television and look at this knife I found on eBay," whispered the voice of the faceless old woman over Diane's shoulder. She turned and looked down the hall, more out of habit than out of interest. It was empty and unnaturally dark. She felt a finger brush her cheek.

The faceless old woman does not like it when people watch television. Diane didn't see her, had never seen her, but she looked down and there was a long hunting knife on the table. It was dull from use, but clean and otherwise in excellent shape.

"It's a nice knife, Faceless Old Woman. Did you get a good deal on it?"

No reply.

She turned off the television. The anchors remained on-screen, talking about tornado safety in the desert, and her mind raced with the possibilities of how to better express her love to Josh.

A good person is a person who does good things. It was a deceptively simple prescription because it implied that she or anyone else knew what good things are. What could she do in this situation that was good, and by what standard?

She grabbed her phone and typed, "Son, I'm sorry I can be difficult. I'm sorry for whatever you are going through, and you don't have to tell me. But I'm your mother, and if there's something we—" She reached the text character limit.

Diane does not like sending a single message in multiple texts. She deleted words. She wrote words. She changed the part about not needing to tell her anything to something about how there are some things mothers need to know about, and if it's a serious prob———

Character limit.

She deleted things and retyped things, something about setting aside one night. Just one night. An hour even. To talk. Even if they just talked about TV shows.

Delete.

Rewrite. Something about knowing how hard it is to be a teenager.

Delete.

Something that started with "How's class?" but then devolved into wanting to talk later.

Delete.

Diane stared at her phone. The last text exchange between Josh and her was from a couple days ago. The final message was her: "what time u home?" The text before that was also from Diane: "running late; stopping for food; want anything?" She scrolled back through her and Josh's texts. A few weeks prior, there was this one from Josh: "sorry sent to the wrong person." The text before that was Josh on the same date: "i definitely want to meet him."

Diane had forgotten this misdirected text. She read it again with the recent context of his note about meeting a boy. Invasive, she thinks, when she sees something not meant for her. Good parenting, she thinks, when she has concern for her son's well-being.

Josh wanted to meet a boy. It wasn't complicated. He was having a difficult time allowing her into a world that was already fraught with self-loathing and discomfort. Josh simply wanted to meet some boy, and her prying put him on edge. A crush. A teenager in an early approximation of love. It was sweet.

She did not cry, but she pre-cried.

"Reminder: I love you very much. That is all." She sent the text.

The pre-crying turned to crying. A good cry. A sad, but good cry. The anchors on the television glanced over at her with concern but continued to report the news. She felt a hand rub her back gently.

"Thanks, Faceless Old Woman," she said. "That feels nice."

Her phone buzzed. She looked down. Josh had texted back.

"I want to meet Troy."

THE VOICE OF NIGHT VALE

CECIL: And now, the community calendar.

Saturday is a softball game between Night Vale Community Radio and Night Vale Local News TV. I don't mind telling you, this is not a game I enjoy. The creatures that work in television news, because of the shape and quantity of their appendages, often hold the bat in ways that are unsettling to the human eye. They usually win by creeping out the other team so much that the opposing team all goes to sit mutely on the bench while the TV News team plays their way to a win on an empty field. Come out for what should be a great game!

Sunday is the annual Imaginary Corn Festival and Fun Fair, celebrating our town's most important crop. Come try out some simple and healthy imaginary corn recipes and take part in a costume contest sponsored by the *Night Vale Daily Journal*. They are asking that everyone dress up as the decline of the printed word in a society reverting to a state of brainless animality. The best costume wins one year of not being forced to purchase several *Daily Journal* subscriptions by newspaper employees armed with hatchets. There will also be rides and carnival games and apprehensive excitement and hoped-for futures and stomach pains and sweat and disappointment and sweat and sweat and love and glances that mean more than they should but less than they need to and a dunking booth.

Monday will be free-sample day at the Sheraton Funeral Home.

Tuesday will be reversed. We will rise tired from sleep to find that it is night and brush plaque onto our teeth. We will move backwards to work, where we will undo spreadsheets, lose ideas to dissipating meetings, and unsee hundreds of cat pictures. Then, returning with a buzz of caffeine to our homes, we will spit liquid alertness into cups and, refreshed but groggy, return to dreams that we faintly, just faintly, remember.

Wednesday is Smell Like a Pirate Day. Everyone in town is encouraged to get in on the wacky fun by not bathing for weeks and rubbing yourself with ash and blood.

Thursday, the employees at Dark Owl Records will be holding a séance to reach the ghost of Patsy Cline. If you'd like to come by and help, just enter quietly and please wear a bolo tie. We're all wearing bolo ties now. And don't wear those shoes. God, do we have to tell you everything? Maybe it's better if you don't come by. Records are not for sale, as usual.

We are skipping Friday this week, but we'll make up for it by having Double Friday next week. Mark your schedules.

This has been the community calendar.

I've just been handed an update. The Secret Police would like to retract their earlier statement that they will be out in large numbers tonight. That was not meant to be known.

"You think you want to know things, but then you know them, and it's too late. You didn't want to know that. You didn't want to know that at all," the Secret Police's press release reads. "This is one of those things you will wish you had never known."

The statement goes on to say that memory is a tenuous human construct, and nothing matters in the Grand Scheme, so whatever.

In other news, a man in a tan jacket, holding a deerskin suitcase, was seen. I don't remember anything about him or why this was news, but it had seemed important at the time. I wrote it down: "Say the important thing about the man in the tan jacket." What was it? What was I supposed to say?

20

"It's not a good idea, Josh."

"Why?" His shouts were muffled behind his locked bedroom door.

"Because—"

In the space after the word *because,* Diane thought through what the next words could be.

Because he is a dangerous person? Maybe. Troy doesn't seem to be a danger. But anyone could be a dangerous person.

Because he will only let you down? Probably. He had disappeared before, he could disappear again. He could also just be a terrible father.

Because it is complicated. More complicated than you can process with your young brain, she wanted to say.

Because she didn't have a reason exactly but felt a storm on its way, a confluence of Troy's reappearance and Josh's interest and the disappearance of Evan, and she wanted to wrap herself around Josh and keep him from all of whatever was going to happen next.

"Because I said so," Diane said.

There was no audible response.

"I have to go," she said.

"Where are you going? It's seven o'clock."

"Out."

"With who? With Don?"

They both took the expected tone and said their lines as if

from a script, but the scene had gotten mixed up and reversed somehow. They both wanted to put it back the way it was supposed to be, but neither of them knew how to do that.

She was going out to try to find Troy again, perhaps make another visit to the movies. She needed to confront Troy now, before Josh did. Josh would inevitably find him, so it would be better if she could facilitate that on her own terms, rather than her son's or, worse, Troy's.

Also, given that she had hit a dead end in her search for Evan at work and with Dawn, the only place she could get any more information was at the hall of records, but citizens were not allowed to know where public records were kept. She figured they were somewhere in City Hall basement, but unless you had high-level clearance to get into the records offices, you would become stuck in the elaborate, tricky mazes designed to trap news reporters and nosy genealogists.

The other option was to go to the public library. Few people came back from a visit to the library.

There was one girl a few years ago that survived the Summer Reading Program at the Night Vale Public Library. The girl, Tamika Flynn, defeated the librarian that had imprisoned her and her classmates, using the switchblade hidden in every hardback edition of Eudora Welty's touching homecoming novel *The Optimist's Daughter*.

But few who have seen a librarian up close have survived or been in a physical condition to communicate.

Perhaps Diane could use Troy. Police officers have access to all kinds of databases. If Diane could just have a few minutes searching Troy's office computers, she could probably find something about Evan. Just something to point her in a new direction: real estate records, a birth or wedding announcement, any number of the mandatory dream journals that he would have had to file with the city if he were a legal resident and, if he didn't, some kind of prison record.

To do that she needed to be away from Josh more than she had been in his entire life, and in order to do that, she needed to keep up the imaginary thing with Dawn.

"Yes, with Dawn."

"Why don't you have Don over for dinner?"

Diane did not reply. Josh opened his door, his wings flapping in an effortless blur.

"Mom, there was no Ty. DeVon helped me figure out that my dad's real name is Troy Walsh. We couldn't find a photo, but DeVon's seeing if his friend can get one. I want to meet my dad. So now I've told you the truth. I've opened up like you keep asking me to do. Now you. Now your turn. You've been going out on dates. Sometimes these dates go all night, and, okay, so that's a thing, I guess, and I don't need those specifics. But I've never had a dad, and you won't let me meet him, and now you're dating someone seriously and you won't let me meet him either."

"Dawn's a she," Diane corrected automatically, based on a reality that was irrelevant to her lie, and regretted it immediately.

"So you just really don't want me to have a dad, do you?" he said, also automatically, based on a hurt that was not irrelevant to his life, and then immediately: "No, I'm sorry. No, that's fine. I didn't mean . . . That's fine."

He was flustered, back on the defensive and unsure of how he had gotten there.

Diane did nothing. She breathed, unintentionally. The faceless old woman who secretly lives in their home crawled by on the ceiling, but neither of them noticed.

Josh matched Diane's stare for a second, then slithered backwards and shut the door.

There are a lot of things we don't understand about orange juice, the house thought.

Diane walked to the kitchen and swung open the fridge. She did not want anything from inside it, and so stood in front of the open fridge for several moments, unsure of what she was doing next.

Her phone buzzed. A text. "Hello."

She texted back to the unknown number, "Hello?"

Diane stared at the carton of orange juice in the fridge, at the bright round fruit logo, its straw hat shading unseen eyes on the pocked face, a tight grin with perfect human teeth, separated slightly, and a pink, leaf-shaped tongue. She didn't know why she was fixating on the orange juice, but she didn't know why she was doing anything.

Troy was everywhere. There were so many of him, and Josh wanted to meet just one of him. It was a meeting she didn't think she was going to be able to prevent, so she needed more time to understand who Troy was now, and what he wanted. And then there was Evan. Why was she looking so hard for Evan?

It seemed to her that her life had slipped loose somehow, its progression all off track. Josh and Troy, that was one thing. But she felt a larger shift, and that shift had all started when Evan disappeared and became forgotten by all but her. There was something wrong, in her life, in Night Vale, maybe in the world. The magnitude of the thing was unclear, but wherever it was, she was inside it.

Her phone buzzed.

"it's been a while"

She didn't know what that meant, and didn't want to reply. She should go to the movie theater. She was going to go to the movie theater.

She walked back to Josh's closed door.

"Josh, I'm sorry. I know this all doesn't make sense to you. It doesn't all make sense to me either."

Nothing.

"I love you."

A long nothing.

"I'm not perfect. I'm not. I'm sorry."

There came a faint "Love you, too."

She exhaled. Her phone buzzed again.

"do you remember me?"

She stared at the phone. The area code of the texts was a postage-stamp-size photo of a burnt-out forest alive with luminescent snails in an array of vivid colors. She didn't recognize that area code, but it wasn't local.

Buzz.

"you remember me diane"

"Who is this?" she typed.

Nothing.

Nothing.

She was tired of waiting for things to happen to her; she would make something happen. She would just call the number. She put the phone to her ear.

It buzzed warm in her ear, and she yelped at the proximity. Another text.

"evan"

There was a photo attached.

It was a man. She was sure she had never seen his face before. He was wearing a tan jacket and holding a small brown suitcase. It looked to be leather. He had dark gray slacks and a light blue shirt, open at the collar.

She looked at his face. She stared for a long time, trying to recall his eyes, his mouth, the curve of his nose, his hairline. It wasn't that he was unfamiliar to her, it was that she couldn't keep her eyes focused on him. Every time she would look at his cheeks or his ears or his chin, she found herself instead looking at his tan jacket or his leather suitcase.

And when her eyes did land on his face, it was like the first time she had ever seen him. There was no recognition.

Buzz.

"remember?"

"evan. i remember, but no one else does."

"no one ever does diane"

"i've been looking for you. where are you." Diane was reaching for a pen to write down this number. She needed physical, not just digital, evidence of his existence.

"i'll come to you"

She began to type "actually I was just heading out. let's meet up in town" while grabbing her purse and walking to the front door.

Halfway into writing that: Buzz.

"Here!" said the text.

There was a loud knock on the front door directly in front of her. Diane suddenly remembered that she had left the fridge open.

21

Diane was sitting in a corner booth at the Moonlite All-Nite Diner without any clear idea how she got there. She glanced to her right and saw her car parked in the lot.

"Don't turn your head."

Across the table sat a man wearing a tan jacket. He looked familiar.

"Keep your eyes on me, Diane."

In her lap were some notes in her handwriting. One said "Evan McIntyre." One said "King City?" The second one was circled twice and underlined.

How had she ended up here? Think back through it. What had been done to her? Or what had she done to herself? She felt like she was outside of herself, looking at her life through a stranger's eyes, and she didn't love what she saw.

She looked back across the table, and the man was not there. She blinked for a second, and he returned.

"Keep your eyes on me," he said, "or you will forget."

"Evan," Diane said uncertainly.

"My name is not Evan," said the man whose name was not Evan. Then he said his name.

"Evan," Diane said uncertainly.

He repeated his actual name.

"Evan, I don't care what your name is. I'm sorry, I don't. Why did you disappear from the office?"

She wondered how long she had been at the Moonlite, and

if Josh was worried about her. She worried more about his worrying than she worried about him. At the same time she felt a victory inside herself that Evan was real, that he was sitting in front of her, that there was some confirmation that he had existed and had worked at her office.

The man sat up straight, widening his shoulders, a gesture simultaneously receptive and defensive.

Laura came by the table and poured them both coffee. Diane ordered lunch. Laura drew a picture of a cow skull on her notepad, using her finger and a small pot of ink clipped to her pad. It was a detailed picture that took her a few minutes, while Evan and Diane patiently waited for her to be done, and when she showed them, they both agreed it captured the beauty and impermanence of physical life.

Before heading back to the kitchen, Laura said, "I'm sorry, dear, what did you order again?"

"Just the coffee," Evan said. "Thank you."

"You have pretty eyes," Laura said. She didn't know why she had said it. She also did not believe in free will, but that is not important to mention.

"Me or him?" Diane said, jokingly, although she did want to know.

"What, dear?"

"Which of us do you mean?"

"I don't understand."

"Did you mean me or Evan?"

"Who's Evan, dear?"

Diane looked back to Evan, but he wasn't there.

"You came here alone, Diane. Just a few minutes ago."

There was only one coffee cup on the table. Only one place setting. The Naugahyde chair across from her was empty and pushed snugly under the table.

"Never mind. Thanks," she said.

Laura turned to leave, her branches swinging through the empty air where Evan had been.

Diane breathed with effort.

She looked where Evan's eyes would have been. She could not recall what they looked like, but she could guess their approximate location. She did not see him appear. He was just there again, matching her gaze. She wanted to look away.

"Focus," he said, visible again.

"This is hard for me."

"This is hard for me too. Almost no one remembers me. Not even back where I'm from. But you do. You remember me. I need your help, Diane."

Diane gripped her coffee cup hard. She thought of the last time she'd talked with Josh, and she let that anger carry her through the strangeness of the conversation.

"You don't just get to ask me for help. I don't know you. You show up at my office. You insinuate yourself into my memories and then you vanish from my life. You keep vanishing even now."

"It's not something I can control."

"I don't want excuses." She slid a pen and a piece of blank paper across the table, her eyes still on his. "I want you to write your name down."

He opened his mouth.

"Do it quickly. No talking."

Diane is a nice person. Nice people are not good at being direct. Nice people do not like to make others feel rushed or indebted or insulted. Nice people like to make others feel nice. It is difficult to maintain niceness while being assertive. You can be respectful and assertive, of course, but that has nothing to do with being nice.

"And while you're doing that I'm going to take pictures of you. I'm not going to be put in this position of ridicule again."

She held her phone up.

"I'm not trying to ridicule you, Diane. I'm happy to help you in whatever way I can," he said, writing out his name on the page. Diane looked at the name, nodded, and immediately forgot it.

"Help me? Evan, I don't remember how I got to this diner. Do you know how uncomfortable that makes me?"

Laura returned before he could reply. She placed a bowl of fruit and a pile of pumice stones in front of Diane. She refilled both coffees.

"Here's your Greek salad," Laura said. "And here's more coffee, handsome." She glanced at the man and raised her eyebrows at Diane, grinning. Diane did not move her eyes from the man. Laura shrugged, walked away, and forgot what had just happened.

Diane took several pictures of him.

"It's hard to expl———," he said.

"Try," she interrupted.

The man in the tan jacket holding a deerskin suitcase explained. Diane understood. She nodded. She protested. She decided she would never do what he said, and then she agreed to think about it.

She took a sip of coffee. She had no memory of what he had just said.

"You'll need this." He handed her a slip of paper that said "KING CITY."

"What is this?" she said.

Instead of answering, he pointed at the man in the white apron with blond hair walking past their table.

"That is who I mean. That is who I mean," the man in the

tan jacket whispered in Diane's left ear even as he sat across the table from her, his mouth not moving.

"Troy?" She followed Troy with her eyes. "How do you know him?"

She turned back to where the man in the tan jacket had been sitting. He was, of course, gone. His chair was pulled out, his coffee half empty. Some currency that was clearly marked as American but that she did not recognize lay on the table.

"I already explained that to you. Remember?" came his whisper in her right ear. "Give that paper to Josh. I want to meet Josh."

"What do you want with Josh?" At her son's name, her bewilderment tunneled into a feeling of intense protection. Like hell would anyone be dragging a child into this mess. There was no answer. She looked out the window.

The man in the tan jacket was running out to the desert. She could just barely see him at the edge of the parking lot's radius of light. His arms were swinging wildly, his suitcase swinging along. His legs were flailing, great puffs of sand kicked up behind him, his head thrown back, sweat running down his face visible even from where she sat. The kind of run that was from something and not toward. Then he left the faint edge of the light and was gone.

She looked down at the slip of paper in her hand. It read "KING CITY." She gathered up her things, hiding the pen in her bag, mortified that she'd left a potential misdemeanor out on the table for anyone to see.

She was still uncertain how long she had been at the diner. Had she said good-bye to Josh? Did he know where she was? She would text him.

Before leaving, she scanned the diner for Troy. She couldn't see him.

Jackie waved at her from the counter. They exchanged pleasantries. There was something odd about the way Jackie considered her. Thoughtful and suspicious. Diane tried to seem completely at ease. They exchanged some words that didn't mean much. Then things turned. Diane said, "What?" and Jackie shook her head impatiently.

"Never mind. What do you got there?"

She nodded at the paper in Diane's hand. Diane realized that Jackie was holding an identical paper, but couldn't get her mind to rest on that fact long enough to become curious about it.

"Nothing," said Diane, and stuffed the paper into her purse. It stayed in her purse.

"Lucky," said Jackie, and turned back to her coffee, tapping the edge of her paper against the counter.

Diane still didn't understand, but Jackie seemed grumpy, and so Diane let the conversation end there. She said some sort of casual good-bye, and Jackie threw it back in her face as a sarcastic joke, which Diane thought was unnecessary and rude.

As she walked to her car, she reached into her bag for her keys.

Her hand came across some crumpled paper. She pulled it out. "KING CITY," it said. Why did she have that? Where would this piece of paper have come from? She tossed it on the ground and then, feeling guilty, picked it up to carry around to the dumpster. Before she could toss it in, there was a crashing sound next to her, which made her jump.

Troy was there, throwing big bags of trash into the dumpster.

"Oh, hey," he said, and ducked quickly through the back door.

She seemed to be holding a piece of paper. She did not know what it was or where it could have come from or how much she would later regret keeping it. She put it in her purse.

22

Jackie was at a dead end, investigation-wise. In terms of tacos, she was doing fine. Judged on her ability to never be able to let go of a slip of paper with her left hand, it was all going great. But trying to figure out what the hell was going on was not going well at all.

She had spent the night with open eyes, trying to will her mind to be just as open. There had to be something she had missed, some connection to be made in the events and individuals moving about in the memory of her day. But if there was, she couldn't see it. Maybe she wasn't smart enough. Or maybe the world wasn't. Maybe the world wasn't smart enough to put together a story that made sense. Maybe it could only stick together random elements randomly, forming, as Shakespeare had famously written, "a show of senseless movement and circumstance that ultimately doesn't amount to much at all."

The next morning found her with only one lead left. She had seen that blond man at her mother's house. And she had seen him outside of the mayor's office. And she had seen him at the Moonlite All-Nite Diner. It was time to talk to that man and to find out how he was involved in whatever it was this whatever was.

She drove to the Moonlite All-Nite. It was the same crowd as always, which is to say that there were many of the regulars, and also to say that certain people were always in the Moonlite All-Nite, always at the same booths, always working on plates of food that never seemed to go away. It's a sign of a good diner to have customers who are stuck in time. A well-known rule of eating is that if there are no time-loop customers, the place probably isn't worth even ordering a plate of fries.

Jackie sat in her regular spot at the counter.

"Hiya, Jackie," said Laura, moving with difficulty behind the counter, her thick, woody branches scraping against it. "You hungry?" She bent a fruit-laden branch toward her invitingly.

"Thanks, Laura, but just a coffee."

Laura pushed her way toward the coffee machine, her branches knocking over tubs of ketchup and mayonnaise and stacks of empty water glasses as she went.

Jackie watched the kitchen. There was no blond man.

She turned to survey the room. Diane Crayton was getting out of her booth. It seemed like there was probably someone with her, but Jackie couldn't remember who. She looked back at Diane's table, and her heart began to pound, and then she looked at the kitchen again and couldn't understand why her heart was pounding.

Diane walked by her. Jackie decided to stop her, talk a little, make it seem casual. She needed to know if Diane actually was involved somehow.

"Hey! Diane!" Jackie said with a casual half salute.

Diane jumped and gasped.

"Easy," Jackie said, bringing her saluting hand down to pat the air with a "Whoa." "Just saying hi."

"Sure. I was . . ." Diane took a breath. "I was all caught up in my thoughts."

She waved her hand to indicate where her thoughts were. She laughed to indicate that she was fine and unbothered. The combination of hands and laughter indicated she was startled and uncomfortable.

"Totally get it. Cool."

"I am sorry. I have to go. I hope the tear I gave you is working out okay."

"Yeah. The tear. It's great. I'm sure it'll fly off the shelf real soon. Always a demand for tears."

"How's your mother?"

Jackie gave her a hard look.

"What do you know about my mother?"

Diane frowned with her whole face.

"What?" she said.

The conversation went wrong from there. Jackie felt Diane hiding something from her. It felt like everyone was hiding something from Jackie, the whole world a game of hide-and-seek she had never consented to play. She gave up on the conversation and turned back to the coffee.

Diane smiled, but only with her mouth.

"I'll be seeing you, Jackie."

"I'm completely visible." Jackie thought this was a pretty good joke, but Diane didn't laugh.

Jackie's coffee had arrived in a mug with the logo of a strangely proportioned giant of a man leering out at the world. Underneath it was a phrase that had been vandalized by some sharp object, chipping most of it away and leaving only

CALL 4 6 TO M   E.

The mug had a smudge where blood had been incompletely wiped off.

She sipped and she waited. She waited and she sipped. The act of sipping was an act of waiting. Sometimes she didn't even put the coffee in her mouth, only held her lips to the rim and then put the mug back down.

The woman with the clipboard was there as usual, and each time that Jackie took a sip the woman would write something down. She appeared to be working with a woman with an earpiece standing outside, as she would occasionally wave wildly to her, and the other woman would wave wildly back, and then they would quickly and nonchalantly look away, loudly whistling and saying, "I don't know that person. If you asked me to define a stranger, I'd say that lady. Couldn't know her less."

Jackie looked back at the kitchen, and there was the man again: blond, handsome in all of the expected ways (and in this way not handsome), staring at her and flipping endless amounts of burgers into the air, a fountain of burgers with a meat-splash pattern in a five-foot radius around him.

She hopped up from the stool. The woman with the clipboard started writing frantically on the clipboard, and Laura said, "Hey, Jackie, where you going?" but couldn't get up because her branches were caught in the ice cream freezer door.

Jackie ran to the back, where the steel swinging doors of the kitchen were. She slammed through them into a kitchen with no one in it. All the burgers were still there, evidence of the man's recent existence.

She walked slowly past the prep table, stopping to look under it, where the pans and plates were stored. No one.

There was no back door that she could see. He had to be in here.

A soft clank. Some hanging spatulas moving. She crept toward them, looking around at the large dishwashing sink and the cold storage room.

The cold storage room. A heavy magnetized door. Was it slightly ajar?

She reached out her hand, slowly, so slowly. Fingers around

the handle. The kitchen was empty and silent. No one out in the diner seemed to be watching. Even the woman with the clipboard had returned to her usual business of marking off new entrances. She was alone and no one would help her if anything went wrong.

"Story of my life," she said, and flung open the magnetized door. Shelves of meat and produce, nothing else. There was nowhere she could see to hide.

A crash from behind her. The blond man pushed away the pile of plates he had been hiding behind in a shout of broken ceramics. She tore after him, and they both slammed through the steel swinging doors. She was just behind him as they weaved through tables and surprised customers.

The clipboard woman was adding something up on her clipboard, mouthing the equations as she went, apparently uninterested in the chase.

Jackie sprinted through the diner as quickly as a person can sprint after a stranger through a diner, which was not quickly at all. The blond man burst out the front door and Jackie was moments behind him. She was younger and she was faster and she would catch him. Her feet slapped hard on the asphalt, so hot in the midday sun that she could feel the heat through the soles of her shoes.

"I've got you," she shouted, before she had him.

"Troy!" Diane shouted, running from her car. "Troy, I need to talk to you."

The blond man broke right, toward the road and the abandoned gas station across the street.

Diane and Jackie both turned to follow, and collided with each other. Subsequently they both collided with the ground.

"Goddammit!" Jackie shouted into the blacktop, a long red

scratch on her face. Diane had the makings of a bruise on her thigh but didn't know it yet. They both looked toward the gas station, but the man was gone.

"Goddammit!" Jackie repeated with her mouth. "Goddammit!" she repeated over and over with her palm onto the asphalt.

Diane glared at her, rubbing her leg.

"Why were you chasing Troy?" she asked.

Jackie glared at her. *Diane Crayton,* John had said. Diane was involved, and didn't this prove it?

"Why was I chasing him? Why do you have that paper?"

Diane didn't understand what that question had to do with anything that had just happened. Jackie looked back at the gas station.

"I almost had him, Diane. That weird dude."

"You almost had him? What did 'that weird dude' do to you, Jackie?"

Jackie tried to come up with an explanation as to why her actions made sense. Her head hurt. "He just stares and smiles. What's his deal? I mean . . ."

"Maybe you're too young to understand this, but you don't just run after people because you want to know what their deal is."

Diane had slipped into didactic mom voice without meaning to, and they both heard it.

"Ah, so the mature approach is to body-tackle people in parking lots. Awesome. I'm sure when I'm as old as you I'll remember that."

Diane sighed and stood up, seeing if her body could still do that. She looked the teenager up and down.

"If you want to be treated as an adult, Jackie, you have to act like it."

In her head, Jackie heard the voice of her ex-friend Noelle

Connolly, brimming with parental condescension: *Oh, Jackie, did you ever think of just turning twenty?*

"Screw you," she said.

"Oh, good. That's good."

Diane turned and walked back to her car. Jackie walked after her.

"Hey, where do you think you're going? How do you know that guy? How did you know his name was Troy? Like, seriously, what's his deal?"

Diane collected herself and spoke with only a mild tremble.

"This is none of your business. Troy is someone from my past, and I'm trying to talk to him so that things will be right with my son. My son, who is the only child I am interested in raising right now. You'll have to find someone else to do that for you."

She slammed herself into her car. Jackie made a gesture through the window that succinctly responded to many of the points made. Diane shrugged and reversed the car out of the spot.

"I'm finding out who that guy is and what you have to do with him," Jackie shouted after her. "I'm getting to the goddamn bottom of this. You just stay out of my way while I do."

Diane responded with acceleration. Jackie threw the paper after her.

"Screw you," Jackie said.

"KING CITY," the paper said, back in her hand.

"She has no idea what she's talking about," Diane and Jackie said simultaneously and separately, but about this they both had their doubts.

Sitting in her car, which sat in front of her house, which was not thinking anything at the time, Diane took out her phone and the paper that Evan had written on.

Diane did not remember much from her meeting with Evan at the diner. But she did remember he had texted her. She had also taken photos of him. She had also asked him to write down his name.

She remembered Jackie chasing after Troy. Diane, thinking of this moment, rubbed the burn marks on her left forearm. Why was Jackie looking for Troy? There was a great pit of the unknown under the rickety bridge of her and Josh's relationship, and every time she looked down the pit was deeper than before. She felt annoyed with Jackie but furious with Troy. Another young person caught in the wake he was creating as he moved lightly through his careless, carefree life.

She looked at the piece of paper. It said "KING CITY," and on the back it had Evan's name. His name was not Evan. She looked at the name on the page and said it aloud. She said it again, and then put the paper down.

"Evan McIntyre," she said aloud, and shrugged. "That's just what it's going to be then."

Diane opened her photos and looked at one of the pictures she'd taken of Evan at the diner. He was wearing a tan jacket. She stared at the picture, then closed her eyes, hoping to burn the image into her mind, or onto the backs of her retinas, or into the mystic cloud of the collective unconscious, whatever it is that makes us remember images. She was no scientist.

She muttered his name with her eyes shut, trying to hold on to the image of him. His eyes, nose, mouth, hairline. Nothing. She looked back at the photo. She took in his lips, and thought about the many adjectives that could be used to describe them. Then she looked at his nose, and took in the adjectives that could be used to describe it.

Upon staring at the nose, she forgot those adjectives she thought about the lips. She looked back at the lips and forgot the nose. She never even got to the ears.

Diane searched her text history and tried texting Evan back. Another way to remember someone is to create more memories with that person. The more there is to forget, the longer forgetting takes.

She typed: "Hey, good talking to you the other night. Let's do it again."

It sounded like a date. She deleted the text without sending.

A horsefly sitting on the right rear headrest flew to the left rear headrest.

Diane saw it do this.

She wrote a different text: "Evan, I can't remember what we talked about. Can you come back?"

She hit send.

Her thumb seized up in a sharp moment of pain. She didn't cry out, just winced. Her text remained unsent. She tried again. Another sharp pain, almost to the bone. A small bead of blood ballooned on the middle of her right thumb.

This is a common feature on smart phones. If a person is unreachable by text or if the underground government agencies that control the phone companies don't want a person to be reachable, the phone is allowed to cause mild physical harm. She put the thumb to her mouth to clean it off.

The day before, the phone had caught fire while she tried to call him. She smelled burnt hair most of the morning, and had to stop by the drugstore to get calamine lotion for the top of her ear and then stop by a garden nursery and place the side of her head onto aerated topsoil for fifteen minutes, per her doctor's orders. She didn't know why the doctor would tell her to do that, but no one knows why doctors do anything they do. Doctors are mysterious creatures.

Diane looked at the horsefly on the left rear headrest through the rearview mirror. She stared at the fly. She could feel the fly staring back. It shuffled its half dozen legs. It moved a little left, a little right. It stood tiny and alone in the middle of what was, to it, a vast cloth field. There was no place to hide.

"I see you," she said.

"It's not what you think," the horsefly said.

"What do I think?"

"You think I'm spying."

"Yes, I do. And what is it you are doing instead, Josh?"

He flew to the front of the car and landed on the dashboard.

"I wanted to hop a ride with you."

"I'm going to work."

"Then I'll just fly."

"You will do no such thing. You walk or ride. You are not to fly outside until you are eighteen. It's dangerous."

The horsefly moped.

"Josh, you can't hide in my car. How am I supposed to trust you if I can't trust that my private space is private?"

"I didn't think you'd see me."

"That's the trust thing I'm talking about."

"I'm sorry."

Despite the fact that horseflies are incapable of dropping their heads in a gesture of penitence and submission, and despite the fact that, even if they could do this, it would be so subtle as to be unnoticeable by human eyes, she heard this action in Josh's voice. She didn't need to see her son in human form to understand his physical language. Even when Josh took the form of a sentient patch of haze (he rarely did, only once or twice after watching a scary movie, when he had felt that, if he had no physical form, no monsters or ghosts could get him), she could still tell when he was rolling his eyes or slumping or smirking or not paying attention.

"I can always see you, Josh. I'm your mom. You could be anything, and I would know it was you."

Josh didn't say anything. He vigorously rubbed his legs together because that was something he had seen flies do, but he didn't know why they did that.

"Why did you want to ride downtown with me?"

"Just to hang out. Maybe go to the video store or something."

"First, you don't get to skip school. You understand me?"

"Yes."

"Second, you don't get to hide from me. That is deceitful, Josh."

"Okay. Okay."

"And third." She hesitated. "You were going to dig up records on your dad, right?"

Josh didn't respond.

"I don't want you doing that. He's your father, yes, but I don't trust him."

"You did at one point."

"I raised you for fifteen years. I fed you and clothed you. I loved you and still do. I love you because you have been with me for fifteen years. I am your mother because we have been together your whole childhood. I have earned you as my son.

"Troy does not get to be your father simply because he participated in your creation. Troy does not get to earn your love as a son because you are biologically his. I have done the work. I have put in the time. I have loved you. Troy does not get to be my equal in your life because he has not earned it. I need to protect myself. And I need to protect you.

"So promise me you will leave this all alone. And I will promise you that I will find out more about him, and, when the time is right, I will tell you."

"Okay," the horsefly said. He didn't sound like he thought it was okay.

"Get moving, so you don't miss your bus. No more of this, okay?"

Diane pressed her finger to the automatic window button for the front passenger side. With a robotic whir, the window cracked open. The horsefly flew up and out in a loose spiral.

"I love you," she called out. "No flying."

"Okay," came back the soft buzz from the human boy with the horsefly face.

Later she would go over this conversation again and again in her head, one of the last they would have before he disappeared.

Jackie hit the steering wheel of her car, which did not hurt the car at all. Sometimes it is easy to forget which things in the world can feel pain and which cannot.

What *did* Diane know about this? What was her connection? Could she be the mastermind behind the blond man and the man in the tan jacket holding a deerskin suitcase and maybe even Jackie's mother's strange behavior?

John Peters certainly seemed to think she was involved. And why not Diane? Wasn't Night Vale a town full of hidden evils and the secretly malevolent? That was what the Tourism Board's new brochures said right on the front ("A town full of hidden evils and the secretly malevolent") along with a picture of a diverse group of townsfolk smiling and looking up at the camera in the windowless prison they would be kept in until enough tourists visited town to buy their release.

If it was possible that Diane was behind any of this, then Jackie needed to talk to someone who knew her. Sure, she seemed nice, but lots of people and things seem nice yet are terrible underneath: like poisonous berries, rabid squirrels, or a smiling god. (Is that a smile?)

This was how it was that Jackie ended up at the Night Vale Elementary Multipurpose Room, which was, among its multiple purposes, the headquarters of the Night Vale PTA. Diane had been the treasurer since back when her son was a student at the school, and had kept it up even as he had gone on to high school and puberty (and the myriad physical forms it had brought him). Josh was just a few years younger than Jackie, and she liked him well enough. Some of his shapes were a little scary, especially the dream forms, but in general he was a good kid. Jackie had always hoped that things would turn out well for him, in the vague way one feels goodwill toward semi-strangers. May his life turn out better than hers had.

The multipurpose room was a cluttered space befitting its many uses. There was a small stage where school plays could be put on. There were stacks of folding chairs for PTA meetings and the various support organizations (Alcohol, Narcotics, Immortality) that used the room after school. There was a full bloodstone circle for bloodstone demonstration and worship, and a child-size bloodstone circle so that the students could try out the rites on their own. There was also a popcorn machine, but no one was allowed to touch it. No one was quite sure why touching it was disallowed, but warnings like that are worth heeding in Night Vale, and so it had been left alone for decades, in its supremely inconvenient place in the center of the room.

"Diane?" Jackie said, hoping she wouldn't be there. The best person to run into would be Susan Willman, who was known to be chatty and who was not on friendly terms with Diane. Susan would be thrilled to pass on any gossip she had about Diane. She also, Jackie knew, would be only too happy to make up gossip about Diane, so perhaps she wouldn't be the best option after all. Jackie would have been fine with an empty room, so she could root around in PTA records and check for files or notes from Diane that might give her any new information. Her worst-case scenario was:

"Oh, hi, Jackie!" Steve Carlsberg said. "Diane's not around. I'm just tidying up for a meeting in here."

He gestured, and in gesturing knocked a cardboard box of files off a table, spilling them all over the floor.

"Whoopsie-daisy! Let me just pick those up. Now what can I help you with?"

Jackie sighed. Steve was fine. He was a nice man. But he was so . . . he was just . . . well, he was Steve Carlsberg. There's always that guy. And Steve was him.

"Hi, Steve," she said, and helped him pick up the files. As she did, her paper did its mystical yo-yoing bit, which she had ceased to even notice. Steve gasped.

"Woooow. So you got one of those papers? Luu-uu-uuucky." He whistled, hands on his hips.

"Lucky?" she said. "I can't work, I've been seeing visions, and some creepy blond dude is following me around town. Plus, some days I feel like I can't walk, can't hardly breathe. Yeah, so this paper is superlucky."

Steve nodded. "That sounds like a blast. Nothing strange ever enters into my life, turning it upside down and forcing me to go on a journey of discovery in order to right things again. Not that I mind, of course. The PTA is rewarding in its own way, and it's nice to get involved with what Janice is up to."

Janice was Steve's stepdaughter. Her mother was the sister of Cecil, the local radio host. Steve and Cecil did not get along at all. It was something of a local joke, although Jackie guessed it was less funny if it was your family that had that kind of feud in it. She'd always felt bad for Janice, but Janice wasn't the type of kid who let you feel bad for her.

"So you know about these papers?" Jackie said.

"KING CITY," the proffered paper said.

"Oh boy, yes," Steve said. "Lots of folks have been getting those. Some fellow with a tan jacket, oh, what's his name? I forget. I keep forgetting a lot about him. He's been handing them out. I saw some folks at the bowling alley the other night. A whole team on lane nineteen just sitting there crying and clutching their left fists. I saw some of the stockers at the Ralphs standing in front of empty shelves, staring to the sky, small slips of paper hanging from their slack fingers. Every now and then I'd see someone shake the paper away, and it would spiral toward the linoleum floor, only to flutter back up into their hands, and collectively they would moan.

"Once you get one, you can't let go of it. Suppose that guy handing them out has a reason, but it might just be a hobby. I've been thinking of taking up beekeeping, but, you know, bees need a lot of space to run around and they're expensive unless you keep them on a farm, and then what's the point of having a pet you can't keep in your apartment?"

This was how it was what with Steve. The important bit buried in a lot of meandering digression.

"A man in a tan jacket?"

"Sure. Holding a deerskin suitcase. Don't remember much more about him than that. I took a picture of him. I think I have it around here somewhere."

He stuck the upper half of his body into a shelf and started shuffling papers around. As he searched, several other stacks of paper fell on the floor, and he came back up, sweating a bit from the exertion.

Jackie felt repulsed by Steve. She had no idea why. He had never been anything other than kind to her, kind to everybody. As the old saying went: "Not all windowless vans have residential surveillance equipment." In other words, not everything can be as good as it seems.

"Well, isn't that funny? I just can't seem to keep it in my

mind where that photo is," Steve said. "It's the darndest th—
— Whoa!"

He waved his arms at her. She held her hands up, fingers splayed.
The paper dropped, and dropped again, and dropped again.

"You were almost leaning on the popcorn machine there,"
Steve said. "Don't want to do that."

"It's not even hot, man," Jackie said, about to touch the machine to demonstrate.

"No, don't!" His voice cracked.

She sighed at the oppression of conventional wisdom but
dropped her hand.

"So the man in the tan jacket has been giving the paper to
lots of people?"

"Not sure how many, but certainly a good amount. Old
Woman Josie has one, but I suppose you know that. I hear even
Stacy got one recently, and she's a sentient patch of haze. Lovely
being. Once told me the best way to pickle grapes. It was a fun
recipe. Never did try it."

"How well do you know Diane Crayton?" Jackie pressed.

He laughed, although not at a joke. He laughed because he
was happy. Jackie winced, although she could not say exactly
what it was that annoyed her.

"Great woman. Been working on the PTA with her for years.
Never could get her to come around on invisible pie, but other
than that we've never had a real difference on anything. We've
talked a lot lately because she needs someone to talk through
the whole Josh thing with. And all that stuff with Troy."

"Oh?" Jackie said. She failed to make her voice casual or patient. "Who is Troy?"

"I really shouldn't say." Steve frowned. "Not my story to tell
and all that. Hey, so can I see your paper?"

"Yeah."

He sat down across from her, taking the paper from her hand. He studied it, admired it. His face was so full of excitement it was difficult for him to keep the words in order as they came barreling out of his mouth.

"So you know how we're always being watched by agents of a vague yet menacing government agency right? ("Sure.") And how they're linked somehow with the World Government? ("Mm.") Well. Sometimes I feel like I'm the only person in Night Vale who thinks about this stuff but have you thought about why the World Government is interested in us? Or why there are always lights over the Arby's? Or what those ghost cars are that come roaring down Route 800 late at night at impossible speeds and angles? I don't know why those questions don't eat at other people. Cecil gets downright mad when I ask them. ("Oh yeah?") No one else sees them. But I do. Glowing arrows in the sky. Dotted lines. The entire world is a chart telling you how to understand it if you just look for them. ("Cool. Sure.") Anyway, so what I think is that the World Government was so unwieldy at first that the leaders, green-skinned, yellow-eyed creatures that do not blink and refuse to ever physically look at the world they rule, they got together and split it into eight committees. And those committees were split into six subgroups each. And each of those subgroups had three chapters. It was all done to keep things organized, but in this way everyone lost sight of what they were supposed to be doing. (" . . ." [Jackie had given up even trying to pretend she was paying attention.]) Instead of governing the world, the chapters and the subgroups and the committees just bickered with each other over who was in charge of what, and which Red Roof Inn the World Government holiday party would be held in. And all of their agents no longer understand whose agenda they should be following, let alone have even the smallest idea of what that agenda would look like. So these agents are as vague as their agency, practicing their skills without any direction but keeping whatever competing committee or chapter or whatever is in the area out of its way, even though they've lost track completely of what they're competing over. What is terrifying, I think, about the World Government is not that the world is held under an iron fist, but that the world is sand scooped up in a sieve. The people running it have no more idea than us why there are lights in the sky above the Arby's or why there are ghost cars. Terrifying, right? I think the grand conspiracy of our world is just an argument between idiots."

Deep breath. Both of them. Jackie had been watching a leaf on a branch outside wave back and forth, almost falling but not.

"And this piece of paper." Steve held up empty, pinched fingers attempting emphasis. He looked at his paperless hand. Jackie showed him the paper in her own.

"What about it?" Jackie asked.

"What? Oh. I don't know." He shook his head. "I forget. There are so many things to know, so many things to find out. I lose track of where I am in the maze."

He used his hands to indicate a maze. (Think of the common gesture for *maze*.)

"The main thing," he said, "is to just enjoy what you have. The paper trick is cool. Do it again."

She did not.

"But definitely don't go looking for King City," he said. "People like to think that there are places other than Night Vale out there what with all the desert, but it's just not true. You try to go to a place like King City, you probably would never come back."

Steve paused.

"I don't think that man has given the paper to the person who was supposed to get it yet," he said.

"Oh yeah?" she said, trying to encourage without seeming too eager.

"I think he's looking for one particular person, and he hasn't found them. It's a message, and the message hasn't been received yet, you know? I wonder what happens when whoever is supposed to get that message finally receives it. Could be something very bad. Real bad."

The door opened. Diane walked in. The noise brought Steve back to himself.

"Hey there," he said. "Your friend Jackie and I were just talking about you. Good things, of course."

Diane glared at the nineteen-year-old, who returned her glare defiantly.

"Not my friend, Steve. Jackie, whatever it is that fascinates you about my life and the people in it, I need you to let go and leave us alone."

Jackie felt herself regarded not as a woman or a human, but as a teenager. She had a rush of anger that felt embarrassingly young but that she couldn't suppress.

"I'm looking after my own life, man. What I want to know is why you always seem to end up involved."

"I'm sorry, Diane," said Steve. "I thought. I mean, I didn't know."

"It's okay, Steve," said Diane. "I know you love a good conversation. Jackie, what are you doing here? Are you researching me? Following me?"

"You'd love it if you were that interesting." Jackie stood up so quickly that her folding chair tumbled backwards into the popcorn machine. Steve and Diane winced, but nothing visible happened, and so they relaxed.

Jackie didn't like how the situation was going, but she also didn't know how to change the momentum. She came right up to Diane's face, like a child fighting on a playground, or like a larger, older child fighting in a bar. Jackie felt unsure and silly and young, and she channeled the discomfort of that feeling into anger and projected that feeling onto Diane.

"I already have one sullen teenager in my life. Go home, Jackie."

Jackie felt stupid (*Oh, Jackie, did you ever think of just turning twenty?*), and so she yelled: "Do you have to show up everywhere I am all the time?"

"This is the PTA room. I am on the PTA."

"Whatever. I'm out of here," Jackie said, and then pointed at Steve. "Steve, we'll talk more about King City later. Tell Janice I said hi."

"Okie doke. It sure was nice to chat." And he meant it, which was the worst part about Steve Carlsberg.

Jackie stormed out of the door, not wanting to leave this way and hating herself for doing it.

Diane stared at Steve with new curiosity, wondering if this was the first time she had ever actually wanted to know something that Steve could tell her.

"Steve. What *do* you know about King City?"

There was a Troy who swept up at the movie theater.

There was a Troy who never left his home.

There was a Troy who was a therapist.

There were so many Troys, and Jackie tracked them all. She had a notebook and a camera, and soon she had a record of every Troy in town. She kept a lot of notes, not because she was good at investigating, but because it gave her something to do, and helped keep her from drifting off into confusion and despair over the terrifying implications of Troy's multiplicity.

If she stopped note-taking long enough to think, she would grow dizzy in a spiral of questions: Do they know each other? Are they the same age? Were they all born, or were they just there one day? When she found herself thinking for too long, she would make another note, maybe about how humid it was ("neck feels sticky, even in the shade") or what color the clouds were ("green with purple stripes—looks like rain").

Today Jackie was following the Troy who was a loan manager at the Last Bank of Night Vale ("We put our customers second, and our apocalyptic prophecies first!"). This Troy had very regular hours, not just at his work but in his life outside of work, and so he was especially easy to tail.

It was the third hour of work for him, and he would be going to lunch soon. Lunch was usually a salad or something light, except for the one day a week he went to Big Rico's Pizza. She watched him through the window, humming and smiling at customers.

There was a Troy who drove a cherry red Vespa while wearing a light blue helmet.

There was a Troy who drove a 1997 Plymouth minivan.

There was a Troy who drove a taxi.

Do some of them live together? Are they working on a single plan? Were they artificially created by the government?

Too much thinking, she was feeling nauseous. She wrote a note about the lunchtime crowd in the street ("it's lunchtime. there's a crowd in the street.").

Troy was eating at his desk today. Salad. He did nothing unusual with the salad. He ate it. She watched him eat it from her car. No one cared about a woman staring through binoculars from a parked car. It was a common sight. There were three other cars with binoculared, watching women just on that block, and that was light by Night Vale standards.

She hadn't been able to get Troy to stop and talk to her. They always avoided her, most not with the same sprinting desperation as the Troy who worked at the Moonlite All-Nite, but with the same result. Not a single Troy would get close enough for her to ask questions. She had even tried making an appointment with the therapist Troy, but when the time had come a short, balding man in a vest had been sitting across from her instead.

"I'm afraid there's been an illness going around," he said. "He's asked me to cover his clients for a bit. Now tell me, what do you remember, specifically, about your childhood?"

She had gotten up and walked out without saying a word. She would stay focused. No matter what Diane had said, she was old enough to concentrate and do this. It was probably better that she was young. Her body was stronger and faster, her mind was more open. Youth was better than age. It was good that she had been young for so long.

The next day the Troy therapist had been back at work, no sign of an illness. But Jackie knew that, if she burst into the building, the balding man would be back, asking her about her childhood.

There was a Troy who lived in an apartment building near the community radio station.

There was a Troy who lived in the housing development of Coyote Corners and collected windowsill cacti.

There was a Troy who simply vanished for long periods of time, and so she wasn't sure where he lived. That was the Troy who did lawn care and gardening.

She made notes and intentionally breathed. Troy ate his salad.

"Eating salad," her notes said. "Still eating it."

One of the notes was a doodle of a cat. She didn't know how to be an investigator. All she had ever known how to do was run a pawnshop. She looked up, and stopped writing in her journal.

Troy wasn't eating salad anymore. He was talking to someone. Or he was turning away and shaking his head while someone was trying to talk to him. She couldn't see who it was. Troy got up, tossed the rest of his salad in the trash, and walked quickly out of the bank, still shaking his head. Jackie got out of her car to follow, but stopped when she saw Diane approaching Troy on the sidewalk. Of course Diane was here. Who else could it have been?

She watched Diane follow Troy until they turned a corner and were gone. She threw down her notebook and swore. A man in a suit seated on a folding chair next to her car and making notes on her every action winced.

"Relax, man," she said, and then cursed again, deliberately, louder than before.

There was a Troy who knew what all this was about.

There was a Troy whose actions had somehow led to the end of the routine that sustained her.

There was a Troy watching her, and now she would watch him until he slipped up, until some part of the mystery was revealed to her, until she understood.

When she came the next day to watch the Troy who worked at the bank, he wasn't there. She went in and asked. The woman at the teller's desk stopped chanting, "And thus the world falls," from a book bound in strange leather long enough to tell her that he had resigned last night without giving a reason. But Jackie knew the reason. Another lead lost to Diane.

There was a Troy. There was a bunch of them. And one of them would answer to her eventually.

THE VOICE OF NIGHT VALE

CECIL: . . . I couldn't taste anything at all for weeks afterwards. No one does a dinner party like Earl Harlan.

Folks, I'm pretty excited about this next bit of news. The staff of local advocacy group Citizens for a Blood Space War have put together Night Vale's first ever flea market. This Friday at the Rec Center, crafts-people, artisans, antique trainers and breeders, and cold patches of air indicating the likely presence of a ghost will bring their wares to town.

The Last Bank of Night Vale will be the title sponsor of the flea market. There will be plenty of free parking and helicopters monitoring all shoppers from above. The Last Bank Flea Market will also bring in food from some of Night Vale's most popular eateries, like Big Rico's Pizza, Pieces o' Glass, Shame, Tourniquet, and Pinkberry. Admission is five dollars and supports our local charity Citizens for a Blood Space War.

The Last Bank of Night Vale will also be offering no-fee checking accounts to those looking to follow local laws, which were recently changed to require every single person to have a checking account at the Last Bank of Night Vale. You can bank wherever you like, as long as you bank at the Last Bank of Night Vale.

The City Council would like to remind all citizens to please use proper methods for organizing regular trash and recycling. For instance, recycling must be divided into paper, plastic, feathers, teeth, and glass, each in a color-coded bag. Also, regular trash pickup is every Tuesday and Friday morning, whereas recycling is taken from your home at unannounced intervals. You will know recycling has been picked up because your recycling bags will be gone and there will be a large, reddish brown smear across your front door roughly in the shape of an X. Or maybe it's a cross. It's not clear in the brochure I've been handed, which has no words, only dark black-and-white photographs of angled shadows along brick walls. I mean, municipal one-sheets are kind of useless, but this one is at least haunting.

And now let's have a look at traffic.

There is a man with a gray pin-striped suit and without a job. He is sitting on the hood of his nice car, looking at other cars as they go places. He is not going anywhere. He knows that now.

All this time he had lived for the future. The future had been the firm ground he stood on, and the present was only the slight haze in the air. But now he understood that the future was a joke without a punch line and that whatever he had in the present was what he would have always. He did not have much in the present. He had a very nice car.

He called someone. It doesn't matter who. It was his lover. They called each other that. It was the name they preferred. It didn't matter to them what anyone else thought of the word.

"Where are you?" his lover said. "They said you didn't come in."

"Yeah," he said.

"Are you okay? Are you hurt? When are you coming home?"

Was he hurt? He stopped to consider this. He didn't think so. He examined his body. He took off his suit and his silver watch, laid them in the dirt, and stood there with his phone, naked, looking at himself. No, he wasn't hurt, he thought. Not physically.

He opened his mouth to answer, but looking up he saw something in the sky. It was a planet of awesome size, lit by no sun. An invisible titan, all thick black forests and jagged mountains and deep, turbulent oceans. It was so far away that he couldn't be sure he was even seeing it, and yet it felt more real and present to him than the cars driving on the highway below him.

He hung up without answering, which was, in its own way, an answer. He looked up. He couldn't see the planet anymore. He put his suit back on. He picked up his watch. It was covered in dirt. He got back in his car and drove.

This has been traffic.

And now a word from our sponsors. Or not now, but later. Much later. You won't know it when it happens. It'll be just one of many words you'll encounter that day. But it will come leaden with unseen meaning and consequence, and it will slowly spread throughout your life, invisibly infecting every light moment with its heaviness. Our sponsors cannot be escaped. You will see their word. And you will never know.

When the phone rang, Diane flushed.

That morning she was at work, but she was not working. She was looking up information about King City on her computer. It seemed like a normal enough place. A highway. Some restaurants. Houses. Probably filled with people who have dreams and wishes and nightmares and crippling doubt and feel things similar to or exactly like love.

Diane was making broad assumptions based on the small amount of data that was her entire life. She was lost in her research, face close to the screen.

When the phone rang, she closed her browser and opened a spreadsheet, out of instinct. Her face felt warm as she pressed her office phone to her ear.

"Can you come in here, Diane?"

"Sure, Catharine."

"Everything okay? You sound out of breath."

"I'm fine." Diane remembered to exhale.

Catharine's door was open, but Diane knocked anyway. Catharine turned around in her desk chair and cut a line through the air with her upturned palm. "Sit, please," her hand said.

Diane sat. The tarantula was perched in Catharine's thick, wavy hair. It wasn't moving much. A slight stretch of a front leg every so often. Catharine, from time to time, would scratch the side of her head with a letter opener. The tarantula would change position by an inch or so to avoid being hit.

Catharine had felt her scalp itch all morning. She thought about the qualities of various shampoos, whether she was using the correct brand. She thought about the dry air here in the southwest desert. She did not think about the tarantula hanging from her hair, because she did not know about the tarantula hanging from her hair. Had she known at all that there was a tarantula in her hair, Catharine might have behaved in a surprising and unsafe manner.

The tarantula had no idea where it was or what was happening. It felt movement from time to time, and it would, in turn, move carefully to accommodate for a possible predator or a possible prey. The tarantula knew about hunger and gravity.

"Diane, I'm troubled by something," Catharine said. "Someone was in my office the other night. I'm not accusing you of snooping around in my office the other night after work, but what were you doing snooping around in my office the other night after work?"

She slapped the desk with her palm, and Diane jumped. The tarantula did not react visibly.

Diane regularly lectured Josh about trust, and now she had violated her boss's trust in much the same way. Just be honest, she told herself. Be honest and accept the consequences.

"I might have looked in here, yes," she said.

"You might have looked in here."

"Yes."

Catharine sighed and put her hands together. At that moment the tarantula put its front legs together, but the timing was coincidental.

"Why might you have looked in here, Diane?"

Diane started to talk about Evan McIntyre, but Catharine waved her words away.

"Entering my office without my permission was inappropriate behavior. We can agree on that, right?"

Diane hated this. She hated being talked to in the way she talked to Josh. Except she was right when she talked that way to Josh. And Catharine was right in what she was saying now. But still it was awful to receive. She understood how Josh felt being talked to like this, whether the reasons were good or not.

"Yes. I'm sorry, Catharine."

"We can't have people behaving inappropriately. The office is not a place for inappropriate behavior. This is a place for appropriate behavior, right?"

She was right, and Diane told her so.

"Diane, I need you to leave the office. You're not fired or anything. We never fire anyone here. Let's call it a 'permanent unpaid leave' while I consult the relevant agencies."

Diane couldn't make herself believe what was happening, even as she completely understood it. Her life was changing, here in front of her, so casually, and in a few simple words.

"You know there are relevant agencies, yes?" said Catharine.

"Yes."

"There are always relevant agencies."

"I'm sorry. I just got carried away."

"You can go now."

Catharine scratched at her hair again. The tarantula moved again.

Diane stood up, still staring down.

"I'm sorry, Catharine."

"Close the door on the way out."

Diane did. As the door shut, she could see Catharine scratching her head vigorously with the letter opener, her teeth gritting and neck wrinkling with tendons and veins. The tarantula—

having apparently had enough—dropped down to the desk behind her.

Diane gathered up her belongings as unnoticeably as she could. She wanted to look like she was just leaving for lunch, which in one sense was all she was doing. She just was never going to come back.

It wasn't until she was outside that the gulf of what had happened opened up inside her. She didn't even like this job, but she didn't dislike it. It was a large part of her life, and now that part of her life was over. She felt adrift, but also, she felt hungry. The hunger was unrelated, but it became tied up in all her other feelings.

After a quick stop to use the ATM at the Last Bank of Night Vale, Diane walked toward the Missing Frog Salad Bar. She wasn't sure if she wanted salad or not, but they also served richer fare, like bowls of capers and orangemilk. She just needed to clear her mind, and if that meant eating something a bit heavier, so be it.

It took her a moment, but she realized that the man down the block from her was Troy, wearing a dark suit. He had a shoulder bag and a burgundy-and-silver tie, and was absently looking at his phone as he came toward her.

It made her furious, her life coming apart around her, let go from a job where she had always been quiet and responsible and respected, and her son at a distance that had never existed between them before, and here was Troy, in yet another guise, walking down the streets of her city like he belonged here. Like he had just as much right to be here as she did.

She walked faster, not sure what she was going to do next.

Just a few feet away, Troy glanced up. She could not tell if he saw her or not. His upward glance turned quickly to his watch.

He stopped, and, in one complete gesture, like a short modern dance, he looked from his watch to the street signs while pivoting his body in the opposite direction, a complete movement phrase that told the story of a man who was late and accidentally walking down the wrong road.

She followed him, thinking about what she would like to do to him, and also about what she was actually going to do to him. When she had difficulty catching up to him (how fast was he walking? She was practically running now), she called out, "Troy!"

As she said this, a car revved nearby, the driver grinding the wheels over the concrete, a great screech, a tiny puff of smoke, and burning rubber stench that hid her shout.

Diane looked at the car and the dark black marks and the thin white puffs of smoke. The driver was Jackie Fierro. Of course, Jackie would be lurking, always watching. Jackie was swearing, and looking past Diane down the street.

When Diane looked back to where Jackie was looking, Troy was already lost in the lunch crowd.

And it was at that moment that she knew there was only one other possible option. She needed information, and she couldn't use the resources at work anymore (there was that shame shuddering through her again).

It was time to go to the library. The library would have records on Troy Walsh.

Diane had survived librarians before. She and Josh had gone on many quests to the Night Vale Public Library, as well as the less treacherous, but still life-threatening, libraries at Josh's schools.

She drove home and grabbed the things she would need to check out a book: strong rope and a grappling hook, a compass, a flare gun, matches and a can of hair spray, a sharpened wooden spear, and, of course, her library card. She couldn't remember exactly, but she made a silent prayer that she had no outstanding fines.

She put on all blue clothing. (It was widely known that librarians could not see the color blue. This was probably just an urban legend, but Diane was willing to do anything to put the odds more in her favor.)

On her bed she spread out four different maps of the library. She noted the inconsistencies in each map, trying to determine which paths were truth and which were certain death. All four maps indicated that the European history section was located on the second floor, northeast corner, but Diane knew this to be untrue, as there has only ever been one book of European history ever written, and it was a pamphlet about the small country of Svitz and it had been lost to a fire during last year's Book Cleansing Day festivities. The pamphlet was not meant to be burned, but it had a picture of a giraffe on the cover (the national tall mammal of Svitz), and the Book Cleansers mistook the giraffe for a handgun. A giraffe can look a lot like a lot of things to someone wearing a hazardous materials uniform and a welder's mask, so the mistake was understandable.

Without that book, there couldn't possibly be a European history section anymore. She threw the maps out as obvious forgeries. Realizing she wouldn't know what to do with them even if they were needed, she tossed the pile of supplies and makeshift weapons as well.

She would have to go off memory and instinct. Mothers of teenagers are good in libraries. They are wise and attentive from their years of experience, and they are unrelenting and fearless because of their focus on a good education for their kids.

Before getting in her car, Diane stopped by Josh's room. That day he was a desk lamp.

"Josh, I love you. I just wanted to tell you."

"What? Where is that coming from?" He was a vase full of sunflowers now.

"Nothing. Just saying that I love you."

"I love you too," he said, his petals cocked to the side in wary confusion.

"Everything'll be fine," she added, not knowing at all if everything would be fine.

Jackie pulled the supplies from her car. The parking lot of the library was otherwise empty, as it usually was.

The entrance to the public library was through an unassuming pair of glass doors that said PUSH. Above that a blue plastic sign said NIGHT VALE PUBLIC LIBRARY. That was all. The dramatics of its reputation were not echoed in its architecture.

She took a breath, and then another. Each one was a moment in which she was still breathing and not inside the library.

The building itself was squat with tall windows that looked onto an empty checkout area and a tiled area with drinking fountains and a bathroom. Everything was quiet and still. There was no sign that anything had ever lived there. It had the feeling of a tomb or a shopping mall that had run out of money before the first store opened.

She pushed through the doors. Inside the air was cool and dry. She listened carefully. Nothing. The doors led to a long entrance hallway ending in another pair of double glass doors. Off the hallway were various reading rooms, for reading, and community rooms, for communing, and bloodletting rooms, for a different kind of communing. Those were also empty and quiet.

Jackie traversed the entrance hall in silence. The only sign of her movement was her shadow through the bands of sunlight on the floor.

She passed a bulletin board advertising community events:

PUMPKIN PICKING COMPETITION. THREE OBJECTS.

DO YOU KNOW WHICH ONE IS A PUMPKIN??

GARAGE SALE. EVERYTHING'S FREE. MOSTLY NOT DANGEROUS. SOME DANGEROUS. YOU'LL FIND OUT WHICH.

I'M HIDING SOMEWHERE. CAN YOU FIND ME? NO, NOT THERE. OH WELL. YOU'LL FIND ME SOON. I PROMISE.

Stuff like that, with tabs where the phone numbers could be taken and reported to local government agencies or the Sheriff's Secret Police. The flyers all looked to be at least ten years old. They were brittle and warped and barely hanging off rusted thumbtacks.

No movement ahead of her. No movement behind her.

She put her hand on the push bar of one of the inner doors, but paused when she heard footsteps behind her. What person would brave this sterile tomb? Besides her, of course?

Jackie turned and found herself inches away from Diane, who was looking down at her phone.

"Aah!" Jackie shouted.

Diane looked up, her eyes wide.

"Aah!" Diane shouted as well.

Her fingers were scarred, and her phone had traces of blood on it. She must have tried to contact a forbidden number.

"Hello, Jackie."

"Did you follow me here?"

"Of course not."

"Then why are you everywhere I am at the same time as me?"

Diane thought about that. It was a fair question, although the problem with fair questions is that they are asked about an unfair world.

"I suspect," Jackie said, "that we are looking for the same

sorts of things about the same sorts of people. Which is why we would keep crossing each other's paths. Also, Night Vale isn't a very big town, is it?"

"I don't know. I've never thought about it."

They both thought about it. Then, as is safest in Night Vale, they stopped thinking about it.

"All right. Well, cool seeing you," said Jackie, hand on the door, her body blocking Diane's entry.

"Jackie, as little as I like spending time with you, and I want you to know that even though I am trying to be the adult of the two of us here, because I am the adult of the two of us, I do not like spending time with you much at all, but as little as I like this, the library is a dangerous place, we both know it. And since we both apparently need to go into it, we should do the right thing and go together."

Or words to that effect. Jackie had lost interest around "I am the adult." No, not interest, patience.

Jackie wanted Diane to go home. She did not need another parent any more than Diane needed another child.

Diane knew the girl needed help. Diane lowered her face, keeping eye contact and giving a slight grin, something that usually worked when Josh was acting sullen or distant.

Jackie turned her head and looked through the doors into the empty checkout area. A fake velvet rope marking where the line would go if there were any people alive in there, and beyond that the shelves of dangerous books. Jackie did not feel fear, but she was aware of herself. She knew that it wasn't healthy, what she was doing.

"Okay fine," Jackie said.

"Okay fine what?"

"Okay. You can come."

"So, just to be clear. We're in this together?"

"Yeah, man. Fine. Whatever. Come on," Jackie said without looking back.

Diane went in first, Jackie holding the door. By the door was the return slot for books or for anything else a person might want to return to the library. Jackie, being who she was, lifted up the metal lid for a moment, just to see. Inside it was dark and damp and there was an intermittent crackling or crunching sound. Diane shuddered and, putting her hand over Jackie's, gently closed the lid. Jackie pulled her hand away from Diane's and kept walking.

The checkout area had printers and computers that looked to be twenty or more years out of date. Nothing like the cutting-edge machines regularly released into local computer stores and immediately outlawed by City Council. There were stains of indeterminate origin all over the counter. Jackie touched one; it was still sticky.

The stain ran in a sloppy streak across the counter and up a pencil holder. Jackie rose up on tiptoes and peered into the cup, which at first appeared empty, but the longer she stared into the small darkness, the more she could make out a pattern—or texture—at the bottom. She could not be certain, but there seemed to be a small lump of wet hair in the bottom of the pencil holder. She lowered herself back onto her heels.

"What are you here for?" Jackie asked.

"Public records. You?"

"Newspaper archives."

"Good. Should be right next to each other."

"Sure. I guess."

According to Diane's most trustworthy map, the archives were about halfway back into the library.

"Well, good thing is we don't have to go all the way to the back," she said. Jackie didn't reply.

They kept moving past the racks of the *Night Vale Daily Journal* by the windows. Due to spiraling printing costs and the necessary layoff of nearly its entire staff, the *Journal* had long ago moved to an imagination-based format. The racks were empty except for a small note reminding you that if you imagined what a hypothetical Night Vale newspaper might look like, then you needed to send a check for $19.95 to the *Daily Journal* to cover your monthly Imagination Subscription.

The library was shaped like a stubby lowercase b, with the entrance hall and checkout area forming its neck. Ahead was the start of the lower portion, where the bulk of the library was. First was the reference section, with thick books full of dangerous words and binders full of classified information. The shelves of the reference section spanned back into the shadows of the deepest parts of the library, and the two women made an immediate left to avoid it.

Diane kept her eyes forward, following the unwavering trajectory of her steps, but Jackie couldn't help but stop and look. Deep within the shadows, she thought she could see the echo of movement. Not exactly movement, but the suggestion left in the air after movement is finished. She hurried after Diane. As they passed a section of geological encyclopedias, Jackie saw a scattering of white teeth in the aisle. She stared at them, hoping they would become something less awful, less human-looking, but the teeth remained teeth. After that, she kept her eyes forward, mimicking Diane.

Beyond the reference section was the large central reading area, sloping gently downward to a fountain. The fountain was out of water. Had probably broken years ago and no repairman had survived trying to fix it. It occasionally made a buzzing growling hacking sound, like its pipes were trying to cough something up.

Around the fountain were oak tables with upholstered chairs. These had never been touched. Crossing an open area like the reading area was guaranteed to draw every librarian in the building, so any hypothetical reader would never get ten steps, let alone all the way to pulling out a chair and sitting down. The reading area was a beautifully crafted trap set by the librarians, but it was too perfect. Even the dumbest book lover—and anyone who would regularly choose to come in contact with books could not be a bright bulb, Jackie thought—wouldn't fall for this.

Diane and Jackie hugged the edge of the reading area, crouching behind the public internet-access tables, served by the same ancient computers as the checkout area, none of which appeared to be plugged in anyway. They looked at each other, faces pale but focused. Without speaking or breathing, but with the urgent set of their jaws, they communicated that they needed to keep moving. The answers might be available on the old computers, but it would be too dangerous to wait around in one spot, trying to retrieve them. Even leaving aside the usual danger that any computer might develop a spontaneous and malicious sentience, like what had wiped out the entire Computer Science Department at Night Vale Community College.

After the computers was the children's section. The beanbag chairs were new, as were the realistic lava-stone statues of children. The section had no books at all, but it did have twenty or thirty child statues, with faces contorted in terror and pain. It was the one part of the library everyone in Night Vale could feel good about. "Well, at least we have those statues," they'd say to each other. "The library might be a threat to the lives of all who use it, but it has a great children's section. And comfy beanbag chairs. At least there's that."

"BRRGGHHHHH," said the fountain.

Diane paused for a moment to look at the statues. One of them looked a lot like Josh, back when he was younger, and used to be made of stone sometimes. He was rarely ever made of stone anymore. Did she have any pictures of him made of stone? No, she didn't think she did. She should take more pictures of him. Or try to remember him better. Or remember more of him.

Assuming she would make it out of the library.

"Why are we stopping?" Jackie hissed. She looked around the children's section for movement or shadows, but it seemed as empty as everywhere else.

Diane shot Jackie a silent look that said, "Shut up."

"Then let's go," Jackie replied with her own silent look.

"Patience. Have some patience. I was simply seeing what the new children's section was like. I've heard a lot of good things about it. Besides, it wasn't like we weren't dawdling earlier at the front desk," Diane argued with just her eyes.

"That was different. It was, it was different. Just . . . dude, keep moving," Jackie countered wordlessly.

"I'm moving. This is me moving." Diane moved.

Jackie glared, but Diane didn't see it happen, so the glare only had an effect on herself.

They were almost to the city archives, but to get there they would have to cross from under the computer desks into the space between the children's and the architecture and science sections.

Diane held back, taking in the apparent emptiness of the room, preparing for what might happen next, but Jackie was already out and running for the microfiche shelves. Diane gasped, unable to grab Jackie, to protect her from her own bravado.

Jackie, all teenage breathlessness, broke her run on the archive cabinets with a dull slap and whirled around, arms out, eyes wide, ready to take what would come. Nothing. Diane held her breath. No one.

"See? No one." Jackie's grin was edging toward smug, but Diane had developed a patience for this kind of thing from years of her son. She scuttled over in a crouched position from her hiding place under the desk, standing only when she made it to the cabinet. They put their backs to the archives and looked at where they had come from. Children's section, then computers, then reference section, then the turn toward checkout and escape.

If they needed to run, they wouldn't make it. So they would just have to not be found.

"All right, what are you looking for?" Jackie mouthed, trying to whisper without sound.

"Troy," Diane mouthed.

Jackie made a face.

"It's for Josh's sake," Diane mouthed.

"What?" Jackie mouthed.

Diane wasn't sure if Jackie had not understood or was expressing incredulity; either way she waved her off. Finding information on any citizen of Night Vale was as simple as looking under their name and sorting through the comprehensive life details kept on record.

And there he was. "Walsh, Troy," between "Vos, Natalie" and "Winged Creature, First Name Unknown." Here was his birth certificate with everything but his name redacted. His death certificate, postdated to the correct time. A cool rock that someone had found and had written "Troy" on with a black permanent marker. Blood samples. Urine samples. Saliva samples. Writing samples. Fingerprints. Photos taken while he was sleeping. A paragraph-length, poetic description of his aura. A video of the same description presented through the language of dance.

Diane shook her head. Nothing unusual or useful.

Jackie placed a hand on her shoulder, patient as she could, and squeezed gently, trying to convey all of "That's cool. But there's nothing. Sorry you came all this way and wasted your time. Let's go."

Diane poked a finger at her but then reconsidered and lifted the defensive gesture into a plea. "Just one more moment?" her finger asked.

"Whatever." Jackie crossed her arms and returned her bored stare to the empty room behind them.

Diane searched through the whole file again, flicking quickly, looking for whatever it was she had missed, because surely she had missed something.

A fluorescent light flickered on the high gray ceiling above them. Jackie squinted. She hadn't seen anything. That had been nothing, she was sure.

BRRGGHHHHH. The fountain. But was that a noise hanging on for just a moment after the fountain's moan?

Jackie turned and put her hand back on Diane's shoulder.

"We need to go."

Diane looked out over the reading area. It looked no different than it had the last time she had looked or, anyway, almost no different.

"Why don't you just do whatever it is you need to do and let me do this? I'm sure you'll be just fine on your own."

She had adopted a mom's voice, and they both heard her do it. Jackie gave one last look to where the noise had come from, which, as far as she could tell, was the magazine room in the complete opposite corner of the library. The angle was such that she couldn't see into the room. She might have been able to see the shadow jutting out on the floor from its doorway, but she didn't want to see that so her brain skimmed past it.

One aisle over, Jackie found the archives of the *Daily Journal*, back when it had had physical form. She started flipping through the binders of old issues. A microfiche system had been deemed too expensive by city government, and anyway would likely just have been ruined by librarian fluids or the blood of one of their victims.

"King City has to have come up at some point."

"Mmm," Diane said.

She wasn't listening because she had found something she'd missed earlier. Stuck to the back of the aura report was an old photo. She couldn't tell how old, because it was stuck image-side down. She picked at the edges of it, trying to get it to come off, but the photo was stuck firm.

"Dammit," Jackie said, not in response to anything but just to have something to say as she searched, tediously, for information that might or might not exist.

Diane yanked at the photo, and it came unstuck with a pop. She turned it faceup. It was a photo from the era where people are stiffly arranged through the long minutes it took to register their image on chemical paper. She considered it as carefully and rationally as she could before coming to the verbal conclusion: "Oh, shit."

"Why 'oh, shit'?" Jackie popped her head up from behind a binder.

Diane held up the photo, and Jackie studied it closely, bringing her face in toward the flat faces looking back from long ago.

"Oh shit," Jackie said.

"Yeah."

"Well, my news isn't great either."

Jackie held up an index card that said, in neat block letters,

ALL MATERIALS ON KING CITY HAVE BEEN CATALOGUED
UNDER GEOGRAPHY, FORBIDDEN.

And then another sentence that had been blacked out with a scribbled marker, so much so that the black ink leaked through to the other side of the card.

Diane nodded, unsurprised. It had seemed too easy up to that point, and so she had been expecting something like this.

"The forbidden materials shelf is just past the biography section, near fiction."

She pointed. The area where she pointed was as far from them as the entrance, in the opposite direction. There would be no escape if they were noticed. They both considered this. Jackie sat down on institutionally patterned carpet, her head in her hands, and allowed herself a few seconds of self-pity. Then she stood up, her eyes steady on her destination.

"Listen, Diane," she said softly, clearly. "It made sense for us to do this together because we both need something. But you can go now. You've found . . ." She looked again at the photograph in Diane's hand and shuddered. "Anyway, you have a son who needs you. You have to go home to him. I can do this."

Diane thought about Josh, and she wanted to agree. The important thing was to get out of the library to her family, her sullen, solitary, teenage family. And so she felt furious about what she was going to say next.

"No. We came into the library together, we'll leave it together."

"Diane, you don't have—"

"Jackie, if I left you here and you died, I would feel bad about it. I'd probably feel bad about it for the rest of my life. And I don't like to feel bad. So let's go."

Jackie smiled. She didn't mean much by it, but she meant some by it. Diane smiled back, meaning mostly the same.

She looked at Troy's useless file and shrugged, deciding to take it with her. There wasn't much to it, and they had come this far. She tucked it under one arm.

They started out for the forbidden shelf, past the biography section and, terrifyingly, the fiction section near it.

Nothing attracts a librarian more than fiction, as even the smallest child of Night Vale knows.

"I hope there is anything there about King City," Jackie said.

"BRRGGHHHHH," the fountain said.

This time there was definitely another noise along with it. Like a laugh but angry. Like crying but aggressive. Like a claw or a tail or a wing moving against bookshelves.

Diane and Jackie didn't hear it, although there was nothing they could have done differently if they had.

THE VOICE OF NIGHT VALE

CECIL: . . . or anyway, all of them that had survived. And that is why police and emergency medical crews no longer feel obligated to search for remains in any public library.

We are getting confirmation from several concerned citizens that something is very wrong with those cute plastic flamingos everyone bought from Lenny's Bargain House. Those who get too close to the flamingos or, worse, touch them, are disappearing. Some of these unfortunates appeared again just moments later, sagging into shriveled skin with long gray hair, as though a lifetime had passed.

"Oh, I'm back! I'm back!" those people all said. "I thought I'd never see this place again."

When asked where they had gone, many promptly died of old age.

Others have not reappeared at all.

Even those who were lucky enough not to disappear still reported odd side effects of the flamingos.

"Yeah, I touched one," said Sheila, the woman who always marks people's activities down on her clipboard at the Moonlite All-Nite. "And the world shown clear for the first time in my life. Like I had never seen any of it before. I *had* never seen any of it before, and I understood none of it. Which is when I realized that I had become myself as a baby again. I lived my entire life over again, making the same choices, surviving the same tragedy and surviving the same joy, and going through all the same mistakes, unable to stop myself, until I reached the moment again where I touched the flamingo, and then I was an infant again. I have gone through this loop hundreds of times. My life, which once seemed like an organic movement, now has become a hideous script that I must play out, with an ending that is forever forestalled. I won't ever die, but I won't ever live. Please help."

And then, weeping, she touched the flamingo again.

There have also been some complaints that the plastic on the flamingos is cheaply produced and warped. Has Lenny's Bargain House been selling us substandard and possibly time-bending decorative birds? We will investigate at some point in the future, when we feel like we are maybe more interested than we are now. Until then, we will continue on in ignorance, happy as we ever were.

And now, we are pleased to present three commercial-free hours of advertisements.

They ran past the nonfiction shelves, filled with informative books on every subject not currently outlawed by city government, or the Sheriff's Secret Police, or the World Government. The shelves were mostly empty. They tried to keep their footfalls as soft as possible.

In Jackie's case, this resulted in only her usual heavy-heeled thuds.

Gently. Silence over speed, Diane thought, glaring at the teenager's back but not wanting to say it out loud.

Hurry the hell up, Jackie thought, as Diane lagged behind.

After nonfiction was science fiction. No one knows why science fiction is kept separately from the rest of the nonfiction. Tradition is a powerful thing. These shelves were much less censored than the main nonfiction section, since science fiction tended to be about day-to-day stuff that everyone already knew.

They hid against a long row of novels, most titles unreadable under a gnashing of teeth and claw marks. Diane looked up to see a shelf full of Ursula K. Le Guin books, streaked with four long, brownish stains. Poor book lover, Diane thought, dragged away just as they found that perfect read.

Jackie smelled something. It was different than the usual library smell of basement closets and bleach. This smelled like burnt coffee during a sinus infection, a stale sting in her nose. She turned to Diane, whose eyes were pointed down, cheeks flushed, nostrils flared.

"You smell it too."

Diane nodded, putting her finger to her lips.

A distant hum. They looked around. Diane took Jackie's hand. Jackie didn't notice. The distant hum was perhaps a nearby growl.

"Keep moving," Jackie said.

Diane did nothing. Jackie stood, pulling her up by the hand. The noise was between distant and nearby. It was between a growl and a hum.

"Hiding won't make whatever that was go away," Jackie said.

Diane clutched at the science fiction shelf as Jackie led her, heel-toe, heel-toe, quiet, into the biography section.

The section was extensive, taking up most of the wall leading to the back of the library. The only book in the section was the *Official Biography of Helen Hunt*. There were a lot of copies. It was a well-stocked biography section. If anyone needed to know about the life of a person, for instance Helen Hunt, then this section was extremely helpful.

A few turned-out copies of the book revealed a smiling Helen Hunt on its cover. Helen's eyes stared back directly at the viewer. Helen's smile had a hard edge, a tight anger to it. Her hair was pulled back to display the intricate clover-shaped forehead tattoos that Helen Hunt is known for. Between the actor's teeth, Diane could see a gray smudge in the famous dark of the famous maw. The gray seemed to move, to flicker. It was pacing to and fro. Jackie saw it too. A bright glint, like a cat's eye in a dark room, flashed out from between the award-winning actor's teeth. Jackie put one hand to her own mouth and tried not to breathe. Diane pulled herself close to Jackie's shoulder. Helen wasn't smiling at all. They must have seen it wrong. She was frowning, angry, still showing all of her teeth. Or no, the woman on the book covers was definitely moving.

Her mouth was opening and the gray movement inside became fast and agitated. Diane gave a light shove and they ran out of the biography section before Helen could do anything more.

Now they were deep in the fiction section, surrounded by books that told nothing but lies. They breathed heavily from their run, but tried to keep their breathing as quiet as they could. They could not keep it very quiet at all.

From one of the shelves, an arm reached out to them. It appeared to be more or less human. Diane made a sound that was not quite but similar to a scream. Jackie stopped, turned, and put her hand over Diane's mouth.

"Librarian," Diane said into Jackie's palm. The human arm was connected to a figure that was leaking out of the wall, with wet skin and sandpaper eyes and a body that shimmered variations on the human form.

Diane sank into Jackie's body in terror, feeling a moment where she just gave up. Jackie held her up, eyes steady on the figure.

"Too human-looking to be a librarian," Jackie whispered. "I think that's just the specter that haunts the biography section. It's harmless."

The bit at the end of the specter's arm that wasn't quite a hand reached out toward them. Its body dripped out of the wall like oil, black and viscous.

"Are you sure?" Diane said. The figure hovered closer. Its face was cratered and oozing, its eyes rough and gray. She pushed back into Jackie, unable to help herself.

"Oh, you know what?" Jackie said. "The specter regularly

takes people. It's taken a ton of people. Presumably they're all dead. We should go."

She took Diane's arm and moved her down the aisle, toward the creature. A cleft opened below the thing's eyes, splitting into a distorted mouth stuck in the shape of a final, mortal scream. Diane tried to lead Jackie into another run, but Jackie kept the pace even and slow. The creature loomed and Jackie leaned out an elbow, pushing it sharply aside. They tumbled forward, into, through, and beyond the specter. Diane turned to see if the specter had followed. It was gone.

"That wasn't funny," she said.

"It was kind of funny." Jackie considered Diane's face. "Oh, come on, dude. It's not like knowing would have helped you any. I've had to do school reports on Helen Hunt enough times that I've learned to deal with the specter. Its intentions aren't good, sure, but it's too slow and weak to be much of a problem."

Diane glared at Jackie, with irritation but also with a new respect. Jackie was braver than she, Diane knew, suddenly and solidly, as much as she had ever known any fact in her life. And while, as the older person, she was more responsible, still Jackie was capable in ways that Diane was not. She didn't know what to do with that information, but she knew it.

They had made it past the books, past the ghost, to a beige metal shelf, bolted to the wall, a few dozen books and folders on it. There was a stepladder available for the convenience of shorter patrons or those seeking information from the top shelf. Handwritten on a piece of paper taped to the shelf was a note: FORBIDDEN MATERIAL SHELF.

"According to the index, should be here."

"Probably it's that," Diane said, pointing. On the shelf, between a teach-yourself-calligraphy book (the powers-that-be worried it would serve as a gateway to pen ownership) and a

1988 calendar called "Mountains of Our World," was a shoe box marked KING CITY.

"That's probably it, yes, I agree."

Jackie grabbed it.

"Cool, well, this has been fun, but let's go," Jackie said. They turned toward the exit but didn't move.

The distant hum had returned. Between them and the exit was the fiction section, and inside the fiction section was the noise. A gurgling, like a person trying to breathe with severe lung trouble, and a clicking like bad joints moving in old bodies. A growl and a hum; threatening crying and angry laughter. All sounds happened at once, coming from the one huge form, a shadow defining its way into the light. Tendrils whipped in and out between the books. The smell of burnt coffee was overwhelming.

"Is that—?" Jackie asked, and a ropy white limb wrapped around her neck. Jackie had no air to register her distress, so she widened her eyes, and heaved back and forth. The limb was glistening, and whatever sticky substance was all over it stung her skin. She started to go pale; her head seemed to be miles above her body. She saw shapes and colors but couldn't be sure if that was still the world or only the inside of her head.

Diane froze. She had never physically fought off even a human being. She had never been attacked. Even in the hypothetical imagining of being attacked, even just by a human, she imagined failing to defend herself. Jackie was braver than Diane, but if she didn't do anything, Jackie was about to die. That was it really. She was about to die, and Diane was doing nothing, was too scared.

Jackie dropped the King City box and held out her arms as she was pulled toward the shadows. She reached for anything that might slow her journey backwards.

The librarian made a gurgling howl, and there were matching

howls from all over the library. Soon there would be more of them.

Diane looked around desperately, but all that surrounded her were books. Useless books. She looked down into Troy's file, cradled in her arms. There. The rock that had reminded someone of Troy. One edge of it had eroded into jagged sharpness.

She pulled it out and stabbed it into the ropy limb that was dragging Jackie away from her. The limb slackened.

Diane stepped forward against every instinct and shoved her arm between it and Jackie's neck. She pulled as hard as she could, and Jackie wriggled frantically. It seemed that even with Diane pulling, the gap was not nearly big enough for Jackie to escape, but the limb was so slimy with its toxic substance (now burning through Diane's jacket) that Jackie was able to slip her head out.

They stumbled backwards. Jackie's neck and face were a mess of purple blotches, and she was sweating hard through her clothes. Still she remembered to scoop the King City box back off the floor. Diane took off her rapidly dissolving jacket and tossed it to the ground. The librarian's limb recoiled, curled back into the massive body, then shot out at them again.

As they ducked and ran down a parallel aisle, Diane saw, through the gaps between the books, the librarian emerge from the shadows. She saw, exactly and in full, what a librarian looked like. Her stomach lurched.

She would not forget the sight, recurring in dreams and panic attacks, until the moment she died, at which point she would forget it. Eventually, on the day she finally died, one of things that ran through her mind was: Well, at least I won't have to remember that anymore. It made her happy, and she died smiling.

But that was much later.

Jackie did her best to keep up with Diane. She was younger and faster, but the poison was coursing through her. Her gait was unsteady, and she hissed hard through clenched teeth.

They tore through the fiction section, and into biographies. Helen Hunt's face was completely gone, replaced by a gaping mouth, distended from chin to hairline, a buzz of gray rushing at them from its depths.

Then the shelves ran out and there was only space. Ahead was the wide open reading room. A death trap. The moment they stepped out into that, every librarian would see them, and then it would be over. They turned to look, and that white, ropy limb was hissing toward them, leaving a thick, oily trail on the carpet.

They looked at each other. Jackie leaned on Diane's arm, struggling a bit now with standing up.

"We can do this," Jackie said. "Just move before you can think about consequences."

Diane nodded, and they ran as thoughtlessly as they could manage into the reading area. There was a bellow from all around them, and more of the white limbs seethed out of the floor and the shelves. Bulbous shapes loomed at them from the ceiling. The librarians had all come out to greet them.

The skittering of hundreds of spindly legs. A buzzing. Red eyes, maybe, or red spots or blood squirted into the air. There were primary jaws and secondary jaws and tertiary vestigial jaws, and each of them turned to two women running toward the exit.

They couldn't run straight because of the broken fountain, and so they curved around it. Jackie, even with her body weakening, had found a reckless energy inside and was running faster. Diane was gasping and slowing, cursing years of intended workouts that had never happened. The younger woman took her by the shoulders and pushed her ahead. They became a four-legged animal of escape. Fangs and stingers and those boneless white limbs slapped the tile of the fountain just behind them. There was buzzing all around.

To the left was the reference section. Jackie didn't look, but she could hear whatever had been in the shadows rushing out at them. Then the checkout area. The return slot's lid was lifting up, a tentacle-like tongue, or tongue-like tentacle, glopping out of it like sludge.

There was a roaring, incoherent voice. It sounded like the entire building, the walls and floors and metal skeleton of its structure, telling them they would die.

Diane watched the front doors of the library approach, and the boneless limbs of the librarians worked their way in and through the handles, shutting the doors with their bodies.

They weren't going to make it.

"We're not going to make it," Diane said.

"We'll make it."

Jackie turned her shoulder forward, putting her entire flung weight into the glass doors and the poisonous limbs. Broken glass and toxic librarian blood spat out onto the tiles of the entrance corridor. Jackie landed in a pile of the glass and a puddle of the gray ooze. Diane ran through the resulting hole and scooped Jackie up. She was so light, really.

They were out of the foyer, out into the empty parking lot. The building behind them expanded and then came back together with a humf. They turned, but nothing was pursuing them. The front doors were unbroken, and there was no sign of any creatures. It was quiet and waiting once again.

Jackie gasped as much air as she could into her throbbing lungs. Her legs were shaking, but she was standing.

"I said we would make it. Who was right?" Jackie said at the ground, bent in two. "Who was right?"

"Are you okay? Do you have any glass in you?"

"A little bit, man, but I'm okay."

Diane smiled at Jackie. After a moment, Jackie smiled back. Then they started laughing. They couldn't stop. They stood and leaned into each other and laughed. Jackie was still covered in purple blotches and pouring sweat, but they laughed about that too.

"You were right," said Diane. "You were right. Oh my god, we're actually alive, aren't we?"

Jackie waved it off.

"More important, we have answers." Jackie nodded to the box in her hand and the folder in Diane's. "I mean, god, I hope we have answers."

Diane nodded and sighed. The sigh held neither despair nor relief, only air. "Guess back to dealing with this mess now."

"Guess so," Jackie said.

Jackie looked at her car and Diane looked at the sidewalk, and they both almost walked away.

"Hey," said Diane. "Do you want to look at this stuff together? Just see if there's anything we can both learn from it?"

"Yeah, sure," said Jackie, still looking at her car. "That'd be cool, I guess."

Diane put her arm around Jackie's shoulder to help her to the car, but her energy was almost gone in the panic of having nearly orphaned Josh, so Jackie put an arm around Diane. Limping, but moving, they carried one another away from the library.

The shoe box marked KING CITY had a book and a small stack of newspaper articles. The book was called Fun Facts and Anecdotes Related to King City and Environs. It was written by noted actor and civic historian Harrison Ford. It was cheaply made, and even a skim of its contents indicated a lack of careful copyediting and layout in its production.

Jackie flipped open to somewhere in the middle.

King City Fact #1061

Did you know? King City is the only city in California to have had a mayor right from its very founding. It has never gone a second without a mayor. It has always had one!

Again.

King City Fact #702

The fad of playing "Dark Side of the Moon" over "Wizard of Oz" was popularized by King City's own George Taylor Morris.

Again.

King City Fact #986

We have the most oranges.

"What the hell?" she said, flipping faster through the useless book. "I almost died for this?"

King City Fact #3

No animals were harmed.

She tossed the useless book on the car floor and picked up the stack of newspaper articles.

KING CITY REPORTS SERIOUS TROUBLE WITH CONCEPTS OF EXISTENCE, LOSS

JANUARY 23, 2003

BY LEANN HART
Senior Life and Style Reporter

A city in central California with no apparent connections to our town of Night Vale or the vast, flat desert in which we reside is reporting trouble with ideas like existence and loss. They are reporting that reality isn't what it used to be, and that life seems somehow empty, or that it always was, and they just never noticed.

In a press release sent only to Night Vale for reasons we do not understand, King City indicated that it feels out of sync with cities only a few miles away and that perhaps everyone they know are just variations on the same, single person. Everyone is one person, says King City. There are a lot of that person.

Also, they need to elect a mayor. They haven't had a mayor in so long. It's time to elect a mayor, they said.

The local paper, the *King City Rustler*, has been printing large glossy photos of some man in a tan jacket holding a deerskin suitcase. They have not been printing anything else. No one knows who he is, and no one can remember the photos after they look at them.

These glossy, color photos seem expensive to print. This is a waste of the newspaper's funds, everyone thought, but no one said.

When reached for comment by an angry mob of King City citizens bearing torches, the editor of the *Rustler* hid.

Those outside of King City are saying that it is getting harder and harder to find the town, like it is slowly sliding off the map. Roads that used to go into town do not go into town anymore. And those attempting to reach town simply disappear.

"I'm pretty sure we didn't used to disappear in King City," said Wanda Nieves, a local resident who issued her own press release, consisting only of that quote.

We at the *Night Vale Daily Journal* are using the massive amount of funds gained in the ever-lucrative newspaper business to investigate why people from King City are sending us annoying press releases and also, if it comes up, why King City is slipping out of our reality under the watchful eyes of a mysterious man in a tan jacket.

As always, this article contains additional reporting by agents of various unnamed government agencies, who add and subtract words and sentences from newspaper articles in order to send coded messages to compatriots living deep undercover in distant parts of the world.

Directly after that was another article, with the same layout and the same photo illustration, a self-shot portrait of Leann Hart that she was apparently quite pleased with and so had, for much of 2003–2004, used as illustration for most of her feature stories.

KING CITY TOTALLY FINE AND BASICALLY NOT THAT INTERESTING

JANUARY 23, 2003

BY LEANN HART
Senior Political Reporter

A city in central California with no apparent connections to our town of Night Vale or the vast, flat desert in which we reside is totally fine. It has a population of about *[a brown smudge]* and an unemployment rate of *[scribbled out with pencil]*.

The sun shines there, much as it does here. Sometimes the

sun does not shine, and people there refer to this as night. In this respect, and in all others, it is totally normal.

We at the *Daily Journal* are not clear why we are reporting on this story, as the fact that King City exists is not in and of itself an interesting fact. If truth be told, and it often shouldn't be, the town itself is not interesting.

Good mayor.

Citizens of King City, when asked via phone, wanted first to know who was calling.

"Oh, I'm a reporter," I said. "I was just checking to see if you had anything to say."

"Huh," said the citizens. "Okay. Like, are you asking about something specific?"

"No, no, no. I don't even know what the story is here. Maybe if you started talking we'd be able to figure that out together."

"Most people don't ask me to talk about anything," said the citizens. "Well, I guess my job isn't fulfilling, but I'm not unhappy about it. I never expected my job to be fulfilling. We're told so often that employment won't be fulfilling that the surprise would be if it suddenly turned out to be. I'm not happy about it, but I'm okay with it."

"That wasn't interesting at all," I said.

"I'm sorry."

"Me too."

The citizens of King City may have commented further. I hung up, so I don't know.

I'm not sure what this information does for you exactly, but just know that King City, a city in Monterey County, north of Mexico, south of Oregon, underneath the sky, over a lot of dirt, and then over a different part of the sky, is doing totally fine. Nothing more to report. It's been a slow day here.

As always, this article contains additional reporting by agents of various unnamed government agencies who have murdered an innocent man they did not know just so that one of their fellow agents, out of contact but with access to a newspaper, will read the man's name and realize that the name of the murdered man is itself the message.

Jackie held up the two stories. They were identical in every way except the reality they were reporting on.

"This is not encouraging at all," said Diane.

"Dude." Jackie meant a lot by that, but she had no other way to say it.

"And this doesn't help," Diane said, holding up the photo from Troy's file.

"Nope. Makes everything worse. I don't see another car. You need a ride?"

"Yes, please. I walked here. I needed to get my blood pumping for a library trip. But I think I've had enough for today."

"Yeah," said Jackie. She found there was nothing to add to that, no modifiers or scorn or jokes. So she just said it again. "Yeah."

Diane studied the photo as Jackie started her car. Every time she looked at it, she could feel her head start to throb. Maybe she did have migraines.

"Can you develop migraines later in life?" she asked.

"Why the hell do people keep talking to me about migraines?"

"You too?"

They shared a confused glance.

"Fine. I don't care. I don't need another stupid mystery to solve," said Jackie.

The photo in Diane's hand was old, yellowing and cracked, and bending at the edges. In it, there was a man who was definitely Troy. He could not have been anyone else. He had his arm around a little girl. They were posed in the middle of downtown Night Vale, but a downtown that had not existed for probably more than a hundred years.

Diane studied the face, blandly handsome, smiling blandly. Definitely Troy.

"Maybe we should talk to Leann Hart," Jackie said.

"Yeah." There was a lot she could add to that, but she didn't have the energy. So Diane just said it again. "Yeah."

She thought she might throw up. If not right then, later. At some point in her life she would. It was a statistical thing.

Diane and Jackie quietly read the clippings on the wall, displayed around a large, well-used hatchet. It was one of many hatchets Leann Hart kept as part of her business. It was a failing business, but Leann kept it alive.

The clippings showcased some of *Night Vale Daily Journal's* most famous headlines:

Glow Cloud Threatens Farms:
Dead Animals Falling from Sky

City Council Approves Humming:
Private Residences Only, Max 50 Decibels

Everything Is Fine
Totally Fine
Carry On

Feral Dogs Actually Just Plastic Bags, Says Mayor

Scientists Announce "Relax. Sun Is Not Real."

WORMS!

All Hail the Glow Cloud!

Wheat-Free Night Vale
Wheat and Its By-Products Turn into Snakes, Cause Deaths

Street-Cleaning Day: Run for Your Lives. Run! Run!

As editor of the *Night Vale Daily Journal* for the past three decades, Leann had been present for the steady popularity and then sudden decline of print news.

Many of her ideas were cost-effective (cutting back to four issues a week). Some seemed like good ideas but failed for unexpected reasons (replacing newspapers in street kiosks with 2 percent milk, which apparently spoils quickly in sunlight). And some were hugely successful (attacking independent news bloggers with hatchets).

The last was a controversial decision, as attacking a person with a hatchet (with anything really) is technically a crime. But Leann made it work by engaging in semiotic arguments with law enforcement about what is assault and what is a business plan. One of her degrees is an MBA, she often told law enforcement officers. Few officers have an MBA, so they rarely argued with her.

Leann's office featured an entire wall of hatchets, held up at angles by screws drilled into the faux wood paneling. Most of them were new and shiny. There were five in the center that were old, with curved gray wood handles. Their heads were smaller than those of the other hatchets. They were flinty, dull, with inscriptions depicting each of the five Ws of Journalism (What? What! What!? What. Why?).

On another wall were her college diplomas, both of which were handwritten in Cyrillic. Neither could have been her MBA, as, since the early 1960s, all MBA degrees have been issued via subdermal microchip.

Having read everything on the wall twice over, Jackie broke the silence. "Let me do the talking, okay?"

"That's fine," Diane said.

"I mean, you can if you want to."

"No, really, you do it."

"You obviously want—"

"Hello."

This last was from Leann, who had entered the room with her hatchet. Her voice sounded distant, like she was still in the other room even as she sat on a couch underneath the wall of hatchets and gestured for the two of them to sit across from her in the smooth, white chairs. (Were those ivory? Unlikely, especially since ivory had been outlawed, and even living elephants had had their tusks confiscated by strict regulators.) The chairs were tall and rigid with thin seat pads but were surprisingly comfortable. Diane and Jackie did their best not to move around much in them. (Definitely not ivory. Perhaps some kind of bone? The knots where the legs met seemed almost like joints.)

"Well?" said Leann. Her voice sounded even farther away, like she was shouting from down a long corridor.

Diane looked at Jackie, who was looking at Diane.

"Go ahead," Diane said, and Jackie laid out the two news articles about King City.

"Hi, Leann. I'm Jackie, and this is Diane C———"

Leann snatched the articles from the table and held them to the light.

"Where did you get these?"

"The library."

Leann widened her eyes and mouthed "Library." It was not clear whether she was impressed or skeptical.

"King City, huh?" she said. "Quiet town. Suburban without the urban. Not much to say about it."

She set the articles down on the coffee table. Jackie opened her mouth, but Diane spoke first.

"But what about this other article? Which article is telling the truth?"

Jackie closed her mouth and looked at Diane.

"A good journalist doesn't have to discuss the truth," said Leann, waving toward her diplomas. "Some details are secret or off the record."

"What—" said Jackie

"So what stuck out to you about this mayor?" Diane asked. "You don't mention his name in either article. You just say 'Good mayor.' You wrote that here as an entire paragraph: 'Good mayor.'"

"Well, they have a good mayor," said Leann.

"But—" said Jackie.

"Hang on, Jackie," Diane said. "Leann, we need any information you have. This is important."

"And why is it so important?" said Leann, testing the edge of the hatchet against her finger. It drew a dot of blood and she smiled.

"I don't know who I am and I don't understand the progression of time as it relates to me," said Jackie.

Leann nodded. "We've all been there."

"I lost my job," said Diane. "I've distanced myself from my son. I'm teetering. I feel like the breath before a scream."

"Listen to me, young ladies." ("Young ladies," Diane mouthed but did not interrupt.) "Good reporting is not wasting words or space. I can't afford the column inches to describe every insignificant detail about a story or all the information that might be pertinent."

"But what about—" said Jackie, but Diane spoke over her.

"We'll make this simple. Which of those two stories is true? Which one can we trust?"

Leann thought about this.

"I don't know. Or I don't remember. Or a journalist never reveals her secrets."

"That's a magician," Jackie said. "A magician never reveals her secrets."

"Isn't a journalist a type of magician?" said Leann, lifting one eyebrow. The effect was very irritating.

"No," said Jackie. "Definitely not, no."

"I think what Jackie's trying to say, Leann, is that—"

"I'm trying to say this," said Jackie, standing.

She reached over Leann's shoulder, grabbed a hatchet (the one inscribed with "What!?"). Jackie hefted the hatchet over her head and put her hand down on the table between all of them. Before either of the other women could do anything in response, she swung the hatchet down and chopped the slip of paper in her hand in two. Then up again, this time a series of quick, light hacks, like a chef cutting up a chiffonade. Once the slip was shredded, she swept all the paper off the table, scattering it into the air and onto the thick carpet.

"Look," Jackie said. She held up the intact piece of paper that said "KING CITY."

"Now, I need to know everything you know about this place," she said, waving the paper.

"How did you do that?" Leann said.

"A magician never reveals."

Diane had of course noticed the piece of paper in Jackie's hand, but this was confounding. She found she had nothing to ask, or she had many things to ask but no way to voice them.

"Why didn't you tell me?" was all Diane could say.

"There's a lot of us with these papers," said Jackie. "Diane, I saw you had one, but I don't know what you did with it."

"He wanted me to give it to my son. But I didn't. I threw it away. Or no, I— I don't remember what I did with it."

"Lucky." Jackie dismissed Diane. "I keep mine in my hand,

because it won't leave. Now, Leann, which of these stories is true? Do you have any idea?"

"I imagine they both are," said Leann. "I'm imagining that because I don't have any idea."

She narrowed her eyes to better assess Jackie. Definitely impressed this time.

"You've obviously been there," said Jackie. "You wrote two articles about the place. Can you put us in touch with anyone there?"

"Oh no, I never actually went there or talked to anyone there. I'm a reporter, not a snoop."

Jackie pulled up to the front of Diane's house. She looked down at her hand, which was crumpling up the paper and then letting it spring open uncreased again and again. The drive had been quiet since she told Diane the story of the paper.

"I know the man in the tan jacket you're talking about," Diane broke the silence. "His name is Evan."

"If you say so. I don't remember the name he gave me. Efran maybe?"

"I used to work with him, I think. But I'm starting to feel that what we think may not be the most reliable test of truth."

"John Peters. You know, the farmer? He told me that you were involved with the man in the tan jacket."

"John said that?"

"Well, nah, not outright. But he implied it, sure."

Diane shook her head.

"That man. He always loves to be ahead of the gossip. So much so I think he makes up half of it."

"All of these men," said Jackie. "Each one carrying a mystery that's not as interesting as he thinks. I don't want their mysteries. I want a life on an even level."

Diane nodded. Jackie's exhaustion was also her own.

"Or maybe I want to grow older," Jackie said. "Maybe that is what I want. But I want to do it because I'm ready, not because someone else is ready for me."

She found that when she looked at Diane now, she saw a

woman who, yes, happened to be older than her, but, yes, also had her own worries, her own worrying lot in life. Jackie softened her voice.

"Who are we following, Diane? Who's the blond man at the diner? And at the bank and the movie theater and who knows where else?"

"He's a police officer too," said Diane.

It's amazing how much a roll of dimes weighs, the house thought.

"So who is he?"

"Josh's father. Left town when Josh was born."

"Asshole."

Diane smiled. She hadn't talked about Troy leaving since shortly after it happened. It always felt somehow like a mistake she had made. An embarrassing moment for her. Jackie's response was honest and simple, and in just two syllables put all the onus on Troy.

After all the back-and-forth with Josh, the weird business at work, it felt good to have a person on her side.

"He showed up again recently. I don't know why he did. I'm worried that he wants back in Josh's life. And of course Josh is interested in knowing his dad, whatever that word means."

"Ah, let him. He'll just find out his dad's a jerk. Like, Troy was cute. You got pregnant. He skipped town. He's an asshole. Josh can figure all that out on his own. He's not much younger than me."

He wasn't, it was true. The limited scale of the human life startled Diane. There was so little actual time between ages that felt vastly different. She had categorized Jackie as different than Josh, and herself as different than Jackie, but the span of years between any two of them wasn't much of a span at all.

"None of us knows what we want to do when we're his age. When we're your age, when you're my age," said Diane, "any age, I guess. We think we do, and sometimes we're right, but only ever in retrospect."

Her tone was halfway between reminiscence and lecture. Jackie sighed but let her talk. She knew that messages were for the sender, not the receiver.

"Troy and I loved each other. We called it 'unconditional love,' which was true. Once conditions arose, the love dissipated."

"Everything that's happened has gotten me thinking about a lot of stuff I've tried hard to not think about. Like, I've never loved anyone," said Jackie. "Not that I can remember. I know this town, but I don't feel like I'm on the same time scale as it. Something went off."

"Love is hard," said Diane, who hadn't really listened to what Jackie had said. "I wish Josh could love his father conditionally."

"The kid is smart. He'll know what to do."

"How old are you, Jackie? If you don't mind."

"Nineteen, I guess."

"You guess?"

"I don't feel nineteen." Jackie looked out the window at the houses across the street that were thinking nothing at all. "A woman who calls herself Mom asked me about stuff from when I was a kid, but I couldn't remember any of it. People think I'm a child, but if so, I've been a child for a long time. I don't know how old I am."

Talking about this made Jackie feel like she was looking down from somewhere high, or like she was staring straight up at a cloudless point of sky.

"People look at me and call me a girl or tell me I'm too young to run a pawnshop. They wonder how I'm able to handle a tough business like that, and I don't know. I just do. Always have. It's the only thing I know how to do. Far as I can tell I've been doing it for centuries."

"Well, when you're nineteen, everything feels like forever," Diane said, staring at the dash and lightly touching the air-conditioning vent. "I don't know. Did you ever think of just turning twenty?"

"I gotta go," Jackie said.

"Okay."

"Meaning this is my car."

"Right."

Diane grabbed her belongings.

"Hey," she said. "I said I was going to let you ask the questions at Leann's, and then I didn't let you. That wasn't right of me."

"Guess we all suck sometimes."

Diane and Jackie held a look for a moment, and this changed nothing about how they felt about each other. But there was a kind of simple peace that came from holding a gaze.

Diane broke it off and shut the door. As she raised her hand to wave and opened her mouth to say "Good-bye," Jackie's car drove off.

She walked into the house, set her things down, and turned on the radio. Cecil's voice relaxed her. He was announcing some upcoming events in town. There was a new exhibit at the Museum of Forbidden Technologies that sounded interesting. Unfortunately, Diane had never been able to go to the museum because all of its exhibits are classified, and no one is allowed to see them. It is a felony to go to that museum.

Diane flipped through the day's mail as Cecil continued on.

It didn't matter what he said. The world is terrifying. It always is. But Cecil reminded her that it was okay to relax in a terrifying world.

The mail was junk: a couple of furniture catalogs, a credit card offer, a dead mouse, and a flyer with coupons for 50 percent off the moon. The faceless old woman who secretly lives in her home had censored the credit card offer, using charcoal to blot out entire lines and amounts. Diane looked through the coupons, considering what a great deal it would be if anyone actually wanted the moon. It's a hideous rock, Diane thought. You couldn't pay me to take it.

The moon is a trick of light suggested to us by the seas, the house thought.

From the radio, Diane heard the word "Chuckwalla." This was the street she lived on. She stopped thinking about the moon and the mail and made her way to the living room. She stared at the radio. In lieu of her ears' inability to open up, she widened her eyes to better hear Cecil's voice. She listened to what he had to say, moving from distant unease to personal unease to panic.

There are not a lot of blue Mazda coupes with double red stripes. Diane had just been sitting in one.

There are quite a few burgundy Ford hatchbacks. Diane owned one of them.

Everything she was afraid of was happening at once. She was only afraid of one thing.

"No," she shouted. She shouted it over and over because she didn't know what she could do to change anything and at least shouting made her feel better. No one could hear except the house and the faceless old woman who secretly lives in it.

Diane opened the door to her garage. She turned on the light. There was no burgundy Ford hatchback.

"Goddammit, Josh."

Diane ran to Josh's room. She knocked. She knocked again. She opened his door. He was not there.

She worried for Jackie's safety. She seethed over Josh's disobedience.

Josh did not answer his phone. Neither did Jackie. The calls went straight to voice mail.

Diane texted both of them. No response. She ran out her front door, down Chuckwalla Road, past several crisscrossing streets, toward the crash.

Is the roof the head of the house, or the hair, or is it a hat? thought the house.

"This is just the start of it," whispered the faceless old woman from behind Diane's washing machine.

THE VOICE OF NIGHT VALE

CECIL: . . . accident at the corner of Lampasas Avenue and Chuckwalla Road. All westbound lanes of Lampasas are shut down, and EMTs are at the scene.

While there is only one damaged car at the scene, a blue Mazda coupe with double red stripes, which rode up the median and wrecked headlong into a light pole, witnesses described a second car, a burgundy Ford hatchback, that had run the Mazda off the road and then sped away. The driver of the Mazda—a woman in her late teens, early twenties—was taken to the hospital.

There are no other reported injuries.

The Sheriff's Secret Police are suspecting this may have been a hit-and-run and are asking anyone with information to contact them. They're also using this time to learn a little bit more about three-dimensional chalk art.

Several of the officers have already drawn an orca leaping above a frothy ocean wave. The whole thing's like ten feet wide. It's remarkable because it looks not only photorealistic but also like the whale is coming right out of the street. Very impressive to have drawn that in the last fifteen minutes while also investigating a major accident. Wow.

And now a word from our sponsors.

Having trouble sleeping? Are you awake at all hours? Do birds live in you? Are you crawling with insects? Is your skin jagged and hard? Are you covered in leaves and gently shaking in the gentle breeze?

You sound like a tree. You are perfectly healthy. Also, you don't need to sleep. You're a tree, a very very smart tree. Are you listening to the radio? Is a human assisting you? What plan do you have for our weak species? Please, tree, I beg of you to spare me. Please, tree. Spare me.

This message has been brought to you by Old Navy. Old Navy: What's Going to Happen to My Family?

Jackie woke up confused, as is usual. Sleep is confusing. Dreams are baffling. The concept of transitioning from one perceived reality to another is a tolerated madness.

So far, normal.

But the beeping and the various clear lines with fluid in them, those weren't right. The cot she was in was not her bed. She tried to move and felt someone pull at her arm. Their fingernails were sharp, tugging at her skin. She looked down at the IV in her arm, not understanding what she was seeing.

A nurse came in.

"Look who's awake," the nurse said brightly. All the cameras in the room obediently turned to look. There were several cameras in the room. In this way, it was like every other room in Night Vale.

"Where the hell is this?"

"You had a touch of an accident," the nurse said. "I wouldn't worry about it. But then it didn't happen to me. You should probably worry. Have a great day!"

She trilled this and whisked out the door. She was the type of person to trill and to whisk.

The hospital room was small. Just a sink and a cabinet of supplies and a window looking out on the abandoned coal mine. The hospital had been built next to the mine for the convenience of the mining company and their many, many injured miners. It was not a safe mine. Fortunately it had been closed down years ago after a great deal of public outcry. Now it had been converted into a prison for the Sheriff's Secret Police to keep people who didn't vote correctly in municipal elections, its sordid past long behind it.

Between the door and the window was Jackie's bed, and on it, her. Above her were several cameras and a loudspeaker. Her left arm was in a cast. How did she get here?

The loudspeaker crackled. An authoritative voice of indefinite gender issued from it.

"Ask your doctor if she has a plan for the future," the loudspeaker said. "Ask her what it is. Criticize it."

"Hello?" Jackie said.

There was a doctor next to her. The doctor had presumably entered through the door and walked up to her. Jackie just hadn't seen the doctor do that.

The doctor rubbed her hands together.

"Well, what do we have here?"

The doctor was washing her hands, although Jackie did not remember her walking to the sink. Then she was by the bed again, her face quite close. There were no transitions, just her in one place and then the other.

"You've been in a terrible accident. Are you in a lot of pain?"

"I don't know. No?"

"We have you on a lot of drugs. The drugs keep you from feeling the pain. But the pain is there. You'll have to believe me. But can I tell you a secret?"

Jackie wasn't sure.

"Yes?"

"The secret is that you don't have to believe me. You have no reason to trust me at all."

The doctor winked, and then she was gone again. Or she

walked out the door, is presumably what she did, only Jackie hadn't noticed her leaving.

The loudspeaker came alive again.

"Ask your doctor a question only she would know the answer to.

"Ask your doctor if you'll be able to play the piano after. After everything. After it's all finished and there's nothing left. Will you be able to play the piano then? Ask your doctor that."

"Sorry," the doctor said. She was hovering over Jackie again. "We're not sure how to turn that off."

She waved vaguely at everything in the room, including Jackie.

"You'll have some trouble for a while," she said. "It will be difficult. You might notice some problems with walking and with life in general. You should look at the sky and scream about how empty it is at least twice a day."

"What kind of accident?" said Jackie.

The doctor smiled. "The accidental kind," she whispered. She was gone again.

"There was a slip of paper in my hand. Where is it?" Jackie asked the empty room. "I can't feel it. I can't feel it in the cast."

The nurse came bustling in. She was the kind of person to bustle.

"Did you find a slip of paper in my hand?" Jackie said.

"Do not fret for a sec," she chirped. "Before we put the cast on, I set that paper safe and sound in this box here."

Jackie used whatever energy she had to sit up. Her face was warm. The nurse felt around in the box, frowning. Then she held it upside down. She smiled at Jackie.

"Looks like it's gone. Sorry, dear. You look sad. Was it important?"

Jackie felt the blood leave her face. She couldn't feel the paper in her hand, but she knew.

The nurse shrugged and then zipped out the door (she was the kind of person to zip, too).

Jackie moved her fingers inside the cast. Her fingers hurt so bad. It served them right for going numb and making her hope that the paper was finally gone.

Various machines beeped. None of them seemed to be attached to her. There was a gurgle from the loudspeaker.

"Ask your doctor a direct question with an unambiguous answer. Try to get your doctor to commit to something for once in her life.

"Ask your doctor a rhetorical question and spread your hands out despairingly. Put your doctor in a position where he feels he can't help you even if he can."

Jackie was alone.

The doctor was standing beside her.

"You'll be fine. I think," the doctor said. "I don't know you, though. Maybe you'll make a lot of mistakes and end up horribly unhappy. But the injuries will go away eventually. That's the good news. There is also bad news."

Jackie was alone again.

The voice from the loudspeaker came out as a whisper.

"Ask your doctor why. Say it like that: 'Why?' See if you can find out for us, okay? See if you can find out why."

The machines beeped. Jackie closed her eyes and returned to the relative normalcy of dreams.

33

Diane stood near Jackie. She had first gone to the accident site, but there wasn't much to see. Just some skid marks and an elaborate piece of 3-D chalk art. Then she had a cab take her by a few of Josh's favorite hangouts (the video store, the Desert Flower Bowling Alley and Arcade Fun Complex, the sand wastes outside of town), but he hadn't been at any of them. He was probably (if he was not injured as well, but she couldn't bear to even think of that) at one of his father's several jobs, doing exactly what Diane didn't want him to do. There would be consequences when Josh came home tonight. There would be a reckoning.

In the meantime, she needed to see how Jackie was doing. It had been Josh, not her, that had done this, but still Diane felt the guilt personally, as though she herself had been at the wheel.

Jackie had broken off the tip of the plastic knife the nurse had given her with her dinner and was using the jagged edge to hack away at her arm cast.

She had not seen Diane come in, but she had grown used to that. Most results have no visible causation. You wake up, and there's a friendly face above you, or a part of you you had never seen and will never see again has been taken from you, or a part of you you never had before you now have. This is how hospitals work.

Everything about Jackie looked sore to Diane. Her skin hung

from her skull, her hair lay flat. Even her teeth looked loose. Her neck and face were still covered in angry purple blotches from the librarian's poison. What little strength Jackie had was being used to cut at her freshly cast cast.

Diane had a cast when she was twelve. She had fallen out of a tree and broken her leg. This is a common injury for children, as trees dislike young humans and are notorious for picking them up and dropping them if they get too close. She had been grabbed by a ficus tree in her mom's office. Ficus trees are not tall trees, but they are muscular trees, stronger than they look. Diane had been able to break its grasp, but when she fell, she stumbled forward to the top of some steps, where she tumbled down to the lower floor, landing on that floor's emergency secret trapdoor, which had opened up onto the basement's jagged rock pile. She had, like most people, feared and loathed houseplants ever since.

"It itches like crazy, I know," she said.

"Not trying to scratch it. I'm looking to see if that paper is still there." Jackie had gotten a good-size hole in the cast. "But now it also itches, thanks."

"Ask your doctor if he is a cop. He is legally required to disclose this information if you ask," the loudspeaker said.

The nurse buzzed into the room.

"Oh, it looks like the cast didn't set right," the nurse singsonged as Jackie openly hacked away, using the full motion of her arm to chisel at the plaster. "We'll just have to reset that, won't we?"

Jackie put her swollen, sunken eye up to the hole in the cast. She couldn't see anything. She sawed at the frayed edge of the hole with the impotent edge of the knife.

"I think I almost got it."

"Ask your doctor if she is you. Ask your doctor if everyone is in your mind. Ask your doctor for tips for living in lucid dreams," the loudspeaker said.

"Reset the cast," the nurse said with a voice like a tolling church bell, her arm landing hard on Jackie's free hand. "Reset the cast."

The nurse's pupils went vertical, and Jackie let go of the knife, relaxing her hand.

"I would rather have the pain than the fatigue," she said.

Her head rolled back and her arms flopped open.

"Just relax," the nurse said, although she was no longer in the room.

"You don't look well," Diane said.

"I don't feel well."

"How long are you supposed to stay here?"

"Dunno. Probably until tomorrow morning. Maybe tonight. Didn't even know this place was still open. Did you?"

Diane did not, but she was too distracted by her worry for Jackie and her frustration with Josh to care.

"What happened?"

"Driving up Chuckwalla, leaving your house. I got to Lampasas. Then all of a sudden, I'm lying in this cot."

"You didn't see the car that hit you?" Seeing Jackie's condition, Diane began to worry more about how Josh was doing. And why hadn't he stopped after the accident?

"Nope."

"I'm sorry about earlier. I think I upset you. I can't talk to younger people. I've failed a lot with Josh."

"Here's the problem, dude. You keep seeing me as a number, and I'm not that. Or not just that. Or, oh, I don't know. Jesus, everything hurts."

"Jackie, I want to help you find the man from King City. There's a directness, a forcefulness to you that I just don't have. I need that. I need you to help me understand what Troy and Evan and all the rest want with Josh. I need to protect my son."

"I'm tired, Diane." Jackie wanted to yawn, but her jaw couldn't open wide enough.

"He's my son, Jackie. You need to . . . I'm sorry. I can come back later."

"No, in general. Tired. Broken."

She held up her cast, newly reset, although the nurse had never come back into the room.

"When this comes off, I'll be holding a paper that says 'KING CITY,' and I'll keep on holding it for centuries, not growing old, not growing at all, still in Night Vale, like I always have been. I'm never going to get my life back. I'm never going to get a life. I'll be nineteen-year-old Jackie Fierro, no purpose, one slip of paper, forever."

Her entire body was a vibration of pain and frustration. Diane was silent. The nurse came in, pacing back and forth at the foot of the bed. After a couple minutes, Jackie fell asleep, from the drugs and from the energy spent on her speech.

The television turned itself on to talk about some local weather issues. The news anchors bantered back and forth about what weather they liked best. One said "warm sunshine" while the other said "cool sunshine." They both laughed, and the ground shook a little bit.

"How's she doing, Diane?" one anchor whispered to Diane.

"She's having a tough go of it, but she's going to be okay, I think."

"That's good to hear."

"It sure is, Tim," said the other anchor. "How are you, Diane? How's Josh doing?" A picture of Josh appeared in the top left corner of the screen. In this picture, he was a French press coffeemaker.

"That your son?" Jackie managed. She was awake again, but barely.

"Yes." Diane felt concern. No, not concern, dread. No, not dread, terror.

"Looks just like you." Saying this seemed to take a lot out of Jackie. She closed her eyes again.

"He's fine," Diane said to Trinh. "He's fine," she said again, as if that made it more true than before.

"We heard he was on a search for his birth father," Tim said.

"Yes, exactly yes," Trinh agreed.

"Josh and I have been talking about it. I don't want him looking for his father. But the important thing is—"

There was an orchestral fanfare from the TV, cutting her off. An animated graphic flashed on the screen, below Josh's photo. The graphic said, TEEN SLEUTH. The letters were red and yellow with a silver-lined bevel, and there was a grotesque digital arpeggio hammering home each letter as it appeared.

Diane rubbed her forehead. "Is this going out to everyone?"

"More news tonight on local teen Josh Crayton, the amateur sleuth in search of his birth father," Tim said.

"We're getting reports now that the junior private eye has gone missing," Trinh said. For emphasis, the word MISSING appeared over Josh's photo.

"What?" Diane stood up. "No, he's just driving around looking for his father. It's only been a couple hours."

"For a report on this breaking story," Tim said, "we go now to Ben, who is live at Night Vale General Hospital."

"Yes, thank you, Tim," another voice said. "I'm reporting live from just outside the ICU of NV General."

She could hear Ben's voice both live outside the door and a

few seconds later from the television. She felt like there was a gap where her chest had been.

"Are you guys . . ." She turned. The nurse was gone. Jackie was asleep.

Diane cried. As long as you have some control over your situation, her father used to tell her unhelpfully, there's no need to cry, only to take action. That statement made sense right up until the tears came.

"Jackie." Diane's voice cracked. "Are you hearing this?"

There was a knock at the door.

"Can we come in, Diane?" said the voice behind the door.

"What's up?" Jackie said, her eyes still closed.

"Can we come in, Diane?" the same voice repeated from the television.

"The TV news. They say Josh has gone missing."

Jackie opened her eyes and forced her body into an upright position. Her face went pale with the effort and pain.

Diane was still crying, and did not cover her face. She let the tears fall openly. She thought of all the minutes, each individual minute, that she had left Josh home alone while she had chased useless ghosts all over town. If she had been home, he wouldn't be gone.

The Ben on the television screen was knocking on a hospital room door.

Jackie turned her legs off the bed with slow, careful effort. "He's a teenager. Probably ran away for a little bit. Call him. Get in a cab. Get home. Call him."

"He wouldn't have run away. He just took the car without telling me. That's all."

"Sometimes kids run away. You can sit here watching the TV talk about it, or you can do something."

Diane's tears stopped. Her dry red eyes looked into Jackie's tired, bruised eyes. She eased Jackie back into bed, gently helped her lie down, and pulled the cover up over her. She placed her hand on Jackie's forehead and stroked her temple. Jackie let her eyes close again.

"You're right," Diane said, trying to keep her panic from showing. "Okay. Okay. Okay."

Jackie closed her eyes and was instantly asleep again.

Diane opened the door and walked out into a completely empty hallway, hurrying toward the elevator. Behind her on the TV, Ben stood in an identical hallway frantically knocking on an identical door.

"Ms. Crayton, a word about your missing son," the reporter on the screen said into his microphone, pounding on the door. "Ms. Crayton, are you in there?"

Diane stood in the elevator as the doors slid shut on an unpopulated and silent hallway.

THE VOICE OF NIGHT VALE

CECIL: ". . . the hospital, which of course closed down years ago and is not being run by recognized medical professionals, or even by anyone who is, or ever was, alive. Do not go in there. Do not go," the press release for the new Ralphs deli counter concluded. Well, I for one can't wait to get a sandwich there.

And now a look at traffic.

There is a man with a gray pin-striped suit covered in dirt. His hands are more dirty than the rest of him, but they are differently dirty. They are covered in rust-colored streaks. The last few days have been unclear to him.

There was a time when his life had seemed like a hallway proceeding to a door. Now it was a garden littered with rocks.

How did his hands get dirty? He couldn't remember. But the question made him drive faster in his nice car, even as he did not know why.

He was in a desert. He kept looking at the mirror, which only showed him where he had already been. He wasn't sure why he was doing that either.

Looking at the sky, he saw, much closer now, a planet of awesome size, lit by no sun. Or he didn't see it anymore. It was there, and it wasn't. It was some ratio of literal and metaphorical. He drove faster. How fast can a nice car drive? How much longer could he keep driving faster before he was driving the fastest?

There seemed to be a city up ahead. There definitely was a city up ahead. It was a definite city, and at the speed he was going, it would not be up ahead much longer. He looked again in the mirror. Only a landscape unmarked by his passing. Only a road going back. Nothing he didn't already know. He knew nothing already.

This has been traffic.

An update on the flamingo situation. The flamingos are extremely dangerous and appear to put you completely out of sync with reality if touched. You think it'll be fun being out of sync with reality? It won't be. You're wrong about that, person who I just imagined disagreeing with me.

Old Woman Josie said that she and her non-angelic friends named Erika who live with her are trying to track down all the flamingos scattered all over Night Vale. She had put some in the pawnshop earlier, but she has been unable to reach pawnshop owner Jackie Fierro. Since the pawnshop's doors are removed and buried whenever the shop is closed, Josie and her not-at-all heavenly friends were able to easily walk in and reclaim the flamingos even with Jackie not around.

Meanwhile the City Council announced that the flamingos sure seem like a serious situation, and probably they'd look into it someday.

"Yeah, definitely," they said in a monotone unison, swarming out of the shadows of the council chambers with eyes like flames, and mouths like flames, and bodies like flames, basically they were just giant flames. "We'll get RIGHT on that. Haha sure. It's a big thing for us and we're taking it superseriously. It's just that, ugh, we hate to bring this up. But today is the day where a human sacrifice is made in our honor. And, while the flamingo situation seems dire, it would be super-dire to interrupt something so important as the sacrifice to the City Council. So yeah . . ." the monotone univoice concluded.

We will update you with more news about the flamingo situation as we know things and feel compelled to speak those things aloud.

Sheila, the woman who marks people down on her clipboard at the

Moonlite All-Nite, came by the studio. She is now sitting outside my booth, looking at nothing in particular, and doodling listlessly on her clipboard. I asked her why she came here.

"I just needed to do something different," she said. "Even one different thing will end this cycle I'm in. I can't go back through my life again. I don't even remember what a life is like. I only remember a series of scripted events. I don't remember ever coming to this station before though. I think maybe if I just quietly sit here long enough, not doing what I'm supposed to do, then finally I will be free."

I told her I'm fine with her sitting there. I'm here to serve the community. That's what I said.

Oh boy, she must really be in a state. Here I've been talking about her for a whole minute and she hasn't looked up once. Sheila? Sheila? Okay. Sorry, listeners. I need to go make sure she's all right. I take you now to the sound of a human stomach digesting, heavily amplified and electronically distorted.

34

Diane stood in Josh's empty room, dialing again. Each time it went straight to voice mail. She checked her texts, reading his last text ("Good. Be home later.") again and again.

She called the Sheriff's Secret Police. She called Josh's friends. She called Josh again. She called the comic book and video stores again. She called Josh again. She called Josh again.

He had to have his phone with him. It was illegal for any person to not carry at all times some sort of device by which the World Government could track their location. Most people opted for a cell phone because it also could do useful things like make phone calls and attract birds. A few holdouts still preferred the old tracking collars, bulky and impossible to take off though they were.

She rifled through the papers on Josh's desk and the ones shoved in his books. She found all kinds of sketches and doodles and homework worksheets. She pulled open his drawers, finding his illicit writing utensils (She didn't care. He was a teenager. What are you going to do, stop a kid from writing because it's illegal?), some cockroaches with corporate logos on them, and a partial tarot deck. She confiscated the tarot deck, making a mental note to lecture him about that once he was safely home (he would be safely home soon, she was sure), but also keeping it for her own use later.

There was nothing from Josh, and no one else she had gotten hold of knew where he was. They all offered their heartfelt condolences. She could taste her worry about Josh as an actual taste on her tongue, and it tasted like rotten citrus.

Diane tried texting him again. When she pressed her thumb to send, she felt a familiar sharp pain. She did it again. She felt it again. Her phone's touch screen grew cloudy with smudged blood. He was unavailable or, even worse, forbidden to call by civil ordinance.

She let out a high-pitched yelp of anger and kicked the open desk drawer shut. The framed movie poster above Josh's desk of Lee Marvin in *Cat Ballou* rattled.

She sat on the corner of his bed, put her head in her hands, and let out a sob that swelled her face and burned her eyes. She slid down the side of the bed, her butt thudding to the floor. She intentionally inhaled and exhaled toward the sky. The ceiling fan blew her breath back at her.

From this vantage point, she could see under the desk. There was a pale fluttering, like a white moth.

"Josh?" she asked hopefully, foolishly. He had never been a moth before, but he liked to try out new forms.

She reached under the desk and felt something light, thin, small. Not a moth. Paper?

Paper. Before she pulled it out and held it up to her face, she knew what it said.

"KING CITY." Over and over, as though the writer was unable to write any other words.

It was not the same as the paper the man in the tan jacket had given her. It was lighter, cheaper stock. The lettering was different too. It was shakier; the curves of the *G* and the *C* were bulbous and crooked, written in thin pen. The words on the paper Evan had told her to pass on to Josh was written in a thick, assured pencil.

She reopened the desk drawer. She ran her hand through the illegal writing utensils and found a pen that matched the color and gauge of the writing in her hand.

How did he know about King City? Diane pulled her purse off her shoulder and threw it against the wall. She smacked the desktop with her palms. She cursed. She stomped. Nothing helped.

She looked at her purse, lying open near the doorway. She remembered the paper Evan had given her. She had gone to throw it away behind the Moonlite All-Nite but put it in her purse after seeing Troy. She rifled through the purse. And just like her car keys, the paper was not there.

"No," Diane said again and again on the floor of Josh's empty room.

"KING CITY," the paper said again and again in Jackie's hand and probably now in Josh's hand as well.

Diane grabbed her phone and tried calling him one more time. She could feel the phone burning her ear. She could smell it burning her hair. She let it ring and ring, until the pain was searing, until her hair caught on fire, until she could not physically hold the phone to her head a moment longer, and then she let it ring a moment past that.

Jackie leaned back, her feet on the counter. It was the first time she had been in the pawnshop in days.

When she left the hospital, she wasn't sure where else to go. She didn't love being at the shop, but it was home, and she just wanted to go home.

In most ways it felt like it always did. But now her entire body hurt. And she knew the paper was curled up in her cast like the hidden centipede nests that sometimes appear over-night in people's beds.

The leaning, her usual position at the counter, was killing her back, and so she got off the stool and stood. She had never done that before. She looked out the window, where, not that long ago, she had watched a man in a tan jacket run away.

There were bubbles of light, low to the ground, out in the desert, and a tall building, and voices. As she watched, more buildings appeared, a forest of tall buildings, all glowing, their bulk wisping away to nothing as they approached the sand be-low them. Bubbles of light. And voices. A crowd of voices.

It was King City. She knew it now. Somehow, from all this distance, the city was calling to her. She spat at the lights but only hit her window.

She watched her spit roll down the glass and felt, for the first time in her short and long life, absolute despair. All of her and Diane's investigations had not gotten rid of the paper, or allowed her to write down any words but "KING CITY," or gotten rid of the visions out in the desert. Her life wasn't what it had been, and it never would be again. For a brief moment, spending time with Diane as an equal, she had wanted to grow older. But that feeling was gone.

Her body ached. First the librarian poison and then the accident and then whatever they had done to her in the hospital. Her body no longer felt young. All of her energy had been robbed from her. She felt old, looked young, was neither.

The bell on the door rang.

"We're not open," she said. "I'm sorry. I know it says we're open. But we're not really."

No answer.

She looked up and saw a woman in a business suit. The woman looked at Jackie but did not seem to see her. She was holding a small cardboard box in one hand, and a large metal hoe in the other. The wedge of the hoe had a dark brown stain with a few misshapen hairy lumps sticking out from it.

"Like I said," Jackie said, "closed."

The woman set both items on the counter and began to wash her hands, chanting to herself as she did.

"Hey, I'm sorry, man. I can't take this. I can't do that anymore."

The visitor finished washing her hands. She was shaking, and her hair was over her face. She would not look down at the box or at Jackie.

"Take your things and go, goddammit."

The woman did not go. She stood there, like she was waiting to be dismissed. Jackie sighed. Her back hurt so much, and her hand itched madly in the cast. She had never felt so distant from herself.

"All right. I can't actually give you a ticket because it would just say 'King City' over and over, I won't pay you anything, you won't die for any period of time, and I won't put it out for sale. But just sign here and you can go. Okay?"

The woman signed the name Catharine to the ticket, put the pen down, and asked in a small, shaken voice: "Is it over now?"

Jackie nodded. Catharine shuddered and walked out, upright and smiling, a different woman than had entered the shop.

Jackie took the hoe and, with her good arm, awkwardly leaned it on the trash can next to her. She opened the box. Inside was the mangled body of a tarantula. It had been hacked over and over until most of its body had detached from itself, a jigsaw puzzle way past solving. She looked out the door and watched the lights of Catharine's car diminish into the highway distance. Jackie tossed the box in the trash, wincing as she did.

The lights and voices out in the desert were gone. She sat alone in the dark pawnshop, looking at nothing in particular, thinking about nothing in particular. Somewhere, Catharine felt better. Nowhere, the tarantula felt nothing at all.

36

Diane bought a bus ticket to King City. It was as easy at that.

The bus left at 7:00 A.M. She brought a small suitcase and a little bit of cash. She boarded the bus, which was a standard bus, flint gray, with a long, rectangular body, two flat front windows, seven wheels, and several narrow viewing slots along the sides, so that the passengers could have a heavily obstructed view of the outside world.

The bus pulled out of the station and onto the highway. Diane tried texting and calling Josh again. It was painful, emotionally and physically, to do so, but she kept doing it anyway. She wished Jackie were with her. It would be easier with another person on her side, someone so steady and fearless, as young as she was, but Jackie was on her own painful journey, and Diane would have to do this alone.

The man sitting across the aisle from her was asleep moments into the ride. He was wearing overalls and a wooden hat. He had only one arm, which he kept folded behind his head. There was a tattoo along his tricep of a head of Boston lettuce crawling with ants. From between the broad leaves came two bare human legs, and below it all was a banner that read, CORAZÓN.

She listened to him breathe. His inhale was long and pinched, a thread of breath pulled taut into his sinuses. His exhale began with a muffled pop, like the sound of a freezer door opening, and spiraled out to a wheeze.

Diane closed her eyes. She tried to breathe synchronously with the man across the aisle. She put one arm behind her head, and breathed intentionally.

Yesterday, she had called the Sheriff's Secret Police and reported her car and her son missing. When asked for a description of the car, she described colors and shapes. This matched the police's understanding of what a missing burgundy Ford hatchback looked like. When asked for a description of Josh, she cried. This matched their understanding of what a missing teenage son looked like.

The Secret Police—who were standing in Diane's doorway only seconds after she had said "Secret Police" into the poorly hidden microphone mounted above her refrigerator—had said they would look for him.

"We're looking for him now," they had said, standing completely still. A helicopter had flown over the house, but this had been unrelated. Helicopters were almost always flying over the house.

Helicopters keep us free, the house had thought.

HELICOPTERS KEEP US FREE, the billboards all over town said.

Helicopters keep us free, the Sheriff's Secret Police had said to Diane then, in her kitchen, and also during all routine traffic stops and at community events and through bullhorns mounted atop cruisers cruising through quiet neighborhoods on Sunday mornings.

She had shown the police the paper with "KING CITY" written all over it.

One of the officers had held the paper to his face and then showed it to another officer, who had smelled it and then dropped it to the floor, where another officer had belly-crawled by quickly with a clear plastic bag and thick rubber gloves. The crawling officer had grabbed the paper with the gloved hand, put it in the plastic bag, sealed it, and written "nope!" on the bag in black marker. The officer had belly-crawled away, leaving the bag behind.

It didn't look like they were going to help her at all. The next day she had gotten up early and taken a taxi to the bus station.

As the bus drove on, she tried to sleep but could not. She urged herself to hold still, but would eventually feel an itch on her side and would have to start over. The bus kept its lateral trajectory, which felt flat and straight. Every time she squinted out her viewing slot, she saw desert sameness.

Her phone's battery was almost dead, even though she had charged it before leaving the house. Anyway, it had no signal to call out or in. She wished she had brought a municipally approved book to read, like *Vacation* by Deb Olin Unferth or *The Complete Plays and Verse of Kurt Russell*.

The man across the aisle never moved. His legato breaths stayed constant, a windy metronome.

The bus had been in motion, nonstop, for several hours, and she had not been able to sleep or read or use her phone. There was no visual complexity to the passing scenery or visceral texture to the drive. She was thankful for the man with the lettuce tattoo. She loved him, this man. He was, aesthetically and aurally, perfect. She loved him the way one loves an old bridge or a wool sweater or the sound of a growing tulip.

As she stared at him, the bus slowed and veered right. King City at last. She had only a vague plan for when she arrived. She would first try to find their Secret Police department, wherever it was hidden. Perhaps there was a radio host, some version of a Cecil Palmer for King City, California. She could contact that person and ask for them to put out a call for Josh, the way Cecil generously announced over the radio the location and personal details of Night Vale citizens without even being asked at all.

The bus came to a stop at a traffic light. They were clearly out on the edge of town. There was a used car lot. The bus turned, and her viewing slot showed her an old house that looked similar to Josie's. Diane leaned into the aisle and looked out the front of the bus, at a familiar low skyline: the library, the Rec Center, the Pinkberry, the distant Brown Stone Spire.

She walked to the front of the bus and leaned over the white line, careful to keep her feet behind it.

"Is this Night Vale?" Diane asked.

"It is," said the driver. Her name tag said MAB.

"But this was the King City bus."

"Right." Mab's sunglasses hid any feelings she might be having about the questions.

"But we never stopped or turned."

"Not many turns on that road."

They passed the Antiques Mall. Today the antiques in the window were playful, jumping over each other and wrestling.

Diane stumbled over the white line as the bus turned onto Somerset.

"Feet behind the line please."

She obeyed.

"I don't understand. Why did we never stop in King City?"

Mab eased the bus to a stop at the downtown bus/train/paddleboat terminal. She turned and pulled off her sunglasses. Her feelings about Diane's questions still weren't clear because she had no eyes.

"My bus started in King City. Why would I stop in King City?"

"I'm sorry."

"You got on the bus in King City. It is a nonstop bus from King City to Night Vale. No turns, like you said."

"Okay, I'm sorry."

Diane turned toward the other passengers, hoping someone would join her confusion or plead her case. The bus had started in Night Vale. It had, right? But all of the seats were empty. No one on board but her and the driver. Not even the driver now. Mab was standing outside, sunglasses back on, smoking a clove cigarette.

Diane walked back to her seat and grabbed her suitcase. Before leaving, she knelt down and put her hand to the seat directly across the aisle from hers, where the man had been. It was cold.

She got off the bus.

She called Steve Carlsberg, who had a car. Steve was happy to take Diane to King City. He was excited to go. He complained about not having received anything from a man in a tan jacket and agreed to skip work. He would pick her up from the bus station and they would leave this very morning.

"Morning?" she said. "What time is it?"

"Eight o'clock. Good and early start. Oh, this will be fun!" Steve said. She could hear the dinging of his car. He was already on his way.

She hung up and checked the time. Her bus had left at 7:00 and had been on the road for at least six hours. It was 8:03 A.M.

Mab pinched out her cigarette and swallowed it. She climbed back into her bus, pulled the doors shut, and drove away.

Diane waited. She bought a coffee and a banana in the station and waited. She bought another coffee and waited. She stared at the arrival and departure screens and waited. She checked the time and waited. It was 9:34.

She called Steve.

"Where are you? Is everything okay?"

"What do you mean, Diane?"

"I thought you were coming to pick me up and we were going to drive to King City."

"Drive to King City? Gosh, I'd love to. That sounds so exciting. When did you want to go?"

"As soon as you can."

"Listen, I'll take the rest of the day off. Where are you?"

"I'm at the bus station downtown."

"Okie doke!"

Diane waited. 11:15 A.M.

"Steve! Where are you?"

"Work. Why? What's up?"

Diane called a cab and asked the driver to take her to the airport.

Yesterday, she had called her insurance company. She was hoping she could get a replacement car to drive to King City.

The insurance company had asked her where her car was.

"I don't know."

"If you do not know where your current car is, how can we replace it?"

"It was stolen."

"So you don't see your car right now?"

"No."

"If you cannot see a thing, how can you be sure it exists at all? Are you familiar with Schrödinger's c—"

Diane had hung up and called back, hoping for a different agent.

"You did not answer our question." There had been only one ring, and the voice had immediately started in. "We cannot replace a vehicle that does not exist."

"You have my VIN number and all of the pertinent information in your system."

"This? This is just ones and zeros. This is just lights flashing various colors and shapes. There is nothing physical or real about data. Here. I just changed your middle name to five *f*'s in a row. 'Diane Fffff Crayton.' It says right here on my screen: 'Diane Fffff Crayton.' Do you accept that is your name because it is in our quote system?"

"No."

"No, you do not. Just as we would not accept that a vehicle exists simply because there is a number here in my quote sys———"

"Shut up and listen!" She had shouted this. She wasn't sure she had ever shouted on the phone before. "My son is missing. My car is missing. I need to find him, and I need a car to do that. I have no time for your absurd logic."

"Absurd logic is an oxymoron."

"Absurd logic!" she had screamed into the phone.

"Hisssssssssssssssss!" the representative had replied.

"You are an insurance company. I pay you to replace or repair my vehicle, or compensate me in the event that something happens to my vehicle. Something has happened to my vehicle."

No response.

"I need a car because I need my son. Can you understand me? Can you sympathize here? Just a small amount of compassion to get this done?"

Another long silence.

"Are you—" she had said.

"Yes. We're still here."

"Have you—"

"Quiet, Diane. We heard you. We are sorry. Give us a moment. This is difficult for us. Hearing that a customer has a missing child hurts us deeply. Please give us some space."

Diane had held back another eruption. Of the stages of grief, Diane had already gone through denial, sadness, and despair. Now she had been on the verge of the final step, vengeance.

The voice on the other end, clearly crying, had said: "We'll see what we can do. It will take no more than two weeks."

"Two weeks."

"This is hard on us, too," the representative had sobbed. Diane had hung up.

The cab pulled up to the airport. Night Vale Airport is not big. Most of the planes are propeller planes, private planes, secret military drones, and government planes that are used to make chemtrails, but she found a commuter airline to fly her from Night Vale to King City. She was one of four people on board the twenty-seat plane.

She had never flown before, having never left Night Vale. She wasn't sure whether she was a nervous flier or not, but the plane certainly felt small and fragile. It took off with a whirring shudder, and she felt dizzy as it rose through the clouds. She leaned her head against the window, but the rough ride caused her to bump her head against the hard plastic, making it impossible to sleep, so she watched the red flatness of the desert pass slowly below them. She looked out to the horizon, wondering if she could ever believe in mountains again having seen this flatness from above, and whether anyone would ever learn what clouds were made of. It was probably best we never know.

She glanced about at her fellow travelers, finding it interesting that they were all wearing blue earphones and horn-rimmed glasses. They were most likely part of a vague, yet menacing government agency. Diane wasn't sure if they were following her or the pilot or what, but they looked bored and tired.

After a two-hour flight, the plane touched down. It had been a long and expensive day, and she had only enough money for a few more cab rides in King City.

As the plane taxied to the gate, which was simply a wood stepladder on the tarmac near the terminal, Diane watched the world scroll from right to left across her window. Behind the airport, she could see a small city watched over by a distant Brown Stone Spire.

"Ladies and gentlemen, we have reached our final destination of Night Vale. Please remain seated until we come to a complete stop and the captain turns on the Free Will sign."

Diane punched the window, crying, "No. No!" her voice cracking and eyes watering. She couldn't help it. She turned to look around the cabin, conscious of the scene she was causing. There were twelve other passengers on the plane. They all wore baseball caps and knit shirts. They were sitting together in the back rows, not showing any awareness at all of her outburst.

"Thank you for flying with us," said the pilot, as Diane dragged her suitcase off the plane. She put down the suitcase and sat on it, right there on the tarmac, having no idea at all what she should do next.

THE VOICE OF NIGHT VALE

CECIL: . . . at a loss for words, at a profit for hand gestures, and more or less break even on eyebrow movements.

Night Vale Auto Insurance Co. announced today that because of rising costs, they will no longer offer replacements, repairs, or compensation for any accidents involving automobiles. "It's really expensive to fix or replace a car," said Bob Sturm, vice president of finance. "I mean, think about how many accidents there are. Those add up. How are we supposed to pay for all of that?"

When asked if they will lower premiums since they are no longer covering any form of repair, Sturm said no, but they will send customers kindly worded sympathy cards, and customers who have been in an accident can come by any one of their ten area locations for a hug and an it'll-be-okay pat on the shoulder.

Sturm concluded the announcement by coughing up a little bit of blood and laughing.

And now an update on Sheila, down at the Moonlite All-Nite, with her clipboard and pen, living her life over and over in a sad, empty reenactment of what was once an organic experience. She said that the loop finally seems to be broken, and that things are looking up.

I asked her if it wasn't then maybe time to leave the studio and return to her life, but she said she couldn't imagine doing that. Not anymore. So I offered to let her become a station intern instead. Isn't that just the best? I gave her the intern tunic and told her about the usual duties (mimeographs, making coffee, editing my slash fiction). I think she'll do just a great job, and she'll learn a lot while working here.

I'm pretty sure that all of our interns have gone on to do great things with their lives. I haven't followed up with any of them or even thought about it for very long, but I'm sure they are all better off for having done their internship here.

Sheila is so happy, she took the clipboard she had once used to mark down people at the Moonlite All-Nite and broke it over her knee. Which is a waste, Sheila. Do you think community radio stations have the kinds of budgets that allow us to just waste clipboards like that? Don't do that again, Sheila.

Moving on, many of you have written to the station asking for more information about our annual fund drive, which was held two months back. It seems that the tote bags and mugs and DVD sets of *Mad About You*, Seasons 2 and 5 have still not arrived for many donors.

We here at Night Vale Community Radio apologize for the delay. Please know that all donor rewards have been mailed out—were mailed out weeks ago—but, as we all know, time is weird here in our beautiful community. As a result, those weeks may have been experienced by you as mere seconds and the delivery would seem instantaneous, or those weeks may be experienced by you as millennia, and you will be a terrible, vacant, ancient form of yourself by the time you receive your reward. These possibilities and all other possibilities remain . . . possible.

Please know that our station exists because of donors like you. It also exists because a long and terribly improbable series of galactic events over the course of billions of years conspired to bring us to this very moment in our station's existence. And we thank you for your support. Again, we apologize for the delay in receiving your items, and also for the absurdity of time.

Next on our program, I will describe a boring photo in a thousand slow, interminable words.

37

Jackie knocked on her mother's door. After a moment, it opened.

"Hello, dear. Come in." Her mother turned and walked back to the kitchen, and Jackie limped after her. She tenderly sat down across from the woman she did not recognize.

"Mom," she tried calling her. "Mom, it's been a rough couple days. Let's start there. I can't work anymore. And if I'm not working then I'm not sure who I am. Maybe that's not healthy. Probably isn't. But it's all I've done as far back as I can remember. Which. Okay. Memory. Wanna talk about that in a moment.

"But I've been trying to figure all this out. Feels like running up a slide while other people are trying to slide down it."

Jackie picked up one of the perfect, wax-looking apples. She sniffed it. It was real.

"I've been spending some time lately with Diane Crayton. Not like that, but. You know, Diane? Does stuff with the PTA? Works at that office no one is sure what they do? Anyway, Diane and I got into this thing where we didn't like each other. But I think I was wrong about that. I think I'm wrong about a lot of things.

"My car got hit, and the other person just drove away. And I think that other person was Diane's kid, who's missing now and I sympathize with him. I do. But my body feels as wrecked as my car. I can't move right and I feel slow and tired.

"I understand that kid. Sometimes you need to run away.

I feel bad because I said that to Diane, but it's true. I'm sorry, Mom. You probably feel different, but I think maybe he's right to leave. Diane cares so much for him. It's not other people that hurt us, but what we feel about them."

Her mother didn't respond. She wasn't even looking at Jackie. Her eyes rested on the ceiling.

"It got me thinking about what you said to me. And I don't. I don't remember my childhood. I don't think I've ever been in this house. I don't know who you are. I don't remember ever being any other age than what I am now, and I don't remember doing anything but what I've been doing. I'm not normal, am I? I mean, I understand that many things in Night Vale aren't what they are in other places, but, even for Night Vale, I don't think I'm normal."

Her mother took the apple from her and put it back in the bowl. She stood.

"Let's step out into the backyard, shall we?"

They did. Her mother put a hand on her arm.

"Jackie, what I want you to understand, about both me and Diane, is this. It's not easy raising a child in Night Vale. Things go strange often. There are literal monsters here. Most towns don't have literal monsters, I think, but we do.

"You were my baby. But babies become children, and they go to elementary schools that indoctrinate them on how to over-throw governments, and they get interested in boys and girls, or they don't, and anyway they change. They go to high schools, where they learn dangerous things. They grow into adults, and become dangerous things.

"But none of that is as difficult as the main thing. We all know it, but most of you don't spend any time thinking about the consequences of it. Time doesn't work in Night Vale.

"You were a child, and then you were a teenager, and then you were old enough that I thought it might be time for you to run my pawnshop for me. Just some days. Just sometimes. I could use the time off, after running it for years while also raising a child on my own.

"I taught you how pawning an item works. 'Pawnshops in Night Vale work like this,' I said. I showed you the hand washing, and the chanting, and the dying for a little while, and how to write out a ticket. I showed you how to bury the doors at night so they wouldn't get stolen. I showed you this and then you started running the shop on your own, and I was so proud.

"But time doesn't work in Night Vale. And so one day I woke up to find you had run that shop for decades. Centuries, even. I'm not sure. You held on to the pawnshop but let go of me. I happened to offer eleven dollars to the first customer we helped together, and in the years of being nineteen you forgot that moment between us and only retained the offer of eleven dollars as a meaningless, unchangeable ritual. People in town couldn't remember a time when you weren't the one running the store. But I could. Because, from my point of view, you've only been running it a couple months. It's all so fresh for me. The course of your life is so linear. But meanwhile you. It had been so long for you that you'd forgotten me, and forgotten the house you moved out of last month. Your entire childhood, gone for everyone but me. All those years spent with me. All those years I gave up everything to spend with you."

Her mother was crying. Jackie suddenly remembered that her mother's name was Lucinda. Lucinda was crying. Jackie was crying too, but wiping it away as quickly as it came, even now uncomfortable with the feeling of it.

"Dear, be kind to the mothers of Night Vale. Have pity on

us. It'll be no easier for Diane. Things go strange here. Your children forget you, and the courses of their lives get frozen. Or they change shapes every day, and they think that just because they look completely different you won't be able to recognize them. But you always will. You always know your child, even when your child doesn't know you.

"Maybe Josh thinks it's right to run away. Maybe you do too. But all I know is Diane is in the same place I am. We don't have our children. We have the faint, distorted echoes of our children that this town sent back to us."

Jackie took Lucinda into her arms, not sure of what she could say but sure that a gesture would say it as well as any stuttered cliché. Her mother cried, but not into Jackie, still turned away from her, and Jackie started to feel as though it was her mother comforting her. Maybe Jackie needed comfort.

Jackie looked up, eyes bleary, to see that Troy was standing there, watching them. His face was not expressionless, but his expression conveyed little. Lucinda did not seem surprised to see him. Her expression also conveyed little. Jackie's expression conveyed anger and confusion, mostly with her eyes and eyebrows. Troy was already gone again.

"Who is that man, Mom? Why is he in your backyard?"

Her mother waved in the direction where Troy had been standing like she was waving off a fly or a small surveillance drone.

"Don't worry about him. Come, let's go inside. That's just your father."

"Troy is my father?"

Jackie perched uneasily in her chair. Lucinda sighed.

"Depends on what you mean by father, dear. He contributed some genetics to you, yes. Never was much good for anything else."

"But Troy was with Diane. He's Josh's father."

"Yes, he went on to her some time after me. He was still so young then. He's a strange one, and I'm not sure that time works for him either."

Jackie leaned forward. Her mother leaned back. There was nothing aggressive or defensive about the movements, but they happened in response to each other.

"Josh is my half-brother."

"I think you'll find, dear, that relationships like that don't come in halves. He's not at all your brother now, but if you wanted I suppose he could be entirely your brother. It would depend on how you related to him."

"And Diane is sort of my stepmom?"

"She is the mother of the person who could be your brother, if you both wanted. It sounds like maybe she's also a friend. But that's it."

Jackie opened her mouth, but Lucinda cut her off.

"Dear, please don't ask me why I didn't tell you this earlier. You always do that. I've told you this so many times, and every time you are stunned and swear you won't forget. But then the memory recedes for you and you don't know me again. You can't remember me making you lunch when you were five, or tying your shoes for you, or helping you through the awkward lessons of puberty, or even where I keep the silverware."

"Where *is* the silverware drawer?"

"I don't have one, dear. You knew that once. I have a silverware trapdoor. It's under one of the hot milk drawers."

"Under the hot milk drawer." Jackie tried to say this as though it were something she was finally remembering, and not something she had just learned.

She thought about Diane and she thought about Josh, and Diane's face when she found out that Josh was missing.

Good for him, she had thought, even as she had sympathized with Diane's pain.

[bottomless chasm of regret and pain], she thought now, thinking back on it. Jackie loved Diane for missing Josh. She loved Diane for living her life in spite of Troy.

She also felt more uneasy about Diane now. Was she a mother, a friend, a sister, a stranger? Jackie didn't know how to proceed with this new knowledge.

Diane experienced time in a normal progression. Her memories were immediate and consistent. Her actions begat reactions and consequences. She could feel the terror of loss or the fear of pain or develop complicated and loving relationships with those around her. Jackie could not. Even things that had happened moments ago would start to fade away into long-ago distance for her.

"I'm sorry," she said, and she took her mom in her arms. She held her tight, as though this would keep their experience of time from diverging. "I'm sorry I don't remember, Mom."

Lucinda smiled.

"You will age someday, dear. We all age. Some of us take longer than others. You are always nineteen now. Someday you will never be nineteen."

Jackie moved over to the couch to sit next to her mom. The couch was spotless. Her mother just really liked things clean.

"I'll remember for as long as I can," she said.

She hugged her mom tight, and, after a moment, her mom reciprocated.

"I'm sorry that it was this way, Mom. Not I'm sorry like an apology. I'm sorry as in sorrow."

"Me too, dear. Me too so very much. Oh, I suppose you should have this."

She opened a drawer in the coffee table and rummaged around. Finally she pulled out an old photo. An extremely old photo, yellowing and cracked, and bending at the edges. In it, there was a man who was definitely Troy. He had his arm around a little girl.

"That's you and your father."

She handed it to Jackie, who made a strangled sound.

"I took that when you were quite little. Before he left both of our lives."

"But, Mom, this photo. This photo had to have been taken at least a hundred years ago. That's City Hall downtown, but there are dirt roads and wood cabins instead of stores, and instead of cars there are horses with huge wings. People haven't flown wild horses in, well, in I literally don't know how long."

"Well, dear, you've been stuck the age you are for so many decades. I took this photo just fourteen or fifteen years ago. It was a regular Polaroid then. Now look at it. It has changed to match your years, and I still remember it as it was. It's very much like you. You should have it."

Jackie put the photo in her pocket. Lucinda smiled weakly.

"It will be different from now on," Jackie said.

She looked earnestly at her mother.

"I promise."

She looked waveringly at her mother.

"It will."

She looked away.

"The effort is what counts, dear. That's certainly what we tell ourselves."

"Mom, I have to go." Jackie grunted through the strain of lifting her injured body from the seat. "I'll see you again soon."

"He's not a bad man, your father. He's just not a very good man either."

Jackie walked to the door. She felt the firm flatness of the photo in her pocket and the sharp crumpled edges of the paper in her cast.

Lucinda sat where she had been left, but soon she would move on to other things. She would clean and read and work on the car in the garage and all the other things she did to fill her days. She had a life of her own, after all.

Steve Carlsberg left a couple of messages saying he wondered if maybe Josh's disappearance had something to do with King City and that Steve had this great idea that Diane should go to King City and that he could drive and to call him back when she could.

No one else had called. Diane tried saying "Secret Police" into the microphone above her fridge, but no one came.

She went to the garage and grabbed Josh's bike. She had never had much money, and, given the loss of her job, she thought it best to not keep getting cabs. Plus, Night Vale cab-drivers couldn't always be relied on to pick you up or drop you off in a timely manner, as they stopped constantly to take improv classes and pottery workshops.

Josh's bike was dusty and the rear tire was nearly flat. He had been anxious to leave the bike behind. It was definitely a kid's bicycle, with a thick frame and smaller wheels and brightly colored decals of scenes from Pieter Brueghel the Elder's *Landscape with the Fall of Icarus*.

She stuck to side streets, riding slowly, with care. The trip took a little under an hour, and Diane was feeling a pulsing pain in her calf by the time she pulled up to the front of the pawnshop. There was a black sedan with tinted windows at the end of the lot—the windows cracked down enough for her to see two sunglassed agents of a vague yet menacing government agency. One of them raised her camera and tried to take a photo of Diane, but the camera flashed, only reflecting the car window back at the lens. The agent swore. Diane waved a cursory hello at them and walked into the store.

Jackie slouched over the counter. She had her eyes closed and was breathing slowly and was inattentive to the living world around her and was deep in a complexity of vivid, nonsequential mental imagery, but she was not asleep.

Diane put her hand on the glass counter.

"Jackie?"

No response.

"Jackie." Diane slapped the counter.

Jackie's eyes opened and focused on the counter. She knew that Diane was there but was too overwhelmed by the new information she had learned to care. It was an issue she was having with the world in general that day.

"Jackie, I need your help."

Diane reached into her bag and pulled out a plastic bag marked "nope!", and took out a piece of paper with "KING CITY" all over it in Josh's handwriting. She placed it on the counter.

Jackie winced. She batted the paper off the counter.

"Jackie I need you to—"

"Why did you bring that here?"

Diane didn't know what to say. There were a lot of reasons, but it sounded like Jackie didn't think any of them would be good reasons.

"This is not an arts and crafts project, Diane. I am living with this. This is real." Jackie shook her cast, and they could both hear the rustle of paper inside. "I only just got out of the hospital."

"I didn't mean—"

"You don't dress like a person and suddenly you're twins.

You don't get the same haircut and suddenly you're best friends. I'm not going to King City, okay? I can barely move. My mind doesn't seem to connect the way it used to. I don't have a car. I can't do my job. If no one would remind me of that goddamn paper I could sit here forever and never think of it or anything else again."

She shook her head.

"I'm sorry. I know this is hard for you. I know this is so painful. You're a mother and you're trying very hard. But I can barely hold it together to just sit here. I can't help you. I can't even help myself."

"I found that in Josh's room." Diane did not raise her voice. She did not flush in anger or frustration. She did not cajole or cater. She said what she knew as she knew it and hoped it would be enough. "I don't know if it's somehow related to Troy, but I know that Josh has gone to King City. I don't know how I know, but I know. He's not in Night Vale anymore. One of the last things Ev . . . um . . ."

"Evan."

"Evan mentioned to me was Josh. He tried to give Josh a paper like yours. I didn't give him the paper, but I think Josh got it. And I think Josh went to King City."

Diane felt at a loss to the depth of her, an exhaustion that was not physical but that slowed her body all the same. Jackie felt the same exhaustion, her body a single, dull ache. They felt this next to each other, neither woman realizing it.

"But everything I do circles me back to King City," said Diane. "Every attempt I make on my own to get there fails. I don't know what else to do. I think if we went together, I think if we worked together, then we could get there. We could make it."

Diane leaned across the counter, meeting Jackie in her slump, so that their faces were very close. They felt each other's breath.

"Jackie," she said. "Jackie."

Jackie heard, but did not indicate it.

"I pawned that tear to you all those weeks ago for a reason. And I don't know what that reason was. Everything I do is for a reason, and I know none of them. Everything makes sense, and the sense is hidden from me. We live in a pattern that we'll never detect, and that will shuffle us through invisible hierarchies to the actual death of us."

She had thought none of these thoughts before, exactly, but it was like a script before her. The sentences were obvious and immediate, and she said them as she came to know them.

"We are together on this. And I don't know why, and I never will, and we just are. Jackie?"

"Yeah, Diane?"

"I'm sorry I do such a bad job of expressing it, but I respect you a lot. There's no one I trust more to help me find my son than you. There's no one, okay?"

Diane felt warm around her eyes.

Jackie shrugged. "I feel bad for you, man, I do. I've learned some things today that I didn't remember before. I wish I could help you. But I hurt all over. I'm slouching onto my bones."

"I can't heal you. You're going to hurt, hurt bad, either way. But I think if you come with me, we can find answers, Jackie. We made it out of the library together. We work well together, for whatever reason. I'm not asking you to . . . I'm just asking . . . I just want us to try."

She drew her hands together in front of her chest like a person in prayer. Jackie considered this woman, the mother of what could one day be her brother. She thought of what Lucinda said about being a mother, slowly losing a child.

"Put your hands down. I don't know why you're doing that, it looks weird. Fine. Yes. I'll come with you."

Diane clapped once and hugged her.

"I'll do my best to help," said Jackie, "but my best might not be anything at all."

She pulled herself gently from Diane's hug and pointed out the window at the bike.

"Neither of us has a car now. So how are we getting there? We gonna take that cute ride of yours, or what?"

Diane frowned.

"No, I don't suppose."

Diane considered several options. The obvious was to rent a car, but she was basically out of money. Diane's only credit card was an American Express Uranium Card, which was a dangerous card to use because it does not allow revolving credit and is made entirely of enriched uranium. Few merchants accept American Express Uranium Cards, or even allow them in their stores, but she did get double mileage points if anyone accepted it and survived.

Diane leaned her head back, exhaling upward, hoping for a solid thump of a thought to fall into her mind. She blinked. She stared up. Nothing.

"Is there anyone whose car we could borrow?" Jackie said.

"Steve would definitely do that. He's always so helpful and nice. But he's not been so reliable these da—" A solid thump of a thought. "What about that?"

On one of the highest shelves, there was a Mercedes, only a few years old, and once offered with urgency by a young man wearing a gray pin-striped suit stained with dirt. The luxury sedan was perfectly balanced across the drive train, resting perpendicularly on the ten-foot wooden shelf.

Jackie smiled, and then winced. It hurt to smile. It hurt not emotionally but physically, due to the trauma to her muscles. She had not smiled since the accident.

"Keys are in the ignition," she said.

"Great," Diane said but didn't do anything because: "How are we going to—"

"I don't know."

"But how did you in the first place?"

"I don't remember."

"So we're stuck again."

"Looks like."

No time passed and nothing happened, but the Mercedes was down from the shelf and out in the parking lot. Around them was an open toolbox, a trail of feathers, and a large quantity of ball bearings. The air smelled like a burnt match.

They took a long moment to absorb this new reality, and then, like good Night Vale citizens, categorized it as unexplainable and set it aside forever.

"Guess we took it down the same way I put it up," said Jackie.

She couldn't remember what way that was.

"Wow," said Diane. "I'm impressed with us. I hope I helped somehow."

"Dude, I'm sure you did."

"That's sweet of you."

"Shall we?"

While Jackie headed upstairs to her desk to pack a couple of personal items, Diane wandered around the store, looking at what had been pawned. She found her tear, and was disappointed that no one had bought it yet, but pleased that Jackie had displayed it so prominently on her shelves. And then she saw something that gave her pause.

Below a series of cute porcelain figurines depicting young

couples committing thought crimes and hiding evidence, there was a trash can. Resting on top of the trash can was a box. It was a simple brown cardboard box. She knew exactly what kind of box it was. It was the box that No. 9 envelopes come in. She was familiar with this kind of box. The only office that used No. 9 envelopes in Night Vale was the one that she had, until recently, worked at.

She crouched down to examine it. There was a long wood handle leaning against the side, belonging to a four-foot garden hoe. The metal edge of the hoe was stained and sticky with clumps of dark brown fur.

She set down the hoe and touched the lid of the box. She grew sad. She did not know why she was sad. She grew scared. She did not know why she was scared.

She lifted the lid and saw. She saw. And she felt. And for a moment she was not. And then she was. She held her hand to her mouth.

When Jackie got to the Mercedes, slow and limping, Diane was already in the passenger seat.

"Let's do this," Jackie said.

Diane's elbow was on the window ledge. She had lost some of her color and was staring out the window at nothing in particular.

Jackie did not know exactly what it must be like to have a son go missing, but it must be exhausting. She knew about exhaustion. She knew about pain.

"You feeling okay?"

"I pawned that tear to you because school was starting and I needed the money," Diane said. "That was the only reason. I made up that other stuff because I thought it might get you to come with me."

"I know."

"Okay then."

Jackie started the car, pressed her feet to both pedals, and backed out with a squeal of vulcanized rubber and a puff of gray smoke. The agent in the black sedan nearby snapped photos of their going, each one ruined by the flash, each ruin followed by a muttering of curses. The women drove away leaving two black curls, like horns, across the crumbling asphalt lot.

Two beings, definitely not angels, both named Erika, stepped out from behind the pawnshop, where they had been hiding. They were drenched in sweat and their hands were covered in black grease.

Jackie guided the Mercedes onto Route 800. It drove so differently from her old car. Her old car had felt like making a plan, whereas this car felt like an improvisation. Or maybe it was that she was driving with one arm.

Diane grinned at her and she grinned back. It was hard to fight the feeling of triumph. Diane clutched hard at the slip of paper that said "KING CITY" in Josh's handwriting. She couldn't let go of it. Or, unlike Jackie, she could, but, unlike Jackie, she wouldn't.

They passed Old Woman Josie's house, next to the used car lot. She was standing in the front yard with all the Erikas, as if she knew they were coming by. The Erikas seemed out of breath. Josie had her hand up but she wasn't waving. She was gesturing, but Jackie couldn't understand what the gesture was. She gave her own meaningless gesture back. A used car salesman stood on the roof of an old Toyota hatchback and howled. Jackie howled back. She hadn't been this happy since before the trouble had begun. The highway was a simple path laid out for her.

Diane turned around, watching Night Vale retreat into the distance.

"Seems small," she said. "I mean, not just from here. It just seems so small now. Such a small place to live a whole life."

"You haven't lived your whole life yet."

"I really hope you're right."

Larry Leroy's, out on the edge of town, was the last house they passed. Larry was nowhere to be seen. His house sagged into itself, an unmaintained heap of wood barely holding the shape of a house. It thought about nothing at all.

Then they were out in the open desert. Jackie tried to think of a time she had been even this far outside of Night Vale. All she could remember were endless days at the pawnshop. For the first time, she felt sad thinking about those days rather than nostalgic. She didn't know what that meant.

"Diane, what does it mean when you know you're feeling something but you don't know what that feeling is?"

Diane considered this seriously for a long time.

"It means you're growing older."

"I never grow older."

"I guess we all thought that once."

The desert went on so far out into the distance that it was easy to imagine that it constituted the entire world. But Jackie knew, even though she didn't quite believe it, that the desert was barely a fraction of the world. It frightened her, the possibility of space. The tininess of home. Her chest felt like a bubble about to pop, and she tried to hold still.

"Is it hard getting old?"

"Only as hard as you let it be. Easier than the alternative."

"Dying?"

"Oh no. No, that's actually easier than anything. I meant getting younger."

Jackie laughed, although she didn't find it funny. There are other reasons for laughter.

They settled in for a long drive. Diane was closing her eyes for a nap before it was her turn to drive when Jackie pointed, swerving the car since her pointing hand was also her steering hand, straightened the car back out, and said to the now wide awake Diane, "Look!"

There was a sign that said KING CITY with an arrow pointing at an exit looping away from the highway out into the sand.

"I guess we take that."

Jackie pulled the car onto the exit. As she did, she felt her stomach start to rise, like she was being carried.

"Do you feel that?"

"Yes. Something's not right."

The exit loop kept turning. She couldn't see how the loop could possibly be that long. The curve just wouldn't end. They went and went. For ten minutes they did a long, slow curve along the exit loop.

"This isn't good," said Jackie.

"Well it's not great."

Jackie started to wonder if she would be turning the car in to the gentle curve for the rest of her life, and just as she started to wonder that, the road straightened them out and spat them out on a highway. They drove past a house sagged into itself, an unmaintained heap of wood barely holding the shape of a house.

"Oh goddammit."

Up ahead was Old Woman Josie's house, and the used car lot. This time Josie was alone. Her arms were crossed. She nodded at them, as if this, and everything else, was exactly as she suspected.

"Turns out working together doesn't make King City any easier to get to," said Jackie.

"I was wrong," said Diane, furiously staring at the paper in her hands. Tears were pouring from her eyes, but she didn't make a sound.

She looked up at Jackie, not making any move to wipe the

tears. Jackie held her gaze for a long moment, letting the car roll down the highway without watching where it was going.

"Okay, we'll find another way," Jackie said.

"There is no other way."

Jackie nodded at the houses and strip mall parking lots they were passing.

"This is Night Vale. Our mayor once led an army of masked warriors from another dimension through magic doors to defeat an army of smiling blood-covered office workers. There is definitely, definitely another way."

They continued into Night Vale, without aim, listening only to the sound of the wind in the windows and the voice of Cecil Palmer from the radio.

THE VOICE OF NIGHT VALE

CECIL: . . . fate worse than death. Most fates are. This has been health news.

Listeners, I'm excited to have here in my studio this afternoon two of my favorite people, Old Woman Josie and Carlos.

Josie, you have been a lifelong resident of Night Vale.

JOSIE: Everyone in Night Vale has been a lifelong resident of Night Vale.

CECIL: Not everyone, Josie. A certain handsome scientist comes to mind, as he often does. But anyway, you headed up the board of the Night Vale Opera for many decades until the puppy infestation in the late 1990s. You claim to know several angels.

JOSIE: They're here in studio with me today. Say hi, Erikas.

ERIKAS: *[off mic, distant]* Hi. Hello. Good to be here.

CECIL: You are all very tall with beautiful wings. I do not believe in angels, of course, no one does or can, but if I did, I bet they would look a lot like you.

We also have here today Carlos, who is a scientist.

CARLOS: Hi, Cecil. It's good to be here.

CECIL: An attractive scientist who is a good cook.

CARLOS: Stop.

CECIL: An attractive scientist who is a good cook who maybe can pick up some toothpaste and paper towels on the way home this evening?

CARLOS: Already done. Also dog food.

CECIL: Scientists are so vital to our community. Now, Josie, you're here today with Carlos because of something to do with flamingos?

JOSIE: Right. Plastic lawn flamingos. Everyone is familiar with these things.

CARLOS: Flamingos, a common desert bird, have six long legs, and are well known because of their bright pink feathers and double beaks and many eyes.

JOSIE: These plastic ones are basic, cheap lawn decorations.

CECIL: Josie, you garden quite a bit. You bought these ornaments for your place?

JOSIE: Yes, we were going through that new place, Lenny's Bargain House of Gardenwares and Machine Parts, trying to find something new for the garden to replace the buried idol dedicated to long-dead gods we had recently taken out. It's fun to collect those idols, but the long-dead gods demand so much worship and sacrifice, and if you don't do it, they start throwing a real fit, causing the idol to float and speak to you and sending terrible visions to your dreams. Blegh. Not worth the bother just to have something decorating your lawn. It was Erika over there who discovered the flamingos.

ERIKA: [off mic, distant] Hey.

JOSIE: They were just too adorable to pass up, and they seemed like they couldn't possibly be as much trouble as those damn idols.

Erika over there—

ERIKA: [off mic, distant] Hey.

JOSIE: Hi, Erika. They took the plastic flamingos from Erika to put them in the grass, and as they lifted their mallet, Erika disappeared from our view. Just vanished. Only to reappear what seemed like a few minutes later standing next to us. Erika said— Erika, tell everyone what you said.

ERIKA: [off mic, distant] I said, "Hey, y'all, what's up?"

CARLOS: Erika had jumped back in time and also in space after touching the flamingos.

JOSIE: Right.

CARLOS: And at other times, Erika jumped forward in time and into a different physical space. Josie called me to run tests and experiments. So we brought all of the flamingos to my lab.

JOSIE: There were more than two dozen of them now. Every time Erika jumped in time, the flamingos duplicated.

CECIL: How did you get them to the lab? Does anything that touches them become affected by their . . . what's the scientific word for it . . . weird magic?

CARLOS: That's not the scientific term for it, but it's cute. So we're examining the time-shifting pink flamingos and—

JOSIE: Oh, to answer your question, Cecil, we had to wrap them in blankets and towels and marley, which is the rubbery material modern dancers perform on. Erika was not pleased that we took up part of their rehearsal studio floor, but science is important.

CARLOS: Right, and we took them to the lab and I hooked the plastic flamingos up to a wall-size computer that was covered in blinking lights and big red, green, and yellow buttons while a single strip of paper filled with numbers came out of a small slot on the front.

CECIL: Science is remarkable. So complex and mysterious. I'm always in awe of what you and your team can do.

CARLOS: Thanks. But it's pretty simple. We just follow the scientific method. No matter how advanced the scientific field gets, the foundation of scientific discovery is the scientific method we all learned in elementary school.

CECIL: I'm not sure I ever learned that.

CARLOS: Oh, it's easy. Here, I'll tell you and your listeners right now. The scientific method is four steps:

1. Find an object you want to know more about.
2. Hook that object up to a machine using wires or tubes.
3. Write things on a clipboard.
4. Read the results that the machine prints.

CECIL: Of course. I totally remember this now.

JOSIE: What Carlos found was that the flamingos were from another place, and obviously another time. They must have been brought here by an outsider.

CARLOS: Their parts are not made of materials indigenous to Night Vale. Plastic does not grow naturally here in the desert, nor do long, thin metal stakes.

JOSIE: The reason we wanted to come on the air with you today was to let others in Night Vale know about the danger these plastic flamingos pose. We've managed to gather a lot of them up, but there could still be more about town.

Before I knew what they were, I had tried giving them away and selling them, but they kept reappearing.

If you see a plastic flamingo, do not touch it. Call Carlos at his lab and he'll come get it.

CARLOS: Yes, I have a storage locker next to my lab where I am safely keeping them all. We are managing to get them all off the streets. Fortunately, we have locked away all of the ones we could find in my lab storage so that they can no longer threaten Night Vale. We're pretty certain we've found them all, but just in case you find any, do not touch them. I repeat, do no−

"Let's touch them."

"What?" Diane was enjoying listening to Cecil. She loved the end of his show, where he said, "Good night, Night Vale, good night." No matter how difficult her life was or how troublesome the news he was reporting, his voice and his sign-off put her at such ease.

"The flamingos."

"Touch them?"

"They jump people into different times and spaces. Maybe that's the thing we need to get out of Night Vale and into King City."

"Maybe." Diane, sounding off mic, distant.

"We've got to try something."

"Sure. I thought working together was the key too, but it didn't work at all."

"If we didn't work together, we wouldn't have this car. We wouldn't be listening to the radio."

Diane sat up. "The tear. When I sold you my tear. On the shelf behind you. There was bundle of plastic flamingos. I remember this now. I remember thinking about the color of those beautiful birds with their double beaks and six stringy legs. About how Josh loves flamingos. Jackie, they're in your shop."

Jackie was quiet.

"They're not? Who'd you sell them to?"

"No one." Jackie had pulled the car to a stop in the parking lot of Patty's Hardware and Discount Pastries, just a few blocks from the barista district of Night Vale. "When I came back to the shop after the hospital, they were just gone. A lot of things were gone actually. Maybe stuff was stolen, but that seems impossible, because I make sure to remove and hide my doors anytime I'm not there."

"Then I don't know where we can get a flamingo. Carlos said he's got them all."

"Can you hang on, Diane? I need to run into this store and get something."

"Sure. Oh, if you're going into Patty's, can you get me a croissant?"

"Got it." Jackie shut the door.

Diane considered the ways they could get a plastic flamingo. Driving around town looking would take all day, especially if Carlos and his team of scientists and Josie and her team of angels or whatever they were had already done a lot of searching.

The radio station was not too far from here. They could head over there and see if Carlos would let them have one of the flamingos. This would be a tough ask, but considering how much Cecil cared for Diane and for her search for Josh, she might have the ally she needed to convince the handsome scientist to hand over a bird or two.

No, she realized, that wouldn't work. He's a scientist. Above all things, scientists are protectors of our world. "Scientist is another word for hero," Mayor Cardinal was fond of saying. They use science to not only learn things but also to change those things so that everything is better going forward. Just like the scientist who cured polio, or that couple who invented radiation, or the astrologers who write our futures for us.

A good scientist would never compromise societal good for one person's needs.

Jackie opened the door to the car.

"Here's your croissant." She handed Diane a cup full of melted butter, yeast, salt, and cold water as well as a spoon and napkin. After wheat and wheat by-products became illegal in Night Vale, Patty continued to make her pastries using the same ingredients and techniques, minus the flour.

"Thanks," Diane said, desperate for a snack. "Hey, Jackie, listen. I've been thinking about how to get a flamingo. It's a long shot but . . . What's that?"

Across Jackie's lap was a metal crowbar, solid black save for a small yellow price sticker.

"We're going to go to the lab to get some flamingos. If Carlos is on the radio, who's going to stop us?"

Diane bit her lip. She stared at the crowbar.

"I've never thought of myself as a person who steals things."

"Well, what's your plan?"

"Never mind. It wouldn't have worked. Let's steal them."

They drove to the science district and pulled up to Carlos's lab. Diane was on lookout while Jackie tried to crack the combo lock with her crowbar, which was not as easy as it looks in Lee Marvin films.

Loud metal thwack after loud metal thwack made Diane nervous. Surely someone would come to see what the noise was. Or worse, someone would summon the Secret Police using the poorly hidden microphone in their house. They would surely be arrested, or maybe even vanished.

Jackie had not made any progress when a woman with long, wild hair and long, wild nails and long, wild eyes touched her shoulder. Jackie pivoted around and raised the iron bar in an automatic defensive response. The woman did not flinch.

"The world ended over thirty years ago," the woman said.

"Did it?" Jackie said. She kept the crowbar up.

"I live inside the Community College. I should know."

"Are you a scientist?" Diane asked, moving between the woman and Jackie, waving for her to lower the crowbar. Jackie did not.

"1983," the woman said.

"Is 1983 when the world ended?" Diane said, in the way a mother might ask a child if a picture of a train is a train.

"No! Are you crazy?" the woman said. "Well, maybe. Hard to say exactly what date."

"What's 1983 then?" Jackie said, finally lowering the crowbar because her arm didn't have any more strength to keep it up.

"Combo to that lock you're trying to smash."

"Who's trying to smash a lock? I was just checking how strong it was," Jackie said while smashing the lock once more.

"The good-looking guy keeps snacks in there sometimes. Mostly crap though. You want the tasty stuff, go to the biomed neighborhood. They almost always have beef jerky."

"Thanks," Diane said. "We will."

Jackie shrugged and tried the code. The door opened with an electronic whir. The woman pushed past them and rummaged through the fridge while they grabbed a couple of the linen-wrapped plastic flamingos.

They locked the lab back up, hopped into the Mercedes, and drove.

Diane drove to give Jackie a rest after the exertion of failing to break the lock. Soon they were back on Route 800, heading the same direction as before.

They passed Old Woman Josie's house, next to the used car lot. No one was in the front yard. The used car salesman still stood on the roof of the old Toyota, howling. Diane did not howl back, but she felt hopeful, once again. Every time she was hopeful.

"Jackie."

"Mm."

"Thank you for keeping me company in my nightmare."

Jackie grinned at her.

"Nah, it's our nightmare now."

Diane smiled a little, meant it a lot. Jackie took the flamingos from their wrapping and laid them across the center armrest, and they both put a hand on them. For a moment they both separately thought about holding the other's hand, and both separately decided not to.

Jackie could not remember the highway exactly, but she knew she was in a car, and that car must have come from somewhere. She cast a rearward glance. Empty fields and low hills and the 101 freeway, a distant, growling ribbon with no obvious way to get from there to here.

"How did we get here?" she asked.

"What do you mean?"

"Did we take a highway?"

"We took the highway. We used these." Diane indicated the flamingos under their hands. Somewhere during the journey they had grasped each other's hands after all.

A sign by the road said, KING CITY WELCOMES YOU across a drawing of two dolphins leaping in fat, blue arcs over a faded sketch of a factory. The wooden sign had grown pale with water damage and disrepair, so the factory building looked hidden in its own smog.

Below the factory was a banner that read MAYOR E . . . But the remaining letters had long ago lost their legibility. There was a very large crow standing just below the sign in the red desert dirt, but, as they drove slowly past, Jackie realized it wasn't a large crow at all, but a very strange dog.

The dog (or perhaps it *was* a crow; it was tough to tell) stared at Jackie as they rolled by, mouth agape, displaying small, sharp teeth and a thin, red tongue.

"Guess it worked," Diane said, smiling, but not feeling any joy.

"Yes," Jackie said, cringing, but not feeling any fear.

There were few cars on the road as they entered what seemed to be the business district. The cars that were there were taupe, long, flat-hooded with short windshields, and they moved slowly, well below speed limits. No pedestrians were on the streets.

The dusk brought a sandy mist to the hot air, turning the sky ocher. There was a dull roar from above, as if a seashell had been placed directly atop the town.

Diane drove past the post office, which was a one-story stucco building with no front door, a splintered parapet wall with letters missing from its marquee, and a tree that had grown through the broken sidewalk and into one of the many shattered windows lining its front. There was no sign of movement inside.

The hum of the sky did not let up. It sounded like a low-flying jet in a never-ending holding pattern. Diane began to hear whispers in the noise, the way one sees patterns in clouds. The whispers were not words but had the rhythm of language, the tone was needy and desperate, but no matter how much she concentrated she couldn't understand any of it. The whispers sounded like her own voice.

Diane felt both here and elsewhere. Like she was in the car with Jackie, but also entering addresses into a spreadsheet at work. She was sitting at her desk, clicking keyboard keys, with headphones in listening to soft rock. Diane felt two of herself. She had never looked at herself before, not like this. She did not recognize herself, but she understood who she was. Diane looked at her hand on the flamingos and felt her hand on her work desk.

Jackie's good arm was out the window, the sandy air tickling her skin with hundreds of inconsequential stings, a tangible Morse code saying something meaningless. Jackie could almost hear the staccato pings of grains, the sound traveling through her skin into her body, bypassing her ears. She closed her eyes, partially to force rest on herself, partially to block out the deep amber of King City's early evening.

Neither told the other what she felt.

Diane noticed a store with a charcoal canvas eave with bold silver sans-serif font reading VHS AND VHS AND VHS . . . She parked the car in front of the store. Neither of them knew exactly where to begin, but if Josh were here out of his own free will, he would certainly find his way to a store like this. He had the teenage attraction to petty bravery, like doing skateboard tricks and watching unmarked VHS tapes.

Jackie stuck a quarter in the parking meter, which was bent in the middle, like it was bowing. There was a hollow clink followed by a hiss. The meter hissed continuously. She circled it, trying to find the source of the noise, and realized it wasn't coming from the meter but from a few feet to her right.

The hiss was coming from the very large crow, or the very strange dog. It had four legs, but stood on only one. It had sharp teeth and a sharp face.

The dog's mouth (Jackie was going with very strange dog) was open, and it was hissing. It didn't seem to need to stop for breath. She took a step backward, and its three unused legs unfurled from its thick barrel body. The legs dragged its body toward her, and then curled back into itself like landing gear. The hiss continued.

Jackie yelped and limped around the back of the Mercedes, grabbing Diane with her good hand. They crossed to the VHS store, Jackie turning to see the dog following them, disappearing and appearing like a figure in a badly constructed flip-book, a little closer each time she looked at it, still hissing, still staring.

Diane was alarmed by Jackie's alarm as she was firmly pushed into the shop. The store was dark. It was unlocked and the lights were on, but the lights were dim and inconsistently placed, leaving pockets of deep shadow throughout.

There was no clerk's counter at the front of the store. Only tall shelves full of loose tapes, some labeled and some not. Some shelves were densely packed to the point where tapes lay horizontally across the tops of the vertically pressed rows. Others were nearly empty save a couple of loose tapes scattered on their sides.

They walked down the best-lit aisle toward the back of the store. After several feet, the light grew dimmer, and their aisle grew dark. There were no side aisles to turn down, so they kept walking. Jackie, a teenager herself, couldn't help but run her hand over the tapes on the shelves. Most had stickers with handwritten titles. She did not stop to browse the selection, but she was certain that some simply had rows of Xs instead of titles or descriptions.

The dog, or whatever it was, was not visible through the shop window, but Jackie could still hear the hissing coming from somewhere. She hurried them down the aisle. It was too dark at this point to see the dead end until they were right up on it. Diane extended her hand just before running into the shelf. She expected her hand to hit a wall of tapes but instead felt something damp and soft and cold. It gave way slightly to her touch. Her jaw tightened and she pulled her hand away. It was wet, and in the low light she could see her fingers were covered in what looked like soil.

As they headed back to where they had entered, there was the hissing again in front of them, source unseen in the distant light or, worse, unseen in the nearby dark. Diane walked behind Jackie, Jackie's hand on her own shoulder, fingers intertwined with Diane's. As they walked faster, the hissing grew louder. Ahead was a deep shadow in the aisle. Neither could see anything beyond it.

Jackie's left arm pulsed. Her body hurt badly. Her legs wobbled, and her eyes felt tender and loose in her skull.

"Diane," Jackie whispered. The hissing was only a few feet in front of them. She heard the soft click of claws on the floor. "Diane. Grab those tapes."

"What?" Diane was alarmed by Jackie's alarm. Jackie was grabbing tapes off the shelf near her waist, and so Diane did the same.

The sides of the tapes were all marked with strings of Xs or Js or Ps or Us. As she pitched them to the floor, she felt the same cold dampness as before. The tapes came apart in their hands, falling away into soft clumps of wet soil. A long beetle crawled out of one and tentatively made its way across the pile they were forming.

There was another soft click on the wood floor as they tore away enough tapes to reveal an open passage to another aisle. Bright light poured through. The hissing stopped.

In the dark quiet of the store, Diane felt the wet tapes pool around her ankles. Jackie felt her atoms letting go of one another. They both watched the shadow where the hiss had been.

"Jackie." Diane's eyes filled but did not flood. She placed her hand on Jackie's back.

They stood, hand to back, teeth together, feet apart, faces parallel to an unknown unseen. They waited for an attack. A tear came loose and trailed down Diane's cheek. They waited.

A scream came from the shadow ahead of them, a scream like that of a terrified child.

Jackie crouched and dove through the hole in the shelves. Diane stayed, staring, streaks down her face as her mouth loosed itself open, silent, lip-synching the scream she was hearing. Her ears hurt. The scream burrowed into her head, splitting her brain, crawling down her throat, and coming to rest deep in her guts.

She felt a soft touch. Something was tapping lightly at her hand. It was wrapping around her little finger. She could not look. She wanted to follow Jackie, but she could not move. She was trying to scream, but could not find space for it in the continuing, sobbing scream from the shadow around her. The thing grabbed her hand tightly and pulled.

"Diane! Diane, please!"

Jackie, reaching through the hole in the shelf, was pulling on her hand. The moment broken, Diane crouched and crawled through the hole. The other side was bright, fluorescent lights and well-organized, clean shelves. She grabbed a stack of the tapes and used them to fill the hole they had come through. Jackie helped, and soon the hole was completely gone. The scream was muffled, but it continued.

They sat up, leaning against the opposite shelf. The scream stopped. There was no scream. No hiss. Jackie thought she still heard the quiet click of claws on the wood floor, but she couldn't say for sure.

They exhaled, and then again, over and over until they were exhaling together, Jackie's arm around Diane's shoulder.

"I'm sorry," Diane said after however long, seconds or minutes, they had sat there breathing. "I'm sorry I froze. I'm sorry I brought you here when this is my problem."

"No, man. I'm sorry I'm broken. I'm sorry I'm weighing you down."

"Jackie, I know what that was."

"Seriously?"

"When I was a child, I would, like all children, cry because childhood is traumatic and confusing. And when crying wasn't enough? When I felt that despair children feel because they don't understand and won't be able to for years? Well, then I would scream. I would scream as loud and long as I could. That scream from the shadows was my voice. That was me screaming."

"Diane, shh." Jackie's head rolled onto Diane's shoulder. "Shh. Let's just rest for a while."

Jackie didn't sleep, but she closed her eyes and wheezed through the pain. Diane looked at the way Jackie's legs curled outward from the knee across the dusty floor, the way her right arm lolled loosely over her torso.

Diane felt herself standing in her kitchen at home, heating soup on the stove, listening to the radio. She could smell the vegetable broth. She could hear Cecil's voice. She could feel the steam on her face. She could see herself. This was not a memory but a moment happening now. Lying with Jackie on the floor of a King City video store, she felt herself splitting, becoming multiple, and, in doing so, becoming less with each iteration.

She stood up. Jackie had rested enough. Diane helped her, groaning, to her feet.

"Hello," Diane tried calling to someone, anyone, in the store who could help.

"Hello," came a voice past the shelves.

"Hi, how do I find you?"

"What are you looking for?"

"You."

"What do you need me for?"

"We're looking for someone. We're new to town and we just wanted to see if you can help us. We just have a couple of questions."

"So ask them."

Diane decided not to walk any farther, not wanting to get lost in the aisles again.

"Do you have a Secret Police? We're looking for a missing child."

"I'm sorry to hear that. The Secret Police sounds secret. I wouldn't know about that. We have nonsecret police."

"We're looking for a police station. Also the City Hall. Maybe the mayor's office. I mean, if you just had some phone numbers that would be helpful." Diane was half shouting. She had no sense how far away the voice was, or from which direction it was coming.

"Well, City Hall is where the mayor's office is. It's four and a half blocks down Pleasant Street here. That's the street you're on now. Of course, we haven't had a mayor in years. Gonna be an election soon, I hear. Don't know why, but we haven't had a mayor, for, oh, I don't know how long."

"Where are you?"

"If you got a missing child, I'd try the police first. I think there's gotta be one nearby. I mean, I don't know for sure. I've never been arrested, you know?" The voice laughed the insipid laugh of casual conversation.

"Okay. We'll try that. My son's name is Josh. He's the one who's gone missing. We're not from here. We're from a town called Night Vale, but I think Josh may have come to King City. And if he's here, he certainly loves VHS stores. Also comic book stores. Have you seen any fifteen-year-old boys here? He probably would have been shopping by himself?"

No reply.

"Or maybe a comic store nearby. He definitely would have gone there."

The shop was silent.

"Hello?"

She looked at Jackie.

"It was real, don't worry," Jackie said. "I heard it too."

Some of the shelves just had empty cardboard VHS sleeves, no sign of their corresponding tapes. There were puddles on the floor and cobwebs along the top shelves. The more Jackie looked around, the more she thought they should leave, as soon as possible. Diane did not believe Jackie to be frightened, just impatient to go. They hobbled together to the front door with no hissing, no screams.

As they stepped outside into the sandy dusk, the bell on the door jingled faintly in Jackie's mind like a favorite song to which she could no longer quite remember the tune.

There was no police station in sight. Diane and Jackie leaned into each other. They walked as one, their arms intertwined so it wasn't clear who was holding up whom. They entered one of the few other stores that appeared open: FISH AND BAIT. The shelves were full of empty jars. A man stood behind the counter. He was towering, the tallest man either of them had ever seen.

"Hello," managed Diane. Her head seemed to be several feet behind her, and her hands floated in front of her like balloons. "We're looking for a boy, a teenager. He looks like . . . well, a lot of things. He's—"

The man nodded absently, saying nothing. Jackie's entire body felt liquid and heavy, sloughing off her fragile skeleton. She had never been in more pain. Each step was a decision that she had to make, every time.

"Feel free to look around," the tall man said. He gestured with an open palm. Behind him one of the empty jars exploded with a pop. A few shards of it went into the back of his hand. It began immediately to drip blood. His face did not change at all.

"We're looking for a boy. My son." Diane couldn't stop looking at his fresh wounds.

The man frowned. He looked closely at them, as though they were not who he had thought they would be.

"Who did you say you were?" he said. Another jar exploded. This time some of the glass went into his face. Blood went down his cheek like tears, dripping with loud taps onto the counter. He frowned at the sound.

"We're just looking," said Jackie, pulling with all of her strength, which was not so much at all, on Diane, who was frozen staring into the man's eyes. The man was staring at Jackie. "Nice shop you have here. Have to go."

The two women hobbled out. Two more jars exploded. The man had quite a lot of blood coming from all different parts of him. He looked down at their leaving from the height of his body.

"We try to remember but we always forget," he said.

Diane turned, hand on the glass door.

"What was that?"

"Have a nice day and thanks for shopping with us," he said.

His words were coming out slurred. There was a long shard of glass through his tongue.

The two of them pushed their way back outside, nearly falling over one another.

"This is all wrong," said Diane. "This is not a safe place for Josh to be."

"It's not like we haven't been in stores where clerks bleed a lot," said Jackie, "but—" She trailed off, her gaze focused on no fixed point.

Most any bath gel or greeting card store in Night Vale has a full staff of bleeding salesclerks, struggling to maintain consciousness and constantly mopping the floors. But somehow in King City, it felt incorrect, like the people were not supposed to be bleeding constantly. Like they had once been normal, whatever that meant outside of the only context she had ever known.

In her mind, Diane saw a different man than the one covered in glass shards, or it was the same man, but he was running a store in which he did not bleed, in which nothing exploded, in which he sold supplies for fishing and at night went home to his family, watched old television shows, one episode right after the other, and then slept, one episode right after the other. She saw that man and this man at the same time. He was multiple, and becoming less with each iteration.

"We can't hear the freeway," said Jackie.

"What?"

Jackie pointed at the 101, so close they could see the writing on the big trucks carrying things from the north of California to the south.

"There's no sound."

She was right. It was completely silent. Even their footsteps seemed to be absorbed by the sidewalk. The loud hum from the sky was gone. They walked in silence past planters teeming with drought-resistant succulents blooming big purple flowers.

Diane felt herself carrying clothes from her dryer, organizing the warm cotton piles into manageable squares on her bed. She felt a King City street full of cars and shoppers, ordinary stores run ordinarily. She felt these things, and at the same time she felt Jackie against her, felt the empty horror of the silent city.

The next store had a sign saying GUITARS. An elderly woman sat in a folding chair at the back. The store was otherwise empty. No furniture, no merchandise, just walls that had been sloppily painted into streaks of different off-whites, and a hideous green carpet traversed by a pink, jagged line and speckled with yellow diamonds. The carpet was torn and fixed with silver duct tape here and there, the tape bright under bare fluorescents.

The woman looked up from what she was doing, which was staring at her hands. She now stared at Diane and Jackie.

"We're looking for a boy about fifteen."

The woman squinted.

"We're looking for a boy who might have come here. He was—"

The woman opened her mouth and stuck out her tongue. Her tongue and gums were gray. Her eyes were squeezed shut, and her mouth was as wide as she could make it. She started making a wet, huffing noise, like a drowned engine trying to start.

"Okay," said Jackie. "We're going to leave now. Thank you."

Jackie turned Diane around and leaned on her to get her to leave the store. Diane's eyes never left the clerk. She saw a wall full of acoustic guitars, a middle-aged woman behind a counter selling a set of strings to a customer. She saw blank walls and, as the door swung shut, an old woman, eyes squeezed shut, huffing and wheezing with that wide gray mouth. She saw both, equally real before her.

"What now?" said Jackie, wincing into the words as she leaned against the hot stucco of the guitar shop wall. Her ability to hide her pain was faltering.

"One more store. Then City Hall," said Diane. Her ability to hide her despair was faltering.

"I'm worried we won't make it out of the next store if we go in it."

"That's a worry, yes. Yes it is."

The next store said CELLULAR in red letters. Inside were display cases full of the newest models of cell phones. There were signs explaining about contracts and data plans. A young woman in a baseball cap and gray polo smiled at them as they walked in.

"Hello!" she said.

"This isn't what I expected," said Diane.

"Oh, did you read our sign?" said the woman. "We're a cell phone store."

"We read it," said Jackie.

"We also do repair. Do you need a phone repaired?"

"No," said Diane. "I'm sorry. We've come a long way in a very short amount of time."

"Dude, what's up with your town?"

"King City?" said the woman. Concern passed briefly through her expression, and then it was bright again. "It's a great place."

"Great . . . how?"

"Not sure," said the woman. "Not a lot sticks in my memory. First thing I remember is you guys coming in. Do you want a cell phone?"

"No," said Jackie.

"We're looking for my son. He's about fifteen years old," Diane said.

One of the phones in the case started ringing. Concern returned to the woman's face, and stayed.

"Those don't even have circuits in them," she said. There were sweat rings on her shirt. "They're cardboard boxes with stickers to simulate the display. All the real phones are in the back."

"Do you mind if we try answering it?" said Diane.

"Just don't tell me what you hear, okay?" She no longer looked at all happy to see them. She pulled a key from a green rubber belt loop and used it to unlock the case.

The phone that was ringing was an older touch-screen model. Diane picked it up. Definitely empty cardboard, and the display was a faded sticker. She pushed on the sticker where she would push to answer a cell phone, and then held the cardboard phone to her ear.

"Hello?"

"Stop being so obvious about yourselves," said a man's voice, one that she was familiar with although she could not place it.

"Obvious about ourselves?"

"Everyone knows you're here. It's not safe." Diane pulled the cardboard phone away from her ear. Printed on the fake phone's fake cardboard screen was a familiar-looking name.

"Evan?"

"No, it's Evan."

"That's what I said. Evan."

"Meet me at City Hall. Head straight back. Ignore what anyone tells you and ignore any signs. Just go down the hall from the front door and turn left when you see a door marked MAYOR. I'll be waiting for you there."

There was a click. She guessed he had hung up, but she didn't know how he had called a cardboard phone in the first place.

"Evan," she said to Jackie. "He asked us to meet him in the mayor's office at City Hall."

"Please. I don't want to know what any of that was about," said the woman. Her face was a grimace and her shivering arms were crossed over her chest. "Please just leave."

"What is this town, really?" Jackie said tenderly, hoping to coax a memory out of her.

The woman relaxed and exhaled. Jackie felt a breakthrough, a confession or revelation coming, but there was only another, weaker "Please leave." The woman's face tightened back into sweat-drenched angst.

"I'm sorry," said Diane. "Can you just tell me which direction down Pleasant Street to get to City Hall?"

The woman grunted and ran through a door marked EM-PLOYEES ONLY, slamming and locking it behind her. Her voice came muffled through the closed door: "We don't even have a mayor. We haven't had one in years."

"So. City Hall?" Jackie said, once they were outside.

"That's where he is, I guess," said Diane. She shielded her eyes and looked down Pleasant Street. "Let's just start walking this way and see if we can find it."

"It shouldn't be hard to find. City halls are always huge and ornate and topped with ancient volcanic stone towers. Or, I mean, the only city hall we've ever seen is like that."

There was nothing that looked remotely like that. There was a Safeway that was boarded up. CLOSED FOR RENOVATIONS, said a sign hung crookedly on the boards, and then someone had crossed out RENOVATIONS with a paint pen and written in GOOD.

There was only one building left. It was low and small, with curtained windows, like a storefront church or a campaign office.

"I don't suppose that could be City Hall," said Diane. She started to move to it.

Jackie was looking the other way.

"Troy," she said.

"What?"

Troy was casually trotting across the road, and then he was gone down a side street.

"You go meet the man in the tan jacket. I'm going to find out what Troy's doing here."

Jackie took off after him, running as hard as her pain-racked body would let her, which wasn't fast, but it was going, all right, and in the right direction, dammit. Shock waves of agony exploded up her legs as she ran.

"Wait, Jackie," Diane called. "We shouldn't get separated. This place is wrong. I don't know if we'll be able to find each other again. Jackie!"

But Jackie was gone. Diane started after her but stopped, thinking of Josh. Josh was what mattered. Jackie could take care of herself. She needed to find Josh. She sighed and walked across the street to the building. It was brick, with a mirrored front window, and a small plastic card that said CITY HALL on the door.

"Okay," Diane said, as loudly as she could. "Here we go."

She pushed open the door. Somewhere else, at that same moment, she was petting a kitten in a shelter pen. The kitten purred and rolled on its back. "I have to take this one," she said. Somewhere else she was repainting an old dresser. Somewhere else, she was standing in a fish market, overpowered by the smell. Somewhere else, at that same moment, she was dead. She did not feel anything at all from that version of herself. It was just a gap in her consciousness, a nothing superimposed on her multiplying selves. The door of City Hall shut behind her.

Inside City Hall there were stacks of files and papers around a groaning titan of a copier, the machine constantly churning out paper, collating it, and then pushing it aside onto the floor as more came. A woman in a dress with a dizzying pattern of blue roses repeating against a white background sat at a desk next to the copier. As Diane pushed open the door, the gust from outside caused the sign-in sheet in front of the woman to flutter into her face. She did not seem to notice.

Behind the woman's desk was an enormous oil painting of a man in a tan jacket. His face was clear. It was more or less symmetrical. He was not quite smiling, but not quite frowning either. Was that not quite a smile? She could remember everything about the painting when she looked away from it. She looked back and then looked away again. Her memory retained all of it.

"Can I help you?" said the woman, without looking up. She was typing away at her computer, which did not appear to be on. She was crying, silently and profusely.

"I don't think so," said Diane, feeling herself here and elsewhere. Without Jackie the feeling of becoming more people and less of a person was worse. Without Jackie she had no one to lean against, to touch, to reinforce with physical contact that she, the Diane in King City, the Diane looking for Josh, was the only Diane that mattered.

Another version of herself was eating shredded wheat at the

counter of an unfamiliar kitchen, trying to decide what to do about some information she had just received by phone. Another version of herself was driving and had to swerve. She had only seconds to swerve. Her heart pounded and she wondered if she would swerve in time, and if she would be able to regain control after she had. The version of herself that was dead was still dead and had been for a long time, a blank spot sitting in the way of her other thoughts.

"All right," said the City Hall receptionist. Tears poured down her face. Her body shook.

"Are you okay?" Diane asked.

The woman looked up. Her eyes were red and hollowed out by the sheer quantity of salt water passing through them.

"No. I don't think I am."

She looked back down and continued to type on her switched-off computer.

"What's wrong?" Diane wanted to help, but the woman did not respond.

A man who looked identical to the large oil painting above her stuck his head from around the corner down the hall.

"What did I say about trying to interact with anyone else?" He sounded tired and annoyed. "Get down here."

His head disappeared, and Diane couldn't remember what he had looked like. She could remember the painting, though, and grafted the painting's features on that blank in her mind.

"I have to go," Diane said to the woman at the desk.

The woman didn't seem to hear or see Diane anymore. She typed away on her useless keyboard.

Diane went down the hall. The building was bigger on the inside. There were many doors, some marked with abstruse letter and number combinations. Most were unmarked. She could hear no one else in the building besides the weeping woman and the man down the hall. Nothing except the roar of the copier, an avalanche of paper tumbling from its maw. Had it been the copier they had been hearing since coming to King City? That distant, ceaseless roar? She dismissed the thought.

The hallway continued in seemingly unending bends. Left turn after left turn. Strangely labeled door after unlabeled door. Then a door marked MAYOR.

"Come in, come in," he said from his desk. His office was piled high with more paper. There were several corkboards with papers thumbtacked to them, and a whiteboard covered in frantic, illegible writing. Some of the writing was circled with arrows pointing to other parts of the writing. A window was open onto a back alley, and there was a garbage can just outside. The room smelled rich and earthy, like decay just turning to loam.

His deerskin suitcase was open on the desk beside him, between the piles of papers. Hundreds of large black flies were inside it, crawling over each other in heaving, buzzing piles. Flies were leaving the suitcase and flying out the window to the garbage can, and other flies were returning through the window. Diane felt dizzy, frightened that her fear would overtake her body, even more frightened that the flies would. Somewhere another version of herself was sitting at her bedroom window in the morning, looking out at a tree she liked, and this kept her together.

"Sit down," said the man, continuing to tell her what she should do next like it was the most natural thing to him.

"No, I'll stand I think," she said. The man rolled his eyes. The flies buzzed louder.

"Suit yourself." He swept a pile of papers off his desk and replaced it with another pile of papers from the floor.

"Where's Josh?"

"We have much to talk about."

"No we don't. Where's Josh? I'm taking Josh and I'm going home."

"I'm sorry, Diane, but you're not going to do that."

He folded his hands in front of him. A fly landed on his shoulder and also folded its appendages in front of it.

"Anyway, I don't know where Josh is precisely," he said. "Around, I suppose. The important thing is that he's in King City. And he'll stay in King City. For now, at least. Until everything is right again he'll have to stay here. I've worked for a long time to get him here."

Some other version of Diane was running, although this Diane wasn't sure whether it was for exercise or to flee. She didn't have access to the other Diane's emotions, only her speed. She had trouble focusing with so many versions of herself in her head.

"Where is Josh?" she said, and moved at the man with her hand up. She wanted to destroy him. She had never wanted to destroy anything before. He sprang out of his chair, face red. The flies formed a furious, pulsing black cloud between her and him.

"Attacking me won't help," he shouted, and the flies echoed his words with their buzzing. "Now sit down, Diane Crayton."

She did not sit down, but she didn't move forward either. This wasn't because of what he said but because the large black cloud of flies made her anxious. The other Diane in her head had stopped running, although she didn't know whether this was because the exercise was over or because she had been caught.

"Josh is completely safe," he said, sitting back down. The

cloud of flies lowered with him, still staying between him and Diane. "But this town needs him."

"You're the mayor of this town, if you can call it a town. Why can't you work out the problems on your own? Why would you need a fifteen-year-old boy from some other place to do your work for you?"

"This town doesn't know that I'm mayor. Ever since the problems started, no one can remember me." He reset himself to a milder tone, a gentler posture. "I was mayor when that man came to town, and ever since then the people of King City will regularly decide they need to elect a mayor because they don't have one. They will go through all the motions of that: setting up the polling places, arranging candidates, talking to each other about who would be right for the job or mostly not paying attention and not talking about it. And then on the day of the election, someone involved will look at the paperwork and realize they already have a mayor. Confused and frustrated, they'll take everything down, cancel the whole election, and go home unsatisfied. Then, a few months later, they'll start again, having forgotten completely that I exist."

He gestured to the cloud of flies in front of him, and they settled back down as a squirming ball in the open suitcase.

"It's been so long since anyone could remember me at all. To be remembered is, I think, a basic human right. Not one that occurs to a person when it is there, but like a parched throat in a desert when it is gone."

Diane didn't care about the man's problems. But there was one part of what he had said that interested her.

"Who do you mean by 'that man'?"

Jackie followed Troy to a bar. She knew what it was because it had a large sign saying BAR outside. It was in a wooden building that it shared with an insurance agency. The building itself looked old and worn but also like it might have been built recently to look old and worn.

Troy went inside, and Jackie followed after.

She couldn't see him. The long bar was full even though the working day wasn't quite over. All men, of course. She rolled her eyes. All the booths were full too, all men, all hunched over.

There was the gurgle of a tap. The bartender, whom she couldn't see over the line of men at the bar, was pouring a beer. Maybe for a newcomer to the bar, one who had just walked in. She headed in that direction.

Her eyes were still grappling with the change from glaring sunlight to dim bar, and so she could not see what was happening when shouting started from the back of the bar.

"You son of a bitch."

"Say it again."

There was the thump of a person falling over. The men at the bar were turning with interest, and she noticed something odd about them, but it was lost as the fight in the back became more violent.

"I'll say it as many times as I want."

A few punches. A clatter of people running into chairs. More punches. The men were starting to get up and run to the back.

"If you break anything that belongs to the establishment, you will pay," shouted the bartender. "Cash or jail time, means the same to me."

But he too started to run to the back.

"Gentlemen, please," he said.

He was blond.

Blond. That was what she had noticed. All the men in the bar were blond. Her eyes started to focus in on dim shapes. She followed the last of the running men to a small open area with a pool table and jukebox in the back.

There were two men on the floor, wrestling and flailing. Their faces were red. Both of them were Troy.

"Gentlemen, take this outside at once," said the bartender.

"Ah, let them fight," said one of the bystanders. "What else do we all have to do out here?"

She recognized both voices. The bartender was Troy. So was the bystander.

Her vision fully adjusted. She was surrounded by an enormous circle of Troys, watching the two Troys fight in the middle. Every person in the bar was Troy.

The crowd around her swayed in empathetic motion with the fighting men. She was jostled in the wave of Troys. As she tried to squeeze herself from the crowd, the group of alike men next to her lurched left and knocked her to the floor.

They were laughing and cheering and attempted but failed to step gingerly around her tender legs.

She grunted and cursed. One of the men made a barely attentive hand gesture toward her, but otherwise they ignored her, so, with great pain and exasperation, she lifted herself to her feet and edged her way behind the moving mass of men back to the exit.

She sagged against the wooden facade of the building. She wished she had Diane again. The pain in her left arm was making it hard to think or move. She worried that pain meds would cloud her mind, and so she paced herself with them. Anyway, the pain meds the hospital had given her were just a bag of wood chips, and so she doubted their effectiveness.

A blond man with a future shiner across his right eye staggered out of the bar. He stopped near Jackie and looked down the street, cursing under his breath.

"Hey," Jackie said, pushing off the wall with her back in hopes of not looking so weak, although her pain and the shock of meeting Troy after everything she had learned about him made her sag right back against it. Without much practice to this point in her life, she tried, clumsily, to make casual adult conversation: "You smoke?"

"No, sorry," he said, looking at her without recognition.

"Neither do I. Don't know why I asked. I'm sorry. My name's Jackie. What's your name?"

"Troy." His eyes narrowed. "How old are you? Your parents know you're out at a bar?"

"My dad does."

He looked out over the empty fields and low, brittle-grassed hills to the always busy 101 and the deepening sky of late dusk behind it, rubbing the back of his head vacantly. He looked concussed, but, more than that, he looked like he knew something he didn't want to know.

"All right, kid. I got clocked and just needed some air. Gonna head back in and—"

"What's the deal with everyone here? Why do you all look the same? Are you all named Troy? Do you know Diane Crayton?"

She had so much to ask, like when you run into a favorite actor or author. How do you say everything you've wanted to say to a person who has been a big part of your life and doesn't know you at all?

"Diane," Troy said, frowning nervously.

"Diane Crayton. From Night Vale. She's raising your boy Josh."

"Oh. Well." Troy nodded, edging toward the door. "How is she?"

"Why don't you ask her yourself?" She let him hear the bitterness in her voice.

"Yeah," he said, not exactly in response to what she said but just to make a sound.

"There's dozens of you. Why doesn't one of you go talk to her? Do you do anything but sit here and drink?"

"This is just who I am . . . um."

"Jackie."

"Jackie. I am who you see. I don't know how to explain it. How to . . ." He grunted. "It's hard, okay. It's just a thing I deal with."

The door to the bar opened and another Troy came out. And then several, if not all, of the Troys came out. They all stared sideways at Jackie.

"Whatever, it's fine," she said, not afraid of any one of her fathers, but nervous around so many.

"Of course it's fine," the Troy with the bruised eye said. "I don't have to explain myself to you. I don't know you. How'd you break your arm? Why does your dad let you drink? Why're you bothering me about Diane?"

The Troys stepped forward. One of them said, "Is this girl bothering you?" Another one said, "Give a guy some room, lady." And another one said, "Back off, guys." And another one—and Jackie wondered if she imagined this one, it was so quiet—said, "Jackie?"

The crowd of Troys were all speaking at once to her, to each other. She backed up.

"Listen, man," she said. "All of you . . . men. I just . . . all right. I gotta go."

Her father was so many, and all of him did not know her. She limped away as quickly as she could. Once out of sight, she fell against the stained stucco wall of a store with a sign that said PLANTS, slumped and aching. None of him called after, and none of him followed her. One by one, all of him drifted back into the bar.

45

Jackie pulled on the front door of City Hall, but it was locked. She shook it a couple of times. She knocked. She tried bleeding on it. Nothing.

"Open," she shouted at the door. "Open up." But it was not a shouting door either. The buildings in King City looked mostly the same, mostly cold and colorless, but City Hall, the breath of life for any living city, sat small and shriveled like a smoker's lung. "C'mon," she whined, helpless.

Nothing in this town made sense. Nothing makes sense anywhere, she supposed, but the difference between the comforting nonsense of home and the alien nonsense of King City made her feel deeply the miles between there and here, and the time that had passed since she had felt comfortable anywhere. She kicked the door, and the only result was a searing wave from her toes up her leg and through her arm.

She walked around the building. On the far side was another door. Unlike the front door, it had no signage and was plain and heavy and dark. Also unlike the front door, it was open.

Instead of a trash room or storage closet, the back door led into a classy, if dated, reception area. The left and right walls were lined with paintings of people in chronological eras of dress. Under the paintings on each wall was a plaque that read, FORMER MAYORS.

The receptionist sat at a metal desk, and on the wall behind the receptionist was a painting of a man wearing a tan jacket. On the desk was a guest sign-in sheet.

"Hi, did a Diane Crayton come in this way?" Jackie said, leaning over the sign-in, scanning for Diane's name. Every line was blank. The receptionist grabbed the sign-in sheet away from her.

"Do you have an appointment?" she said, her voice hoarse and her eyes swollen.

"My friend was here to meet with the mayor. E-Ev-Evan?" Jackie said, curling his name into a question. "Everett. Elliott. Your mayor. She came to meet with the mayor."

"We don't have a mayor." The receptionist smiled, as if this had been a convoluted icebreaker and now they could have a real conversation.

"You do, though."

"I'm sorry. We do not currently have a mayor. We're an un-usual town in that way, I guess. If your friend said she was coming to see the mayor of King City, she was either lying or disappointed."

The receptionist's smile turned from friendly to smug.

"No. You do. Look." Jackie pointed to the painting behind the receptionist.

"I have never seen that painting before."

"Read the plaque."

The receptionist read the plaque aloud. "Current mayor."

"That's who I'm here to see."

"How did I not know that we have a mayor?" The recep-tionist frowned, looking neither friendly nor smug. She stood and said, "Wait here," before running out the entrance of the building, leaving a ring of keys on the desk and an unsecured computer, which on closer inspection was unplugged, and on even closer inspection was a painted model carved of wood.

Jackie shrugged, grabbed the keys, and headed down the hallway next to the reception desk. There were few doors along the long hall. What doors there were had no knobs or hinges, which made them not doors but door-like walls. They had frosted-glass windows and etched room numbers that followed no simple logic: 43-EE was next door to AX-6, which was across the hall from L. Jackie tried pushing on them and sliding them and knocking on them, but nothing happened.

The hall was long and winding. There were no tributary hallways. Given the small size of the outer building, and the incredible length of the hallway, Jackie was certain the hall was spiraling underground, but every few feet there was a window facing outside. Jackie could peer out and see trees and buildings and taupe, slow-moving traffic. The last light of dusk mixed with the anemic low-watt fluorescent lighting.

She knocked on each door hoping to find someone, hoping to find Diane or the mayor or whatever he was. Sometimes she thought she heard voices in soft conversation behind these non-doors, and as she would knock and push and shake the wall, the voices would go silent.

She pressed her face to the frosted glass when she heard voices, hoping to see inside, hoping just to catch movement of some sort. Even if it meant a terrified or irate employee bursting into the hallway to confront her, that would have been fine by Jackie. She would at least have someone to talk to.

But each door, nothing. Nothing at door 55. Nothing at door T9. Nothing at FLX-8i.7. Nothing at 2. Nothing at SUPPLIES. Nothing at 3315. Something at CTY. REC. Something small.

It was one of few doors that had meaningful lettering. She listened at first, then pushed lightly, then heavily. She tried lifting and sliding the door. She knocked. She pressed her face to the glass. She didn't know why, but she did something she had not done at any of the other non-doors. She put her hand to the glass.

She set her palm against the glass and spread her fingers. When she lifted it away, it left its ghost upon the glass, a hand raised to say, "Stop." Or "Come here." Or "Hello." Or "Help." Or maybe only "I am here. This hand, at least, is real."

Behind the handprint she saw a shadow approaching the glass.

"Diane?" Jackie stepped back and prepared whatever energy was left in her to flee whatever might be behind the door.

As it neared the glass, she could see that the shadow had what looked like antlers—sleek, tapered antlers from a bulbous skull.

"Diane?" Jackie asked, less hopefully.

"No," said a voice, and the door began to crack. A yellow sliver of light split the black floor near Jackie's feet and began to widen. Jackie could not move. The door opened and she saw.

"Who do you mean by 'that man'?" said Diane.

"Troy," said the man in the tan jacket.

"Troy," she said.

"Diane," he said, "let me tell you a story about Troy."

A STORY ABOUT TROY

There once was a town called King City that was completely normal. Or it had many small abnormalities, minor secrets, moments throughout its history that didn't quite add up, and events that no one ever talked about. And, in that way, it was completely normal.

It sat on a stretch of the 101 freeway between a town called Greenfield and a state wildlife area. This stretch of the 101 was not interesting to anyone. Citizens of King City would dispute this, because they had been born there, or had fallen in love or had gone south of the law or gone above expectations, had lived full lives along that stretch of freeway. But for most anyone else driving past on their way north or south it was nothing and then a town and then not a whole lot more.

The mayor of that town was a young, energetic man, with a wife and a daughter and a house. There were people he loved and things he owned. There were also people he did not love and things he did not own. He lived a full life.

Not long after he was elected, a new man arrived in town. People arrived in town all the time. It wasn't that distant from other places, and it was along a major thoroughfare. There was a Taco Bell where people could pee. There was a gas station where people could pee. There were all sorts of things. The mayor was proud of his town.

But the stranger wasn't passing through. He was coming to live. He said he came from a town, not that far away, or possibly quite far away. He wasn't sure.

"Distance is confusing," the stranger would tell people, anyone who would listen. "So is time."

He would shake his head and invite them to join him in considering the folly of space and time.

This was not why he was noticed.

Why he was noticed was that he was very helpful. As it turned out, he was that rare combination of nice and competent. There didn't seem to be a lot he couldn't do.

Car troubles? Sure, I know a thing or two about engines. Nothing much, but I can take a look. And the car would be running in no time.

Bill troubles? Actually, I know a bit about the law on that stuff. Let me just talk to them for a second, see if there's anything I can work out. And the bill collectors would never call again.

Broken heart? Buddy, you don't know how much experience I have in that area. Let me buy you a drink and we'll talk about it. And while alcohol never fixed the problem, it certainly made the person feel better for the time that the conversation lasted.

Everyone in town grew to like him very much.

"That Troy," said Ynez, an older retired woman who worked weeknights at the music shop. "He is a helpful one, though, isn't he?"

"Sure is," said the mayor. He was wearing a tan jacket. The mayor sometimes wore a tan jacket, but often did not.

Then the trouble started.

It began with Troy being helpful. He was carrying groceries for an old man who possibly could have carried the groceries himself, but it had been a long day, and he was tired, and if Troy wanted to carry them then he would let Troy do that.

As they walked out through the parking lot, the old man and Troy passed another Troy who was jump-starting a worried teenager's car. The teenager hadn't been allowed to take the car, and now she couldn't get it to start, and she was worried about her parents coming home to both her and the car missing.

"They're going to call the cops," she was saying, aloud but to herself. "I'm going to be in so much trouble."

Troy had hooked the cables to his battery and was in the process of hooking up the other side to her car when Troy walked by with the old man and his groceries.

"Hello," said Troy.

"Oh, hi there," said the other Troy.

The old man and the teenager gaped at the Troys and at each other. Troy kept carrying the groceries and hooking up the jumper cables. He turned and looked back at the old man, who had stopped walking.

"What's wrong?" Troy asked.

And with that, Troy started to multiply. First a little, and then more than a little. He was everywhere. He was competent, and friendly, and helpful, and there were so many of him.

The citizens of King City had no idea what to do. They looked to their mayor for guidance. Their mayor had no idea what to do.

He put on his tan jacket, because it happened to be chilly that day, and he went to visit Troy. Or one of the Troys. The one he thought was the original, although it was difficult to tell at that point.

Troy smiled when he opened his door.

"Oh hey," Troy said, lounging back in toward his living room. "Come on in, man. Do you want something to drink? Water? A beer?"

"No, that's okay," said the mayor. "Listen, Troy, I have some questions."

"Sure, no problem."

"Troy, where did you come from, exactly?"

Troy frowned.

"Place called Night Vale. Great town. Grew up there. Never actually lived anywhere else. But got a lot of heartbreak back there. Lot of bummer life decisions. King City is nice. Plus I feel like I'm doing real good here. Hey, speaking of which, anything you need to get done? I'm feeling productive today."

"No, Troy. Thank you." The mayor sat uncomfortably in a comfortable chair. "Troy, there are more of you."

"Yeah," said Troy.

"There are lots of yous. There are multiple Troys."

"Well, sure," said Troy. "I think we're all being pretty helpful though, right? Listen, if any of them aren't helpful, you come talk to me. I'll set myself right."

"Helpfulness is not the problem, Troy. The problem is that people do not multiply. There is never suddenly more of a person."

"Of course there is. Look at me." He frowned again. "I dunno. Where I'm from, you just kind of roll with things. I guess I assumed this place would be like that too."

"We like you, Troy," said the mayor in the tan jacket. "But we're confused."

"Oh, hey, I like you all too." Troy got up. The mayor got up too. "This is a great town you have, and I'm going to keep doing my best to make it better." He started to guide the mayor out the door. "Thanks so much for coming by. Feel free to come by anytime if you have something needs doing or if you just want to talk. I love talking."

The mayor left the house, feeling uneasy and like he had not accomplished anything at all.

The Troys continued to multiply. Soon there were entire neighborhoods full of them, smiling and waving and offering to help each other out.

The other people in King City changed too. They became forgetful. They found they were talking less to people that did not live in King City. They would get calls from their mother, telling them that they hadn't called her in so long, and they would realize that until the moment she called, they had forgotten that they had a mother.

It wasn't just their memory. There was something happening physically. They were finding it harder and harder to leave town.

They would try to do just a quick twenty-minute drive out of city limits and find that all the roads led back to town, that the sky for a moment looked like video static or maybe just a lot of stars, more stars than anyone had ever seen, but either is strange in the middle of the day, right? The 101, so closely tied to the life of the town, became impossible to reach. There didn't seem to be any entrances, and no matter where they drove, it didn't seem to get any closer. Soon they couldn't even hear it, as close as it was. Silence descended on their town.

And the Troys continued to multiply. The mayor tried to warn the town about Troy, but no one could hold that thought in their minds long enough to do anything about it.

"We need a mayor," they would say. "A mayor would be able to lead, would know what to do," and then they would discover that they had a mayor but had forgotten about him. And then they would forget that they had discovered that.

The man who happened to be mayor the day that Troy came to town felt these changes too. He went home less and less. Sometimes he would forget where his home was, and even when he did go home, his wife and daughter and he would all stare at each other with wide, blank eyes, unsure of who any of them were, terrified of the strangers in their home.

Every time he looked down, he seemed to be wearing that tan jacket. He would decide to take it off, and then he would forget until he noticed again and the process would repeat.

Soon he stopped going home at all. This was not a decision, it was just what happened. He always seemed to be at City Hall, with a staff who did not know who he was or that they even had a mayor.

The only thing he could hold clearly in his mind was the place that Troy was from. A town called Night Vale. So he went looking for Night Vale.

Night Vale is not an easy place to find, but he had a lot of time. In the infinite weirdness that had descended on King City, time was an inexhaustible resource.

He made it to Night Vale and began trying to see if anyone

could help him save his city from Troy. He spent months, maybe even years there, he wasn't sure. No one could remember talking to him, or what they talked about. No one could help him. And then he talked to Diane, and she, for whatever reason, mentioned Troy in passing.

So the mayor, whose name was not Evan McIntyre, began working at Diane's office to learn more about Troy, a man of many selves but only one form, and in time learned about his son, Josh, a boy of many forms but only one self. And the mayor knew what he had to do.

He wasn't happy about it, but then nothing made him happy anymore.

"Your Josh is the son of the man that took my town from me," the man in the tan jacket said to Diane. "Your son Josh is also an unusual person, but he is different than his father. I need his help to understand Troy and save my town."

He sighed, looking out his window as though the view were anything but a wall and a garbage can.

"I feel as though we have been replaced by some other King City that has gone on with the normal progression of its life as a city, right where we left it, diverging from us as we have spiraled out into whatever part of space and time you would call this."

Diane stood. She didn't care about the man or his town.

"Tell me where you took my son. I want my son."

The flies swarmed again, catching Diane off guard. She stumbled backward into the leather chair. The man in the tan jacket shook his head.

"Space and time are weird, right?"

He was right.

"Listen, Evan, or whatever your name is, it's terrible what happened to your town. But I need my son back. Because as much as I care about the world, I care more about my son. You have a daughter, you understand."

"I do. I do have a daughter," he said, turning back around to face her. "And as much as I care about your son, I care more about my daughter. You, I'm sure, understand. We've all had family taken from us because of Troy."

She pointed at him. She meant it.

"Understand this. I will find my son. I will find my son right away."

Which is when her son walked in with Jackie. He had a squat body and enormous antlers.

"Hi, Mom," Josh said.

THE VOICE OF NIGHT VALE

CECIL: . . . break into his storage locker? Who would do such a thing? Feral dogs probably. They are notorious thieves.

In other news, a recent report suggests that things may not be as they seem. The report explains that things are definitely what they are, but never what they seem. Many scientists contributed to the report. They studied numbers that were on computer screens and wrote out long equations and drew many diagrams that helped prove their point.

"Even these pages you think you're reading could be quite different from what you think you see," the report explained. "It's possible this report is just a sprawling aloe plant or a mid-century modern maple credenza. You could try to study it more closely, but you will never know for certain."

No word on whether or not things have been what they have seemed before this report or whether they will be what they seem at some point in the future.

And now, traffic.

There is a man walking out into the desert. He doesn't have much. At one point he had a new job and a nice car and people in his life. Now he only has his gray pin-striped suit stained with dirt and a five-dollar bill. Soon, he thinks, he will have less. The less he has the more things make sense to him, although he doesn't understand why.

He thinks back to the men he had been in the past. The man with a lover. The man with a job. The man driving without a destination. The man with a fancy watch in a place where time doesn't work. The man standing out in the desert with blood all over his hands. The man entering a pawnshop. They all seemed to be different people, people who didn't know each other although they might vaguely recognize each other from different corners at a party none of them liked.

But he also knew that they were all him, that all of them still lived inside his body, somewhere. That they could never leave, just recede into a background hum in his mind.

The young man is in the desert. He is looking back at a world that does not belong to him. Nothing belongs to him. He is looking around at a landscape that desolates outward forever. So he stops where he is, as good as any other place.

He looks up. Again, it is there in the sky. The planet of awesome size, lit by no sun. An invisible titan, all thick black forests and jagged mountains and deep, turbulent oceans. It is very close now. So close that he wonders if he could touch it. As he reaches up, he thinks he sees movement on its surface. Through the canopy of the forests and upon the slopes of the mountains and on the shores of the churning ocean. People maybe. Crowds of people all wrapped in white cloth. They are leaning into each other like dropped puppets. They sway lifelessly. He feels horror in the back of his throat, but still he reaches up.

He can't help himself. It's just what he does next.

This has been traffic.

And now a word from our sponsors.

Do you have lost memories? Are there any memories that once were there but have since been misplaced? Or taken? Forcibly taken from you? Well, of course, how would you know if you had?

So let's try this a different way. Do you ever feel like there is a gap in yourself? Do you ever act in ways that you do not understand and then immediately regret? Do you feel like there is a great abyss of meaning in your very core that will never be filled, and yet you cannot help but try to fill it?

Then yes, you have had many things taken from you, memories among them. And what you need is Lifelock.

After signing up for Lifelock, you will be immediately picked up by our friendly, armed technicians and transported in protective restraints to a secure and heavily guarded facility, where you will be safely locked away in an unmarked cell with no windows or lights, so no one will be able to see you or get to you. Once you are locked away and your identity has been destroyed in all possible records, you will be forever safe from identity theft, impersonation, assassination, assignations, and, of course, memory removal. You will never do anything again that might put you at risk of harm. Everything you could conceivably do puts you at risk of harm. You must stay still in the darkness. We will hold you close to our chest, almost suffocatingly close, in the warm still of our empty forever.

We'll protect you from this world by completely removing you from it. Lifelock.

This has been a message from our sponsors.

Oh, I don't know if I've mentioned my boyfriend Carlos on the air before, but . . .

47

"Mom," Josh protested as Diane wrapped her arms around his sloped, furry shoulders.

She gripped his body tight, placing one hand across his wide back and the other hand to the back of his head, between the tall, pointed ears.

"Josh," she said over and over. "Josh. Josh." Jackie placed her casted hand on his mother's back.

Diane concentrated on breathing deep, full breaths. "Thank you, Jackie."

"Mom." Josh blushed. "It's okay. It's okay."

"Josh, it's not okay. I haven't seen you in a week. What have they done to you?"

"Nothing, Mom. I'm fine." He gently removed her arms from his body.

She looked into his eyes, or into the eyes of his body, looking for him. Her own eyes hardened. Her tears dried. Her pupils contracted, lids narrowing. He felt the moment turning.

"I took your car for the afternoon," he said, pleading the case in what he failed to keep from a whine. "I'm sorry. I found out that my dad had moved to King City and then I found that paper in your purse and then I thought I could take the car to King City to look up stuff about my dad. I thought you would be gone the whole day. You've been gone a lot lately.

"I mapped it out, and it looked like it was maybe only a couple hours' drive. I was planning to come back tonight. But I ran up on the curb into someone's lawn. I wanted to have cool-looking wings, but it was hard to drive with them. I was all pushed forward and they kept getting in my eyes. I dented your fender, and ruined their shrubbery and crushed this row of plastic garden flamingos that got stuck in the bumper, and apparently I ran Jackie off the road, but I didn't see that. I'm so sorry, Jackie. The wings were in my eyes and I didn't know.

"I was scared you'd be mad about your car, so I tried to drive home, but the city around me wasn't familiar-looking anymore. I saw this building marked CITY HALL, which is where Ty told me I could find all kinds of stuff out about my real dad. So I came in here. That was like an hour ago."

"Josh, you've been gone for days."

"Mom, you just texted me a couple hours ago, and I said 'Good. Be home later.' See?" He held up his phone.

"Time is weird in Night Vale," the mayor said.

"Shut up," Jackie said. The cloud of black flies rose, but she moved at them without hesitation. They buzzed louder and retreated to the other side of the room.

"It's not his fault, Diane," Jackie said. "It isn't. You and I both know that. We know it together."

Diane continued to stare at Josh. Her eyes burned on the cusp between crying and yelling.

"But maybe, Josh," Jackie said, "we finish driver's ed when we get back to town. Or maybe you don't need hooves when you drive, straight up hands will do the trick, all right? Full human form when you drive."

"I'm sorry. I didn't know. I didn't know." Josh lowered his head. He saw the deep yellow and purple bruises around the edges of Jackie's cast and along her neck, and cringed in shame.

"Let's just go home," Jackie said. "You and Josh can take your car, and I'll follow in the Mercedes."

"That is absolutely not possible," said the mayor in the tan jacket.

"Shut up," Jackie said again.

She moved toward him, her face set. The flies regrouped into an opaque cloud between her and the man. She stepped forward into them. The flies swarmed onto her skin and into her clothes and onto her face and into her eyes and her nose and her mouth. Their guts oozed onto her tongue as they crunched between her teeth. She batted at them with her uninjured arm, but they wouldn't release even as she got to his desk and grabbed the pair of scissors leaning against the rim of a coffee mug.

She held up the scissors. The mayor moved back, gawping at her fly-covered body, everyone else in the room forgetting his look of terror the moment they looked away. She brought the scissors down, driving a blade into her cast, and sawing. The cast resisted and the blades were not sharp, but she hacked with a fury. The flies retreated one by one as she worked herself into a sweat fighting against her own cast. Her skin was swollen and red where the flies had been.

Finally, dull blades and all, she ripped off the top of the cast, exposing a hand still clutching a paper that said "KING CITY." She held it up to the man in the tan jacket.

"Oh yes, of course." He walked over and plucked the paper from her hand, like a person taking a slip of paper out of another person's hand, and tossed it into the trash can, where it stayed. He did the same with the paper in Josh's hand.

Jackie stared at her empty palm, breathing hard from exertion and relief. She clasped and unclasped her sticky, sore fingers, reveling in the emptiness of them.

"Now then," said the man in the tan jacket, "that's done. And Josh will be back to you sooner or later, I'm sure."

"No," Diane said. Jackie was too struck by the burden that

had just been lifted from her, and would not be able to do this confrontation for her. She would have to do it herself.

"You awful, forgettable man," Diane said. "You will not keep him. You've infected my town with your blank face and your false memories. I am sorry no one knows who you are, I really am. I'm sorry that no one remembers you are mayor. I'm sorry for your town."

She felt another Diane crossing a street somewhere else, arms full with groceries, and yet another, looking idly at the passing scenery outside of a bus window.

"I am sorry you've resorted to taking other people's children—"

"I wasn't taken, Mom."

"Josh, honestly, you are not old enough to know the difference. I'm sorry you have to resort to taking other people's children. Maybe the problem isn't with Troy. Maybe the problem is with you. Maybe if you were a better mayor, you wouldn't be forgotten. Good deeds don't go unnoticed. If there was an economy and good roads and schools, no one would try to elect a new leader every few months."

The man in the tan jacket's eyes darkened. Jackie saw his eyes. They were unforgettable.

"And maybe, just maybe," Diane said, her hand waving in asynchronous rhythm to her speech, "a good father only has to be a good father, not a good mayor, not a man with a memorable face. Look at yourself, Evan, or whatever the fuck your name is. Josh, I'm sorry I cursed. Evan, be accountable to your wife and family, and they will care enough to know who you are. Govern your city, and you won't have to infect mine. Be a father to your child, and you won't have to steal mine."

The mayor backed up to his seat but did not sit. His flies stacked themselves in a subdued pyramid on his shoulder.

"Diane Crayton, I have infected no one. You misunderstand the situation. I came to Night Vale because there was no place weirder, and I thought someone there would understand. But my long conversations were forgotten. My pleas went unnoticed. So I started to write it down. A simple message that would stick better. That, in fact, it would be impossible to put down."

He winced apologetically at Jackie.

"I'm sorry about that. I didn't think people would mind that much. I need the people of your weird town to tell me how to unweird my own. I was desperate. Desperation does not breed empathy or clear thinking."

"You ruined my life," said Jackie.

He shrugged. That was all he would have to say on that.

"Please understand, I didn't want to force Josh. I knew he would be curious about his father. I just wanted to give him the information he would need to find him. I just wanted to give him the opportunity, a piece of paper with a town's name on it, and I knew somehow, once given it, that he would take it."

Jackie was trying to understand the implication of what he was saying.

"All of that, all that I went through," Jackie said, "it wasn't even for me? You were trying to get the paper to Diane and Josh? Why would you give it to me?"

The man shrugged again.

"I didn't know what Josh looked like. He could have been anything. So I gave the paper to as many people as I could, hoping that one of them eventually would be him. None of them ever were. That's when I decided that, as much as I didn't want Diane knowing about this, I would have to get close to her and see if she would give Josh the paper."

"So you understood that what you were doing was wrong?" Diane said.

"If you had just given that paper to him, it would have stuck. But you tried to keep it from him. Or maybe you just didn't remember that you had it. I should have made it so you couldn't get rid of it, but then you wouldn't have been able to give it to Josh, and anyway I'm just a mayor of what is, after all, only a small town. I can't think of everything."

The flies buzzed sympathetically. Or that was their intention. It sounded no different than the rest of their buzzing.

"Mom." Josh put a tentacular arm around Diane. "I want to stay. I want to help. It's not dangerous. It's a chance for me to meet my dad, to talk to him. I can really help these people."

"Josh, we're leaving. We will talk about your father later."

"This town needs me to stay. Mom, I—"

"No," said Jackie. "No. They just need one of Troy's kids to stay. And we have another one of those. Troy's my father too."

Diane and Josh and the man in the tan jacket all turned to face her. Even the flies stopped flying, landing on the closest surface and turning to face her.

"You?" said the man.

"Anything you could learn from Josh, you could learn from me. And if you're not putting me in some lab, I don't mind helping you. You're not like a mad scientist, right? This is just a research project?"

"Jackie, no."

"Diane, yes. Josh has you and you have him. You are a family. What do I have? Years of repetition and a mother I can barely remember. This is no better, but this is no worse, and if I keep your family together, then at last I'll have done something that isn't running a pawnshop. Take Josh, okay? Take your son and leave."

Diane did not want to do that. She saw the waver in Jackie's posture, the way she leaned her hand on the wall. She was not well, and she needed Diane to help her. They needed each other. But there was Josh. And as much as she loved, and maybe she did, maybe she loved Jackie, she loved Josh more.

Dusk had turned to night, and the cheap overhead lighting in the office accentuated the unimpressive realness of this man's life: his ballpoint pens, his worn-out coat (probably one of only a couple of jackets he owned), the chipped paint on the walls, the wrinkles streaking out from his eyes and nose.

Diane felt herself at that very moment getting a thick piece of skin removed from her back. The doctor was taping the wound closed and telling her to come back for results next week. Diane felt herself filling out a pet adoption form at a shelter. Diane felt herself falling off a ladder. She felt herself riding an elevator. She felt herself living in a moon colony hundreds of years in the future. She felt so many of her, but still she was alone with this decision.

"I'm young, yes," said Jackie, "but I'm also much older than you can imagine, Diane. I'm older than I can imagine. I have all the time in the world. I'll continue being nineteen with no connections, no one to give me a reason to grow a day older. I have a mother who will miss me, sure, but she already saw me through childhood. You need to have the same chance. You need to help your son be a better man than his father."

Josh opened his mouth to protest.

"Josh, I get it, man, I do," Jackie said. "I grew up without a father, same as you. But you will have time. Later, after your mother has finished what she needs to do. The next time you see me, maybe you and I will be the same age, and we can have this talk again. I'd like that."

Diane turned to her, but before their eyes met, Diane saw the window. The night reflected everything in the room back at her.

There was a woman in the window, translucent and warped, wearing what she was wearing, standing the way she was standing, making the same small movements she was making, and looking deep into her eyes. She did not recognize the woman in the window, even though she had seen her many times.

"You know I'm right," Jackie said.

"I'll accept whatever decision you make," said the mayor in the tan jacket. "Either one is fine with us. You just have to make a choice."

Diane put her hand out to Jackie, who took it. Jackie was crying, but calm. She accepted what would have to happen next. Diane did not break eye contact with the woman in the window.

"No," Diane said, "I don't."

"Oh, come on," the man said. "Yes you do, get on with it please."

"This is not about King City and it's not about Troy's children. It's about Troy. He has infected King City with our town's weirdness."

"Asshole."

"Exactly, Jackie. What an asshole. And what an asshole this guy is." She pointed at the asshole in the tan jacket.

He seemed much taller than before. His flies spread out behind him, an angry, buzzing aura.

"You must choose," he roared. "You must choose who will stay, or I will choose for you."

"You're not staying here," she said to Jackie, ignoring him, "and Josh is not staying here."

Jackie nodded. "You're right. It's not our fault. It's not us should be solving these problems. It's time for Troy to do it."

"And Troy's not staying here. It's time for Troy to go home."

"Damn right it is."

"Stop talking and choose which child," the man shouted. No one was listening.

"I met a group of him at the bar. Good a place to talk to him as any."

"Then let's go." The woman in the window walked away, but Diane did not move. She had a sudden moment of doubt. What if she was wrong? What if she was making a mistake? Her reflection was gone and she still could not move. And then she felt Jackie take her hand.

"I'm with you," Jackie said gently. "Let's go." She hooked her injured arm through Josh's tentacular arm and led them both out the door and back up the hall.

The man in the tan jacket followed them into the hallway.

"Where are you going? Come back here at once." The flies buzzed around him. None of the three looked back, and the buzzing grew faint as they pushed open the front door into the dusty night air.

"You must choose. You must choose," said a distant voice, and then the door closed and it was silent once again.

48

"Troy," Jackie shouted.

"Get out here right now, Troy," Diane shouted.

The first Troy who emerged from the bar was the one with the shiner, bloomed now to violet. He looked dazed, possibly concussed.

Jackie held the door open and ushered them all out, helping with a pull on the sleeve or a shove on the shoulder in case any of them hesitated. Some were wobbly from the beer. Others strong and chipper and ready to drive home. Troy Walsh was prepared for all contingencies. Troy Walsh was confused about what was happening.

"Troy. Get out here. Come on." Jackie herded them all outdoors.

Imagine a thirty-two-year-old man. Imagine a thirty-two-year-old man who is many men. They all look like the same man because they all are the same man, have always been the same man. Imagine a thirty-two-year-old man who could fix your car and file your taxes and mix you an intoxicating cocktail and paint your miniature collectibles.

Imagine a thirty-two-year-old man born with the ability to be all things to all people but nothing to any one person. Imagine the look on his face when he steps out of a bar, a multitude of him, and sees the woman he, for a short time, always loved fifteen years ago.

Imagine the look on his face when he sees a boy he does not recognize, but knows exactly who he is.

Imagine his mouth opening slightly. Imagine the crack of verbal thought widening across his many countenances. Imagine the words visible in his eyes as he looks up, trying to shake out the logic and dislodge the emotions as the crack opens wide and humid breath hums in to prepare for a flood of words.

"Shut your mouth," Diane said. "Don't say a word."

She extended her arm in front of Josh, who had also stepped forward to speak.

"I will let you speak in a moment, Josh."

Diane looked at Troy. She looked at each and every one of him. Stay there, her eyes said. If I can see you, you cannot move.

"This is your son: Josh. I call him your son because words can mean certain things. It is not the right word but it is the correct word. Behind you is your daughter: Jackie.

"I am not here to ask for support. I am certainly not here to ask for anything on behalf of Josh or Jackie. I am here to tell you something on behalf of me and all those you are affecting.

"You are to come home, Troy Walsh. You are to come back to Night Vale and leave this town. You are many, and you are helpful, and you are kind. But meaning well is not doing well. You mean well, but you do not do well. You are destroying this time and space by bringing the strangeness of our time and place into it. We belong in Night Vale, all of us. It is our home. Go home, Troy."

The Troys all glanced at each other. Some had looks of sincere grief and shame. Some had doubtful grins and smug elbows. One waved her away and staggered back toward the bar, but Jackie kicked him in the shins and shoved him back to the group. Diane persisted.

"You have helped many people with your many skills, but also you're an irresponsible little shit. Both of those are true. Truth can be contradictory. You are not forgiven your lapses by your nonlapses. How many children do you have? How many have you left behind? Forget it, I don't care. What I care about is: What is Jackie's mother's name? How old is Jackie? What does your son look like? Behind all the physical forms, what does your son look like? What's his favorite food? Is he dating? What's the person's name?"

Troy looked at each other. One scratched his head, one burped, one stood straighter, uncertain but willing to give the questions a shot.

"No, don't try to answer. You don't know the answers. Don't waste our time guessing. Here's another question you can't answer: What does a father do? What kind of job is that? In all your infinite incarnations, is there one single good dad or partner in there?"

"Hey now, hey." The Troy who had tried to leave was stumbling forward, the sober Troys unsuccessfully trying to restrain him, shaking their heads and muttering discouragements. "No, hey, I'm going to respond. I'm not just going to listen to this. I did come back. I'm living in Night Vale again."

A few of the other Troys nodded, although they said nothing.

"I was going to come see you guys, come see Josh, but I just hadn't gotten around to it. There were some other jobs to do first. People needed my help. But I was coming. I would have been right there."

"No one needs your help," said Jackie, sneering at her father, a man who expressed multitudes but contained nothing. "It's you that needs the act of helping. You do it for yourself and not for anyone else, or you would have left this town when your 'help' knocked it off the map. Instead you nudged a smatter of you back to Night Vale, like crumbs at birds. That's not a return. That's a toe in the water. That's a minimum of effort. You help and help, but you're lazy. You're goddamn lazy."

The more drunk Troys glanced at each other, nervous. One of the sober Troys stepped forward.

"I didn't feel I had earned that yet," Troy said, looking only at Diane, who he seemed less intimidated by. "I didn't feel I was ready to see you. I was really young, you know, and that's a terrible excuse, but it's what I was. And now I'm older. I can be many things. I've learned I don't have to run. If you would have me. All of me." He gestured to all of him around him. "I would happily be part of your lives again."

"This is not an invitation to be part of our lives," said Diane. "This is a demand that you return home."

"Asshole," said Jackie.

The Troys, en masse, turned to Josh. "Josh, this is a strange way to first meet, and you don't have to let me be your father. I need to earn that, but I'd like to earn it. I will be there. I will do my best, much better than before, to be a man you can trust as a father. Or whatever relationship we can build. I owe you that."

Diane allowed her son to answer for himself, against every instinct. Jackie nodded reassurance at her. Josh didn't answer, instead turning to Diane, his eyes pleading, his face looking similar to Troy's for the first time in his life.

"You don't have to ask permission," she said. "Speak your mind. Say what you want."

Josh swallowed. He was quiet. The Troys were quiet. Everyone waited. When he spoke, the words were soft but clear.

"Okay," Josh said, and the Troys flashed proud grins. "But you've been gone fifteen years. She raised me just fine without you, so it's a little, um, it's a little shitty for you to talk to me like I need you. Sorry, Mom, for saying 'shitty.'

"I mean . . . Jackie. Jackie runs her own store, and she's awesome. She's doing great. Right, Jackie?"

"You tell him, antlers." Jackie smiled with her voice, not her mouth. Josh blushed, one hand gently and unconsciously touching the structure coming out of his head.

"I'd be interested in getting to know you," Josh continued. "But you don't get to send four or five of yourselves. You don't get to be everywhere. You live in Night Vale or nowhere. And when you're there, it's all of you or none of you."

Troy opened his mouths. He closed his mouths. He looked, with sober eyes and drunk eyes, around at himself.

"Lucinda," Jackie said.

"Huh?" he said.

"My mother's name is Lucinda," Jackie said. She turned and limped away, having nothing left to say or any desire left to hear.

A few, but not all of the Troys, nodded knowingly at this. A few, but not all of the Troys, looked at their shoes.

"Is this all of you?" Diane said.

"Most of us," the Troys said, in unison.

"Get the rest of you together. You're moving home. Now, Troy Walsh."

Diane followed Jackie, but Josh stayed, watching the men, all of them gaping at him, doing nothing. Then, one by one, they went back into the bar. The especially drunk one leaned on the doorframe and held his son's stare for a moment, then he was gone too.

"I don't think he's coming, Mom."

Diane and Jackie just kept walking. There was nothing left to say. Either the right thing would be done or it wouldn't.

Josh stayed where he was, watching the empty outside of the bar. He felt like crying, but his current physical form wasn't able to do that. He had thought for a moment that things would be different, but they were the same. He looked down at his hooves for a long time, trying to gather himself enough to give up and leave. He brought his head up at the sound of a door opening.

The drunk Troy was back. He nodded at his son. And the Troys, one by one, came out of the bar, a slow, staggering army of them, following the women back home.

Diane and Jackie and Josh stood near Diane's burgundy Ford hatchback, with its recently crumpled fender.

"Quick question," Jackie said. "How do we get back to Night Vale?"

"Huh," Diane answered. The three of them stood for a moment, staring at the two cars and the pile of flamingos, waiting for an idea to come to them. A voice from behind them interrupted their thought.

"Hey," the voice said. It was the man in the tan jacket. "Troy told me that he's leaving for good."

"I don't care," Jackie said. "How do we get back?"

"That's what I was coming to say," he said. "It might be impossible. I'm sor——"

Jackie punched him.

The man in the tan jacket holding a deerskin suitcase fell down into a sitting position in the dirt, but said nothing. The flies did nothing.

"I'll let you know when you're sorry enough," she said.

"It's not my fault," he said. "I just drive to where I think Night Vale is, and sometimes I get there. Sometimes I don't. I wish I could tell you——"

"Jackie," Diane said, "Night Vale has a way of bringing home its own. I think we could drive in any direction and still get home. We live in a weird place."

"Man, we really do."

"It's superweird," said Josh.

"The best kind of weird," said Jackie. She waved to the mayor, who was still sitting in the dirt. "See ya."

They got in their cars: Diane and Josh in the Ford, Jackie in the Mercedes. They would drive out the direction they had come. They would stay together, not losing sight of the other car. They would keep a plastic flamingo and a cell phone in each car, just in case.

Jackie rolled down her window and looked down at the man in the tan jacket.

"What's the deal with the flies anyway? Why does a mayor have a briefcase full of flies?"

"You don't make much money as mayor of a small town. I have to have a full-time job to make ends meet."

"Fly salesman, huh?"

"Fly salesman."

"Makes sense."

Without breaking eye contact, Jackie gunned the engine until a fog of white smoke enveloped the fenders. There was a sharp squeal, and the smoke lifted like a slow curtain, revealing her absence.

THE VOICE OF NIGHT VALE

CECIL: . . . City Council announced today that, in addition to history, the following other things are also "bunk": memory, timepieces, walnuts, all hawks (obviously!), most advanced mathematics (trigonometry and higher), and cats. The City Council clarified that they are not announcing this to anyone in particular, and that if anyone in particular should hear this announcement they can do with it what they will. Although they added that the only legal thing to do with it is to forget it. Forget it immediately, they repeated, swaying together and moving their digits around in a "sparkle fingers"-like motion.

Before dismissing the press conference, the City Council, looking somewhat emotionally hurt, said that it's a nervous tick—that thing with their fingers—and that they wish people wouldn't make fun of it by calling it "sparkle fingers."

Oh, bad news, listeners. Our newest intern, Sheila, fell into the pit that Carlos was using to bury the dangerous plastic flamingos. Rather than touching one and reliving her life, she touched hundreds as she rolled down the side of the pit, while at the same time dying not from the length of her fall but from the subsequent change in velocity at the end of it. She awoke again as a baby in hundreds of worlds at once, all of the infant versions of herself having awareness of the gaping silence that was her one true dead self.

To the family and friends of Intern Sheila, we extend our greatest condolences. Know that she was a good and hardworking intern, and that she died doing what she loved: simultaneously living and dying in infinite, fractal defiance of linear time.

If anyone is looking for college credit or to prepare for the life-threatening dangers of a career in community radio, come on down to the station. If one of the intern shirts fits you, you're in.

The Night Vale Council for Language Management would like to remind you of this last month's word definition changes.

Fork now means a momentary feeling of evening as a cl[BEEEEP] passes in front of the sun.

Loss now means whatever the opposite of loss is.

Migraine now means a large scorpion perched on the back of a person's neck where they cannot see it or feel it and would have no idea it was there if no one told them.

And of course this week's wild-card word is *brood*. For the next week, it means anything you want it to mean! Which is very, very brood.

Remember that misuse of language can lead to miscommunication, and that miscommunication leads to everything that has ever happened in the whole of the world.

Larry Leroy, out on the edge of town, has announced that he has found many wonderful things in his most recent sweep of the desert. A metallic sphere that fell from the sky and whistles softly to itself as though bored. A double of himself whom he had not seen in years, and whom he growled at until the double ran away. A number of plants, all exactly where they were before, but all a little bit different, as though they were somehow alive. A rock, but he won't tell us where. A body dressed in a gray, pin-striped suit lying sprawled on a dune. A new way of breathing that he says gives him verve and spunk. He said it just like that, punching at the air in front of him. "Verve and spunk," he shouted. "Verve and spunk." He seemed to have gotten off track from his original plan of listing what he had found in the desert, and ran off down the street, breathing with his new method, punching the air, and shouting, "Verve and spunk!" to passersby.

That's it from me for now, listeners. But something in me says that this is no ending. The night outside is bright and breezy and full of dangerous secrets. There is a taste in the air like tarnished silver, like the flesh of an extinct animal now only remembered through our spinal cord and the hairs on our back.

Something in me says that this is only the start. The moment after which all other moments will come. And looking back at the point we are at now, we will know that this was before, and that all of our nows from here on out will be after. This is the only way we know time works.

Stay tuned next for the sound of a creaking spine and the soft collapse of paper onto itself. And as always, good night, Night Vale.

Good night.

Jackie knocked on Lucinda's door. Diane answered.

"Come on in. You look great. How are you feeling?"

Jackie pulled her close with her completely healed left arm and let the hug go long past what is casually comfortable.

"I'm glad you're here," Jackie said.

"Glad you're here too," said Diane, through the constriction of the embrace. It seemed that Jackie had recovered her strength.

Lucinda met them in the kitchen and gave Jackie a kiss.

"It's always wonderful to see you, dear."

"You too, Mom."

In the months since their cars had, only a few hours after leaving King City, rolled across the Night Vale city line, Jackie had hired Diane as a part-time bookkeeper at the pawnshop while she continued to look for a more permanent job. This had allowed Jackie some free time outside of work and given her someone to pass the time with.

She saw every day what an active mother Diane was in Josh's life, talking regularly to and about him, helping him with school and society, allowing him to be a child and to become an adult, and this reminded Jackie to visit her own mother. Diane also often literally reminded her.

"We should stop by and visit Lucinda," Diane would say after work.

Today all of them were at Lucinda's house for a barbecue.

There was everything you needed for a barbecue: a small plastic bucket full of mud. Everything.

"Happy birthday," Diane said to Jackie. "Sounds like someone has decided to finally grow older. How old are you now?"

"Twenty-one. I skipped twenty. Not everyone has to turn twenty. Don't know when I'll turn twenty-two. Maybe in a few years, when I'm ready. Is Troy coming?"

The Troys had settled in the barista district. It turned out that he was an excellent barista, just as he had been excellent at everything else he had done. Carlos had taken to issuing each Troy a pink flamingo, which had the double effect of removing the flamingos from Night Vale for good and taking each Troy out of his current reality and into a reality of his own, where he could be a helpful and competent individual, rather than a helpful and competent horde. It was a highly scientific solution, and Cecil would not stop talking on the radio about how brilliant it was that Carlos had thought of it. "Nothing is more attractive that someone who is good at their job," Cecil often said.

"Josh invited him, but honestly I think even he doesn't really want his father to come. Speaking of which, how about you and Troy?"

"There is no me and Troy," said Jackie. "It's too late for that. Besides. I already have a family."

She took her mother's arm. Lucinda laughed and patted her hand.

"That's nice of you, dear, but I don't mind if you want to spend a little time with Troy. Not for him—I could care less about him—but you might get something out of it."

"Have you remembered any of your childhood?" asked Diane.

Lucinda let go of her daughter's hand.

"No," said Jackie. "We're working on it, but might be it's gone for good."

"Even if we don't have the then, dear, we have the now," her mother said, biting into one of the wax avocados, as she always did when trying to process her feelings.

"You really should stop eating those, Mom," Jackie said. "They're not real."

"'Should' and 'will' are different words," said Lucinda, taking a second big bite.

Jackie shook her head and went out the sliding glass door into the backyard. Josh came barreling into her.

"Jackie!"

He was small, and round, with broad, feathered wings and wide green eyes.

"Looking good," said Jackie. "Have you ever tried flying with those?"

"No," he said, flapping self-consciously. "I wouldn't know how."

"You've flown as a housefly before."

"That's different. I don't go high or far at all. I wouldn't know how to fly with wings this big."

"You won't know until you try, man."

"Can I help you at the pawnshop sometime? I've never had a job. It sounds kind of awful and kind of fun."

"It's exactly both," she said. "Tell you what. If you can fly higher than the roof, I'll let you do a shift with me tomorrow."

Josh grinned nervously, but first he turned to Diane, who was watching the conversation unfold with something less than enthusiasm.

"Is it okay, Mom?"

"It's okay, Josh," she said, not sure if it was okay. She hid her anxiety behind smiling eyes.

I'll always be a mother, she thought, but I'll always be a lot of things. I wonder what the next of those things will be?

Josh looked back at Jackie, who nodded and gave him a thumbs-up with her empty left hand, and then he looked up at the sky. His wings worked and his body slowly lifted off the grass.

"Please try not to hit any windows, dear," said Lucinda from her lawn chair.

"Just be careful please," said Diane.

Josh banked around experimentally. He was a little lower than the rooftop. Diane watched him, one hand over her eyes, one over her heart.

"Watch your head," she said, but to remind him of something he already knew, not to tell him something he didn't.

Jackie gave him another thumbs-up, and he returned it to her. He tried a loop, and managed a wavering somersault instead.

Troy watched all this, sitting in his car just outside the house. He had both hands on the wheel and he was smiling. It was definitely a smile. He had been sitting there for a couple minutes trying to make a decision. As he watched Josh, he thought about what Jackie had said about helpfulness, and what Diane had said about his role in their lives, and he made a decision.

From where he was flying, Josh could see the other red-tiled rooftops of Sand Pit, between the identical rooftops of Palm Frond Majesty and the Weeping Miner, and other housing developments with elaborate names and houses failing to live up to them, and just down the way the strip mall with Big Rico's Pizza and Carlos's lab, and beyond that City Hall, draped in black velvet for the night, and a young woman walking to her car, Mayor Cardinal, yes, but also Dana again for the night, going to meet her recently cured brother for a celebratory dinner at Tourniquet, and beyond that the tall black walls of the forbidden Dog Park, and, in the parking lot of the Desert Flower Bowling Alley and Arcade Fun Complex, Cecil from the radio station and Carlos the scientist with bowling bags in one hand and the other's hand in the other, strolling inside for League Night, a kiss before they opened the door and then they were gone, and beyond that the Moonlite All-Nite Diner, which, true to its name, was as busy then as it was at any other hour, with Laura offering fruit from the gnarled branches of her body and Steve Carlsberg digging heartily into a slice of invisible pie, and beyond that Diane's old office, full of computers and tables where work could be done although no one knew why they did it, where Catharine had stayed late to finish up some work at a desk which was tarantula-free, although she still flinched at imagined light touches on her hand, and beyond that the low bulk of the public library, outwardly quiet, quietly seething with librarians, and near that his own house, which was just now thinking of him, and where a faceless old woman was secretly refolding all of his clothes, and beyond that the *Night Vale Daily Journal* building, whose sole occupant was considering a wall of hatchets, ready to get down to the bloody business of local journalism, and beyond that the movie theater, its blinking lights showing through the sentient haze of Stacy as she prepped the box office for the midnight movie audiences, silent customers who fade into being in their seats at exactly midnight, watching movies that play on the screen even with the projector shut off, before fading back away into nothing without even waiting for the ending credits to finish, and beyond that the hole in the vacant lot out back of the Ralphs, and the Ralphs itself, offering fresh food and low, low prices, although never at the same time, and beyond that Old Woman Josie outside her house, no paper in her hand, and Erika, and Erika, and Erika as well, all outside in the garden, and the tower of Night Vale Community Radio, blinking light atop, and Jackie's Pawn Shop, formerly Lucinda's Pawn Shop, a place that was just then closed, that was now closed more often than it wasn't because its owner wanted to be somewhere else sometimes, and the windows of the hospital, doctors flitting from one to the next in an unexplained instant, and the car lot where used car salesmen loped joyfully over their car-strewn territory, barking at a moon that they did not understand but then no one else did really, and the Brown Stone Spire, ancient and humming a malevolent tone, and a cordon of helpful helicopters keeping everyone free, and out past all of that the sand, a small eternity of sand, desert like there would never be anything else, and beyond that, eventually, something else, because there is always something else, and King City, no longer forgotten, an ordinary town, with an ordinary mayor, who was just then taking off his jacket, a man in a short-sleeve shirt holding a deerskin suitcase, and stepping into his house where a family greeted him with his correct name at last, and beyond it and around it all other ordinary towns, and all ordinary people, who were sleeping or not sleeping, who were metaphorically or literally alive, or metaphorically or literally not, gone but alive in our hearts, or gone and forgotten, all existing somewhere on a spectrum of loss, and beyond them and around them the oceans and forests, momentarily teeming with life before the great planetary hush, and out beyond that a sky that was coming around slowly to the idea of sunset, or was, somewhere else, just having the first thought of day, and beyond that the wavering red lights of spy satellites, watching, and the steady blue lights of unidentified spacecraft, watching, and the white light of what we mistakenly assume is the moon, watching, and beyond that void, and void after that, void on and on, with a scattered vanishing of non-void mixed in, and beyond that so many mysteries that it didn't seem to Josh that he would be able to solve even one of them, not if he had all the time in the world, and he didn't have all the time in the world, and he would never solve even one mystery.

He looked down, past a rooftop which was way below him now, at Diane, who was laughing, with her arm around Jackie, who was laughing, hand in hand with Lucinda, who was laughing.

"Wow," he said. "I'm higher up than I thought."

"Nah, man," Jackie said. "You can go way higher than that."

HOW TO LISTEN TO THE *WELCOME TO NIGHT VALE* PODCAST

This is the end of the book. Either you finished the book, or you flipped right ahead to the ending pages to see what they say. Listen, we're not here to tell you how to read this book.

If you enjoyed this novel, we recommend you join us in our ongoing *Welcome to Night Vale* podcast, which has been telling stories about this strange desert town since 2012.

Our podcast comes out twice monthly online and is completely free. You can download it to your computer or listening device through iTunes, Stitcher, Podbay.fm, Soundcloud, any of the hundreds of free podcasting apps, or by going to welcometonightvale.com. You can also stream all of our episodes at our YouTube channel (youtube.com/welcometonightvale), and even watch some bonus behind-the-scenes footage of the *Welcome to Night Vale* cast.

All of the episodes going back to the very start are available to download right now. Or if that sounds like too much time investment, just hop right in wherever we are now. You'll be in the swing of things in no time. Well, some time. It will take longer than zero time.

Interested in more stories from us? Visit nightvalepresents .com to listen to *Alice Isn't Dead* and *Within the Wires*, new serial fiction podcasts from the team behind *Welcome to Night Vale*. And check back for more new podcasts in the future.

We also regularly do live shows all over the world (more than two hundred shows in sixteen different countries at the time of this writing). These live shows are full evenings of Night Vale storytelling, with live music and guest stars, designed so that you do not need to know anything about the podcast to enjoy.

Keep an eye on welcometonightvale.com to join us next time we pass through wherever you live. (Wherever you live is our favorite place to perform.)

See you there.

ACKNOWLEDGMENTS

Thanks to the cast and crew of *Welcome to Night Vale*: Meg Bashwiner, Jon Bernstein, Marisa Blankier, Desiree Burch, Nathalie Candel, Emma Frankland, Kevin R. Free, Mark Gagliardi, Angelique Grandone, Marc Evan Jackson, Maureen Johnson, Kate Jones, Erica Livingston, Christopher Loar, Hal Lublin, Dylan Marron, Daniel Mirsky, Jasika Nicole, Lauren O'Niell, Flor De Liz Perez, Teresa Piscioneri, Jackson Publick, Molly Quinn, Retta, Symphony Sanders, Annie Savage, Lauren Sharpe, James Urbaniak, Bettina Warshaw, Wil Wheaton, Mara Wilson, and, of course, the voice of Night Vale himself, Cecil Baldwin.

Also and always: Jillian Sweeney; Kathy and Ron Fink; Ellen Flood; Leann Sweeney; Jack and Lydia Bashwiner; Anna, Sam, Levi, and Caleb Pow; Rob Wilson; Kate Leth; Jessica Hayworth; Holly and Jeffrey Rowland; Zack Parsons; Ashley Lierman; Russel Swensen; Glen David Gold; Marta Rainer; Andrew Morgan; Eleanor McGuinness; Paul Sloan; John Green; Hank Green; Patrick Rothfuss; Cory Doctorow; Andrew WK; John Darnielle; Dessa Darling; Aby Wolf; Jason Webley; Danny Schmidt; Carrie Elkin; Eliza Rickman; Mary Epworth, Will Twynham; Erin McKeown; Sxip Shirey; Gabriel Royal; The New York Neo-Futurists; Freesound.org; Mike Mushkin; Ben

ACKNOWLEDGMENTS

Acker and Ben Blacker of *The Thrilling Adventure Hour*; the Booksmith in San Francisco; Mark Flanagan and Largo at the Coronet; and, of course, the delightful Night Vale fans.

Our agent Jodi Reamer, our editor Amy Baker, and all the good people at HarperPerennial.

ABOUT THE AUTHORS

Joseph Fink created the *Welcome to Night Vale* and *Alice Isn't Dead* podcasts. He lives with his wife in New York.

Jeffrey Cranor cowrites the *Welcome to Night Vale* and *Within the Wires* podcasts. He also cocreates theater and dance pieces with choreographer/wife Jillian Sweeney. They live in New York.

THE WELCOME TO NIGHT VALE EPISODE COLLECTIONS

FOREWORD BY CORY DOCTOROW
INTRODUCTION BY JOSEPH FINK

FOREWORD BY MAUREEN JOHNSON
INTRODUCTION BY JEFFREY CRANOR

ORIGINAL ILLUSTRATIONS BY JESSICA HAYWORTH

"Brilliant, hilarious, and wondrously strange. I'm packing up and moving to Night Vale!"
—RANSOM RIGGS, AUTHOR OF THE #1 *NEW YORK TIMES* BESTSELLING
MISS PEREGRINE'S HOME FOR PECULIAR CHILDREN

COLLECTIONS OF EVERY EPISODE FROM SEASONS ONE AND TWO OF THE PODCAST, FEATURING GUEST INTRODUCTIONS,
BEHIND THE SCENES COMMENTARY, AND ORIGINAL ILLUSTRATIONS. • WWW.WELCOMETONIGHTVALE.COM